MARGARET THE QUEEN

'Sixty Scots, Pictish and Dalar kings lie buried
on Iona, Highness. All of the most ancient line in
Christendom. Have you forgot?'

She looked at him, her lovely eyes untroubled.
'No, Maldred, I have not forgot,' she said.
'But there is a time and a tide for all things.
For standing still and for moving on. For holding
fast and for pointing forward and renewal. I
believe that God, in His wisdom, sent that great
storm to bring me to this northern land for a
purpose. *His* purpose. In all humility I say it. For
myself, I am nothing . . .'

Margaret the
Queen

Nigel Tranter

CORONET BOOKS
Hodder and Stoughton

Copyright © 1979 by Nigel Tranter

First published in Great Britain 1979 by
Hodder and Stoughton Limited

Coronet edition 1981
Second Impression 1984

British Library C.I.P.

Tranter, Nigel
  Margaret the queen.
  I. Title
  823'.914[F]   PR6070.R34

ISBN 0–340–26545–0

Printed and bound in Great Britain for
Hodder and Stoughton Paperbacks, a
division of Hodder and Stoughton Ltd.,
Mill Road, Dunton Green, Sevenoaks,
Kent (Editorial Office: 47 Bedford
Square, London, WC1 3DP) by
Richard Clay (The Chaucer Press) Ltd,
Bungay, Suffolk.

PRINCIPAL CHARACTERS

In Order of Appearance

MALDRED MAC MELMORE: Second son of the Mormaor or Earl of Atholl.

MALCOLM THE THIRD (CANMORE): King of Scots.

GILLIBRIDE, EARL OF ANGUS: Great Scots noble, former Mormaor.

HUGH O'BEOLAIN, HEREDITARY ABBOT OF APPLECROSS: Great noble.

EDGAR ATHELING: Saxon prince. Grandson of Edmund Ironside and rightful King of England.

PRINCESS AGATHA OF HUNGARY: Mother of above.

MARGARET ATHELING: Sister of Edgar.

CHRISTINA ATHELING: Sister of Edgar.

MAGDALEN OF ETHANFORD: Saxon attendant on the princesses.

INGEBIORG THORFINNSDOTTER: Queen, wife of Malcolm.

DUNCAN MAC MALCOLM: Prince of Strathclyde, elder son of Malcolm.

DONALD BEG MAC MALCOLM: Younger son of Malcolm and Ingebiorg.

DUNCAN MACDUFF, EARL OF FIFE: Great noble. Hereditary Inaugurator.

IVO: Celtic Church Abbot of Dunfermline.

MADACH MAC MELMORE: Eldest son of Earl of Atholl. Brother of Maldred.

COSPATRICK MAC MALDRED: Formerly Earl of Northumbria, cousin of the King.

WALTHEOF MAC MALDRED: Styled Earl of Cumbria. Brother of Cospatrick.

PAUL THORFINNSON, EARL OF ORKNEY: Elder son of Thorfinn Raven Feeder and brother of Queen Ingebiorg.

ERLAND THORFINNSON: Governor of Galloway. Younger brother of above.

GODFREY CROVAN OF ISLAY: Later King of Dublin and Man.

FOTHAD THE SECOND: Celtic Church Bishop of St. Andrews. Chancellor.

TURGOT: A Cluniac monk, from Durham.

WALCHERE, BISHOP OF DURHAM: A Lorrainer.

ELDRED, ARCHBISHOP OF YORK: Saxon prelate.

EDWIN ALFGARSON, EARL OF MERCIA: Saxon leader.

MORKAR ALFGARSON: Brother of above.

THURSTAN, ABBOT OF ELY: Saxon leader.

HEREWARD LEOFRICSON, THE WAKE: Lord of Bourne. Saxon leader.

DUNCHAD, ABBOT OF IONA: Co-Arb or Chief Abbot of the Celtic Church.

WILLIAM OF NORMANDY, KING OF ENGLAND – THE CONQUEROR.

DONALD BAN MAC DUNCAN: Son of Duncan the First. Half-brother of Malcolm.

ALDWIN, PRIOR OF WINCHCOMBE AND JARROW: Saxon.

ROBERT, DUKE OF NORMANDY: Eldest son of the Conqueror.

EDWARD MAC MALCOLM: Eldest son of Malcolm and Margaret.

ETHELRED MAC MALCOLM: Third son of Malcolm and Margaret.

ETHELREDA: Daughter of Cospatrick.

EDGAR MAC MALCOLM: Fourth son of Malcolm and Margaret. Later King.

SIR ROBERT DE MOUBRAY, EARL OF NORTHUMBRIA: Norman noble.

WILLIAM THE SECOND (RUFUS), KING OF ENGLAND: Second son of the Conqueror.

Part One

1

MALDRED, SICKENED AT it all, turned away. He was not a
particularly squeamish youth, but on this raid he had
already seen enough savagery and sheer brutality to last
him for many a day. He did not protest, however, not any
more. Malcolm the Third, by-named Canmore, King of
Scots, was not the sort of monarch who accepted criticism
gladly from any man, or woman, in especial from an
eighteen-year-old — even though he was a kinsman, in
cousinship.

The distraught woman's screams would have drowned
out any protests, anyway. No sound came from either of
the children any more, at least — one, a tiny naked baby
which had been still at breast, now lying crumpled some
forty feet below the cliff; the other, a yellow-haired
two-year-old already beginning to be carried away by the
river's current, where it curved round the cliff-foot — the
Wear it was called, apparently. No sounds either now
emanated from the two men of the little household back
there, lying in their own blood, presumably the woman's
husband and father. They sprawled at the door of their
cot-house, the reed-thatched roof of which was blazing
fiercely and sending up great murky clouds of smoke,
carried on the gusty and chill east wind off the sea to join
the vast pall which lay over all that Northumbrian land
northwards and westwards, whence the army had come,
the product of scores, hundreds of other burning home-
steads in their path, all with their quota of slain.

The King was not looking at the hysterical woman, any
more than at her late family. He stared seawards, into the
south-east wind, pale-blue eyes narrowed, watching the
three ships which had just been spotted and pointed out to
him, far from clear as they were in the poor visibility and
clouds of spindrift of the storm's aftermath. That they
were making, limpingly, for the river-mouth was clear
enough however, whatever else was not. There might be
more behind, as yet not visible.

King Malcolm turned to the group of his thanes and

captains who sat their shaggy garrons behind his own — lords, rather; Malcolm, who had been reared here in Northumbrian England, did not like the old Scots terms, and thanes were now lords, mormaors now earls, after the Saxon-Danish custom.

"What think you?" He spoke jerkily, and in the English tongue, not in his native Gaelic — which for a dozen years now the others all had had to practise. "These ships? Are they in trouble? Are there more?" His eyesight was not of the best. "I can see three only . . ." An explosive curse burst from his lips, and he swung in his saddle to stab a blunt finger towards the screaming woman whose cries were preventing the others from hearing him properly. "Silence me that trull, fools!" he shouted.

One of the dismounted soldiers raised a fist and struck the woman full on the mouth, a great blow which flung her headlong to the ground, there at the edge of the little cliff, her outcry reduced to a snuffling, strangled sobbing.

Malcolm Canmore repeated his questions. He was a stocky, thick-set man of forty-seven, with a head strangely over-large for the rest of him — hence the by-name of *Ceann-Mhor* or Big Head — a shock of dark, curling unruly hair only partially restrained by the gold circlet around his brows, his down-turning moustaches cruel, to join a beard forked in the Danish style. The gold circlet alone distinguished him as monarch, for he was dressed no more finely than many of his men, and some of his nobles were considerably more grand. His whole appearance indeed seemed to relate him to his mother's blood rather than his father's. For, although he was the first-born but illegitimate son of Duncan the First, whom MacBeth had slain, boasting the blood of possibly the oldest line of monarchs in all Christendom, reaching far back into pagan times, his mother had been no more than the miller's daughter of Forteviot, not Duncan's queen. Be all that as it might, Malcolm the Third was one of the most successful warriors and shrewd manipulators of his day, even though the notion of mercy, as of gentleness, was not in him.

The consensus of the Scots lords was that the three ships were damaged by the storm and heading into Wearmouth's bay for shelter. One, a long low galley, Danish by the look of her, of the longship breed, was in front, being rowed in, her great single square sail, tattered in ribbons, streaming in the wind. The two other vessels were larger, but more clumsy, traders, cargo-carriers by the look of them, one with a mast gone. If any had borne the usual markings of flags or painted identities on the sails, these had not survived the storm. The general opinion was that they were not war-inclined.

"There is a fourth ship, Highness," Maldred mac Melmore of Atholl said, his young eyes keenest. "Some way to the south. See, rounding the headland. The spray hides it somewhat . . ."

"If four, how many more? What is it, boy? A warship or another merchanter?"

"Not a longship or galley. One like these other two . . ."

"Good. Better pickings from traders than from soldiers, I say! We will down to this haven and receive them, I think! Suitably. Bide you here, lad. You have good eyes, at least! If not much else. Watch you for other ships. Bring me word if there are more. And if any are war-galleys."

The King reined his horse round to move off, and his eyes lighted on the fallen woman again. She lay unmoving, but whether she was conscious or not could not be seen, for her clothing was now thrown up over her head and shoulders, her white lower half laid bare. The man who had struck her was now kneeling over her, busy, another dragging her ragged clothes higher.

"Animals!" Malcolm roared, heels kicking his mount forward at the same time as he whipped out his great two-handed sword from its sheath at his back. Over woman and active, grinning men he rode, slashing downwards with the edge of his blade as he went, beating both the soldiers to the ground in red ruin. "Curs! I said silence her, not breed on her! Colbain — if these two are not dead, hang them. I will be obeyed, to the word." And he rode on without pause.

This forward section of the Scots punitive force, some twelve hundred mounted men, streamed after him, down towards the harbour and village of Wearmouth in St. Cuthbert's Land, taking the savaged would-be rapists with them. Rape was no offence in Malcolm's eyes; indeed it was so commonplace on that expedition as to be wholly unremarkable. But disobedience and undisciplined behaviour in the royal presence were altogether another matter.

Maldred of Atholl was left on the cliff-top beside the burning hovel, with a twitching, moaning woman and two dead cottagers.

He went to her and pulled down her pitiful clothing, very much aware of her rounded white nakedness and the dark triangle at her groin — but aware also of the great bruising on the soft flesh, bruises he guessed had been caused by the hooves of the King's horse rather than by the rough handling of the soldiers. He sought to comfort the creature, but she was only semi-conscious and beyond his feeble aid. There was nothing that he could do, no shelter even into which he might drag her. Sighing, he left her, and went back to gazing seawards into the chill wind.

Presently he decided that there were no more ships coming. Weakly, uncomfortably, he did not look at the woman again, but went for his garron and rode downhill for the river-mouth.

All four vessels were now in the shelter of the estuary, but standing off a few hundred yards out, as though uncertain of their landfall and reception — as well they might be, with a large armed force drawn up and awaiting them. In England, or most other lands, in the year 1069, it paid to be discreet where numbers of men were in evidence. Perhaps the seafarers contemplated turning and facing the angry, snarling Norse Sea again, rather than risk such a welcome. Yet, seen thus at fairly close quarters, the damage to the ships done by the storm of the last two days was sufficiently evident to make anything such unlikely in the extreme. All four craft were in a sorry state. Even the galley, probably the least affected, was sorely battered, its rearing prow, once bearing a proud eagle's or dragon's head, broken off, the decked fighting-platform at the high bows stove-in at one side, and great gaps amongst the rowing benches.

Maldred reined up and dismounted beside his scowling, heavy-shouldered cousin. "No more ships, my lord King," he reported. "Nor any sign of any enemy force to the south, either. On land."

Malcolm nodded, unspeaking. He was, on the whole, a silent man.

"These timorous shipmen grow tedious, Highness!" Gillibride, Earl of Angus declared. He was a youngish man, dark, saturnine, slightly-built but of a smouldering fierceness of nature, who had only recently succeeded his father, the old mormaor. "Shall we put out these boats here and hasten them somewhat?" He gestured towards the numerous fishing-cobles drawn up on the shingle of the boatstrand nearby.

"They will not sail away," the King said briefly. "We have them, and they know it."

"Why waste men on what will fall to us anyway, with a little patience?" the Abbot of Applecross asked. Knowing Hugh O'Beolain, Maldred did not esteem that to be any gentle reminder of Christian charity towards the unfortunate. All abbots of the Celtic Church were not necessarily that way inclined; the hereditary ones, like this O'Beolain of Applecross, were quite as military as, say, some of the Norman bishops.

Maldred himself spoke up. "They will not know who we are. Any more than we know them. They may be friends, not enemies. If you spread your royal banner, Highness, they might come. Reassured."

Some of the nobles round the monarch grinned at the notion that sight of the standard of the present King of Scots might reassure anyone as to a kindly reception. But Malcolm himself nodded, and signed to young Cathail mac Lachlan, son of the Earl of Buchan, who shared the duties of royal standard-bearer with Maldred, to unfurl the great blue Boar flag of Scotland which, because of the difficulty of keeping it flying in high winds, had been carried wrapped round its staff.

Whether as a result or not, the galley at least made a move shortly thereafter. Long oars were put out and the vessel headed slowly for the boatstrand. It was, of course, the only one of the four which could make land thus, with its shallow draught and forefoot construction able to run up on to a shelving beach, where the heavier conventional trading-ships required quays and jetties.

The damaged vessel drew in, and some of the Scots moved down to the strand to receive her. A gang-plank was run down from the shattered bows-platform to the shingle, as the galley grounded, and three men came down it, their rich clothing wet and weather-stained. It was to be seen that some of those who stood at the plank's head to watch were women.

Of the trio, the one in the centre was youngest, thin, almost emaciated, with a slight stoop, very fair hair, and a way of screwing up his eyes as though short-sighted.

"That looks like the flag of Malcolm of Scotland," he said. He spoke a strangely accented English, with a hesitancy of enunciation which nevertheless did not lack authority. "Is it so?"

"It is," the Earl of Angus agreed, less than respectfully. "Who are you?"

The other ignored that. "Take me to the King," he commanded.

Angus grinned. "Beware how you crow here, cockerel!" he jerked, but turned and led the way back to the waiting Scots leadership group at the top of the shingle-bank.

As they came near, Malcolm, staring, drew a quick breath, leaning forward. Clearly he knew now who came.

"These offer no names, Highness," Angus reported. "And come from beyond this sea, I think." And to the newcomers, "Down, fools — on your knees! Before the High King of Scots."

That was ignored likewise. The pale young man spoke. "King Malcolm — we meet again. I thank God that it is you."

"Edgar!" the King said. "Edgar Atheling!"

Angus stared, and swallowed. He had been telling the man who should have been King of England to get down on his knees. He muttered something, scarcely an apology for it was not in that man's nature to apologise for anything, but in protest that he had not known. The Saxon paid no attention.

"We saw your host and feared that it might be some of the Norman's army. From York. From whom we have fled. We are not in your Scotland here, are we?" he asked.

"No — not by a long road! We are ten miles south of Tyne. In Northumbria. But how come you here, man?" Malcolm demanded. "I deemed you in Deira, with Sven of Denmark. You fled, you say?"

"Fled, yes," Prince Edgar said bitterly. "It was all that was left to us. This William the Norman is the Devil Incarnate." He had some difficulty with that phrase. "You know that he bought your Earl Cospatrick away from me. With great promises . . ."

"Aye — that is William, fiend take him! And why I am here. To teach my Cousin Cospatrick of Northumbria a lesson, not to sit down with the Norman. But that was weeks past. Where is Sven Estridson and his Danes?"

"William has bribed King Sven also. Sent him great quantities of gold, English gold, *my* gold! To buy him off. Danegeld again! Sven has sailed back to Denmark, deserting me. Like Cospatrick. I could not face the Norman alone. So must needs flee. We set sail from the Humber. Back to Hungary. Leaving all. But this storm caught us. Three ships are lost, the rest blown here. Near to Tyne, you say?"

Malcolm Canmore failed to express the sympathies which might have been looked for. He was indeed urgently assessing his own position in the light of these tidings. If Sven's Danish army had sailed for home, and this Edgar's Saxons had dissolved in flight, then his own situation here, in less than major strength, could be dangerous. William of Normandy, with his great host based on York, was only seventy miles away to the south. Freed of any threat of Saxon–Danish arms, he could strike swiftly north against the raiding Scots expedition. He would be well informed by spies — always William was that.

When the Atheling got no reply, he went on. "These are the lords Alfwin of Elmham and Leleszi of Hungary." He indicated his two companions. "I have my mother and my sisters on the ship. And others of my company . . ."

Malcolm nodded. "Yes. They may come ashore. We shall spend the night at this Wearmouth. While I send out scouts . . ." He looked away, frowning. Then turned. "Maldred — go bring these ladies to me. My greetings to them. We shall find the best of such hovels as there are, for them." He returned to Edgar Atheling. "Where was William when you last heard? At York? Or nearer to Humber?"

"We sailed from Ravenspur. The Norman was then said to be at Selby, south of York, burning and slaying . . ."

Maldred hurried down to the beach, and ran up the gang-plank on to the galley's damaged prow, to bow before the party waiting there. He had eyes only for the four women, however, one of middle years, the other three young, one a girl no older than himself. They all looked storm-beaten and weary, but held themselves proudly, and were, in his enthusiastic eyes at least, beautiful. Especially two of the younger ones. Half-a-dozen men stood with them.

"I am Maldred mac Melmore of Atholl," he told

them respectfully. "The High King Malcolm bids you kind welcome. And asks me to bring you to his presence."

"Mary Mother of God be praised!" the older lady exclaimed. "So it *is* the King of Scotland. We scarcely dared hope . . ." She was a handsome, slender woman of almost gypsy-like good looks, but with the lines of sorrow or pain in her features, her appearance no doubt accounted for by her Hungarian blood. "I am Agatha Arpad, daughter of King Stephen of Hungary. And these are my own daughters, the Princesses Margaret and Christina." She did not name the youngest girl.

He bowed again. "Princesses, I am yours to command. I act standard-bearer to Malcolm mac Duncan, my cousin." He could not prevent himself putting that in. "Will you come with me?" He had difficulty in keeping his eyes off those younger women.

Two of these, then, were Edgar the Atheling's sisters, the elder the most lovely creature it had ever been Maldred's good fortune to set eyes on, of a calm, ethereal beauty, flaxen-haired, violet-blue-eyed, notably well-built, seemingly serene, untroubled, despite her wet hair, soaking clothing and all the ordeal they had undergone, all Saxon in appearance this one, with no hint of her Hungarian ancestry. Her sister, younger, perhaps twenty years of age, was darker, more like her mother, but less assured, attractive also but more aware of her dishevelled state, even shivering a little in the chill wind. The unnamed one, presumably only an attendant, was nevertheless almost as eye-catching as the Princess Margaret, although very different, with red-brown hair, sparkling hazel eyes and a slender but quite provocative figure. Never, surely, could monastic Wearmouth have witnessed such a visitation as this.

Giving the Princess Agatha his arm down the swaying gang-plank, in some danger of himself falling off — and wishing that it was one of the others, for Maldred was a very normal youth in most matters — he led his bevy of storm-tossed beauty up the beach towards the village, followed by most of the richly-dressed men, and watched by a great many distinctly envious soldiers, not all of whom kept their admiration and feelings silent or even muted. They found the monarch ejecting a couple of Romish priests from the small St. Peter's church in the village with scant ceremony, and ordering the building to be prepared for his occupation.

Malcolm was no ladies' man, and greeted the new-comers in fairly off-hand style — they in turn looking askance at what he was doing. But even he at second and third glance, clearly became not a little conscious of the pulchritude and refinement in evidence, more especially of the older daughter Margaret, to whom his fierce gaze kept returning. He adopted a more attentive attitude accordingly, although nothing would make that man courtly or other than unpolished.

"You are wet and cold, ladies," he paused to say. "But, never fear, we shall soon have you warm and your bellies full. There are but miserable hovels here, but we shall find you the best." Clearly the church was for himself. But from Malcolm Big Head, who normally never so much as took women's feelings and susceptibilities into account at all, this was significant indeed.

"We praise Almighty God that He, in His infinite mercy, directed the cruel storm and wind to bring us into your good care and ward, Sire," the Princess Agatha told him devoutly.

The King grunted non-committally at these sentiments. Moreover, this term sire was a Continental usage being introduced by Norman William, and therefore to be deplored.

But the praise and thanksgiving was quite quickly interrupted when, presently, Malcolm decided on a cot-house for the ladies — scarcely to be compared with the premises he had reserved for himself but reasonably clean and warm, the central-hearth fire of driftwood less smoky than some. Unfortunately its dark interior proved to be encumbered with a bed-ridden old woman in a sort of cupboard recess, unnoticed at first. The King was having her bundled out when there was protest from one of the princesses, Edgar's elder sister Margaret, the beautiful one.

"No! No — please, Highness!" she cried. "Not that. Do not turn her out, I pray you. Let her stay." She had a low-pitched, almost throaty voice, pleasant to hear and much less accented than her mother's — she had spent much of her youth, of course, at her great-uncle Edward the Confessor's Court in England. "We shall find another house . . ."

"Not so," the King snapped, unused to his commands being opposed. "The old witch can kennel elsewhere, well enough. Out with her."

"Sire," the young woman said, her fine bosom indicating depth of breath and emotion both, "of your royal clemency, do not do it. For sweet Mary's sake! If lodge in this house we must, let her remain in it. In her own bed. She is old, sick I think. There is room for us all."

Malcolm stared, as though disbelieving his own ears and eyes.

"Bear with us, Sire," her mother said. "The dear God would not have us to be unmerciful, selfish. Let her remain."

The King clenched great fists. "No!" he barked. "Take her away." His voice quivered. "Do as I say." As his men hustled the old woman out, he turned to stamp after them. At the door he spoke again, without turning. "Maldred — see to these . . . ladies. Their needs." Then he was gone.

There was silence in the shadowy, smoke-blackened, earthen-floored chamber — into which muffled sobbing sounded from the younger sister, Christina.

"Restrain yourself, daughter," the Princess Agatha said tensely. "And you, Margaret. You should know by now that kings are not to be contraverted so. The good King Edward spoiled you. We are wholly in this Malcolm's hands — and he is named a hard man." She glanced over at Maldred, suddenly realising that he was still in the cottage, and bit her lip.

"Are we not rather in *God's* hands, Mother? Has that changed? Has He spared us the storm for us to refuse His mercy to others? Because the King of Scots is heartless, must we, who need mercy ourselves, be so also?"

Christina gulped and snuffled.

Maldred cleared his throat. "Princesses," he said, "your gear? Clothing, apparel, linen? The King commands me to see to your needs. If you will tell me what I can do . . . ?"

"To be sure." The older woman turned to the young girl, who had stood throughout silent although keenly alert, absorbed in it all. "Bedding, other clothes, we have on the ship. It is dry, I hope. Or drier than these here. Magdalen, take him. Bring what is necessary for the night."

The young woman nodded, proffered an incipient curtsy, and signed to Maldred to follow her out.

Skirts kilted up, she skipped before him down to the beach, ignoring the soldiers' pleasantries. She darted a smiling glance back at her companion.

"What name do they give you? Malfred or Malfrith, was it?" she asked.

"No. Those are Saxon names," he said, a little scornfully. "I am Maldred mac Melmore, of the house of Crinan of Atholl."

"So? Is that so very grand?"

He frowned. "Not grand, no. But of ancient line. My father, Melmore, is Earl of Atholl and Abbot of Dunkeld."

"Abbot! A churchman and an earl both? So you are a bastard?"

"I am not!" he cried. "I am lawful second son. In our Church, the Celtic Church, abbots may wed. Not all, but some. *Our* abbacy is heired, hereditary. Dunkeld is the greatest of all. My father is Primate of our Church."

"Indeed," she said. They had reached the foot of the gang-plank, and without pause she went tripping lightly up the steep incline. She seemed something of a light creature altogether, he decided.

Because she had sounded distinctly unimpressed, he informed her slender back, "Moreover, my uncle was King Duncan. And my great-grandsire King Malcolm the Terrible!"

"The Terrible? Then let us hope that King Duncan was something better than either Malcolm," she called back. "For I think this present one is a brute-beast!"

Shocked, he caught his breath. She could have been overheard. There were sailors working about the galley, and Scots soldiers nearby, seeking what might be found. Even gently-born women could die, and horribly, for such a remark.

"For God's sake, watch your tongue!" he said.

Reaching the decking of the bows platform, beside the broken prow, she turned to grin at him, before moving on.

From up here the damage done to the vessel was evident on all hands, with men already seeking to effect repairs of a sort. The girl led the way down the stair to the oar-deck and along the gangway between the rowing-benches, many of which were smashed, the decking littered with the fragments of splintered oars, some blood-stained and telling their own story.

The stern quarters had suffered less. In a dark small

cabin under the poop fighting-platform, his guide wrinkling up her pretty nose at the sour smell of sickness, Maldred was given an armful of feminine clothing, cloaks and furs, to carry, his companion burdening herself similarly. As they were about to leave, she turned back, to collect an object from one of the chests which cluttered the confined space.

"I should take this," she said. "Perhaps it will serve to protect our virtue from all you rough Scots!"

"We . . . I . . . what is it?" She had produced an oddly-shaped silver casket, richly chased.

She opened it, to show him inside a crucifix, strange in that although it was studded with diamonds, it was made of very rough wood, dark, almost black.

"This is the Lady Margaret's most prized possession," she told him. "It is called the Black Rood — made from a piece of the true cross. Given her by her grandfather, King Stephen of Hungary — *Saint* Stephen she calls him . . ."

"The true cross? Do you mean . . . Christ's cross? From Calvary in the Holy Land?"

"Of course. Whether it is truly that or no, who can tell? But she believes it — they all do. And they are a very holy family!" The girl wrapped relic and casket in a fur rug, and gestured him out.

"How did they get it? This King Stephen? If it is truly Christs's cross." Maldred kept glancing at his companion's bundle with some awe.

"From the Emperor, I think. The Emperor is kin to King Stephen. He would get it from the Pope, at Rome. He is King of the Romans. But — it could be any piece of old wood. It looks no different from any other, to me. Although I would not say so to the Lady Margaret, you understand! She would have me starved for days. If not flogged . . . !"

"Flogged? The Princess? Never that, surely!"

"Perhaps not actually flogged, no." The other flashed her impish smile. "But punished severely, oh yes. She could impose harsher penances than any priest, that one."

"But . . . but . . . I cannot believe that. She is kind, good, beautiful. She pleaded for that old woman . . ."

"Ha — another one! You men are all alike. You see a fair face, fine eyes and a bed-worthy woman's body, and you are lost! For a little, at least! You esteem all softness and mild gentleness. But the Lady Margaret is more than

20

that. She is good, yes — too good, perhaps. But strong too. She has steel in her — as unbreaking as any man's sword. So watch you, young Maldred mac Whatever-it-was! Standard-bearer you may be — but do not try your standard on Margaret Atheling, if you would keep it flying! Or on Magda of Ethanford either. So you are warned!"

"I, I . . . am not . . . I have no such . . . I would not think of anything of the sort . . ."

"Liar! I have seen where your eyes rove. And the look in them."

Sidelong he considered her, over his bundle. He had never encountered a creature such as this, so outspoken, so lacking in modesty, so sure of herself. Scots girls were not like this. Nor any Saxon woman he had met hitherto.

"You are quite wrong," he told her. "Much at fault. About me, at least. I am not a knight yet — but I shall be. I respect women. Seek to cherish them."

"Knights are the worst!" she asserted, but smiling again. "But — never heed me, Maldred — or not overly much. I do not think that you are all bad. Indeed I would say that you are the best of the Scots we have seen here, as yet. Better than that King of yours, certainly. Or that arrogant lord who met us." They were back to the village, now wholly taken over by the Scots host, its occupants banished into the oncoming night. "I am Magdalen, daughter of Oswin, Lord of Ethanford," she confided. "I think my father sent me, to attend the princess to Hungary, to be rid of me! Like most other men he does not like the truth from female lips!"

Maldred did not attempt to argue that.

Reaching the cottage, he did his best to make the interior as tidy and comfortable as possible for its new inmates. There were no real furnishings, only the roughest of built-in timber bunks, benches and a table, some wooden platters and chipped earthenware pots. Not that the ladies were complaining — after all it was a considerable improvement on the cramped, dark and noisome cabin on the galley. He scoured other houses for additional items, and though he did not find much suitable, he was rewarded for his efforts by kind words of praise and thanks from the lovely Margaret — and a raised eyebrow from Magdalen. He said that he would go and see what was the position about feeding. The Prince Edgar did not seem to be concerning himself greatly about his womenfolk's wellbeing.

The entire village smelled of roasting beef, with cattle-beasts being cooked whole above a score of fires. At the commandeered church, Maldred found the King and his lords using the altar as a table, round which they sat drinking ale, and coughing somewhat, whilst soldiers aloft dug a hole in the thatched roof to let out the smoke from a well-doing fire of church furniture — since the building was provided with no fireplace or flue. Malcolm was still questioning the Atheling — who looked uncomfortable — closely as to King William's dispositions and possible strategy.

Men brought in the repast, vast quantities of beef with oaten cakes, and little else. Maldred used the King's authority to have no insignificant portion carried off to the ladies' cottage. With the rough if plentiful ale it was scarcely delicate feeding for princesses, but all that was available — and, as they asserted, better than they would have had on the ship. Again they expressed their gratitude to the young man — as well as to their Creator in a lengthy grace-before-meat, worthy of a better feast. They had a further task for Maldred, after they had eaten. Would he go to try find their chaplain and confessor, one Oswald? He was a young Benedictine monk of Durham, who had been lent to them by Bishop Ethelwin to replace their true confessor, Anselm, fallen sick. They had become separated in the confusion of the flight from the Humber, when the monk had gone searching for his bishop. But they had heard that Bishop Ethelwin was on one of the other ships, and possibly Oswald was with him. They had prayed Almighty God for his welfare.

Maldred was less than enthusiastic about this errand, but said that he would do what he could. There were no quays or wharves for deep-draught vessels at Wearmouth, so the other three ships remained at anchor in the bay. There had been some slight coming-and-going with small boats, but the visitors' reception by the Scots had been cool to say the least, King Malcolm having no wish to be burdened by the useless remnants of a defeated Saxon army. So, other than the royal party from the galley, the refugees were remaining in their ships meantime.

Maldred found a little boat on the pebble-strand amongst the fishing-craft, little more than a coracle, and pulled out in the dusk of the October evening to the three vessels, an uncomfortable proceeding, however short, for even in the sheltered bay the sea was choppy. At the first ship he came to he shouted to ask if the Bishop of Durham was aboard, and was directed to the next craft. There, with a seaman agreeing sourly that there were more than sufficient clerks below, he climbed a rope-ladder and went in search of his quarry.

If the galley had shown damage at close quarters, this vessel revealed greatly more, the decks a tangle of rigging and cordage from a broken mast amongst shattered woodwork, men working everywhere to clear the havoc and make what repairs were possible. There was much more, and better, accommodation here than on the galley however, and Maldred wondered why the royal party had chosen the latter. It was much faster, to be sure.

The sound of chanting led him below to where the clerical company were evidently celebrating the evening office, discomforts and mishaps or none. He found them at least in better heart than most of the passengers in that crowded ship, although two of the eight or nine priests were injured, and the old Bishop Ethelwin had an arm broken when he had been thrown against a bulkhead by the violence of the storm.

The monk Oswald was indeed there, probably the youngest of the party, a sturdy, red faced but serious-seeming man in his early twenties, in the black habit of the Benedictine brothers, his shaven tonsure somehow looking out-of-place on a head more apt for a helmet — on the crown of the head, of course, in the Romish fashion instead of above the brow as was the Celtic Church usage.

When the chanting ended, Maldred explained his mission. Although most of the clerics looked with scant favour on the Scot, the young monk seemed eager enough to return to the princesses, and apparently pleased that they had remembered him. Bishop Ethelwin expressed no objection to his departure, asked heedfully after the royal ladies, and sent the two young men on their way with a rather awkward left-handed benediction — it being the right arm which was broken.

Thankful to escape from the smells below decks, Maldred led his companion down to the heaving boat. There he was positioning the oars to row back to the shore when Oswald insisted on taking one, rolling up the wide sleeves of his habit to reveal quite muscular and hairy forearms. Clearly he was used to handling small boats. He did not appear to be a companionable or particularly friendly character, but he curtly explained that he was the youngest son of a small Northumbrian thane from a coastal area near Alnwick, called Amble, and had used such craft for inshore fishing since childhood. Maldred, who was not strong on monks and clerics generally, thought that this one might be less obnoxious than some.

He was less pleased, however, at the flattering reception accorded to his companion by the princesses, their concern for his comfort, their assumption that Maldred would hasten to find him food and bedding.

His services apparently no longer required thereafter, that young man returned to the church, where serious drinking was now in progress. King Malcolm had a large capacity for liquor — as, in consequence, tended to have his close associates. Not that he was a drunkard; Maldred had seldom seen his cousin actually drunk; but drinking was how he spent his evenings as a rule, and as the night progressed his mood was apt to grow the more uncertain. Wise men were inclined to keep out of his way. Aware of this, Maldred's intention was merely to report that all was well with the ladies, learn if any other duties were required of him — for he acted as esquire to the King as well as standard-bearer — and then retire to the folds of his own plaid in some quiet corner, to sleep.

However, this sensible programme was upset. He had reached the King's side, up at the altar, and was informing Malcolm of the state of the three ships out in the bay — and having to lean over Edgar the Atheling to do so who was sprawled forward asleep over the altar-top — when a guard brought in a weary, travel-stained messenger for the monarch, who had obviously ridden far and fast.

He had, he declared, come down Browney to Wear from the Blanchland and Alston fells, from the furthest west of the Scots expedition's units, under the Thane of Arbuthnott. He brought word of major trouble in the west. The Earl Cospatrick, formerly of Northumbria, the King's cousin — and Maldred's also — was laying waste the Cumbrian countryside with a large host. Far too large for Arbuthnott to challenge with his company of only a few hundreds.

"Why?" The King, shoulders hunched like a bull about to charge, snorted that one word, and reached out a great hand to grasp a bunch of the messenger's clothing as though to shake the answer out of him.

"I know not, lord King," the man gasped. "My lord of Arbuthnott did not know. Only that he, the Earl Cospatrick, had come north from Deira with a host, a large host, and was burning and slaying far and wide in your Highness's province of Cumbria . . ."

Malcolm spat out an oath. "Damn you — to what end? What does it serve Cospatrick, foul fiend burn him, to ravish Cumbria? He has lands in Cumberland his own self — Allerdale, that he heired from his father."

"Perhaps it is not Cospatrick that it serves, but his new master William of Normandy?" the Earl of Angus suggested, who seemed less drink-affected than many. "It could be on the Norman's orders."

"Aye, that is likely. William! If William knows that I am here . . ."

"Lord King — my lord of Arbuthnott sent this word also. That folk he has captured, fleeing from the south, from York and Deira, say that King William is greatly wroth. He is laying waste all that country, right to York, in the fiercest fury. Sparing neither man, woman nor child. For their support of the Atheling. He has even burned the great monastery and church of St. Peter . . ."

"Hear you that, man?" The King shook the sleeping prince. "William makes Deira pay for your failure. And sends Cospatrick north to lay waste *my* Cumbria, a curse on him!" Cumbria, the southern portion of the old British kingdom of Strathclyde, which stretched from Alcluyd or Dumbarton down to Lancaster, had been attached to the Scottish crown for over a century. Indeed, King Duncan had made his son, Malcolm, Prince of Strathclyde and Cumbria at the age of five. That was now the nominal title of Malcolm's own son and heir, the young Duncan.

Edgar shook his head vaguely, looking bemused.

"A third word, Highness," the courier said. "My lord says that he has sure word that the new Earl of Northumbria, Robert de Commines the Norman, is slain. And near a thousand of his people with him. At Durham."

"The Comyn? God — who did this?"

"They say the Durham folk themselves. He was a hard

25

man, hated. But my lord thinks that the Earl Cospatrick contrived it, on his way north. In revenge."

The King stared as though through the speaker. "It could be . . ."

"Aye — that is like that fox!" Angus exclaimed. "He deserts the Prince Edgar here, for Norman William — who had earlier displaced him as Earl of Northumbria and appointed this Comyn in his place. Then, sent north by William to ravage Cumbria, to distract *us*, he pays his debt to the Comyn on the way! With the Norman's men. The man is agile!"

"Comyn is no loss, at least! But this of Cumbria . . . ?" The King tapped the altar-top with blunt fingers. "Why? Why should William send Cospatrick there? To distract me? I do not threaten him, William."

"Perhaps he thinks that you do, Highness," Maldred put in eagerly. "Perhaps he thought that you were on your way south to support Prince Edgar also. With a great host. So, having suborned Cospatrick, bought off the Danes and put the Saxons to flight, he now would be rid of you. He is not to know that you were not aiming at him."

"True . . ."

"You were *not* coming to aid me, then?" the Atheling had awakened sufficiently to demand.

Malcolm ignored that. He could hardly explain that he had just been fishing in troubled waters, taking the opportunity whilst William and de Commines were otherwise preoccupied, to do what he best liked doing, raiding into Northumbria, striking terror into his cousin's former earldom, and gaining great booty, cattle and slaves in the process. Malcolm Canmore, despite his ancient throne, was no more than a robber chief at heart. Abruptly he rose from his bench. "This of Cospatrick, of Cumbria, must be dealt with. At once," he declared strongly. "We will waste no more time in sleeping. We march, Forthwith."

"But, Highness . . . !" Angus began. "This is what the Norman wants . . ."

"But nothing, man! It is what *I* want. Cumbria is mine. I shall not see it destroyed, to serve William's purposes. Or Cospatrick's either. And, by God, when I have cleansed it of my devil-damned cousin and his rabble, I will turn Cospatrick's Northumbria into a smoking desert that will make the Duke of Normandy's ravishment of Deira seem like a bairn's play! So — go rouse the camp. We ride, night or none."

"Sire!" the Atheling protested, rising up distinctly unsteadily. "What of me, in this? What of my mother and sisters? They cannot go riding the night, in war . . ."

"Nor shall they!" Malcolm told him grimly. "Women we can do without."

"What then . . . ?"

"You have your ships. The storm is abated. Go where you will."

"But . . . the ships are in no state to sail, to cross the Norse Sea. All are sore damaged."

"Then bide here until they are repaired, man. Sea-worthy. There is timber here. Pull these hovels down. Their roof-trees will give you sufficient for your needs."

"But William could descend upon us. He will hear that we are here. We are but seventy miles north of York . . ."

"Christ God — then go to Scotland, man! Aye, go to Scotland. It is none so far, by sea. Sixty miles to the mouth of the Scots Sea. Your galley will serve for that, safely enough. Go shelter in my realm meantime, with your women. But, see you — only them. Only the galley. I do not want those other ships, a flood of Saxons to support. Just the galley."

Edgar looked doubtful. "Scotland? I do not know . . ." He gnawed his lip. "What shall we do in Scotland? Where shall we go . . . ?"

"Go to my town of Dunfermline. You have been there before. In Fothrif. You will be well enough there. You can bide at Dunfermline until you know your own mind. Whether you go back to Hungary, or whether you try again to regain the throne of England."

"You are . . . kind. But — you will not be there. In Scotland. We may not be well received . . ."

"Maldred mac Melmore here will go with you. He will look to your comfort, man. Now — I must be doing."

"What of the others? The three other ships . . . ?"

"That is your concern, not mine. What would you have done with them had I not been here? See you to it. Maldred — conduct the prince to his quarters. You will bide with him and his women. Convey them to my palace at Dunfermline. When they have their craft ready to sail."

Maldred shrugged unenthusiastic shoulders. "If you so command, Highness. When will you return to Scotland?"

"When I have taught Cospatrick and the Northumbrians a lesson! Aye, and William too, it may be." The King was stamping for the door as he replied.

As Maldred led the uncertain Atheling — he seemed to have little head for liquor, as for coping with emergencies — through the village to the princesses' cottage, the bulls' horns were blowing the muster, a great wailing, and cursing soldiers were everywhere turning out, expressing their disgust in emphatic terms. At the cot-house, lit now only by the glow of the dying fire and the flickering flame of one candle placed beside the uncasketed Black Rood crucifix on the table, they found the ladies retired for the night but sitting up in their makeshift couches, aroused by the horn-blowing and noise, and wondering what was to do. The monk Oswald had found a decently discreet place to lay himself in that part of the hovel screened off and reserved for the cow — now no doubt eaten.

The prince announced the situation baldly. "There is trouble in Cumbria — invasion. Cospatrick again. King Malcolm marches. Now, forthwith. We are to go to Scotland. So soon as we can sail."

"Scotland!" That was in the nature of a chorus, from the princesses.

"Scotland, yes. Malcolm says it. Only ourselves. Not the other ships."

"But why? Why Scotland?" his mother all but wailed. "We are going home. To Hungary. Not to that, not to that . . ." She swallowed the rest.

"We cannot sail for Hungary, across the Norse Sea, with our vessel damaged as it is. Many oars short. The mast broken. Taking in water. We should never gain the other side. And we cannot wait here while the ship-men affect repairs. William the Norman is only seventy miles away. Less, it may be, by now. He will learn of our presence, nothing more sure. And will come for me. So we cannot, dare not wait. You know how that evil usurper would serve us! Scotland is the nearest, the only secure haven we could reach. We can limp that far north, sixty miles only . . ."

The Princess Agatha buried her face in her hands. "I want to go to Hungary, sweet Hungary," she exclaimed. "Not to that cold and barbarous land. Where they are not even true Christians!"

"Mother!" the Princess Margaret warned, indicating

Maldred. "At least they are offering us shelter and safety. Which is truly Christian."

"I have had enough of exile, of strangers, of war. I am not a young woman any more. I yearn for my father's house, my friends, the sunny land of my birth."

"I do not wish to go to Scotland either," the Princess Christina declared. "It is a rude, heathenish land. Let us put to sea, if William comes. He cannot reach us in the ships. Finish the repairs out in the bay. Then sail for home, when all is secure."

"Think you, girl, that William has no ships, no fleet?" her brother demanded. "You do not know what you say. He could send hundreds of vessels against us. Only the storm spared us from pursuit, I think. Now they will be out looking for us. Malcolm is right. The sooner we are in Scottish waters, the better."

"Besides, Scotland is better for our cause than is Hungary, surely?" Margaret put in. "For Edgar's cause. He will never win the throne of England, from Hungary. But from Scotland he might. That, no doubt, is why this King Malcolm is offering us refuge there. To hold us as a threat against the Norman. Let us *be* threat, then, God assisting us! Not just flee the scene, and leave all to the wicked usurper."

There was silence for a moment or two as they all stared at the lovely speaker, sitting up amongst the furs and blankets of her couch, in a shift which revealed rather more of her excellent upper parts than that piously modest young woman would be apt to demonstrate to male gaze. Maldred, for one, was lost in admiration. And not only on the physical plane. Clearly this princess had the spirit of the family. And shrewdness too, since she had so quickly perceived Malcolm Canmore's advantage in having the Athelings in Scotland.

The monk Oswald spoke, at their back. "What of Bishop Ethelwin and the others, in this, lord Prince?"

"He . . . they are not to come. King Malcolm was very strong on that. They must go . . . elsewhere. I am sorry, but that is his command."

"Go where?"

"I do not know." Testily the other said it. "Perhaps, perhaps to Denmark. Or Norway . . ."

"You — *you* will not leave us?" Agatha Arpad asked the monk, almost pleaded. "Stay with us, in God's mercy. If go we must to this heretical land. Where they do not recognise even the Holy Father in Rome, it is said. We shall need you sorely."

"If my humble services are required, Princess, and if Bishop Ethelwin agrees, I shall be honoured to remain with you . . ."

There was a commotion at the low-browed door, and the King himself stooped to stride in unannounced.

"Maldred," he jerked. "I may need more men. When you win back to Dunfermline, have MacDuff of Fife muster another host. Two thousand will serve. To be ready if I send for them. Ready to march with all speed to Cumbria. You have it?" He turned, to glower at the women. "I march within the hour, ladies. You will sail for Scotland so soon as you may. You will be safe there. Maldred mac Melmore will see to it. Until I return. The Prince, here, can go with you, or ride with me — whichever he pleases."

"Edgar — in sweet Mary Mother's name, do not leave us now!" the Princess Agatha cried. "You *must* not go Sire — we need him. You do not."

"As you will. I but reckoned that he might wish to take a hand in settling his score with Cospatrick."

"No — he has his duty to me and mine, first. In this grievous coil. If go to Scotland we must, Edgar must accompany us."

"Aye. I think that I see why he has not won his English throne!" Malcolm said heavily. But he had scarcely looked at either the older woman or her son once during this exchange, his eyes being concentrated on her elder daughter's delectable person, so much more in evidence than was customary. Margaret must have been very well aware of his assessing gaze, but she ignored it, did not even make any special attempt to cover herself more fully or to huddle down in to the bedding like her sister Christina. Maldred admired her spirit the more.

"My brother did not win his throne because his reputed friends and William's reputed enemies, deserted him, Sire. Or never so much as lifted hand to aid. Although . . . nearby."

"Ha — you think so, girl?" The King stepped over, to where he could look down directly on her. "You conceive all to have a duty to rescue this prince?"

"I conceive that all who profess to hate the Norman

30

usurper and his savage ways should have rallied to send him back to Normandy!"

"So-o-o! You are free with your opinions, for the daughter of a landless man!" he growled.

"But the grand-daughter of two great kings, Sire — Stephen and Edmund Ironside!" she gave back.

He frowned — and then raised surprised brows as the girl Magdalen appeared, to insert herself neatly between him and the princess, to stoop and slip a cloak from her own couch around Margaret's bare shoulders. It was deftly done. As she moved modestly away again, she contrived to make an immodest face at the interested Maldred. Margaret herself acted as though nothing had happened.

Malcolm glared, snorted, began to speak, and then turning, stamped out of the cottage.

"Thank you, Magda," the princess said calmly, into the hush.

After a moment, Maldred followed his monarch out, uncertainly.

2

SCOTLAND SHOWED AT least a scenic welcome for the refugees, as the galley limped up the Scottish Sea between the Lothian and Fife coasts, with all echoes of the storm gone, the late-autumn sunshine golden and the air crisp and clear. Maldred stood, with the three young women and the monk Oswald, on the roughly-repaired bows-platform, pointing out the landmarks on either side, the soaring, mighty Craig of Bass and the lesser islands of its group, with the little red-stone cashel or Celtic Church monastery on Fetheray and the green cone of North Berwick Law behind, all backed by the long heather hills of Lammermuir — this on the south; and to the north the yellow beaches, rocky headlands and fishing-havens of the East Neuk of Fife, with the cave-pitted cliffs of Kincraig, near where the great MacDuff, Earl of Fife, had his ferry. He named for them the great bight of Aberlady Bay on the one side and Largo Bay on the other, the twin breasts of the Lomond Hills, which he took the opportunity of calling the Paps of Fife — and stole a sidelong glance at his hearers to observe any effect — gesturing ahead to where the extraordinary crouching-lion-shaped peak of Arthur's Chair and the fort-crowned rock of Dunedin, or Edinburgh, seemed to challenge a range of taller hills, the Pentlands.

"Hills everywhere!" the Princess Christina said. "I had heard that there was nothing but mountain and rock and bog in Scotland. How can men live in such a place?"

"We live very well," Maldred replied tartly. "As you will have need to discover, perhaps."

"At least it is a beautiful land," Margaret put in soothingly.

It was nearing noon. They had left Wearmouth the previous afternoon, only some twelve hours after King Malcolm had marched off, not daring to wait longer, despite the state of the vessel, so anxious was Prince Edgar — although the other three ships had remained at their anchorage meantime. But they had brought some of the passengers from the other craft with them, so that the galley was much overcrowded — Hungarian and Saxon notables of the Atheling Court. Maurice, the Hungarian ship-master, found them all a trial.

The visitors were surprised when, passing the cliff-girt island of Inchkeith, Maldred signed to the shipmaster not to turn in southwards towards the lion-shaped Arthur's Chair and the cluster of lesser hills around it, where clearly there was a sizeable town and associated haven for ships, but to continue on up into what was now a narrowing estuary. They passed three more islands, on one of which Maldred pointed out the cashel of St. Colm — he was concerned to make it evident to these proud Romish Church travellers that Scotland was indeed a Christian country, with many monasteries and religious houses, even though they did not recognise the Pope of Rome as Christ's deputy. To the monk Oswald's question as to who was this *Saint* Colm, distinctly emphasising the word saint, the younger man declared strongly that he was the devout and vigorous missionary, Columba of Iona himself, from the Celtic Church in Ireland, who had come to convert the Cruithne or Picts here centuries before the English, the Saxons and probably the Hungarians likewise, had even heard the name of Jesus Christ.

The girl Magdalen at least seemed to find that amusing.

Quite soon after this exchange Maldred indicated where, ahead, thrusting promontories on either side narrowed the estuary to little more than a mile across, with an islet in the centre. This was the end of the Scottish Sea, he informed. Beyond it was the Firth of Forth, which continued for many miles more up to Stirling. Here he directed the shipmen to steer the galley in to the north side, where in a little bay behind the cliffs of the promontory, there was a substantial stone jetty at which there were already two vessels moored, and a number of small fishing-craft. The great Highland mountains of the west, some already snow-streaked, had now come into view, blue and jagged in the distance.

When they had tied up, and the protracted business of landing and unloading was proceeding, Maldred went to find a messenger with a horse who would ride the four miles north to Dunfermline, where King Malcolm had established royal residence, to fetch back many garrons and carriers to help transport the visitors. Also, of course, to inform the Queen of the situation.

Inevitably there was quite a lengthy wait, and while their elders sorted out and arranged what was to be taken and what left, the young people decided to walk for at least part of the way, Maldred leading a party of perhaps a dozen, glad enough to stretch their legs after the constrictions of the ship.

They climbed inland by a winding track which lifted and dropped and rose again over a series of gentle ridges of pastureland, cattle-dotted, with small farmsteads and strip cultivation. As the land rose, the prospects widened and became ever finer, all the tremendous Forth valley stretching westwards, the firth narrowing to the river emerging from the mountains of Lennox, while as far as eye could see, to the south, the hills of Lothian reared their shadow-slashed ramparts above the coastal plain. Even Christina Atheling had to admire.

They had covered almost two miles before a convoy of men and garrons passed them, heading for the harbour under one of the palace stewards. Maldred offered to detach two or three of the horses for the young women, but Margaret would have none of it, declaring that the exercise would do them good. They had kilted up their long gowns for ease of walking, to the admiration of their escorts, even Oswald, entrusted with carrying the precious Black Rood casket, hitching his black Benedictine robe to reveal hairy legs.

They rested for a while beside a large isolated boulder, recumbent on the crest of one of the rolling ridges, which interested Margaret sufficiently for her to enquire how it had got there, so great a stone by itself. Maldred explained, pointing to humps in the cattle-cropped turf around, that it was all that remained above ground of a stone circle. The Cruithne, who occupied the land before the Scots came from Ireland, were sun worshippers, and these circles, of which there were a great many, were temples of a sort, usually set on high places, the stones aligned most exactly to point to the sunrise position at certain times and seasons.

"They were great sundials, then?"

"More than that. It is said that they enshrined much knowledge now lost to us. Of the heavens, of other worlds, of the weather and the seasons. Ancient wisdom . . ."

"Heathenish superstition!" Oswald amended.

"Not so. My father says that we have lost much in discarding this knowledge. He says that in some matters their learning and understanding was far above ours . . ."

"Such talk is foolish and wicked, such knowledge sinful — like that of the Assyrians and the Babylonians. Of the Devil. Let us be on our way, princesses — this place is evil!"

"Who are you to say what knowledge is foolish or sinful?" Maldred demanded warmly. "An ignorant Englishman from a Northumbrian village! A mere monk — whilst my father, as well as an earl, is an abbot of Holy Church!"

"You are condemned out of your own mouth, young man — since no true abbot could ever have a son. Holy Church forbids it . . ."

"Is that your Dunfermline we see ahead?" Margaret asked, moving between them. "Up on the terrace, with the trees? It looks a fair place."

Maldred swallowed. "That is the cashel of Saint Ternan. He came from Ireland, with Farlane the Strong, long ago.

34

Farlane built his dun, or fort, further over, to the west. You cannot see it yet. That is where the King has his tower and palace. At the dun. Dun Farlane — it has become changed to Dunfermline."

They moved on, while Maldred told them more of the sturdy, fearless and strong-armed missionaries of the Celtic Church, who had brought Christianity to this land in no uncertain fashion, and of the Keledei, or Friends of God, their present-day successors in the cashels and monasteries. Oswald marched along behind, tight-lipped, frowning.

Prince Edgar, his mother and the others caught up with them as they neared the monastery of St. Ternan. The prince very much took charge now. He had been here two years before, in 1067, after a preparatory expedition to try to establish a base for his attempt on the English throne, in Cospatrick's Northumbria, had suffered defeat at the Norman usurper's hands, and fled to Scotland. He insisted that his sisters be mounted, as befitted their rank, and that they rearrange their clothing and tidy their hair, blown by the breeze. He instructed Maldred to go on ahead and inform the Queen of Scotland of their arrival.

"The Queen's Highness already knows of your coming," he was told. Maldred did not like Edgar, and it is to be feared that he was not very good at hiding his feelings. "If she is ready to receive you, she will no doubt be waiting."

Proceeding along one of the many little ridges of that strangely folded land, presently there were sudden gasps from the ladies. They had reached a point where the ground dropped away abruptly, unexpectedly, before them into a deep, winding glen, its sides scattered with thorn-trees. And rising out of the centre of this glen was a narrow, isolated mound, glacial of origin, steep-sided on all flanks save that to the east where a sort of spine rose more gradually. Crowning the summit of this mound, within the green ramparts of an old fort, Farlane's dun, reared a tall square stone tower, almost in the Norman keep fashion, totally unlike any Scots or Celtic hall-house or rath, stark, strong, uncompromising. Stretching eastwards from it, within a high-walled enclosure, was a range of lesser, lower buildings, part stone, part timber coated with clay and whitewashed in more typical Scots style.

"That . . . that . . . ?" the Princess Agatha exclaimed. "Is that it? We have come to . . . this?"

"That is Malcom's Tower, yes. I told you that it was no palace, no suitable house for a king, Mother. Or even a modest thane . . ."

"The King has houses, palaces, at Forteviot and Dunsinane and Kincardine," Maldred interrupted. "Forts and raths amany. But he prefers to live here. He chose to build this tower and house. He is not a man for great palaces and large Courts. A warrior-king."

Without comment the visitors moved on down into the Glen of Pittencreiff.

There, at the foot of the eastern spine of the central mound, was the first line of defence, a moat, water drawn from the burn that threaded the valley, with a drawbridge. Here the chief steward awaited them, to conduct them through a gatehouse-pend in the perimeter walling and up the slope, zigzagging, to a point where the spine had been cut through laterally with a wide and deep trench or dry ditch, across which was a second drawbridge. Beyond this, the first of the buildings arose, all stone here, with an arched and fortified entrance to an elongated narrow central courtyard. Within the entrance a young woman stood, backed by attendants.

"Greetings, Highness," Maldred called, strongly. "The lord King sends his royal salutes." Which, in fact, was a lie; Malcolm had not so much as mentioned his wife. "I bring the Prince Edgar of England, his lady-mother and sisters and some of their people. Seeking your royal clemency and aid. In flight from Duke William." He turned. "The Queen's Highness, the Lady Ingebiorg Thorfinnsdotter."

"I thank you, cousin," the Queen answered gravely. "My husband is well? Good. I greet the Prince Edgar again, warmly. And bid the princesses welcome to my house." She was a fresh-faced, round-featured, big-boned creature, not beautiful but pleasant-looking and unassuming, only daughter of the great Thorfinn Raven Feeder, Earl of Orkney. Malcolm had married her soon after attaining the throne on the death of King Lulach, as a politic gesture to ensure that the late Thorfinn's sons did not trouble him as their father had troubled his. They were second-cousins, their grandmothers being sisters, daughters of Malcolm the Second, The Destroyer — although the King was now forty-seven while she was only twenty-five. The marriage could scarcely be called a happy one. Maldred bore the same relationship to the Queen.

The visitors dismounted, to make due obeisance to their hostess and to be led within. The ladies all eyed the Queen interestedly, for her story and Malcolm's behaviour towards her were well known.

"So that is the daughter of the famed Thorfinn the Mighty!" Magdalen of Ethanford said quietly, as she and Maldred followed their principals up the climbing courtyard. "She scarcely looks a female Viking!"

"A pity that she is not more like her sire."

"Why?"

"She might do better, live the happier. She is too gentle for the King."

"Ah. I can believe that he would require steel in a woman. They have no children?"

"Yes. Two princes. There they are, waiting in the tower doorway. With the wolf-hounds. Duncan and Donald."

Two small boys, about nine and eight years, watched the procession, one scowling, one grinning.

The Queen led her guests not to the tall stark tower that frowned over all from the crest of the mound, but into the doorway of the secondary and lower building on the right — which proved to be really a fairly typical Celtic hall-house attached to the keep but utterly different from it in style and accommodation, a commodious, comfortable, sprawling establishment. Malcolm had built it on to his tower at his new wife's urging, when he still paid some heed to her wishes, she hating his Norman keep from the first sight of it, however defensively strong.

They came into the great hall of the house, a vast apartment which took up a full half of the entire building, right to the blackened roof-timbers — it had to, in order to allow the smoke from the central fireplace to be drawn up and escape through the necessary aperture in the roof, flues being impracticable in this timber-and-clay construction. Elsewhere the building was two-storeyed, with only the upper-storey bedchambers having heating. A huge fire of aromatic birch-logs blazed now in mid-hall, scenting as well as warming the air notably — but even so the visitors were quickly coughing in the smoke-laden atmosphere. A very long table ran down one side of the chamber, strewn with platters and goblets and the like. For the rest, the place was an untidy litter of benches, coffers, stools, spinning-wheels, rugs, skins, hangings askew and bone-gnawing dogs. It seemed that Queen Ingebiorg was little concerned with keeping a spick-and-span house.

Informed that a meal would be ready for all shortly, the newcomers were taken to their quarters. There was insufficient room in this tiny palace for all the refugee party, and most of the men would have to live either in the monastery or in cottages of the quite large associated township. The Athelings were given upper rooms in the hall-house, whilst stewards took their nobles away to find as acceptable accommodation as possible.

While they were settling in, the Queen spoke privately with Maldred.

"What is the truth of all this, cousin?" she asked. "What does Malcolm want with these? It is not like him. Why are they come? And for how long?"

"I do not know," he admitted. "The King took pity on them. They could nowise sail the Norse Sea in their damaged ship . . ."

"Malcolm does not take pity on any — save to his own advantage," she said factually.

"Perhaps. It may be that he sees gain in holding the Atheling here. As threat against Norman William. Something to bargain with."

"And the women? Malcolm has little use for women — save to breed on. I mislike that Agatha, I think. The mother. She has a proud manner."

"They have been told ill of Scotland, Highness. They believe us barbarians, uncouth. Scarcely Christian, indeed! For they are a very holy family. God's name is seldom off their lips. But . . . the Princess Margaret, the fair one, is different. Holy also, but kinder. And stronger too, with more of spirit."

"To be sure. I can see that she is the one who would have men dancing to her tune! I shall watch her! Holy women of her years require watching. Especially when they are beautiful and shaped as she is! So — watch you also, Maldred mac Melmore! And what of my warrior lord? Who is he slaying now? And when does he return?"

"That I know not, cousin. He is gone to Cumbria now. To repel a raid by Cospatrick."

"But Cospatrick is his cousin. And yours. Displaced by the Normans. That Comyn in his place. Why should he raid Cumbria?"

"He has changed sides once more. A strange man. And Comyn is dead. This time, the King will hang him, I think, cousin or none."

"Malcolm will enjoy that!"

Maldred glanced sidelong at the Queen, and away. She was seldom so outspoken as this. Something must have roused her.

The young princes came running in, towed by their wolf-hounds. Duncan the elder, aggressive, abrupt, true son of his father; Donald, cheerful, happy but easily hurt.

Time for confidences was past.

The next morning Maldred rode eastwards for Kennochy in Fife, to deliver the King's message to the Earl MacDuff. Dunfermline was in Fothrif, the western sector of the great peninsula between Forth and Tay; but the Earl had his main seat at Kennochy twenty miles or so into Fife proper, sufficiently distant not to be too irksomely on the King's back but near enough to be able to rally swiftly to the royal aid. It was indeed the strong presence here of his powerful friend and ally, MacDuff, which had occasioned Malcolm to desert the traditional royal palaces of Fortrenn, in Forteviot and Dunsinane, and to build his tower on Fife land at Dunfermline, for reasons of security, the first monarch to have dwelt in Fife. He and MacDuff had been equally unpopular in 1058, jointly responsible for the slaying of the good King MacBeth and then, six months later, of his stepson and successor, Lulach. MacBeth's seventeen-year reign had been an unusual and prosperous interlude for Scotland, and his killers were hated. So they had kept together for mutual protection, and lived close these dozen years, whilst memories and old loyalties faded. Malcolm would never be loved or popular, as MacBeth had been — nor, probably would wish to be. But he was a strong King, maintained discipline, had few extravagances — and therefore was not heavy with his taxes — and was excellent at providing English slaves and bondwomen from his raids in the south.

Kennochy lay almost three hours' ride to the east. Maldred went by the Hill of Beath and the Loch of Gelly, and thereafter, with the long, high ridge of the Lomonds lifting above him to the north, entered the Leven valley by Kinglassie and Goatmilk.

The house of Kennochy, like most other seats of the

lords and thanes, was built on the site of an earlier Pictish fort, in a strong defensive position commanding a wide prospect over land and sea. Within the old ramparts of stone and turf rose not so much a rath as a village of hall-houses and their subsidiaries, a self-contained community of some two hundred souls. Here he found Duncan MacDuff, sixth Mormaor and now first Earl of Fife, about to set off hawking in the Myres of Balgonie. He was a big, almost gross, red faced man in his mid-sixties, bull-like, short of neck, choleric. He was not at all pleased with Maldred's arrival and message, for he was essentially a lazy man, disinclined to exert himself. Hawking suited him very well, since little effort was demanded of any but the hawk.

But puff and snort as he would, the Earl was not foolish enough to fail the King's command. If Malcolm needed his services, he more greatly needed Malcolm's support. For although senior noble of the realm and Hereditary Inaugurator at coronations, a Pictish dignity, he had many enemies and was looked upon with suspicion by many of his peers. Apart from being so closely involved in the death of MacBeth, he had fought against the Scots many times, on the English side — as, of course, had Malcolm also — and was trusted by few.

"How many men does the King require? Two thousand?" he grumbled. "I cannot raise the like, in Fife and Fothrif. With what he already has from my earldom. I shall have to send to Lennox and Strathearn and Gowrie. Even Angus and the Mearns. What of your own Atholl, boy?"

"My father has already five hundred with the King."

"Then he will have to find more. What are they for, all these men? What does Malcolm want with so many more? It is not a war he is at!"

"He is teaching Cospatrick a lesson — who has changed sides once again. And he fears that Norman William might come, or send, to Cospatrick's aid. In Cumbria."

"Malcolm should have more sense. At his age. He should bide at home, looking to his kingdom. Instead of traipsing off on unnecessary warfare." Belatedly the Earl asked for his son. "Dufagan? Is all well with him?"

"Well enough, my lord. He is with the King, slaying, burning and raping with the best!" Maldred did not like Dufagan MacDuff.

"Aye. That is Dufagan . . ."

While the Earl went about the business of sending messengers around the land calling for the additional muster, Maldred was afforded refreshment in his hall. The Countess was long dead, and he was entertained by the two remaining unmarried daughters of the house, the Ladies Malvina and Medana, both somewhat older than himself. They made quite a fuss of him — for, because of his unpopularity, their father's house was little frequented by folk of their own rank, and personable young men thin on the ground. They were neither of them beauties, but nor were they without their attractions, well-built and quite comely young women, especially the younger. Normally Maldred was far from unappreciative of the excellences and kindnesses of the opposite sex; but today he found himself comparing these two with Margaret Atheling and finding them sadly wanting. Which was perhaps unfair.

He did not linger long at Kennochy, in consequence, before heading back for Dunfermline.

There, the very next day he came to blows, after a fashion, with the same Princess Margaret — with her mother and sister also, to be sure, but Margaret being the more positive character, he identified the clash more with her, however quietly dignified she was about it. It was Sunday, and the day was started fairly early with a procession of Keledei, the Friends of God, wending its way down from the cashel of St. Ternan into Pittencrieff Glen, and then up to the palace courtyard, chanting sweet music of praise — although long before that the customary early morning devotions of the Athelings could be heard emanating from one of the upper rooms. The monks took up their position in the centre of the yard opposite the hall doorway, four brawny specimens depositing a heavy stone altar in the midst, which they had carried down on a sort of poled tray. It was a massive thing, reputedly the blessed St. Ternan's own, richly carved with Celtic floreate crosses, intricate design and fabulous animals, with a hollow scooped in the top, which enabled it to be used as a baptismal font for holy water when necessary. On this old Abbot Ivo reverently placed the communion vessels, the silver flagon of wine, the canister of bread, the bowl and shallow, battered silver spoon. This done, still chanting, the Keledei waited.

Despite the chill east wind and threatening rain, the palace staff — it could scarcely be called a court — with the servitors and cottagers from the rath-toun, mill-toun and farm-touns around, were flooding into the courtyard in cheerful, familiar fashion, children and dogs and laughter all but drowning out the singing. The Celtic Church was not very interested in church buildings, preferring worship to be in the open air. In the great hall the Queen and her immediate household were waiting for their guests. When still these did not appear, she sent Maldred upstairs to remind them that all was ready — although they had been previously informed.

He found the Atheling family together in one bed-chamber, with Magdalen and the Benedictine Oswald, clustered at the window, the wooden shuttering open. He cleared his throat.

"Princesses — the Queen awaits you. Abbot Ivo also. All is ready."

Prince Edgar answered him. "Then proceed. We can watch from here. If so we decide."

Maldred stared. "But . . . but you are expected. To take part. All attend Christ's Holy Mass. This is Sunday."

"We are well aware what day it is," the Princess Agatha said. "When the uproar outside is quietened, we shall celebrate Mass here. With Father Oswald. In decent reverence."

"But . . . all expect you. To attend. All guests. It is the custom. Her Highness stands waiting . . ."

"Then convey our regrets that she has been delayed, young man. We worship God . . . otherwise."

"Maldred — ask that we may be excused," Margaret added, less rigidly. "Say to Her Highness that, not knowing the order and service, we should but confuse all."

Abruptly Maldred hurried away to inform the Queen.

Ingebiorg Thorfinnsdotter was scarcely religiously inclined, as a rule, having been brought up in an establishment which had other priorities — even though, before his death, Thorfinn Raven Feeder had indeed built a stone church in Orkney, the first such there, in which to await the resurrection of his body, as a sort of insurance. But she was the Viking Earl's true daughter deep down, however quiet her ways, and in certain matters could play the queen with any. Listening to the young man, she set her lips tightly, small chin jutting. When he had finished, she sent the chamberlain out to inform Abbot Ivo that they would be a short while yet, and turning, hitched her skirts to climb the stair in no uncertain fashion, Maldred at her heels.

She halted in the Athelings' doorway, eyeing them. "I give you good morning," she said. "This is God's Day. And this is a Christian house. All dwelling in it start this day, one in seven, thus. Attending the Mass of our Good Lord, men, women and children . . ."

"Even the dogs, it seems!" Edgar interrupted.

"We partake of Mass *every* morning, Highness," the Princess Agatha said. "In rather different fashion."

"Perhaps. But you are guests in this house and this land. And guests have their duties, as have hosts."

"Our first duty is surely to Almighty God! We cannot worship Him uncouthly, as though at a, a fair!"

"Lady Queen — we are grateful indeed for your hospitality and shelter," Margaret put in earnestly. "But we pray you, do not ask this of us. If it had not been Mass, if it had been some other worship, we might have attended. But it is a sin against the Holy Ghost to participate and partake of the Mass, unbelieving. Holy Church binds us in this."

"Holy Church? Holy Church is one and indivisible. Only man makes divisions. Is that not so, Sir Priest?"

Father Oswald looked unhappy. "There is one Church, yes — Holy, Catholic and Apostolic But the keys thereof were given by our Blessed Lord to Saint Peter. And his successor, the Holy Father in Rome, lays down due and proper order . . ."

"Do not preach to me, sir, of what is due and proper! I was reared in the Romish faith. In Orkney. But when I wed, it was due and proper that I adhered to the Church of my husband's people, that of Columba. You are now being cherished and protected — of your own will, not mine — in a realm of that Church. It is the bounden duty of every householder in that realm to ensure that all under his or her roof, or in their care, attend this Mass at the commencement of the Lord's Day. I abide by that duty, in my husband's absence."

"You will not force us to partake damnation to our eternal souls, Highness?" Margaret declared, and it was in reality no question.

Ingebiorg perceived a will as strong as her own. "Do not partake, then," she said. "But attend. Down there. All others must. That is my royal command." Turning her back on them all, she strode for the stairway.

Maldred waited for the others to follow, however reluctantly — and waited also to ensure that they did. The girl Magdalen whispered to him, as they brought up the rear behind the Benedictine monk.

"I pray that your Queen knows what she fights in Margaret Atheling! The others she may beat, I think. But Margaret will win — you heed my words. She always does."

The royal party emerged from the hall-house to join the throng surrounding the monkish group. The chatter and laughter died away, all, including the clergy, turning to consider the newcomers with undisguised interest. Abbot Ivo bowed to the Queen, smiling, and again to the Athelings. They took up their position at the foot of the tower, left clear. All remained standing.

The Abbot raised his bachuil, or crozier, a simple ash-plant about four feet long, with an elaborately decorated crook in silver and enamels, his assistant rang a rectangular-shaped bronze bell, rather like a large cowbell, and the service commenced.

It went briskly, starting with a chanted recital of the Apostles' Creed, all joining in enthusiastically. A prayer followed, also chanted, with a shouted response. Then a psalm which all seemed to know, a reading from a well-thumbed scriptural scroll, and a rousing hymn with a repeated rhythmic chorus, obviously much enjoyed. It was all in the Gaelic, of course, and unintelligible to the visitors, who might thus be excused for not joining in. King Malcolm, in his determination to substitute what was known as the Inglis for the old language, had not yet managed to wean the Church from its traditional tongue. Abbot Ivo, however, made a gesture, in the short homily which followed, by repeating in English a welcoming reference to the refugees from the Duke of Normandy's usurpation in England, and a good-going denunciation of the tyrant's savageries — at which all cheered strongly, save for the victims, who looked uncomfortable.

Another prayer heralded the Eucharist. All turned to face the east. A lusty ringing of the hollow-sounding saint's bell, before and after the Consecration of the bread and wine, led to the congregation shouting grateful approval. The administration followed at once, all still standing, children as well as adults being given a broken fragment of the loaves and a sip of the wine from spoons even more battered, from much use, than the one on the altar. The Queen was not served first, but actually near the end, for the administration started at the eastern side of the circle and worked round clockwise, like the sun, and the royal party stood at the tower-foot, to the north. When Abbot Ivo offered the Elements to the Athelings, and they were refused with head-shakes, he looked surprised, but smiled acceptingly and passed on. Father Oswald placed a hand before his eyes, at this stage, so that he did not have to look at the offending substances. Margaret and Magdalen at least smiled their rejection.

When all others had partaken, a final vigorous hymn, with a refrain that set feet tapping, even stamping, followed by the Benediction, crozier held high, completed the essentially simple service which, despite the large number receiving Communion, had not lasted more than twenty minutes.

Thereafter all broke up and became a cheerful social gathering, easy, noisy, unaffected, the children, released from what had been only moderate restraint, making up for lost time, the Keledei mixing casually with the crowd, the Queen and her attendants likewise. Princess Agatha hurried indoors at once, followed by Edgar and Christina and the monk, but Margaret remained and went over to look at the altar, left unattended, Magdalen with her.

Maldred came to them. "Was that so ill, then?" he asked. "So, so uncouth, was it? Barbarous?"

"It was . . . interesting," Margaret said.

"I enjoyed the singing," Magdalen added. "Although I did not understand the words."

"Did it injure you to attend? And could it have harmed you to partake?"

The princess chose her words. "Knowing it to be in error, mistaken, yes, Maldred. When one is aware of the truth, to practise other is sin. It was all sincere, honest, yes. But nevertheless, in error. Those who, in honesty, believe in it will no doubt escape punishment. But for those informed in the truth . . ."

"Error! Mistaken! What is in error here? How can you, princess though you may be, declare what is truth and

45

what is error? Against the teachings of abbots and priests and the ancient saints of God?" he exclaimed.

"There have been saints and saints!" she said. "Heresies can grow, even amongst the elect. The holy Augustine proved that, and purged Mother Church. And more lately the Blessed Benedict. The Devil will insert heresy amongst the unwary whenever he can . . ."

"Are you naming us heretics now? In your English pride!"

"Would you have me to shut my eyes to error? When it is so manifest? I who am grand-daughter of Saint Stephen and grand-niece of Edward the Confessor? Maldred, I do not *blame* you, any of you, since you know no better. But that service we watched was in error from start to finish. It was not held in a consecrated building. It was attended by all and sundry, without any due preparation. There was no confession of sins, so far as I could understand, and so no absolution. So all partaking were still in their sins."

"Save us — but is the partaking not itself to wipe away our sins?"

"Not if it is taken unprepared and unworthily. As it was. Even the children received the sacrament, knowing nothing of what they did, poor little creatures. It was not, to be sure, the *true* sacrament of the Body and Blood of Christ, so we must believe that they will not be harmed . . ."

"Saints in Heaven — may God forgive your arrogance!"

"God indeed forgive me my unwitting sins. In this we agree. But God *has* given us wits. To use. To discern His truths. And to discern error, with His teachings in Christ. And it required little wit to discern on what that ritual was grounded. Not so much on the blessed Last Supper of Our Lord as on ancient pagan sun-worship!"

He stared at her. Even Magdalen looked wondering.

"Can you not see it? The circle, out in the open air. This graven stone in the midst. The turning east, to the sunrise. The administration as following round the hours of the sun's course. The shouting, the standing. Look at this stone, covered with strange animals. What of Christ is there in that? And these crosses, more like flowers, or sun's rays. Recollect that great stone at which we rested, walking here from the ship. This is just such another. Here is the shadow of sun-worship, idolatry!"

"Dear God!" the young man said.

"Can you deny it, Maldred — now that it is shown to you?"

He was no theologian and no more versed in matters religious than most youths of his age. But he had certain basic loyalties, a respect for ancient tradition and his race, some pride — and a resentment at being catechised by mere girls.

"My father — who is abbot you will mind, as well as earl — told me once that the old saints who brought the gospel here from Ireland, the Brethren of Columba, used of purpose to preach at the stone-circles and standing-stones. They used them, set up Christ's Cross within them. Carved crosses on the stones. Built their cashels and churches there. And why not? That was where the folk had always worshipped. They taught them the true worship — but used what the folk knew to do it. Taught the true meaning of what they had groped for. In the sun and the seasons, the stones, the running water, the sowing and the harvest." He shook his head. "They, the old saints, were less proud than you, I think!"

Margaret took a deep breath, eyeing him steadily. "I pray always to be saved from the sin of spiritual pride. For it is damnable," she said. "But in this I believe that you are wrong. Wholly wrong." And she moved off, back to the hall-house.

"You are a very rash young man, Maldred Abbot's Son!" Magdalen told him. "But you will learn, in time."

"Is all the learning to be on my part? None on yours? None on hers?"

"Oh, I am learning a lot!" she assured, as she left him.

Later, there was further controversy when, after the Athelings had held their own Mass, Maldred went to them and informed that he was going to the Abbey of Culross on an errand for the Queen. It was on the firth about six miles away to the west and he wondered whether any of the visitors would like to accompany him, to see something of the country and people? The prince and his mother showed no interest, but Margaret thanked him for the thought. She asked, however, if she might know the reason for the errand.

"The Keledei at Culross are the best beekeepers in the land," he told her. "They keep the Queen's bees for her. And make the palace candles with their wax. Her Highness requires a new supply of candles. I go for them, rather than a servant, for my younger brother, Kerald, is training there to be a monk. Or, at least, one day to be abbot." He grinned. "He should be more learned in matters of the Church than I am. Perhaps he can convince you that we are not such pagan idolators as you think!"

"I did not say that, Maldred," she reproved. "Only that that ritual we saw back there had its roots in sun-worship." She shook her lovely head. "These candles — are they required for worship? Do you light candles? To the Blessed Virgin and other saints?"

"Why should any do that? The saints have no need for lights in heaven, have they? No, they are for the house. You, here, need more . . ."

"Then surely they should not be fetched on the Lord's Day?" she said.

"Why not?"

"Because it is a day for rest. For worship and meditation only. When no work should be done, no travel undertaken, no ventures started. The candles should have been fetched yesterday, surely. Or await the morrow."

"Lord — what harm in carrying a few candles? Or in riding to see my own brother?"

"No harm on any other day. But on Sunday, yes — when it is not necessary. Is that not so, Brother Oswald?"

"Indeed yes, Princess," the Benedictine agreed. "God's holy day is not to be defiled."

"But — where is the defilement? Sunday is a day for joy, not gloom, is it not? Always the Church teaches that — *our* Church. God is worshipped by all, at the beginning, to start His day well. Then folk may do as best pleases them. So long as there is no ill in it . . ."

"Young man, you know not what you say," Oswald told him sternly. "Holy Scripture speaks positively, clearly on this. The sainted Augustine had to reprove and instruct the Church, grown lax in this very issue. Benedict likewise . . ."

"I have had my day's sermon, I thank you!" Maldred interrupted, and nodding only briefly to the ladies, left the chamber.

He rode to Culross with his pannier-ponies alone, distinctly at odds with holiness.

3

IN THE DAYS that followed, Maldred discovered that he was
not purged of his admiration for Margaret Atheling by his
lack of appreciation of her piety. For otherwise she proved
to be a lively and spirited young woman, far from prudish
or stiff, not obviously concerned with rank and station,
friendly, energetic, with an innate dignity and never the
tomboyishness which her attendant Magdalen could
display on occasion. She was interested in what went on
around her, glad to take part in most activities, only
moralising when she conceived a religious aspect to be
involved — which certainly was apt to happen rather more
frequently than occurred to some of her Scots hosts. Yet
even then her attitude was not really so much holier-than-
thou as one of urgent awareness of the dangers of sin and
of a spirited antagonism to it. That she found some things
sinful which others did not was most of the trouble. And
compared with the others of her family, she was much
more likeable, not the least in that she was endowed with
a sense of humour.

Maldred saw a lot of her — and therefore of Magdalen,
since they were not to be left alone, of course. She enjoyed
being out-of-doors, even in a Scots November, seeing
places and people, unlike her mother and sister. And the
Queen, who clearly limited her relationship with the
Athelings to mere civilities, more or less made them
Maldred's responsibility, since he had brought them.
Edgar was, understandably, in a low state, having made his
bid for a kingdom and failed, and did not show himself
much. But despite indifferent weather, Margaret filled her
days. She did not like hunting and hawking, since these
meant killing God's creatures; but went riding for long
distances, walked happily enough, made expeditions to
places of beauty, interest and antiquity, most certainly not
brooding on her fate.

Maldred found her company stimulating, challenging
and only now and again exasperating. Had he not had
other responsibilities, in the matter of the assembling of

the reinforcements for the King's army, he might have made something of a fool of himself over this princess, for he was not good at disguising his feelings. But in this Magdalen helped him to keep his feet reasonably firmly on the ground. She was anything but a cipher in their relationship.

So ten days passed, with, the next Sunday, confrontation carefully avoided. Then, towards dusk one late afternoon, the King arrived home unexpectedly, ahead of his forces, with only a handful of his nobles. And the entire atmosphere and circumstance at Dunfermline was changed dramatically from the moment he rode clattering into the palace courtyard. Everyone was affected, and in major degree, from the Queen down to the lowliest servitor, however differently they showed their reaction. Malcolm mac Duncan was apt to have an impact like that of a mailed fist slammed down on a table.

Maldred and the two young women had been on a visit to Loch Leven, some fifteen miles to the north, to inspect the vast flocks of waterfowl which wintered there, rowing around the loch in a boat supplied by the Keledei of the cashel of St. Serf on the largest of the islands. The King was already returned when they got back. They found him pacing the hall floor, still clad in his metal-scaled leather tunic and long riding-boots, a beaker of ale in one hand and a leg of cold mutton in the other, jerking out mouthful questions, comments and disapproval as he paced, clearly in no good humour. The Queen sat, stiffly, frozen-faced, at the table, half-turned away from him. Edgar stood nearby looking uneasy and depressed; whilst his mother and sister all but cringed beyond the central fireplace, as though to keep its protection between them and their host. The Earls of Angus and Strathearn waited, to the side, travel-stained, watchful.

". . . I tell you no single Saxon was raising a hand against him," he was almost snarling. "What are your devil-damned people? Mice, slugs or men? This William has all cowering before him, stricken as though with the palsy. And you, *you* cower here!"

"What else could I have done . . . ?" Edgar protested.

"You sent the prince and his ladies here, husband," the Queen said, coldly. "Now do you blame them for coming?"

"If you have not better to say than that, keep silence!" the King snapped. "You could have sent on forces to my aid. Spurred on that idle oaf MacDuff! I was faced with William's full strength. In Cumbria. With a bare two thousand men . . ."

"Highness," Maldred put in, from the doorway. "You ordered me to tell my lord of Fife to muster men, but to hold them here until you sent for them. They are at Forteviot and Scone. Another two thousand and more . . ."

"Silence, fool! Speak when you are spoken to!" Malcolm shouted. But he paused, as his pale angry eyes went past Maldred to Margaret Atheling, and for a moment he faltered both in his denunciation and his pacing. "I sent messengers, whenever I heard of the Norman's march into Cumbria," he ended shortly.

"No messenger came here," Ingebiorg said. "And if one had reached MacDuff he would have acted. Your messengers must have failed you, or been intercepted."

"As to that, we shall see." Malcolm Canmore bit into his mutton, and spat some of the skin into the fire. He swung on Angus. "Get you to Forteviot and have MacDuff march for Tweed forthwith," he commanded. "With all his strength. We shall hold Tweed and Esk, if the Norman seeks to drive north into Galloway or the Merse or Lothian. Then on with you to your Angus and the Mearns, aye and on to Mar and Buchan also. To muster more men. Every man capable of bearing arms, I want. Horses too. And quickly. Hang such as will not aid you. You, Strathearn — to your own parts, then to the Lennox and Monteith and Alclyde. Raise me a sufficiency of men — or suffer for it! The Duke William has had to see my back — a thousand curses on him and on all who forced it on me! But he shall see my face and my fist if he seeks to step a yard over my border, I swear by Christ God!"

"Husband," the Queen declared evenly, "if this is to be a council-of-war, I pray that you hold it elsewhere than in my hall. You have guests, ladies, whom you sent here. Have you forgot?"

Maldred for one held his breath at that, in fear for the outburst that Ingebiorg would bring down on her head. She was not normally thus bold. But before the King opened his chewing mouth, a new voice spoke, Margaret Atheling's, quiet, firm, yet soothing.

"The lord King must not allow us weak women to

incommode him, Highness. We rejoice to see him safe returned, whatever trials he has had to bear and dangers to overcome. But we should relieve him of our presence meantime, when he has much on his mind. Do not you agree, Mother? If His Highness will permit our retiral?"

"Yes. Yes, indeed," the Princess Agatha said eagerly, at once beginning to edge towards the stairway, Christina with her.

Malcolm commenced to speak, then closed his lips again, staring at Margaret, head thrust forward. She met his glare fearlessly although not defiantly, indeed managing to smile slightly, whilst the Queen looked from one to the other of them.

There was a tense hush until, at length, the monarch nodded. "So be it," he said. "Off with you. I will speak with you later." It was only at Margaret that he gazed.

Thankfully the ladies departed, save for Ingebiorg who sat still. On her, her husband turned.

"And you!" he jerked. "You will have to learn your place. I would have thought that you would have known it, by now!"

She rose. "My place, Malcolm, is sure, secure, and known to all. I am the crowned Queen of this realm. And sister to the Earl of Orkney and Zetland and Lord of the Hebrides and Galloway. I urge that you do not forget it."

"What mean you by that, woman?"

"I mean that I have borne much from you in the past, of ill-usage and disrespect. I do not intend that I shall bear more."

"And . . . ?"

"And I remind Your Scots Highness that I have brothers! That I am Thorfinn Raven Feeder's daughter — in case you have forgot. Brothers who could set all your north and west alight and take Moray and Galloway from you, if so they desired . . ."

"If so I let them! Your brothers, woman, are weaklings. Made of different stuff from your pirate father! Think you that I care for their puny threat? If they ever mustered the courage to move against me."

"You cared for their threat sufficiently to wed me, in order to counter it, did you not? Eleven sorry years ago, and I little more than a child. Or why else the marriage? When you had not so much as seen me. It was scarce for love and yearning!"

"No, by God! I . . . I . . ." The King seemed to realise belatedly that they were not alone in the hall, and pausing, turned to glare around him. "Enough of this. I have work to do. Maldred — have the Chancellor sent for. Have him here from St. Andrews at the earliest, even if the old fool has to ride all night! Aye, and the Treasurer also. I need money, as well as men . . ."

The Queen swept from the chamber, and thankfully Maldred escaped.

*　　*　　*

The meal that night was scarcely a happy occasion. Not unnaturally the Athelings elected to eat in their own rooms upstairs; and the Queen sat as far away from her husband, at the long table in the hall, as was possible. This produced an awkward dilemma for their attendants, nobles and courtiers, as to where they should seat themselves. Most, for obvious reasons, decided to sit near Malcolm, however bad his mood; and only a small group took their places at the foot of the table beside the Queen, so that there was a major and most evident gap. Maldred, despite being the King's standard-bearer or esquire, to use the new Norman term, chose a place close to Ingebiorg. Being cousin to them both, he was perhaps in a better position than others to take a more independent point of view.

Malcolm drank steadily, eating little, morose, mainly silent, so there was little conversation at his end. The Queen, on the other hand, was much more forthcoming than normally, evidently determined to sustain her access of spirit and to underline her husband's boorishness. Her companions, however, found themselves unable to back up her efforts adequately, especially in view of the scowls from the head of the table, and Ingebiorg's talk took on a somewhat feverish note. Maldred did his best for her, and often the only talk in the hall was in the nature of a dialogue between the two of them, an uncomfortable proceeding.

Eventually Malcolm had had enough of this — if not of his liquor — and smashed down his hand on the table-top, to make the beakers, flagons and platters jump, and most of the diners with them.

"You, Maldred — still your lack-wit chatter and fetch me the Atheling," he commanded.

"Yes, Highness. Bring him . . . here?"

"Did I say otherwere, dolt?"

The Queen rose as Maldred did. "If it is to be more of fighting and war, husband, then I shall retire," she announced. "I bid you, and all, a good night!"

The King snorted but did not otherwise comment.

Maldred was thankful once more to hurry to open the door for the Queen, behind whom he himself made an exit. He climbed the stairs to inform the prince that his presence was requested in the hall.

Edgar came down in evident alarm. And with reason, for whenever he appeared he was subjected to abuse. Malcolm, presumably because he was humiliated by having had to turn and flee before the unexpected eruption of King William — whom he preferred still to refer to as *Duke* William of Normandy, or the Bastard — into Cumbria, was much more critical of the English prince and Saxons in general than he had been previously over their major collapse in the rising against the usurper — in which, of course, he had not been involved personally. He was angry that William could make a forced march northwards through Deira or Yorkshire, Durham, South Northumbria and into his own Cumbria, without apparently an English sword being raised against him; and no single message or warning sent to the Scots King as to his enemy's approach, while he had been hunting down the side-changing Cospatrick. Malcolm, suddenly faced by greatly larger numbers of the puissant Normans and sundry of their Saxon underlings, had been forced into ignominious and headlong retiral for Scotland — and he had to vent his wrath on someone. The fact that, as it transpired, William had actually been making his dash north to punish the renegade Cospatrick, unpopular with all, rather than the raiding Scots, did little to appease Malcolm's ire. His reputation as a warrior-king had taken a body-blow.

So Edgar had to bear the brunt of it, as representing the wretched Saxons — and was in a poor position to defend himself. Wilting, he just had to stand and take it. Malcolm was three-parts drunk, and tired, so that, indeed, the diatribe was more incoherent and less devastating than it might have been — for this man's anger could be deadly, murderous. Presently the spate of it flagged, and the King came to the real reason for Edgar's summons. Were there any Saxon lords or thanes remaining in the north of England with a spark of spirit in them who could be stirred up to rise in arms behind Norman William, and so to cause the usurper to pause in any attempt to cross the Scots border? Only a mere gesture might serve. The Athelings had brought a number of Saxon notables here to Scotland with them — Merleswegen, Archill, Siward Barn, Alfwin, Maurice and the rest. Was there anywhere these might be sent, secretly but in haste, to arouse trouble behind William, in this pass?

Unhappily Edgar had to admit that he knew of no such opportunity, of no such paladins. All who had been disposed to rise against the Normans had already done so. Now that the rising was put down and William triumphant, who was going to put his neck into a noose by making gestures of this sort? He, unfortunately, because of his upbringing in Hungary, did not know many of his Saxon lords personally . . .

Disgustedly Malcolm waved him away, and rose, somewhat unsteadily, to his feet. "Useless!" he snarled. "Vain, posturing daw! I will see some of your miserable Saxons in the morning. Some may have more of wit and spirit than have you — although I doubt it. Now — fetch me that sister of yours."

"Sister?" The prince stared. "What . . . what . . . ?"

"Sister, yes. The fair one. Think you I would prefer your mother?"

"But, Sire — now? She will be retired . . ."

"Then arouse her. I ride in the morning. I shall have no time to await women's hours. I shall see her now."

"Highness — not so, I pray you. It, it is not suitable. At this hour of night. She, a young woman of royal blood . . ."

"God's Blood, man — I shall not rape her. Or . . . I think not! See her I shall. Go fetch her — if from her naked bed, so much the better!"

"Sire — my regrets. But that I cannot, will not, do! In all respect. Her own brother . . ." He drew a deep breath. "I may be a posturing daw — but I will not aid in my sister's dishonour."

"Dishonour is it, fool? To deal with the King of Scots!" Malcolm swung around. "You, Maldred — go you.

55

Request the princess's presence. Not here. In the tower. Bring her to my chamber."

"The saints forbid!" Edgar exclaimed.

"Not them! Go, boy." That to Maldred, pointing.

"Then I shall accompany her," the prince declared. "If she goes, I go . . ."

Maldred hurried off, mind in a turmoil.

Upstairs, doubtfully, he knocked at the door of the Atheling women's room. At first there was no response. His second knock brought a stirring within, and presently the door opened partially, and Magdalen's face appeared at the crack, enquiringly.

"You!" she said, surprised. "What seek you? At this hour. Is it refuge that you seek? From that monster of a King . . . ?"

"No. It is the Lady Margaret. I am sorry. But will you ask her to come?"

"Lord — will you never learn? Have you taken leave of your wits, Maldred?"

"It is the King. His royal command. I am to take her to him. Forthwith. I am sorry, but . . ."

"She is in her bed. You cannot mean this?"

"It is the truth. Think you that I would be here, otherwise? The King requires her presence. Now."

"But, but why?"

"The good God knows! But he is in a strange mood — the King. And, and not to be kept waiting."

Shrugging helplessly, the girl was turning away, to close the door in his face, when Margaret herself, a bed-robe thrown around her, her fair hair falling to her shoulders, appeared.

"Maldred — did I hear you say that I was wanted?" she asked. "By King Malcolm? With Edgar? Only me?"

"Yes. Only you. The prince, he will be there, I think. His Highness requests your presence, lady. For, for some reason."

"Must I dress? I was in bed."

"No, I think not. He said *now*."

"So be it. I shall come."

"And I shall attend you!" Magdalen declared strongly. "Let me get a wrap, to decent me . . ."

In no more tranquil frame of mind Maldred escorted the two young women downstairs, through the hall, now all but deserted save by staring servitors, out into the open courtyard across which they hurried, wrapping themselves more tightly against the chill night air, to the tower doorway and in, there to climb the narrow, winding turnpike stair to the first floor. Malcolm had slept here, apart from his wife, for some time, an obvious convenience when it came to bringing in alternative bedfellows. The door of his chamber stood open. The two men within were well apart, the King sitting on the great bed pulling off his boots, while Edgar stood near the door, set-faced.

"The Princess Margaret, lord King," Maldred announced, and ushered the pair in.

The monarch looked up, peering a little, for the light from the one lamp and the flickering log-fire — here with a chimney fireplace — was poor, and his sight was not the best of him, especially when drink-taken.

"So! Is this to be a council-meeting, then?" he growled thickly. "Would you wish an armed guard to be brought in also, young woman, to protect your virtue?"

"I cannot believe that necessary, Highness," Margaret answered, mildly enough. "It is but seemly that the Lady Magdalen attends on me, always."

"Indeed? We shall see about that!" But he did not actually dismiss her, or the others. "Come here, girl," he said. "I would look at you."

It was indicative of Margaret Atheling's character that she did not shrink back, or even hesitate. Calmly she moved forward to the bedside, not so much as pulling her robe closer around her person. She halted only a foot or two from him, and there proffered the merest hint of a curtsy, with the flicker of a smile even.

"Can you perceive my poor looks from here, Sire?" she asked. "If they disappoint, they are, I fear, all that the good God has endowed me with!"

He stood up, swaying a little, eyeing her closely, comprehensively, unabashed, from her gleaming, cascading flaxen hair down to her bare ankles and slippered feet, lingering noticeably at the long, graceful column of her neck and the fine swelling of prominent breasts, their shapeliness entirely obvious in the low-cut sleeping-gown which her bed-robe failed to cover. If a slight flush did mantle her features and throat at this frank and assessing scrutiny, that was her only evident reaction. Her violet-blue eyes met his own pale ones, steadily, when at length he raised them that high again.

57

"Aye," he said.

Maldred was watching the King's great fists — his hands were notably large, like his head — which were clenching, knuckles white. If they reached out, to touch and grasp and tear, as they might so well do, as he had seen them do so often, God knew what might happen. The young man was aware that Edgar had taken a step forward, and that Magdalen was as tense as he was himself.

Margaret it was, however, who took the situation in hand, slender but capable hands. Raising another smile, she curtsied again, a little lower this time — despite the dangerous effect on her bosom — and almost in the same movement stepped back a little, and drew her robe closer, but in a perfectly natural way, as though it was slipping, rather than any hasty covering up.

"Is Your Highness content?" she asked lightly. "I do not offend? As guest in your house, I would not wish to displease you in anything, even in my looks. But now, Sire, since that is by with, I believe that you wish to speak with me? How can I, a mere girl, advantage you in this?"

His powerful jaw-muscles working, Malcolm eyed her loweringly. "You . . . are . . . sure of yourself!" he grated.

"But no, Sire. Quite otherwise. Since I do not perceive how I can advantage you. All that I am sure of is your royal clemency towards a weak woman, and those in distress. And God's concern for us both."

There were a few moments of silence, save for the hiss and crackle of the log fire.

"I desired to see you," the King jerked. "For sufficient reason." His glance travelled over her, once more. "I find you comely . . . but forward, malapert. And over-fond of deeming God to be yours for the beckoning! I say that such is . . . presumption."

She inclined her head. "I constantly warn myself against the sin of spiritual pride," she conceded. "I accept that, at times, I speak more freely than I should. But I will not, dare not, limit God's love and care. For me, and for you. And all. Sinners as we are."

He frowned. "You are worse than any priest!" He gestured roughly. "But enough of such talk. I ride to Strathclyde in the morning. To Alclyde and Renfrew and Kyle. To raise men. Then south to Tweed and Esk, to confront Norman William in his power. It will be hard fighting. This brother of yours, it seems, can aid me nothing. You, it may be, have more spirit. You were long at the Court of King Edward, so-called Confessor, your father's uncle? Ten years and more, were you not? You must know many of the Saxon lords of the north. Better than this Edgar. Lords who have some valour, some hardihood. Who hate the Norman usurper."

"I know some, yes. But, Sire, if they did not already rise to aid my brother's bid for his throne, will they rise now? For *you*? Or, if they did rise, and are now scattered, like the Saxons with us, will they risk all again? So soon?"

"There is a difference. A Scots army will now be facing William. Two armies, one on Tweed, one on Esk. This has not been, before. And Cospatrick is arrayed against him, in Cumbria. It is to encourage that fool cousin of mine, Cospatrick, as well as to make William look back over his shoulder, that I want the Saxons to muster behind him. Only to muster, as yet. Not necessarily to draw sword. The threat, I need."

"If Your Highness had confronted the Norman with your Scots armies some weeks past, instead of waiting until now, I might now be sitting on my English throne and you not concerned for your borders," Edgar intervened, with an access of spirit.

Malcolm ignored him. "Well?" he demanded, of Margaret.

"Our Saxon friends here in your land will know better than I, Sire," she said. "Names, strengths . . ."

"*You*, I ask! I shall use them as my messengers, never fear. Send them south. By sea. Tomorrow. Merleswegen, Maurice, Siward Barn and the others. But — I want the message to come from the Athelings. Not only from me. Give me names. Edgar here knows none — or so he says. Names, girl."

She looked over at her brother, and then shrugged those fine shoulders. "There is Leofwine of Godmanham — he did not rise, although he has ever misliked the Normans. Eadwulf of Amunderness was said to be coming, but his force never reached our army. Eadred of Lastingham is old, but fierce enough. And the Eald of Craven is powerful, if timid. Athelstan and Eadwig are great Deira lords, of whom we saw naught . . ."

"That is liker it. Can you write, girl? Then write these names on a paper. More, if you can think of them. Also write a command for them to muster. Your fine brother will sign and seal it, as true King of England! Maldred will have it ready for me before I see your Saxons in the morning."

"Sire — we are indebted to you for hospitality, here," Edgar protested. "But this is high-handed! I, and my sister — we are not to be used so . . . !"

"Begone — all of you," the King said abruptly, and turning, began to remove his shirt.

Eyeing each other, they all bowed hurriedly to the royal back, and left the presence, their reactions various.

4

IT WAS ON the Eve of St. Finian, eight days later, that the urgently awaited news reached Dunfermline. A messenger from Malcolm's headquarters in the Merse brought the tidings. William had turned back, without attempting to cross Tweed or Esk, whether because of threat to his rear from reported Saxon musterings, or otherwise, was not known. But the Norman was marching off southwards, apparently in a hurry. There had been no real fighting. The Scots were now, in consequence, raiding happily over into Northumbria again, to recoup themselves for their trouble and expense in coming there, and so would not return home empty-handed. Just when they would be back was uncertain therefore — but as it was late in the season for campaigning, it would not be overlong delayed.

As well as these general tidings, the courier had two especial and private messages to deliver — by word of mouth, since Malcolm was no writer of letters, indeed could do little more than write his own signature. What he said to the Queen was between her and the messenger — although her set face thereafter held its own eloquence. But the royal instructions to Maldred mac Melmore were clear, brief and to the point. He was to escort the Queen forthwith to the palace of Kincardine in the Mearns, and there to leave her. With her household and gear. There was to be no question nor any delay. This was the royal command. The King did not desire to find his wife, or anything of hers, at Dunfermline when he returned.

Appalled, Maldred listened, and then went off to commune with himself for a while, before presenting himself before Ingebiorg. When eventually he did come to her, however, he found her calm and the mistress of her emotions.

"It has come to the parting of the roads, between Malcolm and myself, Maldred," she said. "A road which should never have been started on. I blame my mother and brothers for ever having agreed to this marriage. But that is an old story. I am to be removed, out of sight and sound. Far away. You are to take me to Kincardine, I understand."

"So I am commanded. I, I am sorry, Ingebiorg."

"You need not be. I have not been happy here. It is probably better so. I shall not miss my husband's company, I promise you!"

"It will not be for long. His wrath will cool . . ."

"Do not you believe it. He desires to be rid of me. I have known that for long. I shall not come back, I think. Indeed, I shall not bide long at Kincardine, if I can help it. I shall return to my own Orkney, so soon as I may contrive it. Although tell no others so, Maldred, I charge you. I shall shake the dust of Malcolm's kingdom from my feet."

"But you are the Queen, Highness! Queen of this land. Mother of the two princes."

"That is Malcolm's concern, not mine. He banishes me from his house and home. But, to be sure, I shall take my sons with me. If I am so unloved a wife, I am still a loving mother. The boys go with me, whatever Malcolm says. Did he command you to leave them here, Maldred?"

"No. There was no mention of the princes, to me."

"He is scarce a more fond father than he is a husband. Duncan and Donald will suffer nothing from being deprived of his presence. And — they will give me the wherewithal to bargain. His heirs. Perchance I may need to bargain. Even, it may be, for my life!"

He stared at her. "I do not understand him. The King. I cannot see what he is at. Why now? You have been wed near a dozen years . . ."

"If you cannot see, then you are blind, cousin! It is that Atheling woman who has brought this to a head. He finds her to his taste. Have you not seen how he eyes her? He is not a man for loving women — only their bodies. Most that take his fancy he can bed at will. But not this one, this Saxon. She is proud and sure of herself — and moreover, the sister of the rightful King of England. So she is out of his reach — at present and the more desirable therefore, to a man of his sort."

"But . . . but *you*!"

"Out of his way, he will feel the less constrained. If Malcolm is ever constrained!"

Maldred shook his head. "She is not like that. She is good. Virtuous as she is fair. And strong, too. She would never permit him . . ."

"She is all but his prisoner. And he is the King. Oh, I know that you too think much of her. I have seen you look at her, likewise! You, and others. No woman who affects men so is a saint — however much she talks of God and holiness! Watch her, Maldred my friend . . . !"

The King's orders were explicit as they were imperative, as to an immediate departure — and Ingebiorg was nothing loth to be gone. So only two days elapsed in preparation, whilst word was despatched to Kincardine to have all in readiness to receive the Queen and her attendants. The eventual leave-taking was a strange and strained proceeding, with all aware that something was far wrong, the palace staff most careful as to how they reacted, the local people sad and alarmed — for the Queen was well-liked — the visitors uncomfortable, embarrassed somewhat, and keeping well into the background. The Queen herself was, not unnaturally, tense and reserved. She avoided anything like an admission to the Athelings that she was being *sent* away or that her departure was other than a normal and temporary visit to one of her other palaces. Nevertheless, something of the truth behind this sudden move inevitably percolated through to the guests, although nothing could be said. No especial dissension developed between her and Margaret, the latter being noticeably quiet and withdrawn.

Maldred, in the end, was thankful to be on the road. There were numerous Kincardines in Scotland — the name merely meaning at the head of the rowan wood. Their destination was the royal hunting-seat of that name in the mortuath of the Mearns, near the eastern end of the vast vale of Strathmore, under the foothills of the Mounth, the great mountain mass of Drumalbyn. It was, in fact, the furthest away of the royal residences from Dunfermline — and chosen by Malcolm, no doubt, for that reason — involving a journey of almost one hundred miles, through Fife, Gowrie, and Angus. There were houses which the King could have claimed were his further north still, of course, in Moray; but these had belonged to his predecessors MacBeth and Lulach, of the northern branch of the royal house, both of whom he had slain — and after a dozen years on the throne, he still avoided that country and distrusted the Moraymen and Rossmen, for valid reasons. After all, MacBeth's son Farquhar was still alive and Mormaor of Ross, scornfully rejecting the non-Celtic title of earl.

A less than cheerful party of about a score, with a long chain of pack-horses, they travelled as fast as they might, with a chill November wind and drizzling rain no encouragement to linger. Ingebiorg took only four of her ladies with her, two of them Orkneywomen, two pages and the rest servitors and guards. They went almost due north, over the spine of Fife, crossing the skirts of Benarty and the Lomond Hills to the Tay valley, to pass the first night at the large abbey of Abernethy, where the Abbot Ewan, who had once been High Judex, or Justiciar, of Scotland under MacBeth, welcomed them, the more warmly when the Queen revealed that she went in bad odour with her husband, and indeed was all but being sent into exile. Malcolm was not loved by the Celtic churchmen, for whom he had little use, and who had not forgiven him for the death of their friend the good MacBeth.

They crossed Tay next morning by the ford of Elcho, east of St. John's Town of Perth, and turned north-eastwards to thread the Balthayock pass of the Sidlaw Hills into the head of Strathmore, by-passing Scone, moving within sight of the royal palaces of Dunsinane and Cairn Beth, only a couple of miles apart, the latter built by MacBeth for his Queen Gruoch who had found Dunsinane little better than a barracks. Strathmore, a wide and lovely vale, extended for some sixty miles eastwards to the Norse Sea, second only to the Great Glen of Alba itself in length, and much surpassing it in width and fertility. With the damp east wind off the sea in their faces all the way, however, even Strathmore's fair prospects palled, and

Maldred for one chafed not a little at the comparatively slow pace they had to take. This was not on account of Ingebiorg or her ladies, all experienced horsewomen, but because of the long file of pack-garrons laden with the Queen's personal possessions, clothing and the like. Needless to say, the young princes fretted even more than Maldred.

The second night was passed at the cashel of Resten-neth, near Forfar, where the Keledei entertained the royal visitor to the best of their ability. The hospices of these Celtic Church monasteries were the recognised halting-places for travellers of all degrees, the quarters simple and the fare plain but usually plentiful. Resten-neth was a very ancient foundation, and better equipped than most, on a peninsula thrusting into its loch, having been founded by the Pictish King Nechtan, who was actually baptised here by St. Boniface after defeating the Angles in 685 at the great Battle of Nechtansmere.

In twenty-five miles next day they completed their journey, arriving at the rambling hall-house establish-ment of Kincardine on the Devilly Water, near the village of Fettercairn, as the early dusk settled on the drenched land, with the great heather hills of the Mounth looming high over them to west and north, and a cold mist off the sea rolling in from the east. Colin, Mormaor of the Mearns, a man in his mid-forties and another former friend of MacBeth's, greeted them, his own seat, the Green Fort of Dundevilly lying only a couple of miles to the north.

Kincardine, although pleasingly situated and com-modious, was in a poor state to receive high-born ladies, having been unoccupied for long and consequently neglected. Malcolm Canmore had never favoured it, as his namesake and great-grandfather Malcolm the Second had, preferring as his summer or hunting palace the Ward of the Stormounth on Loch Clunie, between Gowrie and Atholl, much more accessible. The Mormaor Colin had done his best at very short notice to have the place cleaned up and made welcoming, with blazing fires and decorative greenery; but nothing could disguise the bare and unlived-in atmosphere. He indeed suggested that the Queen should come and lodge in his own house of Dundevilly meantime; but Ingebiorg, although grateful, declined, saying that the only way to turn the palace into a home again was to live in it, and that this endeavour could be good for her and her women, keeping them occupied along with the house.

Maldred was undecided thereafter as to his own programme. The King's orders to him had been merely to escort the Queen here, with no further instructions. One part of him was for returning to Dunfermline forthwith, duty done. But Ingebiorg appeared to assume that he was attached to her as aide and friend, as well as cousin — and certainly she was notably short of male attendants. Moreover, the young princes begged him to stay, a while at least. He lingered, therefore — although that was scarcely an apt description of the flurry of activity in which he found himself caught up, playing his part in the rehabilitation of Kincardine Palace, its facilities and amenities. There was an endless succession of tasks for an energetic young man to tackle, the Queen urging him on, and indeed working hard herself, like any housewife.

So the shrinking days passed quickly enough, and long evenings round the hall fire, with music and singing and story-telling, made pleasant relaxation for tired muscles. The youngest of the Queen's ladies, Cathula, daughter of the Thane of Aberlemno, began to take a more than passing interest in Maldred, which he did not actually discourage — although again he found himself not infrequently comparing her unfavourably with Margaret Atheling or even Magda daughter of Oswin. She was sonsy rather than pretty, amiable, cheerful, uncomplicated and good company for any normal young man; but there was little of the challenge, fascination and sheer quality which kept drawing his thoughts back to Dunfermline. Being indeed entirely normal and male, he took what he was offered gladly enough, gave his share in return, but remained uncommitted.

It was not all work, of course — or at least, the work could be varied with occasional hunting expeditions. Kincardine was famous for its deer-drives. The mountains to west and north abounded with herds of red deer, and one of the earlier monarchs had ordered a great wall or dyke, of earth and turf, to be raised, many miles long and with angled bends in it, on the same principle as the defensive ditch and ramparts round a fort, towards which the deer herds could be driven but which they could not cross. Even so, most of the animals escaped, of course, for their fleetness of foot, when they swung sideways or bolted back from the wall, called for skilled archery indeed on the part of the waiting hunters and drivers both. The Mormaor Colin and his younger son Malpender, and some of the older Mearns thanes, co-operated in these drives — the others were away with the King's armies — and Maldred managed to acquit himself adequately enough. It was important for all such lordly households to lay in a store of smoked venison, to be kept in underground ice-houses, for the winter feeding, before the deer grew thin on account of their pastures being under snow. So Maldred helped to stock the palace ice-house as a change from more domestic labours.

December brought different weather, drier, colder, with frosts and clear days, but occasional flurries of snow. It was after a fairly heavy snowfall, one day in the second week of the month, that Maldred decided that it was time that he was gone. Travel in these conditions grew ever more difficult, not only because the snow could close the passes but because the rivers rose, and in a land mainly without bridges, the fords became impassable and the low-lying ground flooded and marshy. He usually spent his Yuletide at his home at Dunkeld in Atholl; but that required the King's express leave-of-absence. So it seemed to be time to take his leave of the Queen — and Cathula nic Neis — and return to Dunfermline.

At eighteen years, farewells were easily effected and quickly over, and promising to return before long, he rode off alone southwards, ice-puddles crackling beneath his garron's hooves. He wondered, in fact, whether he *would* be back, for he had not forgotten Ingebiorg's hint that she intended to contrive a return to Orkney.

Despite worsened road conditions, he completed the return journey in half the time they had taken to come. To his surprise, he found that the King had still not returned to Dunfermline, where a curious vacuum situation prevailed, with the distinguished visitors lacking hosts, and nobody in a position to take major decisions. Almost inevitably, perhaps, the strong-minded Margaret Atheling was doing what she could, supervising the palace steward and his staff, meeting the day-to-day questions and problems. But all otherwise was in a state of suspension. The Athelings were glad and relieved to see Maldred back — at least Margaret and Magda were — as some representative of the reigning house, if not for more personal reasons. So that, young and junior as he was, he found himself the authority at the palace on the rock.

If they were denied the monarch's presence at Dunfermline, they did not lack news of his doings. It seemed that he was very busy in Northumbria, the same Northumbria in which he had grown up, enjoying himself and doing what of all things he liked best, however little his victims enjoyed the process — that is, raiding on a massive scale. The reason and excuse for this change of plan — if such was needed — was that his cousin the Earl Cospatrick, once King William had departed southwards, had refused to submit to Malcolm and had instead left Cumbria and headed eastwards across Northumbria to his own powerful fortress of Bamburgh, which had been his seat when he reigned as earl and which he had managed to retain because of its almost impregnable situation. So now he was inside Bamburgh, with Malcolm besieging it, aiming to starve him out — since he could by no means capture the place — meantime the Scots filling their days by spreading havoc far and wide over the great province, burning, slaying, pillaging, to their hearts' content, all in the name of suitable and necessary discipline and pressure. As an excellent by-product, never-ending columns of slaves and serfs, the strongest of the men and the most acceptable of the women, were being sent back to Scotland by the thousand — along with vast herds of cattle, horses and sheep, of course — to improve the King's popularity at home. Word indeed came daily to Dunfermline to the effect that there was not a village or township or valley in the Merse, Teviotdale and Lothian, without its quota of these useful Saxon captives, to the satisfaction of all.

Such tidings, of course, scarcely rejoiced the hearts of the Saxon Athelings, although they were glad enough to hear that the renegade Cospatrick was receiving his due deserts. But there was nothing that they could do about any of it.

It was apparent that the King was not going to be back for the annual Yuletide festivities. Equally evident that Maldred could not gain the necessary royal permission to go home to Dunkeld for the occasion. Anyway, he could scarcely abandon the Athelings and Dunfermline once again. He felt in duty bound, therefore, to try to organise

67

some sort of celebrations to mark the festive season, however modest — and in this he was encouraged and to some extent aided, by Margaret, indeed all the Atheling women, although Edgar appeared little interested. It was a pity that Margaret's ideas as to what was desirable harped distinctly on the religious aspect, which was not always the most spirited. After all, Scotland — or at least Alba — had been celebrating Yule for long centuries before the missionaries arrived with their Christ Mass, and the pagan festival of the Rebirth of the Sun had been, as it were, amalgamated with the Christian anniversary of the Birth of the Son of God, in highly satisfactory fashion, producing a rousing and prolonged succession of activities to suit all tastes and temperaments, lasting for the three weeks around the winter solstice. The Celtic Church was broad-minded in this matter — as in others — but apparently the Roman Church was not, at least as represented by the Athelings. In these circumstances Maldred felt that there was little point in seeking to assert his Scots point of view too strongly, since it was only a token Yuletide he could arrange anyway; but still he stood out for certain basic ceremonies and observances — and came to recognise still further the qualities of will, determination and conviction in Princess Margaret, and the disadvantages for those who sought to oppose her, however kindly and patiently she marshalled them.

In the end they made do with a mixed and distinctly patchy series of events — it would be inaccurate to call it a compromise, for that was an attitude to which the princess could not subscribe — the least exciting and colourful Yule which Maldred had yet experienced, if the most pious. Even so the Athelings only took part in a selection of what went on, and after due consideration, needless to say those activities wherein they could trace no least hint of pre-Christian or heretical practice, thereby missing much hilarity. For instance, at the very start, at Yule Girth, the seventh day before Christmas, they did not grace the proclaiming-of-sanctuary ceremony wherein all sinners, wrongdoers and felons generally were assured of immunity from arrest and punishment until Up Halie Day — on the grounds that sin was always to be fought to a standstill. Two days later the Mistletoe Bough saturnalia, modest as it was on this occasion, was boycotted for obvious reasons. Log Even's selection and the drawing-in and lighting of the Yule Log, was ostracised in favour of the Mothers' Night adoration of the Virgin, on Christmas Eve. The decoration of doors and windows with holly and mistletoe on the Christmas Day was frowned upon as pagan, although they all did take part in the feasting after an inordinate proportion of the day had been passed by the Athelings in private worship with the monk Oswald. St. Stephen's Day thereafter was of especial reverence to the visitors, because of its linking with the later St. Stephen the King, Princess Agatha's father; nevertheless his family did not participate in the lively business of Stoning the Devil as retaliation for the stoning of the first Christian martyr, or even eat of the Martyr Cakes, with their red jam to represent blood, for which they had some unspecified objection. Hogmanay, of course, with its large-scale drinking, was anathema. And so on up till Up Halie Day itself, the Eve of Epiphany, the twentieth day of the celebrations, with its fires and dancing to be frowned upon as barbarous.

Despite disagreement on such matters, however, Maldred got on very well with Margaret — from whom he could not hide his admiration; and on a different level with Magdalen, with whom he established a close companionship — even though there was challenge, too, in their relationship, and she seldom failed to berate and mock him over his all-too-evident preoccupation with the princess, her beauty, her spirit and her strange authority. With the other Athelings he could find little or nothing in common.

So the festive season passed. And then, in the bleak days of mid-January, King Malcolm came home.

Tension immediately reigned at Dunfermline again. It seemed that it was that man's role, quite apart from his royal status and absolute power, to carry with him this aura of restless unease, a sort of prevailing if unspecified threat. He came back in triumph, the victor, laden with spoils, handing out gifts, in as high good humour as was in his harsh nature. Yet still the tension was there, the menace implicit.

The sense of unease was scarcely lessened, for the palace occupiers at least, by the fact that he brought home with him, of all people, Cospatrick mac Maldred, lately Earl of Northumbria, cousin, former ally, recent foe and now apparently colleague again. At least the Earl did not act the prisoner in any way, cheerful, noisy, brash even. A handsome man of about thirty, in a raffish way, high-coloured, well-built, with an ever-ready laugh, he was the son of the former King Duncan's second brother, where Maldred was son of the third, Malcolm himself being Duncan's own son, although illegitimate. It seemed that, hunted across Northumbria from Cumbria by his cousin, after the Norman had retired southwards, and going to ground in his fortress of Bamburgh, he had fairly quickly wearied of siege restrictions — for he was a man of impatience and constant change — and perhaps concerned at the havoc being wrought in his former earldom by Malcolm, he had made a deal with his besieging cousin, to yield his fortress and all rights he had in Northumbria, for 4500 merks — how they had arrived at the figure was not explained. This to include his own freedom. So here he was, seemingly uncaring and prepared to be on the best of terms with everyone, including Edgar Atheling whom he had so recently abandoned.

Needless to say, he got scant response from that quarter.

While the King made no effusive greetings or courteous attentions towards his neglected guests, he had at least thought to bring Margaret a gift, a handsome gold and jewelled crucifix, no doubt looted from some Northumbrian church. He thrust it at her, as soon as he saw her — and it was obvious that there was nothing brought for the others.

"A trinket — since you like such things," he jerked.

She took it, after only a moment's hesitation. "I thank you, Sire. It is very fine. Too fine for me. This should be in some house of God. Not in a poor woman's hands."

"Better so," he said. "Too good for snivelling priests!" And he glowered over at the Benedictine Oswald.

"Then we shall find good use for it, my lord King."

Cospatrick was eyeing her appreciatively, assessingly. "For one so fair, I would have brought gifts, myself, if I had known," he declared gallantly.

"And had them less gratefully accepted, my lord Earl!" she gave back, coolly.

The faint hint of a smile flickered over Malcolm's stern features. "Beggars make poor givers!" he said tersely.

"What news of William, Sire?" Edgar asked, turning shoulder pointedly on Cospatrick. "Where is he now? And in what state?"

"He returned to York. Without battle. Because of risings in Mercia and the Welsh Marches. Passed Yule at York."

"Risings? God be praised!"

"Is it God to be praised? Or myself who sent emissaries to rouse the risers?"

"These had scarcely the time, I think . . ."

Scowling, Malcolm turned to Maldred. "You, boy — come." He beckoned him aside. "What of Ingebiorg? And where are my sons?" he demanded, but lower-voiced.

"The Queen is at Kincardine, as you commanded, Highness. The princes with her . . ."

"A curse on you! I did not say to take them also, fool!"

"But the Queen did — and she is the Queen. You sent no word as to them, that reached me. She said . . . that they needed a mother's love."

He chewed one of his cruel down-turning moustaches. "They must be brought back. She, she went readily?"

"Very readily, my lord King!"

Malcolm glared at his young kinsman. "She is better away. An ill-minded woman. I should have sent her away long since. How is it at Kincardine?"

"Well enough. When I left, before Yule. The Mormaor Colin aids her."

"Aye, he would. He was never my friend. One of MacBeth's men." He shrugged. "This other — the Atheling? How is it with her?"

"The Princess Margaret? She is well, as you can see."

"Tcha! How did she take Ingebiorg's going?"

"I did not ask her. Nor did the Queen seek the Athelings' sympathies."

Those pale eyes glinted at him. Then the King turned back to the others. "You!" He pointed at Edgar. "What is it to be? What do you do now?"

"Me? Do? What can I do? Here in Scotland . . . ?"

"You could be otherwhere. Slip secretly into England. Stir up others to join in these risings against the Norman. Seek arouse those Saxon lords of yours — Leofwine, Eadred, the Eald of Craven was it? And the rest your sister named. Or you could go to Hungary. Raise an army from your kin there. You will not win your throne sitting here!"

"How could I do that . . . ?"

"He could not bring an army from Hungary," the

Princess Agatha protested. "They would need to march for hundreds of miles, to the sea. Then require hundreds of ships. Whose ships? Hungary has no sea and ships. And to go into England, alone, without an army, would be to go to certain death. It would soon come to William's ears. Every Norman in the land would be searching for him, every Saxon traitor being bribed . . ."

"So, what?" their less-than-pressing host demanded.

"If we overstay our welcome here, Sire, then we can *only* go to Hungary. As first intended," Edgar said stiffly. "But not to raise an army. That is not possible there . . ."

"Did I say aught of overstaying welcome? I spoke of winning a throne."

Margaret intervened. "My lord King would sooner have you here, I think, brother, than sailing for Hungary. His concern is to keep Duke William at bay, is it not? To trouble the Norman by keeping England unsettled and astir behind and around him. He can effect that better by having the true King of England here in Scotland, a threat, than away in distant Hungary where he is no threat. Meantime, I think, better than wandering secretly in England either. For from here you could possibly lead an army southwards. Not merely stir a few Saxon lords to revolt. Am I not right?"

Her brother moistened slack lips at this actue reading of the situation, but said nothing.

King Malcolm looked at her narrowly, thoughtfully.

Then he barked a short laugh, something he seldom permitted himself. And swung on the deferentially waiting steward. "Meat!" he commanded. "Victuals. Wine. Without delay. See to it. I am hungry. As are all here . . ."

Next morning, Maldred sought leave-of-absence from the King, to visit his home in Atholl. Madach, his eldest brother, had returned with the army, and was homing also, much richer than when he had set out. They would pick up Kerald, the second brother, on the way, at the Abbey of Culross — the abbot there would not prove difficult towards his Primate's son. It was a long time since all three had been home together. The King did not refuse the request, although he was less than gracious about the business, Maldred gaining the impression that the monarch was displeased with him over something. He bade farewell to Margaret and Magda, and expressed the hope they would still be there when he got back. Madach, a cheerful, stocky and uncomplicated young man three years older than Maldred, volunteered the information that if *he* had been on such easy terms with two so attractive females, Atholl could well have waited indefinitely for his return.

* * *

Dunkeld lies in the south of Atholl, only just within the Highland Line — otherwise it would have been very hard to reach at this season of the year. As it was, with the broad Tay and all its tributary streams running high, the Pass of Birnam was difficult enough to negotiate — although it would have taken considerably more than that to hold up these three brothers.

The Abbey and College lay amongst the riverside haughs, in splendid woodlands, surrounded by steep forested foothills, the second most holy place in all Scotland after Iona. Around them huddled the quite sizeable township of cot-houses and hovels, with the monks' orchards, farmeries, mills, tanneries, fish-hatcheries, bakehouses and the like, a self-contained community. And high above, on the summit of a jutting rock, guarding the mouth of the Pass of Dunkeld itself, reared the rath or defensive hall-house of the Primate, Hereditary Abbot and Mormaor — now Earl — of Atholl, built on the site of the former Pictish dun or fort which gave the place its name — the Dun of the Keledei, or Castle of the Friends of God.

This eagle's-nest of a house in the very jaws of the Highlands was home to the young mac Melmores, a wonderful place for boys to have been reared, even though it had had a bloody past, abbey and rath having been burned by Norsemen only forty years previously, and their grandfather Crinan, King Duncan's father, slain whilst in revolt against MacBeth at the Battle of Dunkeld a score of years later. Their parents welcomed them warmly, quietly rejoicing in this surprise home-coming. Melmore mac Crinan was a deal more abbot than earl, a gentle and studious man, and much more suitable Primate for Scotland than most of the long line of warriors from whom he descended. Much the youngest of Crinan's three sons by Malcolm the Second's daughter Bethoc, he had been too young to be involved in the wars of succession in MacBeth's time, and had spent the years of exile in a monastery, not fighting and plotting. Now, a man in his mid-fifties, he took little part in national affairs, save those connected with the Church — which, being non-hier-archal and non-diocesan, did not go in for much of organised ceremonial or conclave on a national scale — well content to stay at home and administer his wide-spread mortuath of Atholl. He and his nephew Malcolm had little or nothing in common, save blood. His wife, the Lady Annalie, daughter of a former Thane of Calatria, was a comfortable, motherly soul, as well content with a stay-at-home husband — and who could have wished that her sons were like-minded.

Madach, the heir, was of course full of the recent successful campaign in Northumbria — and had brought home a string of pack-horses laden with booty to prove his prowess. He had the good sense, however, not to dwell upon the savageries and destruction inseparable from King Malcolm's warfare and raiding. Maldred for his part was as full of the situation at Dunfermline, of the Queen's banishment and of Margeret Atheling's excellencies — he tended to play down her strictures against the Celtic Church, for obvious reasons. Kerald, who was a moderate and thoughtful youth, very like his father, had as ever the least to say — but of course he had only recently been home for Yuletide. He did, however, say that his abbot at Culross, Bishop Fothad of St. Andrews, the Chancellor of the realm, and other Church leaders, were much con-cerned over the Queen's situation and anxious to effect a reconciliation. The Earl Melmore agreed, strongly for that mild man, and said that he would write a letter to the King, as Primate as well as uncle.

So pleasant weeks passed, energetic weeks of hunting and hawking and fishing, of climbing amongst the snow-peaks, of skating on the high lochans, of great eating and talking and boasting, after the fashion of young men, of long evenings of story-telling and music and dancing round the hall fires — and if sometimes Maldred's thoughts turned longingly to feminine company back at Dunfermline in Fothrif, he did not express it in words.

Then, in the fourth week of their stay, with the recognition that it could not go on for much longer beginning to colour their thoughts, the astonishing, appalling news reached Dunkeld — the Queen was dead, Ingebiorg Thorfinnsdotter had died at Kincardine.

At first they could scarcely credit it, or take it in. She had always been a notably hale and healthy woman, and was still not thirty years old. But when confirmation of a sort came, in the form of details that she had died of a bloody flux, on St. Matthew's Eve, they had to accept at least the fact of death.

Dunkeld, like the rest of the land, was stunned. The Queen had been well-liked. Popular was scarcely the word, but admired and approved of by the great and the common folk alike, as her husband had never been nor sought to be. And, needless to say, it did not take long for the rumours of poison to arise and grow and circulate. Any sudden death of the prominent was apt to be explained away so, by the sensationally-inclined — but this was particularly fertile ground for it. The King's lack of affection for his wife was well known. The death had happened after messengers from Malcolm had arrived at Kincardine demanding the return of the young princes to his keeping — and being refused. She had shown no previous signs of illness. Thereafter, the King had ordered a swift and private burial, which he had not attended — just where was not stated, but in no suitably prominent place evidently. And, most significant of all, it was recollected by the older folk that Malcolm's father, King Duncan Ilgarach, or Bad-Blooded, had been known as a poisoner, his doing away with certain Danes by the use of meiklewort, or hemlock, notorious.

So the kingdom buzzed with talk and conjecture and apprehension — for if the King could do such a thing, what mightn't he do? Fear also for the consequences. For what would the Norsemen do, the Queen's brothers, the Earls Paul and Erland of Orkney, Zetland, the Hebrides and Galloway, when they heard? Dunkeld was not the only place in Scotland to have been burned and ravaged by the Vikings in the not-too-distant past. The young earls were not so fierce as their tremendous father, the Raven Feeder, but their Vikings were as tough and savage as ever, and if they suspected poison could they do other than launch their dreaded longships?

Maldred, although he did not love the King and had been quite fond of Ingebiorg, refused to believe in the poison theory. Even admitting Malcolm's ferocity in raiding, his utter ruthlessness and contempt for human life, he would not have done this, surely? The consequences were too obvious, the danger to his realm apparent, the entire conception too stupidly heavy-handed. The Earl Melmore agreed, as did Kerald — but Madach was not so sure. Madach said that Malcolm would get rid of anyone who stood in his way, man, woman or child. Ruthlessness was not qualified, save only by expediency. If the King considered the dangers were worth risking, as related to the benefits, he would not shrink at wife-murder or poison.

If Maldred were to accept that, he could in conscience no longer go on serving the monarch as esquire and standard-bearer. So he did not accept it. He said that he would have to go back to Dunfermline. Madach also declaring that if there was trouble with the Orkney earls, he would be needed. Kerald could claim no such urgent recall, but decided that his abbot would expect his return.

The three brothers set off southwards, then, in a different frame of mind from their northwards journey, holiday-making over.

5

IN THE CIRCUMSTANCES, Maldred was surprised at the air of normalcy which prevailed at Dunfermline on his return to Court — surprised and even a little shocked. It was almost as though the Queen had never been. No mourning was in evidence, no sense of loss or even of change, certainly no aura of guilt or apprehension. Presumably stories of poison did not penetrate here, or if so were carefully ignored.

He was surprised, too, at the altered state and standing of the Athelings, as revealed that first evening, within an hour or so of his arrival, at the meal, almost a banquet, in the hall. The King, who had received the mac Melmores back briefly casual, seemingly unconcerned and in comparatively good humour for that man, came in to seat himself at the head of the long table, with Margaret and Edgar on his right and left, and Princess Agatha, Christina and the Saxon and Hungarian lords who remained, at the other end, where the Queen had used to sit. All the visitors, save perhaps Margaret herself, seemed more at ease and assured than heretofore.

Maldred found a seat beside Magdalen of Ethanford at mid-table.

"A change since I went to Atholl," he murmured. "Is it for the better?"

She shrugged. "Who knows? *Some* find it so."

"And you do not?"

"Me? Who am I to judge? A mere waiting-woman."

"But the Lady Margaret's friend. She sits now at the King's right hand. And her brother at his left."

"Think you she chooses that? However well it suits others."

"Edgar? Her mother?"

"He is not now being told to go prowling through England. Or to remove himself to Hungary. And she, the Lady Agatha, sees her daughter as Queen of Scotland, one day!"

"Dear God!"

"You are surprised? After the way your King eyes her, seeks her company, speaks to her? He desires her, and does not hide it."

"But . . . the Queen. New dead . . . !"

"He was at it long before she died. You know it. But now, he is the more eager, more pressing, more hopeful."

"And, and she . . . ?"

"She wants none of him. But she does not reject him out-of-hand. For the sake of her family. And for Edgar's hopes of the English throne. I fear for her."

"But . . . always you said that she could well take care of herself. That she was strong. A match for any man."

"She is, yes. But it is different now. She is not thinking only of herself. Before, the King had a wife. Now he is the more dangerous."

"She would never wed him," he decided, with conviction.

"Not from choice. But princesses are seldom allowed to wed from choice. And there is much at stake. A kingdom, possibly. If Edgar could call his sister the Queen of Scotland, use your Malcolm's name and power to help him against the Normans, he would be greatly strengthened. In rousing the English to fight for him. You must see that."

"Yes. But *would* she? Sacrifice herself?"

"She might well. For Edgar's sake. And her mother's. To turn their dream into truth. If not, what have they? Nothing. Only failure. In Hungary, little to go back to. Safety, that is all, they say."

"So Edgar urges her to this, this infamy! To give herself to Malcolm, fiend take him!"

"I do not know. Edgar, I think, is torn in two ways. For he hates King Malcolm, in truth, and is fond of his sister. It is their mother, I believe, who is eager. She sees it the answer to prayer!"

Maldred snorted, and attacked his venison angrily. It was some time before he could bring himself adequately to appreciate the company he was presently keeping. Which was a pity, for it should have been excellent enough for any young man.

At least the new Atheling influence improved the quality of the evening's entertainment, Margaret managing to dilute and modify the steady eating and hard drinking, with music and song and the like, in a way that Ingebiorg had never prevailed on Malcolm to agree to. Drunkenness, as a consequence, was much reduced.

For all that, Maldred went to bed an unhappy young man.

Next day, he sought to speak with the King alone — and found it more difficult than he had anticipated. Previously it usually had been easy enough to contrive, for the monarch's esquire, for Malcolm was hardly a sociable man and company was apt to keep its distance discreetly. But now he always seemed to be surrounded by the Athelings and their hangers-on. Where formerly he had all but ignored and neglected them, now he sought them out, arranged activities and entertainments for them — in especial Margaret, of course, but she was adept at including others — and behaved generally like any man in the throes of courtship. Which was, his young cousin considered, for a middle-aged warrior-monarch of fierce, not to say ferocious, reputation, ridiculous, unsuitable and quite deplorable.

To add insult to injury, Maldred found himself dispossessed from his accustomed quarters in the palace, his room in the main hall-house having been allotted to the Earl Cospatrick and his family; for while he had been away in Atholl, Cospatrick had brought his children north from Bamburgh, four of them — Dolfin, the eldest and illegitimate, aged twelve; Waldeve and a second Cospatrick, aged ten and eight; and a daughter, Ethelreda, seven. This was quite good going, considering that the Earl himself was only twenty-nine. He had fetched them, not so much because he could not bear to be parted from them, his wife dead, as because of the conditions now prevailing in Northumbria as a result of the Scots activities, famine rife so that even cannibalism was reported and people dying like flies in the hard winter owing to their homes having been burned, their beasts driven off, their corn and forage destroyed. Bamburgh had been unable to replenish its storerooms after the siege, in consequence.

So the little palace on the Forth was overcrowded indeed, and Maldred and Madach, like others, had to go to find lodgings with the monks at St. Ternan's monastery. This was no great hardship, for it was less than half-a-mile away, and the Keledei were friendly and practised hosts; but it was an obvious demotion — and on account of the renegade Cospatrick, to make it worse — and it also meant that Maldred saw less of preferred feminine company, inevitably.

Nevertheless, it was from this other cousin, Cospatrick, that Maldred did learn something of the King's attitude and anticipations, in the present situation. The Earl was scarcely popular at Dunfermline, in the circumstances, and seemed to find his young kinsman preferable company to most of the Scots nobles. His was an extrovert, swashbuckling character which required an audience, and Maldred was sufficiently junior not to be able to rebuff him but at the same time of near-royal blood. After a slightly-veiled insult from Hugh O'Beolain, Abbot of Applecross, the second afternoon, he confided in Maldred that these pestilent Scots lords would be singing another song shortly, when they would be thankful for the services of an experienced soldier who knew more of warfare than burning peasants' hovels.

"You think that there will be warfare? Fighting?" Maldred said. "Soon?"

"Certainly. Only a fool would not."

"The King is no fool, my lord. Does he think so? He shows nothing of it."

"Malcolm *knows* the danger, boy. That is why he is glad to have me here."

"Is it so? This war — where will it come? Where strike?"

"It could come anywhere. At any time. William is no laggard — as I know well! He will not linger, licking his wounds. But now Malcolm has others to look out for. The Norse."

"You mean the Orkneymen? Paul and Erland?"

"These too. But they are scarce the main threat. I mean the true Norse, the Viking host. King Olaf."

"Olaf the Farmer is no warrior. Unlike his father, Harald Hardradi. And what has he against Malcolm?"

"He may deem sufficient. Even though the Orkney earls do not call him in. Our cousin Ingebiorg was also his, you will mind. His mother's sister's daughter. Kings mislike such . . . incidents."

"The Queen's death?"

"Aye — with the putting of her away first."

"I had forgot that Thorfinn Raven Feeder's wife was sister to Harald Hardradi's. The King — Malcolm? Does he perceive this danger?"

"Oh, yes. As you say, he is no fool. Even though *I* say that he has acted foolishly this time."

"Foolishly? Is that how you name it, my lord?"

The other looked at him carefully. "You would say differently?"

Maldred was equally careful. "Many would — and do — say worse."

"This talk of poison, you mean?"

"You know of that? Does *he* know — Malcolm?"

"He it was told me."

"He did? And what did he say? More?"

"He laughed."

"Laughed! Does he not care? Care for his name and repute, if nothing else? Care for the danger this may bring on his kingdom?"

The Earl shrugged. "Who knows? If he does, he does not let it trouble him. But — he is ready to muster at short notice."

"When it might be too late . . ."

The following day, of strong frost — February being the hardest month of the Scots winter — the monarch led his guests to a bonspiel or ice-carnival at Loch Leven, where Maldred had taken the young women to see the birds in November. The loch, being shallow but extensive, was famous for freezing over, and folk flooded to it from far and near. It was a dozen miles from Dunfermline, so that an early start had to be made. Indeed it was barely light when they set out, and to brighten things up in that biting cold, servitors rode with blazing torches in a long double line, very romantic-seeming. Maldred could not remember the King having done anything of this sort before.

The sun had risen over the Lomond Hills to the east by the time they reached their destination, and the loch was a glittering, gleaming expanse which hurt the eyes, morning smokes rising blue against the white from the islands, on one of which was the cashel of St. Serf, an offshoot from Culross, and on another a small Pictish fort, now used as a fishing-station.

Fairly constant movement was necessary for the distinguished company to keep warm, but there was no lack of activities — skating, individually, in formation and in races, curling, a form of ice skittles, sledging, with contests, man-drawn and horse-drawn, fishing for the large loch-trout through holes in the ice. This last was scarcely a warmth-inducing pastime but it could be combined with the bonfires lit on the ice, it being suggested that the heat attracted the fish. This lighting of fires on ice was contrived by insulating the surface with a thick mattress of green yew branches on which were spread layers of fresh, untanned deer-skins, hide-up, the firewood being lit on these and the ice not melting appreciably. There was the music of fiddles and pipes, for dancing, even.

So the sport and vigorous merriment proceeded merrily, the monks joining in, a cheerful lot, indeed leading in much of it, for of course they had more practice than the others. Madach and Maldred were glad to find Kerald there, along with others from the main St. Serf's abbey at Culross, and the three brothers made a formidable team, happily incorporating Magda into their group. They would have included Margaret, but she was pre-empted, the King proving quite expert at getting her to himself, especially in the sledging, with most of the sledges only holding two people. No doubt this had not escaped his anticipation in organising the affair.

Maldred's preoccupation with this situation was somewhat ameliorated by a growing awareness of his brothers' interest and admiration in Magdalen, which he began to feel was in danger of becoming excessive, and due to be countered. He tried to involve them with Christina, but with scant reaction on either side.

Madach did manage to detach Magda and swept her off on a sledge-run round the islands, allowing Kerald to have a private word with his older brother.

"The Abbot told me a strange matter," he confided. "At Culross. He said that the King sent for him. Soon after we were gone to Atholl. Asking him privily if there were relationships where the Church said that men and women should not marry? Cousins, in any degree. The Abbot told him not so, not in the Celtic Church. He said that the Romish Church frowned upon cousinship in marriage, but not the followers of Columba. The King said that he knew about the Roman Church and that he had spoken with a Romish priest — it would be that Oswald, with the Athelings — who had told him that marriage between cousins was no true marriage and could be annulled. He asked if this was not possible in our own Church."

"So-o-o! Ingebiorg was his cousin, as she was ours."

"Yes. The Abbot said no. That a marriage of cousins celebrated in the Columban Church — as was Malcolm's — was true marriage, perfectly lawful, and could not be annulled or set aside."

The brothers stared at each other.

"So — your Abbot may unwittingly have written the Queen's death-warrant," Maldred got out, after a moment.

"It . . . it need not mean that."

"No. But . . ."

"There is no cousinship with this Margaret?"

"None. They are not related. How could they be?"

After that, Maldred found himself actually avoiding any close contact with the King instead of seeking an interview, private or otherwise. Which he realised was foolish, for there was nothing that he could do about it, no means whereby he could alter the situation — even if he had call to, or if it was any responsibility of his. However, he did have opportunity to speak with Margaret herself thereafter, although not alone of course. At the repast on the ice, as the short day faded, with hot soup for all, oxen roasted whole on the bonfires, and folk stamping their feet as they ate, the King had to present prizes for the various competitions, races and contests — which took some little time. Margaret stood well back, while this was going on — and Maldred and Magda moved forward.

"You have won no prizes, Maldred?" the princess asked, lightly. "I thought that I saw you doing well? But perhaps you have been too busy esquiring this young woman of mine?"

"I would not have thought that *you* would have noticed!" Magda returned quickly.

Maldred coughed. "We have had a good day, yes. My brother Madach, as eldest, will go for the prizes. And you, Princess?"

"I also have been well esquired."

"Yes. To be sure." He considered his steaming rib of beef. "It is all good cheer, much merriment. But scarcely right, I think. Suitable. When we should still be mourning the Queen."

"I agree with you," Margaret said simply.

"Yet all this is, is . . ."

"Done for my entertainment? I know it, Maldred. Or for my family's. The King is kind. I do not desire it. But I cannot refuse to partake of what he offers. We are his guests, dependent upon him wholly."

"He may offer more!"

"He has much to offer, yes. Not only for myself."

"That could be dear bought."

She nodded.

"You so God-fearing. Could this be God's will?"

"It could be. God could be pointing me my duty."

"Duty! In this?"

"Why not? Christian duties are not always for our enjoyment. There could be much here that even such as I could do to further Christ's cause."

"I say that it is not right. He is a violent man."

"Was not the Blessed Peter?"

"It was not a woman who tamed Peter!"

"No. Perhaps that was presumptuous. But — I might do lesser things."

"The Queen tried — and failed!"

She looked at him searchingly. "You were fond of the

Queen, Maldred? I did not gain her friendship, I fear. She
was a woman of some strength, able. And comely. Why
did she fail?"

"She failed nothing, as Queen. Only in this of changing
the King, of taming his violence."

"You speak so of your prince and kinsman?" she said,
troubled.

"Not to all. But to you, it is different. I know him. Have
served him since a boy. He has good in him, too. He is
valiant, can be generous. Is not proud as some great ones
are proud. But he has a, a savagery. Like a lion untamed. I
tell you . . ."

The King was turning from his prize-giving and coming
back. Maldred swallowed his words.

"God be thanked that is done with!" Malcolm declared.
"Ha, Maldred — I see little of you these days."

The young man gulped. "You seldom seem to need me.
I am ever at Your Highness's service — if required."

"Aye, you are, boy, you are indeed! As are all. I do not
forget it, never fear!" He turned to Margaret. "You are not
cold? The sun has gone. Time that we were on our way.
We shall have the torches again . . ."

6

IT WAS ONLY a few days later that the King sent for
Maldred. The young man found him for once free of
Athelings, closeted with Gillibride of Angus and Hugh
O'Beolain, drinking deeply of ale.

"Aye, cousin," he greeted, "my standard-bearer and
esquire — who does little of standard-bearing and prefers
to esquire ladies, I swear! How old are you now, Maldred
mac Melmore?"

"I will be nineteen years next month, Highness."

"So advanced! Old enough to use your wits, then. And
old enough to be a knight, I think, and done with this
esquiring. How say you?"

Maldred, surprised, took his time to answer that. Knighthood he had wanted, coveted, for long, the accolade of manhood as well as of chivalry and leadership, a status longed for by all young men of noble houses. But he was suspicious as to why Malcolm should offer this privilege at this juncture, when they were scarcely on the best of terms. Also, he had certain finicking doubts as to the rectitude of accepting the honour at the hands of one whom he suspected of wife-murder.

"It is my hope to win knighthood one day, my lord King," he said cautiously.

"Then this is the day, lad — or tomorrow, since you must needs keep your vigil first. Tomorrow, before you go."

"Go . . . ?"

"Go, yes. Tomorrow you are to go to Galloway. With Cospatrick. And a small force. We have heard that the Earls Paul and Erland of Orkney have arrived there. At Kirk Cuthbert's Town. Erland is often there. He calls himself governor of Galloway. But Paul seldom ventures south of the Hebrides. So this is unusual. And he is said to have brought many longships and men. Something is afoot, winter though it is. I want to know what. And to have it stopped, if it is to my hurt."

"But . . . why? Why me? If there is trouble in Galloway, you need an army . . ."

"I cannot spare an army for Galloway. Meantime. I have William to consider. Perhaps Olaf of Norway."

"What am I to do, then? With this small force?"

"With the force, nothing. Or little. That is for Cospatrick. I do not esteem you one of my most experienced soldiers, cousin, knight or none! Whereas Cospatrick is that — whatever else he is! No, you are to keep watch on our kinsman Cospatrick. I do not trust him. You will be my eyes on him."

"But . . ."

"But nothing, boy! He must be watched. He seems to think well of you. You are kin, to both of us. He will accept you, where he would not others. Heed you, in some measure, perhaps. The more if you are knight, it may be. Restrain himself."

"Why send him then, at all? Whom you cannot trust."

"Use your wits — if you have any! Galloway is in Strathclyde. As is Cumbria. Cospatrick has links there,

85

influence. He is Lord of Allerdale, in Cumberland. His brother Waltheof mac Maldred, is in name my governor of Cumbria — little use as he is! I cannot spare an army to go to Galloway. So one must be raised there, or thereabouts. To counter these sons of Thorfinn. If they intend trouble. Cospatrick can do that better than any. And he is a fair soldier. Better, more experienced than Paul or Erland. And I do not *think* he will change sides this time. They have little to offer him. Whereas *I* have promised him an earldom here. To make up for Northumbria."

Maldred shook his head. "I cannot but think that another would serve your purposes better, Highness."

"By God's mercy Scotland is not dependent on *your* thinking, boy! Leave that to me."

"Watch Cospatrick over Man," Angus put in. "He might choose to fish in *those* drumly waters, I think."

"Man? What of Man?"

"Sufficient. Godfrey Crovan the Pale-Blooded, is in Man. Fled there. A hard man and a fighter. Son to Harald the Black, of Islay. The other Godfrey, Olafson, King of Dublin and Man, is weak, sickly, some say dying. So Godfrey Pale-Blooded will grasp Man if he can, nothing more sure. For his father is bastard brother of King Godfrey. And being an Islesman, from Islay, he owes allegiance to Orkney. What better way to gain Man than by bringing a Manx force to aid his lords in Galloway — weakening Man thereby; then to return with Orkney support, and take over Man?"

"A mercy — all that? And what of Cospatrick?"

"They are friends, Cospatrick and Godfrey Crovan. Have fought many times on the same field. They were together at Stamford Bridge — when Godfrey was wounded and King Harald Hardradi of Norway slain. If Cospatrick is thinking of changing sides again, he could well do it over Godfrey Crovan and Man."

"And then change again, slay Godfrey and take Man for himself!" Malcolm added sardonically.

"And *I* am to bridle this, this treacherous mount!" Maldred exclaimed.

"Watch him, constrain him, be ever at his elbow," the King said. "Earn your knighthood! Off with you, now. Prepare. I shall see you in the morning. Before you move off."

In his doubts, Maldred went seeking his brother

Madach. As all too often nowadays he found him in company with Magda of Ethanford.

"Are you commanded to go to Galloway tomorrow? With this force of Cospatrick's?" he demanded.

"Galloway? Cospatrick? No. What is this?"

"It is some strange venture of the King's." He explained the situation. "But why send me? *You* would have been better, more experienced. And the same kin."

"I have my own command, of our Athollmen. Part of his main array. There is a difference, man."

"There is something else. He would make me knight. Before we go. The, the bait to the hook!"

"Knight, Maldred? You? Splendid!" Magdalen cried. "Well-deserved, I say!"

Madach, who had been a knight for a couple of years, grinned. "As well now as ever. If it is not to be on the field of battle. Malcolm is not usually so amiable. He must think well of you. Better than I believed."

"That is where it is so strange — I do not think that he does. He mocks me always, now."

"It is but his way. Be thankful."

"But . . . should I accept?"

"Accept? A God's good name, why not?"

Maldred glanced at Magda. His doubts over his monarch were not for her ears. "Knighthood is . . . especial. To be held in honour. It must be received in honour, and given in honour. Not, not . . ."

"Honour? What more do you want, man? So be it the King honours you, what is your complaint?"

"I would rather be knighted . . . otherwise."

"Then you are a fool! Knighthood is knighthood, however bestowed and whoever the bestower. It is *being* a knight that is important, not who knighted you."

"Should not a man greatly respect the hand which holds the sword?"

"Watch your words, brother!" Madach warned. "Men have died for less than that. I say, grasp the accolade while you may. Besides, you dare not make refusal of the King's offer. As well spit in his face! Take it and be thankful. Forby, if Malcolm does not knight you, who else is like to do so? Tell me that."

Slowly Maldred picked his words. "As I understand it, any knight can make a knight. *Only* a knight can do so — but the right is with any who has himself been knighted."

"Save us — what are you at? That may be so, as a notion. But in practice only kings, princes and the very great ones, with commanders in the field, do so. What is this?"

"You may think me foolish. But . . . I feel at odds with Malcolm. Once I am made knight, I am so for all my days. I would not wish for so great a matter to be spoiled. For me. Because of this."

"Maldred — you should not throw away the King's knighting because you find fault with the King," Magda said. "If all did that, there would be few knights! Do not refuse this."

"There, there is a way out, I think. If Madach was to knight me first!"

"Wha-a-at! Saints save us — what madness is this?"

"None," Maldred assured, earnestly. "See you, this is for my own mind only, my mind's peace. None other would know — save only Magda here. After my vigil. Do it secretly. Then I know, in my heart, that I have been knighted by a true man, a true knight. Whom I respect. So that afterwards I can go before the King and receive *his* stroke of the sword. Before all. It will not matter, then. No harm in that — the second accolade. It will not wipe out the first and true one. But it will ease my mind. None will know, only ourselves."

"Dear God — what a brother I have! To think of this. Why should I do this, take this risk? If the King were to find out . . . !"

"I swear never to tell anyone. It would cost you nothing."

"Do it for him, Madach," the girl said. "A secret, between us."

The older brother looked from one to the other. He shrugged. "It is a folly. But, so long as none hear of it, I suppose there is no hurt in it. Very well — come to me in the morning, before you see the King . . ."

So that February night of 1070, Maldred kept his vigil. The Celtic Church had its own relaxed way of dealing with this, as with other ceremonial — for knighthood was a religious as much as a military state, in theory at least. Not being building-bound like the Romish faith, night-long kneeling before a high altar was not required; but instead the postulant was expected to go off alone to quiet places and meditate with his Maker — if he could — on the meaning and significance of the new phase of his life he was about to enter, on service to an ideal of chivalry, of defence of true religion, of respect for women, of upholding of justice, of cherishing the weak and helpless and of eschewing cowardice, corruption and treachery at all times. When he had finally meditated on all this to the extent of his capacity — and it was recognised that all, military men in especial, had not the ability for unduly lengthy silent communion on the verities — the candidate was to take himself to some holy spot and there, facing the east, take his solemn vow to carry it all out, God aiding him, to his life's end. He was then considered fit to receive the accolade.

So Maldred went wandering on the Fothrif Moor above Dunfermline on a windy night of showers and a fitful half-moon, amongst the whins and short heather and out-cropping rocks. He did not find the deliberate meditating easy. Natural and spontaneous thought was one thing, but forcing himself to deep and continuing consideration on an abstract theme he found all but impossible. But he tried, came to recognise that he was in fact thinking of nothing very apposite in particular and of everything, haphazard, in general, and sorrowfully came to the conclusion that this was not for him.

So he turned and wended his way back over the rough and difficult terrain to a stone-circle on which he had recently stumbled — there were three or four of these dotted over the high and desolate moorland ridge. Here, in the centre, facing east to the tall index-stone, he sank to his knees and promised his Creator to at least try to fulfil all these lofty conceptions and ideals — while seeking to shut out of his mind's-eye the all-too-clear picture of King Malcolm, the fount of honour, trampling over that unhappy Wearmouth peasant-woman's ravaged body, on his horse, and other similar incidents, surrounded by his knighted warriors. Was it only high-born ladies of one's own nation to whom the protective vows applied? Justice to be upheld only in law-courts? Religion to be fought for only as policy? If this amounted to unsuitable meditation, he prayed for forgiveness. That he did so here in an ancient stone-circle, no doubt Margaret Atheling would brand as heretical and a return to paganism. But much honest worship had been offered up in such a spot. however misguided, and therefore surely it was holy? As holy, anyway, as knighthood conferred by such a monarch?

He found his way back to his cell at St. Ternan's thereafter, soon after midnight, deciding that this was as much vigilising as he was fit for — and slept with his usual alacrity.

When the hollow clanging of St. Ternan's bell awakened the monks for early-morning prayers, Maldred roused himself, washed and shaved, and went to Madach's cell nearby. His brother was still asleep. Wakened, he showed no enthusiasm for the business. But the postulant insisted, fetched him his sword and knelt before him. Owlishly, the other grumbled and frowned and then tapped each bent shoulder with the steel, muttering that he hereby named Maldred mac Melmore knight, and let him be a good and true knight hereafter until his life's end. Maldred rose, took the sword, held it up by the blade, cross-like hilt high, then kissed it. He was a knight.

He left his yawning brother, and went for his breakfast.

Later, all ready for his journey, he presented himself at the palace. The King was no slug-abed and was already briefing the Earl Cospatrick and a group of officers. Maldred did not have to wait long. Malcolm beckoned him forward.

"Here is our knight-to-be. I swear that he was awake all night, making his vigil!"

"Scarcely all night. But I did what I could, Highness."

"I am disappointed in you, cousin — so serious a youth, and that is all you could do? Myself, I mind that I fell asleep after a minute or two. On your knees, then. Cospatrick, man — give me your sword."

There was little more ceremony about it than in Madach's cell earlier. The King slapped the sword-blade down more heartily on Maldred's shoulders, and added a few extra words, that is all.

"Maldred mac Melmore, I name you knight," he said, almost casually. "See you keep your vows, maintain the right, serve my cause and do so all your days. Aye, do that! Arise, Maldred of Atholl, knight."

It can fall to few men, surely, to be knighted twice in the one morning.

Cospatrick was the first to come forward to shake his hand — but his grin was mocking.

Soon thereafter they were on their way, Maldred

disappointed that no one from the Athelings' party came down to see them off. No doubt they were deeply engaged in morning worship. Also, amongst other doubts, he had one about leaving Magda to see much of Madach with himself removed.

*   *   *

They had to cover some one hundred and fifty miles of Lowland Scotland, in diagonal fashion, to reach Galloway, over the high spine of the land, first having to ride fully twenty-five miles up the firth to Stirling, to win across the Forth itself. Thereafter they went almost due southwards, across the grain of the country, though anything but directly, for they had to make innumerable detours to find river-fords, to circle lochs and flooded areas, to avoid marshes and dense forests. This was no time of year for such travel. But though most of the company grumbled, Cospatrick himself was in good spirits. Clearly he was glad to be on his own again, his own master and free of the trammels of Malcolm's establishment. He made himself entirely affable towards Maldred — who did not particularly like him, but found him easy enough to get on with. He was a strange man, with a reputation almost as fierce as Malcolm's to add to his well-known unpredictability as to loyalties, yet cheerful, at least superficially friendly and good company, with little of the proud noble about him. He was good-looking too, in his own way, tall and a fine figure of a man. Although of the Celtic royal house, his mother had been sister to a previous Saxon Earl of Northumbria and he had been married to a daughter of King Harold of England, he who had died at Hastings.

He made a hard-riding commander, and despite the difficult conditions, led them fully seventy miles before halting for the night at the Hospice of St. Bride in Douglasdale, in the former kingdom of Strathclyde. That Cymric-Celtic realm, stretching from the northern Welsh marches and the Yorkshire border right up to the Lennox Highlands and the fringe of the Hebrides, had been an independent monarchy until a century-and-a-half previously when Constantine the Second of Scots annexed it; and still its relationship with Scotland was apt to be uneasy, the latter's sovereignty at times only nominal.

Indeed, Cumbria, its southern province, was now largely English-dominated, although Cospatrick's brother Waltheof was styled Malcolm's governor thereof; and the great Lordship of Galloway was, like the Hebrides, a possession of Orkney, although again the Earl Erland Thorfinnson ranked as governor. In the circumstances, Strathclyde was an unruly and unmanageable entity, more of a source of weakness than of strength to the Scottish crown.

Off again at first light, by noon next day they were actually in Galloway, *Outer* Galloway as it was termed, which extended from the Cumbrian border at Annandale right up to the Lordship of Renfrew on the Clyde estuary. But Inner, or Galloway proper, was otherwise, confined to the great many-pronged peninsula itself which thrust out into the Irish Sea. Their destination was another fifty miles at least.

Cospatrick went more warily now, concerned not to thrust his head into any noose, having a notable sense of self-preservation. His company of two hundred was large enough to be safe from casual interference but not from major assault in a semi-hostile land — and certainly not small enough to escape notice. So they went now by hidden ways, keeping within the closer hills and higher moors, more difficult going as this made and much as it added to their journey.

In the late afternoon they came down from the bleak, snow-streaked Lochinvar Hills, by the Garpel Burn to the Water of Ken, and to the cashel of St. John of Dalry, a remotely-sited monastery in a quiet valley at the hub of waters. Cospatrick had little fear of trouble or betrayal in such places, for the churchmen were entirely sympathetic towards the Scottish crown, in Galloway, feeling themselves somewhat beleaguered indeed. For the Romish Church in England, through the Archbishop of York and Bishop of Durham, were making claims that this area should be under *their* jurisdiction on the grounds that there had once been a diocese of Whithorn owing allegiance to them, even though that was centuries before — an issue which had taken King MacBeth to Rome and agreement with the Pope. But that Pope was dead, and now the English bishops were at it again. The Orkney earls were Romish likewise, if they were anything; so the Celtic churchmen of Galloway lived under something of a shadow and were apt to welcome warmly any signs of attention from the North.

Cospatrick, to be sure, had no religion in him; but he made much of Abbot Cosgreg and sounded the soul of Celtic piety. And to excellent effect, for the monks here were in a position to be well-informed as to the present situation in Galloway. St. John's Town, although deep in the heathery hills, was only a score of miles up the Waters of Dee and Ken from the former's estuary, whereon lay Kirk Cuthbert's Town and fort, the principal place of Galloway, where the governor had his seat. There was a monastery of St. Cuthbert there, and considerable coming and going with that of St. John.

"So the Earl Paul of Orkney is come visiting his brother Erland, friend?" Cospatrick said, conversationally, over an adequate if simple meal in the eating-hall. "And has brought a sufficiency of Orkneymen with him, I am told?"

"My sorrow, yes, my lord Earl," the Abbot agreed. "There are seventy longships lying in St. Cuthbert's Bay. Aye, and another score lying apart, behind St. Mary's Isle. Manxmen, there."

"God — Manxmen? Already? A score of Manx longships, you say? An army?"

"An army, yes. For what, I cannot say, for sure. But I greatly fear. Since their Bishop Roolwer is come with them. Which bodes no good."

"A bishop? The Bishop of Man? What does *he* want?"

"What does any Romish bishop want? To wrest Galloway from us, from our Church. As first step to taking it from King Malcolm."

Cospatrick glanced over at Maldred. "This we had no word of. The Church taking a hand. It could be an added danger."

"Perhaps. But — do we need added dangers? With near a hundred longships. Even though they are not all of the largest, that could mean four thousand men."

"Aye." The Earl turned back to Abbot Cosgreg. "These Manxmen — who sent them?"

"It is said the King of Man. But he is sick, in Dublin. They are under the command of the Lord Godfrey of Islay, Godfrey Crovan."

"I know him. How long have they been here?"

"They came three days past."

"And the Earl Paul and his Orkneymen?"

"Ten days or more."

"So! It looks as though he had waited for them. This was planned between Paul and Godfrey. Four thousand men. For what?"

"For no good, lord. To take Galloway. The Church *and* the land."

"Tut, man — they already have Galloway's land. Paul Thorfinnson is lord here, his brother governor. This of your Church is not the main concern, only to aid in it. These seek bigger things. What? Have you heard talk? From Kirk Cuthbert's Town? What are folk saying?"

The little cleric looked both anxious and embarrassed. "It is only mere chatter, my lord Earl. The clash of idle tongues. Unseemly. And I cannot think that it is all true . . ."

"Out with it, man. We are not bairns! There may be a hint of truth even in such talk."

"It is whispered — by the ignorant, see you — that the Orkney earls intend to make war, large war. Against King Malcolm. To drive north into Scotland. To avenge the death of their sister, the Queen. For which foolish men blame His Highness."

"Aye. But if Paul desires to fight Malcolm, would he not do so better to descend with his longships and Vikings upon the *other* side of Scotland? On the east coast. In Fortrenn. Or into the Scottish Sea. Near where the King is, the heart of the land? Why here, so far away?"

"Because, lord, they say that is for others to do. It is to be a greater war than just this of the Orkneymen. They say that Norman William himself is in it. That — saving your presence, my lord — your own brother, the Earl Waltheof of Cumberland, also. That even King Olaf of Norway, whose cousin the Queen was, is to come. He it is who will land on the east, in Fortrenn. Many onslaughts."

"But . . . but . . ."

"I told you, my lord, that it was idle chatter. Foolishness."

"Yet it makes sense," Maldred put in. "If it could be achieved. A concerted attack."

"At this season? Moving great armies, while still the rivers are high? The campaigning season is two months off, yet. And are these Orkney earls of the worth and stature to lead anything such? Or devise it? Would William

94

dance to their tune? If it had been their father, the Raven Feeder, I might have believed it."

"They may conceive themselves more potent than you do," Maldred said.

"There is more to it — although how much to believe, who knows?" the Abbot went on. "It is said that the plan is for the attack from Galloway here to start first. To give the others time. And to draw King Malcolm away from Fortrenn. Get him south of the Forth crossing, his greatest defence. To have him march southwards and westwards, to repel this invasion of Strathclyde. Whilst the Earl Waltheof invades Teviotdale and the Forest. Then the others to strike behind Malcolm. William by sea and land, from the south, to the Scottish Sea and Tay. Olaf to the north. So Scotland falls . . ."

"As it would, by God! If this indeed could be done. But — do not tell me that Thorfinn's sons could rise to this? Have the wits for it. Or the ability to move kings like pawns on a board!"

"Could it be that it is *they* who are being moved?" Maldred suggested. "That the conception is not theirs but Norman William's? It is not beyond *him* to conceive all this. He has done greater, has he not? And but uses the Orkneymen and the others, even King Olaf, to his own ends. To bring down Malcolm."

Cospatrick looked at him thoughtfully, rubbing his small pointed beard. "I do not know," he admitted. "But if it is so, then we are in a coil indeed." He straightened up at the table. "Tomorrow," he decided, "we go see my good brother at Caer-luel. Discover what *he* knows. Before these others gain word of us. That is best . . ."

That night Maldred lay long awake. There was a sufficiency to think about. And not the least of the questions he asked himself was, if all this proved to be true, even in some measure, what were the chances of Cospatrick remaining true to Malcolm and Scotland? Would not all his advantage be to change sides once again, to throw in his lot with this menacing confederacy, if such there was? In which case, what was his own duty? Or, at least, how was he to carry any of it out?

He could only wait and see what transpired.

In the morning, they were on the move early again, for it was a long day's ride to Caer-luel in Cumberland, especially since they must still keep to hidden ways and high ground, at first at least, to avoid discovery. Later, it would not matter. They went by Corsock and the Urr Water, over to Auchenreoch, and then followed the Cargen Water down to Nith, to ford that great river at Dumfries. This was a fair-sized town at the only available crossing, which they could not avoid. But they were not held up, the banner of Northumbria — which Cospatrick still chose to fly — sufficient credential if two hundred armed men were not enough. On across the great Lochar Moss to the Solway shore, openly now, for none would challenge the Earl Waltheof's brother this side of Nith, to cross the foot of Annandale and so come, over Sark to the two final Solway crossings, of Esk and Eden, into Cumbria. At once, across Esk at Kirkandrews, they were held up and questioned by guards, but allowed to proceed. Yes, the Earl Waltheof was in residence at Caer-luel.

Caer-luel, the Fort of Llewellyn, some Cymric princeling of old, rose in marshland at a major bend of the River Eden some five miles inland from the Solway, in a strong position within triple moats, the site of a Roman strength. Its township, on the firmer ground to the east, although the most important centre in Cumberland, was a poor place, having suffered much from Viking burnings in the past. But on its outskirts was a monastery, a Romish one this, and very different from the Celtic cashels, even though not large as such establishments went. It was built all in stone-and-lime and slating, with a handsome church and quite extensive monastic buildings surrounding a cloister — chapter-house, refectory, dormitories, calefactory, infirmary, locutory, guest-houses, even a scriptorium and library, and a misericord where special indulgences in food could be enjoyed. In the circumstances, perhaps, it was not to be wondered at that this was where the visitors found the Earl Waltheof installed, a deal more comfortably than in the old fort.

Two years younger than his brother, he proved to be a very different man, hesitant, slow of speech, wary, inclined to stoop. He was handsome also, in his own way, but there was an essential weakness about the mouth and chin which was not to be hidden.

He did not appear overjoyed to see Cospatrick or to meet his cousin Maldred for the first time. But he made them reasonably welcome — or at least requested the Prior, one Ulfwin, to do so, and to provide suitable accommodation for his kinsmen in the monastery, and quarters for the soldiers nearby in the town. Unfortunately it was the Fast of St. Matthew, and these being Benedictines and of fairly strict rule, the hospitality would not be of the most lavish.

For all that, the newcomers did quite well at Caer-luel, with better, or at least more varied, feeding than at St. John's of Dalry, served suitably in the misericord chamber. Here Cospatrick lost no time in questioning his brother, having cheerfully if autocratically dismissed all others save Maldred from the room.

"Now — what of this talk of war, man?" he demanded bluntly. "I hear that you are in some way concerned. Which is not like you. What's to do, Wattie?"

The other looked alarmed and unhappy, glanced at Maldred, and closing somewhat slack lips rather more tightly, shook his head.

"Come — out with it," his brother insisted. "Never heed Maldred. He is our close kin. And acts my lieutenant in this enterprise."

As the younger man blinked at this, Waltheof found his voice. "Aye — what *is* your enterprise, Pate? What brings you here, with this Scots company? Who do you support now? Who do you serve?"

Cospatrick laughed. "Say that I support myself. As best I can in this sorry world! As must all, who are not fools. At present I am on an errand of enquiry, see you."

"For Malcolm?"

"And for myself. A man cannot make wise decisions lacking full knowledge. Eh, Maldred?"

That one, as careful as Waltheof, only slightly inclined his head.

"It is not for me to inform Malcolm Big Head," Waltheof said.

"You are his governor, here in Cumbria, are you not?"

"Am I so still? Or ever? I know not. We have no dealings. It was never more than in name — as well you know, Pate."

"So — you have something to hide? From Malcolm. But not from me, brother — not from me, I promise you!" That was almost menacing. "It is this of war? That you are entangled in it with those fools Paul and Erland Thorfinnson — like the fool you are also!"

"No, Pate — no. It is not so, not that . . ."

"Do you deny that you have, of all follies, conspired

with the Orkneymen to invade Scotland? With Godfrey Crovan and others?"

"Not conspired, no. It is at William's express command — King William of England."

"William? Since when has the Norman commanded *you*? Or any of our house? This is Cumbria, is it not? In Strathclyde. Not in England."

"You fought for William yourself . . ."

"When it suited me. Of my own will. Never at his command."

"And look what that gained you! *You* lost Northumbria. I, I will win it back again."

"Ha — so now we have it! That is what William has promised you, to be his man? To do his bidding. You are to be Earl of Northumbria. In *my* place. Or so he says . . ."

"And why not? You have thrown it away. It was ours, our forebears' . . ."

"You think that Norman William would fulfil his word, fool? And that if he did, *I* would leave you in possession of my earldom! Dear God — even you should know better than that! One man has already learned what it costs to try to hold my patrimony — Robert de Comyn. I slew him, you will mind."

"You . . . ?" That was on a choke.

"Did you think that the Durham mob did it of their own feeble wills? So will end any others who think to hold what is mine — whether the Norman gives them it or no." There was an appreciable pause, whilst brother glared at brother. "Now," Cospatrick went on, in a different tone of voice. "This of William's new war? What would he have of you, for Northumbria?"

Waltheof swallowed, looked again at Maldred, and mumbled somewhat. "There is to be invasion of Scotland. From all quarters. The Orkneymen and Manxmen up through Strathclyde. Myself into Teviotdale and the centre. Waldeve Siwardson, Earl of Deira, through Northumbria into the Merse and Lothian. A Norse force to land in Moray and Ross, where MacBeth's son Farquhar is Mormaer and hates Malcolm. And a Hebridean force under Earl Somerled mac Gillaciaran to land in Dalar." For a slow-spoken man that came out in a rush.

"All that! When?"

"It will be in stages. It cannot all be done at one time. The Galloway force to move first. Any day now. They but

wait for word that Somerled of Colonsay has his Islesmen
gathered. Then they strike up towards the Clyde. In the
west. To force Malcolm to come out against them. As he
must, for the Orkney earls have a great army assembled.
Then, when Malcolm has left Fortrenn, I move. I have
fifteen hundred mustered along Esk and Liddel. More to
come. The Earl of Deira at the same time, in the east. We
both make for the Forth. At Stirling. With all speed. To
capture that vital crossing. And to cut Malcolm off from
Fortrenn. Then the Norsemen and Islesmen move into
the north. It cannot fail, I tell you!"

"And the so-clever William? Where is he, in all this?"

"He waits at York, meantime. A great fleet assembles in
the Humber. When he hears that we have secured the
Forth crossing, he will sail for the Scottish Sea. Attack
Malcolm in the rear. Take over Scotland. And appoint
the boy Duncan mac Malcolm, Ingebiorg's elder son,
King. Under his own overlordship. He has promised this,
to myself and to the Orkney earls."

"Aye. So our Abbot Cosgreg was none so far out! A
pretty plot!" Cospatrick suddenly leaned forward, to jab a
pointing finger at his brother. "You!" he all but shouted.
"You believe all this, Christ God! Do you, fool, idiot,
dizzard?"

The other shrank back. Clearly he was much afraid of
his dominant and unpredictable elder brother. "Why . . .
why not?"

"Because, witling, William the Bastard of Normandy is
the greatest liar and deceiver ever spawned! An able
fighter, yes. But an arrant deceiver. As *I* know. A user of
others. He will use you, Wattie, and these others, to do
his work for him. As he has done times beyond number.
You, and Paul and Erland Thorfinnson. And Godfrey
Crovan. Aye, and Waldeve Siwardson. You all will fight
Malcolm, for William, and bring him down — if you can.
And then the Norman will step in and take all. And you
will get nothing for your pains."

"When I get Northumbria, I will share it with you, Pate.
I swear it . . ."

"Dolt — I tell you, you will never get Northumbria.
How think you William has won over Waldeve Siwardson?
His father, Siward the Strong of Deira, took Northumbria
from our grandsire. Became Earl of Northumbria also,
until he died. Waldeve fought *against* William, for the

Atheling. Now he is *for* him. He too will have been promised something — Northumbria, I vow! And he, being one of William's English earls, and a fighter besides, unlike you, will be much the more likely to get it. Can you not see it, man?"

The other was silent, clenching and unclenching his fists.

"So — you will be done with all this nonsense, Wattie. You hear me? It is finished."

"I cannot, Pate — I cannot." That was next to a wail.

"You can and will. I say it. Who is head of our house? You, or I? You will not use Cumbrian levies against their liege — lord Malcolm — you, his governor. You will not raise hand against your cousin at the behest of the Bastard of Normandy. You will, instead, send to warn the King of what is plotted against him. As is your duty. You have it?"

"My word is given . . ."

"*Your* word! Your word, brother, is not worth a snap of my fingers! It is *my* word that counts. And stands. As well that I came in time. Now, will you send and draw back your levies from Esk and Liddel? Or shall I?"

Waltheof sighed, and shrugged, beaten.

"See to it, then. For I have other work to do. Where is Waldeve Siwardson now?"

Both his hearers stared, at that.

"He is . . . he is in Northumbria. At, at Bamburgh. Mustering."

"Precious Soul of God — Bamburgh!" Cospatrick half-rose from his seat. "*My* house! The Dane sits in my house. And you, *you* knew it! You . . . !"

"I could not stop him, Pate. How could I? He is William's man, now. What could I do?"

"As you say — what could *you* do! What could you ever do, to effect? It is ever I who must do — and you whine! But I will do, never fear. You — get me fresh horses. For myself and my men. Get them now, this night — for I ride before daybreak. For Bamburgh."

"Bamburgh? Waldeve . . . ?"

"Aye, Waldeve. I will go reason with your fellow fool, that insolent Dane! My former brother-in-arms! And see if the men of Northumbria prefer to obey their true lord, or him! Go — get me those horses . . ."

Alone with Maldred, the Earl spoke in a different tone, although still urgently. "You, lad — now you have your chance to play the knight! You have sound wits in that head, I think — now show them. While I go see Waldeve Siwardson, *you* must go to your cousins Paul and Erland. And tell them where their advantage lies."

"*Me!* Go to the Orkneymen? To their army?" Maldred gasped.

"To be sure. They are your kin also. Talk with them. Tell them that William cheats them, cozens them, uses them. Tell them that my brother Waltheof will not march. Aye, and tell them that Waldeve of Deira will not march likewise! As he will not, if I can stop him. Tell them that King Malcolm knows all, and will surely defeat them. No surprise."

"But — how can I do this? They will not listen to me, believe me. I am too young, of insufficient stature . . ."

"You are not so much younger than are they. You are the King's cousin, new knighted. You came from *me*, my lieutenant. Aye, and you were Ingebiorg's friend. Tell them, see you, tell them that Malcolm did *not* have the Queen killed. That their hatred and spleen has no justification . . ."

"How can I tell them that? When I do not know it as truth?"

"Tell them it, anyway. This could be the saving of Scotland, man! You do not know that it is *not* the truth. So you would be telling no lie."

"No. That I will *not* do."

"Then, by God's Blood — tell them that *I* say it! That I, Cospatrick, swear it is truth. That I know that the King did not poison the Queen. That I am close to Malcolm. You can tell them that, and save your thin, lily-white skin! But, whatever you say — keep them from marching. Until I arrive. I will hasten back from Bamburgh just so soon as I may. To tell them that William's plans are all agley. That if they attack, it will be alone and will be their end. Give me three days — no, four. It is near one hundred miles to Bamburgh. Even killing horses, I cannot do it in less, in this winter. I need four days — you must win me this, Maldred. Win Malcolm them. For Scotland's sake. For he *is* Scotland, in this, whether you love him or no. Else, I tell you, there will be bloody ruin!"

He strode off, leaving the younger man to stare and chew his lip.

*　　*　　*

So next day, a very doubtful new knight rode, with half their former escort, back across Esk and Sark into Galloway, on to Dumfries and westwards for St. Cuthbert's Bay. He cursed the Earl Cospatrick, in his mind, cursed Malcolm for having sent him on this crazy errand, cursed himself for being so feeble as to allow himself to be committed to it. Yet he did not see what else he could have done, in the circumstances.

One matter at least now seemed clarified and straightforward — Cospatrick's commitment to Malcolm and Scotland. Whatever had decided him, it now appeared to be assured that he was not intending, or even contemplating, another switch in loyalties meantime. It was inconceivable that he could have acted as he had done if he had been harbouring any doubts. He could scarcely have taken a stronger line, indeed, or pitted himself more vehemently against the Norman. And that he would be an effective ally for Malcolm was equally clear. Whatever his doubts and fears, Maldred could not help admiring at least some qualities of this peculiar cousin of his.

Cospatrick, before he rode off eastwards for Northumbria, had advised that Maldred should just ride openly into St. Cuthbert's Town as an envoy should; no more hiding and lurking. Which was sensible enough, but it did mean that he was picked up by the first of the Galloway outpost parties strong enough to challenge his five-score men, at the Haugh of Urr ford, and so escorted to the Orkney camp with some suspicion if a degree of circumstance, in the face of a smouldering sunset.

The army was encamped south-west of the township, around the sprawling fort which occupied St. Mary's Isle — a peninsula into St. Cuthbert's Bay rather than a true island, with a wide artificial moat cut across the neck of it, and the flanking shores flat and marshy. It was a strong place, on account of its water-defences. To the fort, through the savage-looking encampment of the Viking host, Maldred was conducted, by boat finally, for although there was a hidden underwater causeway zigzagging out to the island, this was not to be demonstrated to suspect callers.

The leaders were sat down to their evening meal in the rath or hall-house of the fort when the visitor was shown in by a captain of the guard.

"My lords," he shouted, when he could gain a hearing.

"The Lord Maldred mac Melmore of Atholl. Seeking word with the Earl Paul of Orkney."

A tall fair-haired young man at the head of the long table rose to his feet, ale-beaker in his hand, staring.

"Maldred . . . of Atholl!" he exclaimed. "The Earl Melmore's son? And . . . Malcolm's cousin!" That was hardly a cry of welcome.

"As are *you*, Paul Thorfinnson!" Maldred returned. "I greet you, and all here, kindly."

The other looked uncertain, as around him others rose. He was an open-faced, boyish-looking individual of burly build, still under thirty, undistinguished as to features but with an honest if non-intellectual look about him.

"Kindly . . . ?" he repeated, at length. "If you come from Malcolm, you do not come kindly!"

There was a growl from those around.

"Kindly, yes," Maldred insisted. "Since I come for your good, your welfare."

"Why should we believe that — of one of your house?"

"Would I be here, thrust myself into your armed camp unprotected, if I sought your hurt?"

"You might. If you were here to spy out our strength." That was another and slightly younger man, on the Earl Paul's right, less robustly built but bearing a strong resemblance, undoubtedly the Earl Erland, so-called Governor of Galloway. His was a less attractive face, narrower, lacking his brother's openness.

"No need for that, cousin," Maldred gave back, seeking to keep his voice steady — for he felt a deal less bold than he sought to sound. "We know all your strength, Orkneymen, Manxmen, Islesmen. We know your allies, or your believed allies! We know your plans, and King William's orders to you. We know it all, cousin. No need for spying."

There was a stunned silence as men absorbed that, turning to eye each other.

"So, I have come for your good," Maldred went on. "That this folly may cost the less."

"Where have you come from?" a pale, hawk-faced, lean man of early middle years demanded. "Who sent you? Where is Malcolm Big Head?"

"To whom have I the honour of speaking?" Maldred asked, to give himself a moment to marshal his wits.

"I am Godfrey of Islay."

So this was the notorious Godfrey Crovan, the Pale-Blooded a notable soldier if a scoundrel. "I come from Caer-luel — Earl Waltheof's camp," he answered. "As to who sent me, King Malcolm did, in the first place. But I come here on behalf of the Earl Cospatrick."

"Cospatrick!" Godfrey and the Orkney brothers were not the only ones to exclaim over that significant name.

"He sent me with tidings for you. In goodwill. He will come himself, in a day or two." Maldred looked about him. "But — should we not speak more privily than this?"

"Yes. To be sure." The Earl Paul turned and pointed to a door. "In there." He gestured to his brother, Godfrey Crovan and one or two others, to follow. Then he paused. "Have you eaten, cousin?" he asked.

"Not since morning, no."

"Then you shall eat as you talk." He ordered servitors to bring food and drink from the table through to the small chamber, which proved to be little more than a storeroom. "Now — why are you here?" he asked, when the door was shut.

"Because I bring this message from the Earl Cospatrick. Do not march, he says. For if you do, it will be to your utter defeat. All is known of your plans — or the plans King William has made for you. Malcolm is apprised. He will take steps to confound them. He does not wish your ruin and death, for the Norman's advantage. For that is what it is, *all* it is. The Earl Waltheof does not march. He has thought better of it. Nor the Earl of Deira." God forgive him if that was a lie. "And since these two were to gain the Stirling crossing of Forth before William sailed from the Humber, he will not sail — if ever he intended to. Which we believe unlikely. So, if *you* march, it will be to disaster. For you, with four or five thousand, cannot hope to fight and beat a warned and waiting Malcolm. Alone."

His hearers' consternation was not to be hidden. Anger too, of course; but alarm and dismay were clearly uppermost.

It was Godfrey Crovan who recovered his wits first. "Why should we believe all this?" he demanded.

"Why should *we* devise it? And *how*, if it was not the truth? Send to the Earl Waltheof and ask him, if you do not believe me."

"The forsworn turncoat . . . !"

"I say, rather, a wiser man than you are, my lord! In that he perceives how William the Bastard is using him, using you all, to fight his battles for him, to try to bring down Malcolm at no cost to himself, that *he* may rule Scotland, as well as England. Through the child Duncan."

"Since when has Waltheof been of this mind?" Paul asked. "We had a messenger from him but four days back. Nothing was said of this."

Maldred took up a leg of roe venison. He tried to sound assured. "He no doubt has constant word from the south, from William at York. From those close to William. As has Waldeve, from Deira. He has learned the truth." He feared that was less than convincing. He added. "And Cospatrick, like Malcolm, has his own information."

"Aye, Cospatrick!" the Earl Erland exclaimed. "That one I do not trust. Where comes he into this?"

Chewing, Maldred racked his wits. "Cospatrick has *reason* to mistrust William. He knows him, was his ally. And was betrayed. Dispossessed of his earldom. He aided William and then saw a Norman, de Comyn, given his Northumbria, put in his place. The same will happen again — with Northumbria and Cumbria both. William has done it all over England and Wales. Replaced the Saxon and native lords by Normans. Think you, when he controls all — at *your* cost — that he will not put more Normans as Earls of Northumbria and Cumbria? Aye, and Galloway too, belike. Or Man, for that matter!"

That made an impact, at least. Doubts chased themselves across every face.

"It is not only William," Paul said, after a moment or two. "More than he moves against Malcolm."

"The Norse? King Olaf? Who is now your overlord in Orkney!" He threw that last in deliberately. Olaf's father, Hardradi, had managed to reassert the Norwegian ascendency over the islands, nominally at any rate, on the Earl Thorfinn's death, to the Orkneymen's chagrin. To the brothers' glares, he went on, taking a chance. "Did he, Olaf the Farmer, tell you that he was sending a fleet? Or was it William who said it?"

It was evident from the expressions that he had guessed aright; the word of the Norse participation had come from the Normans.

"If they do come — which, I say, all should doubt — it

will be on the east. And little help to you here in the west. Like to be as much use as was the Danish fleet to Edgar Atheling, at York!" That more or less exhausted Maldred's doubtful armoury of words, his playing on their fears. "So you are left with only the Earl Somerled of the Hebrides. But he is your man anyway — another cousin. Landing in Argyll, Dalar, he will not threaten Malcolm direly. Or serve *you* greatly."

There was a short silence. Then Paul said, "This of the Norman. Even if it is as you say, our quarrel with Malcolm is not only on William's behalf. It is on behalf of our own sister. Whom Big Head misused. And, we are told, slew with poison."

It had had to come to this, of course, sooner or later. "Who told you so, cousin?" Maldred asked, levelly.

"More than one. Whom we trust." Erland said that.

"I say that that can only be idle talk. Hearsay. Who could tell the truth of the matter? The Queen sickened and died. Without known prior illness. But — many do that. I was in Atholl when Ingebiorg died. So I cannot tell you how it was . . ."

"You had been there. You it was who took her to this place, we were told. I misremember the name. Where she died."

"Yes. But that was weeks before. Before Yule."

"So you do not *know* how she died," Erland insisted. "You only say that you *think* that she was not poisoned. You cannot deny it. She was buried hurriedly, secretly. At this place. On Malcolm's orders. He was not present."

"That is no proof of poison."

"It is proof that he had no love for her. And he is a hard and violent man."

"So was your father. That does not make him a poisoner."

"*His* father was — King Duncan. Whom MacBeth slew."

Paul intervened. "On this, you can speak with no authority, cousin," he said. "So we shall use our own wits, make our own decisions. For the rest, we thank you. We must needs confer. Consider what you have said. Decide on our course. We shall leave you to eat in peace."

"Yes. One last word, my lord — do not march until the Earl Cospatrick comes. He will be here in three days, or four. He has more to tell you than have I. I am but his messenger. And, and he who is close to Malcolm, declares that Ingebiorg was *not* poisoned. Him you should ask . . ."

With varied expressions they filed out.

*   *   *

The three days that Maldred spent with the Viking host at St. Cuthbert's Town — for Godfrey Crovan's Manxmen were mainly of Norse-Danish extraction also — held for him a strangely unreal quality. He was in a sort of limbo, idle after all the great and hurried riding of the previous days, largely shunned by his involuntary hosts, with only the Earl Paul in any way civil, all initiative now out of his hands, not knowing what was being decided, what the true situation was outside Galloway, what his own immediate future was likely to be. It was all frustrating, unsettling, for a young man of his active and direct temperament.

At least, the army remained stationary meantime. He could claim little credit for this, however, since he gathered that they had all along been waiting for a further contingent from the Isle of Man; also for great numbers of garrons scoured from all the Galloway countryside, since they could hardly have brought these on their longships.

The days passed slowly, with little enough to occupy his mind, although he made what he could of seeing to the comfort of his five-score men. But the evenings were better, for these Scandinavians knew how to enjoy themselves; and though their visitor was scarcely accepted as part of the proceedings, he was allowed to sit in, as it were, at the nightly feasting and entertainment. There was no lack of provender and good cheer — Galloway was probably being ransacked to provide it; and the divertissements which went on during and after the meal were as unstinted, indeed apt to be uproarious, much wilder, disrespectful, even scurrilous, than was ever the Scots custom. Nothing and no one was sacred to Arnor Earl's Skald and his minions, even, indeed particularly, his masters Paul and Erland Thorfinnson — with parody and ridicule generally taken in extraordinarily good part, although occasionally there was fury, fisticuffs and flagons thrown. Inevitably Maldred came in for some derogatory references from the sagamen, skalds and storytellers, but nothing that he could not grin at or swallow. He came to the conclusion that, given more propitious circumstances, he could get on well with these Norsemen — but that he would not like to have to fight them.

Then, on the fourth evening, Cospatrick duly appeared, with his weary following, travel-stained, all but exhausted with homeric riding. Not that the Earl allowed himself to show it. He came into the great camp as though he owned it, shouting for the Thorfinnsons and Godfrey Crovan, a picture of assurance and cheerful authority. Even Maldred was impressed.

From the start Cospatrick took it that the projected campaign against Scotland was off, that anything else was unthinkable, that he pitied his young kinsmen from Orkney for ever having been so deluded as to consider the matter, whilst hootingly deriding his old friend and fellow-veteran Godfrey of Islay for not knowing better, for taking William the Norman at his word and for not advising the young earls more wisely, he a man of experience. Not for a moment did he give any other impression than that the project was dead, that the others would have come round to realising this in due course anyway — but that they certainly owed himself his meed of thanks for having saved them all from folly and disaster if not ruin. Waldeve Siwardson so esteemed his intervention, he confided — but then, poor Waldeve had never been of the brightest, easy meat for William's wiles. He ought to be on his way back to Deira by this time.

It was rather extraordinary how the others accepted all this as valid, factual — and despite Cospatrick's reputation for untrustworthiness and double-dealing. Presumably it was his personality, allied to his sheer arrogant confidence of manner, which carried the conviction. Maldred had to some extent paved the way for him, admittedly; but the real conquest of the others' intentions and will-power was all his own. At any rate, without it having to be declared in so many words, it was agreed, before they slept that night, that invasion was no longer practicable, and that the offence concerning King Malcolm would have to be assuaged otherwise. Maldred deliberately retired early, not wishing to become involved again in the vexed subject of the Queen's death, so what Cospatrick told the bereaved brothers he did not know nor wished to know.

They had a day of relaxation thereafter for Cospatrick's

tired escort and horseflesh — which that indefatigable manipulator turned to good purpose — as he saw it — by convincing the now distinctly purposeless and at-a-loose-end Vikings, to prevent them having second thoughts, that the obvious thing to do with all their fine mustered strength was to sail across to the Isle of Man and take it over as a suitable appanage and dependency of the Orcades and Hebrides — after all, it had once been part of the Sudreys, the Southern Hebrides; and its present king was unlikely to rise from his sick-bed in Dublin. Godfrey Crovan, needless to say, backed this programme whole-heartedly — as Cospatrick had foreseen — declaring that he would be happy to rule Man for the Orkney earls. The brothers had not actually committed themselves to this adventure when Cospatrick and Maldred took their leave next morning, but clearly they most probably would do so, for it would serve to save their faces, allay the sense of anti-climax in their army, and show some suitable return for all the trouble and expense they had been put to. Also it might conceivably lead to greater things, for the sickly Godfrey was King of Dublin as well as of Man, and who knew what possibilities might arise, with Man as a stepping-stone to Ireland, most of the east side of which was in the hands of second and third generation Norsemen and Danes.

So the Scots company rode off northwards on St. Moluag's Eve, the second day of March, reasonably satisfied that they left a much improved situation behind them — except for sundry folk on the Isle of Man — and took even a sort of grudging gratitude with them.

Maldred was admittedly at a loss as to what to think of this cousin of his, Cospatrick. He did not know that he was any more prepared to trust him than before — less so, perhaps. Yet he could not but admire his agile wits, his genius for persuasion, his dash, courage and élan. It occurred to him that he might, in fact, have made a suitable king for Scotland had Duncan Ilgarach had as eventual successor his brother, the late Maldred, rather than his illegitimate son Malcolm.

After riding a while at the Earl's side, he spoke. "Did Paul and Erland believe you as to Ingebiorg?" he wondered.

"God knows! But I did my best for Malcolm."

"Aye." Maldred left it at that.

A little later, he resumed. "What of the Earl Waldeve of Deira? Was he as easily convinced as was your brother?"

Cospatrick grinned. "He is of a more sceptical turn of mind, is Waldeve. But I think I persuaded him where his present advantage lay, see you. And I won him out of Bamburgh."

"How did you do that?"

"I said that Malcolm would take it unkindly. As might I. And that a Scots army could be at Berwick-on-Tweed, twenty-five miles away no more, in not so many days' time."

"Oh. And he accepted that? And is now on his way back to Deira?"

"He will be — if he believes half what I told him . . . !"

7

IT TOOK SOME time for Maldred to adjust himself to the atmosphere which they found prevailing on their return to Dunfermline. It was as of holiday and celebration, with no least hint of danger or threat of war. It was not normalcy, far from it indeed, because Malcolm's Court and establishment had never been notable for gaiety and good cheer; but it was far removed from the urgency and emergency in which the Galloway party had been steeped. There was a preoccupation with conviviality and festivity. The Princess Margaret Atheling had agreed to marry the King, and the wedding was set for so soon as a month hence.

The newcomers learned this even before they reached the palace, had it shouted to them time and again as they approached and entered the town. If Maldred was surprised, almost shocked, Cospatrick was not, and said so, with sundry cynical, lewd and uncalled-for comments, so that they reached their destination in mutual disenchantment.

The King, they discovered, was away with his bride-to-be visiting the small monastery which St. Columba himself had founded on an island in the Scottish Sea, St. Colm's, called after him — this significant in itself as indicating the influence Margaret was establishing over the monarch, at this stage at least, in that Malcolm had never been one for visiting religious establishments as a means of recreation or enjoyment. Cospatrick had his comments to make about that, too.

Magda was with her mistress, and Maldred was not one to discuss affairs with the Princesses Agatha or Christina — who already seemed to be carrying themselves with enhanced authority and assurance. So he gained no detailed information until the royal party returned, with sundown — and Malcolm, hearing that his envoys were back, summoned them to his presence forthwith.

The King was stamping around the hall fire, sipping at a quaich of whisky, for a chill wind had made the voyage home a cold business. Margaret had gone to her room to change.

"You are back, then," he growled at them. "Both of you!" Undoubtedly he emphasised that, a little. "Your message reached me. That Waltheof's also. Is all well?"

"All is well," Cospatrick nodded. "This time. But William will try again. Nothing surer."

"No doubt — fiend burn him! And the Orkneymen?"

"Sailed after lesser game, I think. But — I hear that you are to wed again, cousin? I wish you good fortune. And you will need it, with that one, I swear! Eh, Maldred?"

Maldred compressed his lips and said nothing.

Malcolm glared. "Watch your tongue!" he jerked. "I mislike loose tongues."

"You owe my tongue a deal!" the other observed, cheerfully.

The King hunched his heavy shoulders in the bull-like way he had, big head thrust forward, lower lip curling down. "I owe *you* nothing — save perhaps a hanging!" he said deliberately. "Remember that. I do not forget who betrayed me, not so long ago. I have a good memory."

"Then, I hope that you will remember what I have saved you, these last days, my lord King! Perhaps your kingdom, indeed." Cospatrick flung that back almost casually, confidence evidently nothing diminished. "How say you, Maldred?"

"I would say that His Highness may have much reason to be grateful, my lord," the younger man said carefully.

The monarch looked from one to the other, assessingly. He was a realist, above all. "So-o-o! Out with it, then. What have you saved me? And how?"

"Why, I have destroyed a most dire threat to this realm. Turned back invasion on many fronts. Talked the Thorfinnssons, Godfrey Crovan, my brother Waltheof and Waldeve Siwardson out of a combined attack, wrecked the Norman's plans against you, and persuaded the Orkney earls to assail Man instead of you. All without a life lost, a drop of blood shed. Is it not enough?"

"All that? So nimble a tongue! Or so great a liar!"

"Have it as you will. But the threat was there. Thousands of men mustered against you. And now is not. William forced to think anew. If you do not believe me, ask Maldred."

"It is true, Highness. All true. My lord Earl did all that he says. By using one against the other. By cozening, yes — but shrewdly. By threatening his brother, first, the weakest link. It was featly done. The Orkneymen had four thousand waiting to strike. Waltheof fifteen hundred. Waldeve I know not how many. Somerled more. Others also. The Norse may still strike, at Moray and Ross, where Farquhar MacBeth hates you. And William waiting with a fleet in the Humber, to finish all."

"While you, cousin, courted!" Cospatrick added easily.

"I have five thousand waiting at Stirling and Scone. Others mustering. Think you I have lost my wits, fool?"

"Men have done that over a pretty face, before this."

"Not Malcolm mac Duncan!" the King said grimly. "Now — from the beginning. Tell me it all."

He listened, weighing each word, as Cospatrick recounted the circumstances and details — the tale losing nothing in the telling. At the end, he stroked his cruel, down-turning moustaches.

"As well that it was witlings, fledglings and cravens you had to deal with! Men of any parts and experience would have required more than a glib tongue to persuade."

"They were the same whom William's tongue had first persuaded! Do not forget it. Nor forget that, like William, I require my price!"

"*Require*, you say . . . ?"

"Aye. For the labourer deserves his hire. And, if refused it, might hire his labour to . . . another!"

"I promised you a Scots earldom. The Merse."

"That, cousin, will be more burden than reward. Since it is your border with William's England, and I shall have to fight for every yard of it. You should *pay* me for holding your March for you."

"You seek more?"

"Much more. I shall *need* another earldom to enable me to hold the Merse. It had better be that next to it. Lothian."

"Lothian! So rich a province? So great? You are bold, man!"

"I am. But then you need my boldness, do you not? And I am not done yet. I am giving you back control over Cumbria. And now Northumbria also, *my* Northumbria, which William promises at large. For these, to help you hold them, I require ten thousand merks, in gold and silver."

The King's intake of breath was audible. Maldred tensed physically for the explosion. But before it came, a stir behind them turned them all. The Princess Margaret stood there.

After a moment Cospatrick and Maldred bowed, the former deeply.

"Lady," he said. "Your most humble admirer. I was felicitating the King's Highness on his good fortune."

"Was that what it was, my lord? To me, it sounded as though your felicitations were becoming expensive!" She turned. "Maldred — I rejoice to see you back."

He inclined his head. "I also must offer my humble duties," he said flatly. "And my good wishes."

At his tone of voice she looked at him searchingly, almost anxiously. "I . . . much esteem your . . . goodwill, Maldred. Your regard. I hope that I shall always have it." For that clear-sighted young woman, that was less than assured.

Malcolm humphed impatiently, such talk not for him. "This fine cousin of mine, Cospatrick, claims that he has saved my realm for me! And asks, *requires*, two earldoms and ten thousand merks for doing it. What say you to that?"

"The Earl Cospatrick esteems his services more highly than do you, my lord King?"

"It seems that he does, yes."

"The buyer need not pay all the seller asks, I think. In any market. Often the seller scarcely expects him to! All depends on whether there is another buyer in sight?"

"M'mm. The only other buyer for these goods, I say, could be William the Norman."

"And he already has bargained with this seller. And lost to him. Twice, has he not? I think that our merchant will . . . chaffer!"

"Aye, by God — you could be right!"

The Earl looked from one to the other. "I perceive that Scotland is going to have a queen of some . . . commerce!" he said. "I admire that. I will take *eight* thousand merks. But I must have Lothian as well as the Merse. There are insufficient men in the Merse to keep your border for you. The March. Insufficient wealth and rents to pay them, also. For you are giving me the Merse as a task and duty, not a reward."

"I will give you half of Lothian, then. The east. Dunbar, with Lammermuir. And the Merse. And *five* thousand merks. Not a merk or an acre more. That is the last of it."

The other grinned. "Very well. Chaffering over! I accept. Earl of Dunbar and March. And five thousand merks. Before these witnesses! I am your true man." He made a half-mocking bow. "And your most deft lady's. You can belt me an earl of Scotland some other time."

Malcolm, however, ensured himself the last word. "At *my* convenience. You have my permission to retire. Both of you."

Maldred went in search of his brother and Magda — and hoped that he might not find them together.

The girl was easily discovered. But it transpired that Madach was with his Atholl regiment at Stirling, and had been for some days. Magdalen was undisguisedly glad to see him, at least, and chattered away like a kettle on the hob. Maldred did not have to steer the subject round to the matter of Margaret and the King. Magda was not long in reaching it herself — and in no uncritical fashion.

"There was no stopping her. Once she had made up her mind," she declared. "I saw it coming."

"But why? Why?"

"She conceived it to be her duty."

"Duty? To give herself to a man old enough to be her father. And such a man as Malcolm."

"Even so. As Queen of Scotland she sees herself as greatly aiding Edgar and her mother. And as Malcolm's wife she thinks that she can do much for Scotland. And even possibly England. The Saxon cause. She says, who is she to refuse, reject, so great an opportunity to serve others?"

"Saints above! How can she believe that? Delude herself?"

"But she does believe it. Has come to. And once she believes, nothing will move her. You do not know her as I do."

"But does she know what she does? In giving herself to the King. Can she think of what it will be like, wed to such a man?"

"As to that, Maldred, no woman will fail to consider! And Margaret is no shrinking flower. She is prepared to accept it all."

"She has no fondness for him, surely?"

"I think not. But princesses are seldom permitted to wed where they are fond. That is for lesser beings! I hope! No doubt she believes that she may grow into some fondness. I know that she prays for that."

"Prays!" He shook his head. "And so soon after the Queen's death."

"She prays over that, also. But the King is . . . urgent. He much desires her. And she will allow him but little, until they are wed."

Maldred made a growling noise.

Magdalen raised an eyebrow at him. "Envy is a sin!" she said succinctly.

"I am not envious," he lied hotly. "But — it is all so wrong. So great a, a waste."

"You will just have to console yourself . . . elsewhere, my friend!"

They left it at that.

With Margaret seldom free of the King's company, Maldred and she were never alone. One day, however, with the monarch visiting the army in Fortrenn, Margaret and a large party with him, whilst Malcolm was speaking with some of the leaders and officers at the old palace-fort of Dunsinane, the princess sent Magda off on an errand, and beckoned Maldred forward to her side.

"Are you avoiding me, Maldred?" she asked. "It seems that we do not now have opportunity for a privy word. I have never told you how rejoiced I was at your knighting."

He bowed a little, stiffly. "I thank you." Then a thought

struck him like a blow. "It, it was not *you*? You who won Malcolm to do it?"

"I had said, more than once, that you were very deserving of knighthood. That is all."

He moistened his lips. "I would not wish, I would not like to think, lady, that I owed my knighting to, to . . . !"

"To a woman? You need not so think, Maldred. Malcolm would not have done it to pleasure me, I promise you. But — why do you call me lady, now? As though we were no longer friends. You did not do that before."

"No. But you are to be Queen. It is different now."

"Different, yes. But not so greatly that we should cease to be friends. I would have you always that, Maldred." She paused. "You do not approve, do you? Of me being the Queen."

"It is not for me to approve or disapprove."

"But you would have it otherwise? That I should *not* be Queen of this realm."

"Say that I would not have you wed to King Malcolm."

"Do you hate him so?"

"No. He is my liege-lord. And my cousin. I serve him to the best of my abilities. He has good qualities. But . . ."

"You think that I am not the wife for him? Yet he needs a wife, and Scotland a queen."

"He *had* a wife. And Scotland a queen."

"Yes. So that is where the trouble lies? You were fond of your cousin Ingebiorg, and resent me taking her place?"

"No. Not that. Although it is too soon. But — he is not the man for you. Harsh. Fierce. Lacking any gentleness."

"So . . . you are concerned for *me*?"

"Yes. For you."

"You are kind, Maldred. And I thank you for it. But this is something that I must do. I have considered it well, endlessly indeed. I think that perhaps I was born for this. For what I may, with God's help, be able to do. I do not fear the, the cost. I am strong, well able to bear what must be borne. Or, if that seems prideful, vainglorious, say that I believe that God will give me the strength I need."

"You are so sure that it is *God's* will?"

"I am, yes," she said simply.

Magda came back — and Maldred was actually relieved to see her. She said that she had found Bishop Fothad, and he would be with them shortly.

"The Bishop of St. Andrews, who is to marry us, wishes

me to see the Abbey of Scone. Which is near here, I understand. After we have seen the army," Margaret explained. "He would have us to wed there. He says that it is the proper place for royal weddings. Where the coronations are held. And where this great Stone is, that you have told us of. But — I would as well be married at Dunfermline."

"Scone Abbey, yes. Since you would scarcely go to Iona. It is the place for great occasions."

"If Malcolm was wed there, the first time, it might be better elsewhere. Might it not? As well Dunfermline, which is to be our home. Ah, here is the Bishop . . ."

* * *

Bishop Fothad, good man, was of course no match for Margaret Atheling, and in due course, on 5th April, Easter Monday, the wedding was consecrated at the cashel of Dunfermline — Malcolm himself having no least care where the ceremony was performed, although Dunfermline was much more convenient for arranging the nuptial feasting and subsequent celebrations than it would have been at Scone. For old Fothad was outmanoeuvred in more ways than just location, and the entire proceedings were made the occasion for great splendour, with no expense spared. This again was at Margaret's instigation. The Celtic Church's marriage service, like all its other ceremonial, was brief and simple; but the bride saw the occasion as demanding a very different celebration — and as an opportunity, Magda revealed, to demonstrate the superiority, colour and significance of the Romish rite. For although, to be sure, the nuptials had to be in essence those of the Columban ritual, the faith of the country into which the bride was being adopted, she managed to introduce considerable innovation of the Roman practice which had never been seen in Scotland before — her groom again concurring, having little concern either way. Indeed, although the service was conducted by the Bishop, assisted by Abbot Ivo of Dunfermline St. Ternans, her own confessor Brother Oswald was allotted quite a prominent role in support, reinforced by another and more senior monk of the authoritative Cluniac persuasion, one Thorgot or Turgot, specially sent north by the new Bishop of Durham for the occasion. It had to be conceded, of course, despite due loyalty to their own Church, that most of the people around the palace found the enhanced proceedings to their taste — especially after the intense gloom of Holy Week which the Athelings had sought to impose.

So, on a bright and breezy spring forenoon of sunshine and high-sailing cloud galleons — confirmation of the Almighty's favourable reaction, to Margaret at least — the great company assembled in the open air before the tiny church of the cashel, to the chanting of choirs of boys and men and the strumming of clarsachs. This, within the monastery itself, was composed of the invited guests, the Court and high nobility, the officers of state, the clergy, the choristers and the sennachies. At this stage, all was under the control of the High Sennachie, as master-of-ceremonies. Outside the perimeter, the populace was gathered in its thousands, in holiday mood, come from far and near.

The King arrived with his own party, dressed more magnificently than any had ever seen him, but scarcely at ease in his finery, scowling and self-conscious. With him were nearly all the mormaors, now earls, the lesser kings who supported the *Ard Righ* or High King of Scots — but not those of Moray or the Mearns, hostile to Malcolm. The Earl of Atholl, uncle of the bridegroom was there, for once coaxed away from Dunkeld, countenancing the marriage as Primate of the Church, his three sons with him on this occasion. Maldred had not wished to attend at all, but he could hardly absent himself — although he had politely rejected the suggestion that he should join the bride's procession.

This, when it appeared up from the palace, a little late, grew later still when it halted amongst the outer crowd and Margaret, gorgeously arrayed, descended from her litter to move amongst the people. She could not actually speak meaningfully to them, for she did not know the Gaelic and these spoke no other; but she could smile and gesture and wave, a move much appreciated by the throng, if less so by the impatient monarch. Her train did not follow suit, save for Magda who stuck close, but merely waited — the Athelings and the Saxon and Hungarian nobles they had brought with them.

When, at length the two parties were before the church-door — but not joined — they were addressed by the High Sennachie Gillemor, after a prolonged blowing of bulls' horns. He proclaimed the names, styles and titles of the parties to this marriage, announcing that Malcolm mac Duncan mac Bethoc nic Malcolm was true *Ard Righ*, crowned on the Stone of Destiny, and was without question or any impediment able, free and entitled to wed the daughter of Edward, son of Edmond. If any held otherwise let him now stand forth and declare it.

This producing only the desired hush, he went on to the important part of the proceedings, as far as he was concerned, the genealogies. He recited with great vigour and sonorous dignity the royal pedigree of the King, seemingly endlessly, back and back into and beyond the mists of antiquity, never stumbling or hesitating, in extraordinary catalogue of the oldest royal line in Christendom, a double line of the Scots and the Picts. It took a long time, as strange, uncouth name succeeded name. The bride's entourage, in especial, stirred restlessly, for of course it was all Gaelic and incomprehensible to them — although Margaret herself listened as though enthralled. And when it was their turn, to be sure, the second recital was comparatively brief and feeble, neither the Saxon nor the Hungarian royal lines being particularly ancient.

This over, in deference to the bride, a move was made inside the church. Only a small proportion of even the most prestigious could gain entry, of course, with a few of the choir — and even so the dark little sanctuary was grievously crowded, with the smoke of the candles breath-catching — these for light rather than devotion, for there was little of window about the wood-and-turf building. Bride and groom moved up towards the altar, the King with MacDuff of Fife and Cospatrick in support, Margaret with her brother and sister.

Bishop Fothad — he was Fothad the Second of St. Andrews — now took over, flanked by the local Abbot Ivo on the one side and the two Romish priests on the other, both these in much more resplendent vestments than the main officiants. Fothad was in rather a peculiar situation here. In the monastic Celtic Church abbots were actually senior to bishops, and this was Abbot Ivo's own church. But certain sacramental duties, including marriage, were the preferred role of the bishops. Partly because a succession of Bishops of St. Andrews had been Chancellors, or chief ministers of the realm, this bishopric had become the most influential in the land, its occupant being known as the King's Bishop. Nevertheless, he was not in any way superior to Ivo or to other abbots or bishops, and they were both junior to Melmore of Atholl, Hereditary Primate, and to the Abbot Robertach of Iona, St. Columba's present successor. Probably only in the Columban Church, so utterly non-hierarchal and egalitarian, could such an unsystematic arrangement have subsisted.

Fothad's part of the service was simple and straightforward, up to a point. He said a prayer, Ivo read a suitable passage from Holy Writ, and the Bishop then turned to address the bride and groom on the sacred duties and responsibilities of matrimony, in lieu of sermon. This was followed by chanting, while the eucharistic elements were made ready on the altar. Fothad then paced forward to superintend the ceremony of the exchange of rings, the clasping of hands and the vow-making. This done, he duly pronounced the pair man and wife, without more ado. All this in the Gaelic, except that Margaret made her vows in English.

This would all have been quite enough for Malcolm; but now the Roman contribution commenced, in Latin, with much intonation, signing of the Cross and genuflection, amounting almost to a second wedding rite, so that the bride could feel truly married. Thereafter, Brother Turgot laid hands on the couple's heads, for which Margaret knelt but Malcolm, who would kneel for no man, even if deputising for the Almighty, remained standing and glowering.

There followed the Nuptial Mass, in this instance a complicated process, for however far the Athelings had gone in countenancing heretical and unsuitable ritual, they would not yield an inch on Holy Communion. So, in effect, two simultaneous consecrations went on at the little altar, Gaelic and Latin, although unfortunately the latter was much the more prolonged, so that Fothad and Ivo had to stand idle and expressionless for some considerable time until administration could proceed. And even that was less than straightforward, for the two rites differed, the Celtic proffering in two kinds, that is the bread and the wine, the Romish in one, the bread only. The royal couple partook first, again kneeling and standing, and while Malcolm received both elements in short order, Margaret got over the difficulty by accepting the bread from her Turgot and the wine from Fothad.

When, thereafter, it was the turn of the little congregation, the other Athelings refused to make any such gesture, taking only the bread from their own priest, the Saxon and Hungarian notables following suit. So there was something of a confusion at this stage, a holy disorder as Cospatrick whispered to Maldred, adding that all this was a foretaste of what they might look for thereafter. The sweet singing of the choir helped however. And the final benediction, from both sources, Turgot's resounding and comprehensive indeed, sent them all out thankfully into the sunshine from the dark, smoky and humanity-smelling atmosphere.

The High Sennachie took over again, hailed the fortunate and potent monarch, and declared that Scotland had a Queen again, Margaret the Beautiful and the Good.

The cheers rose and continued.

The bride, flushed and gleaming-eyed, certainly had seldom looked more lovely. If she was not truly happy, she appeared to be.

The ceremony of kissing the new Queen's hand followed, for the magnates and high nobility. When it came to Maldred's turn, he rose from his knee to find Margaret's eyes keenly scanning his face.

"It is done then, Maldred," she almost whispered. "For better or worse. Wish me well."

"That I do, Highness," he said. "Always. I shall be your true knight."

"And friend . . . ?" she murmured, as he passed on.

The King was wearying of all this, and made it obvious. But his new wife had a strong sense of duty, and nothing was to be skimped. Even when the procession was formed to wend its way back to the palace, this concern for what duty required was demonstrated, for she refused to get into her litter, declaring that she would walk, so that her people could see and speak to her and touch her — for they *were* her people now. What this meant Malcolm soon discovered for, despite the fact that the royal couple were leading the procession, behind the massed singers and instrumentalists, Margaret insisted on darting off to mingle with the crowd, to catch hands, to pause and greet and smile — whilst the King, whose habit was to drive headlong through all crowds, had to wait, fretting, like all the others. Cospatrick again had comments to make.

The wedding banquet at the palace was probably the most ambitious that Scotland had ever seen, the numbers invited almost more than the accommodation would hold, the provision lavish to a degree, the entertainment which went with it and followed after varied to suit all tastes, from music, story-telling and dancing, to juggling, sword-play and performing bears. As well, there were outside feasts, in the courtyard for the lesser nobility and clergy, the magistrates, officers and the like; and in the open Glen of Pittencrieff beyond the walls, oxen were roasted whole, with barrelled ales, for all comers. Malcolm was not normally thus spendthrift, although by no means mean either; interested in neither hospitality nor display rather; but he had been left in no doubts as to what was necessary on this occasion, and he had opened his coffers wide. Moreover, he had had a very successful season in Northumbria. Margaret asserted that wealth was for spending, spending well and for the benefit of others, not for hoarding.

Maldred was unable to sit with Magda on this occasion, having to remain in his father's group, actually nearer to the royal pair than usual, while Magda was further down the table, well squired by appreciative young males — although at least Madach could not be amongst them. He was there, next to Maldred, to be sure, for most of the army leaders were present, from Scone and Stirling, military threat having for the moment receded, the Galloway host having taken over Man, where Godfrey Crovan had declared himself King under allegiance to the Orkney earls; and William of Normandy, thwarted meantime and moreover preoccupied with another Welsh rising. Maldred then was in a good position to watch the King and Queen, and to note Margaret's graciousness and easy assumption of her new role, her suitable attentions to her husband allied to her nice concern for their guests, even it seemed for the servitors. This was something new for that company and could have caused embarrassment; but not once did she put a foot wrong, display or permit undue familiarity, or verge on the officious. The only frowns brought to Malcolm's features were when, once or twice, she gently placed a hand across the mouth of his goblet as he was about to replenish it — but even that surely was a bride's privilege on her wedding-night, and the King's brow quickly cleared.

He, and they all, had occasion to look more doubtful, or at least astonished when, the main eating over, Margaret rose, and raised an uncertain Malcolm also — whereupon of course, everyone else must rise. There were lewd grins amongst the male guests and some lifted eyebrows amongst the ladies, at this presumed over-eager early departure of the bridal pair; but Margaret explained to such as were near enough to hear her, that she now, with the King's consent and she hoped his escort, would go out to see how it all fared with the various companies feasting outside — who were, to be sure, as worthy and entitled to celebrate this joyous day as any in the hall. She urged all to continue with their entertainment here, desiring only her husband's company amongst the people. They would return.

Malcolm stood silent, his face a study. But he could scarcely refuse to go.

With the royal couple gone, the guests were more free to move around. Maldred soon found his way to Magdalen's side.

"*You* are not needed now?" he put to her.

"I shall be," she asserted.

"You, you are not going back to England, then? Now that she is wed? And is Queen."

"I think not yet awhile. Are you in such haste to be rid of me?"

"Lord, no! I but feared that you might."

"Feared? You did? Do I bow my grateful thanks?"

Warily he eyed her, and changed the subject. "This of going off amongst the poor, of choosing to speak with them. Why does she do it? What does she seek?"

"Why, she loves the poor. Or so she says. As Holy Writ prescribes! They are to be cherished and comforted."

"Why?"

"Maldred, have you no Christian charity in you? If you have not, you will not get far with your new Queen!"

"I meant, what is comforting the poor to do with being a queen? I would not harm them, misuse them, tread them under, as some do. But this cosseting such folk, I do not understand."

"I think that she does it as her duty. She desires to be queen not only of the powerful and the rich, but of all. She has seen sufficient of what can happen to the poor. Is that not good, proper?"

He shrugged. "I do not know. But I think that Malcolm will scarcely consider it so."

"Then your Malcolm will have to learn. Like the rest of you! Will he not? Learn much."

He chewed on that for a little, thoughtfully. Madach came up.

It was quite some time before the King and Queen returned. The entertainment and the drinking had gone on apace, and the hall was growing progressively noisier, the company less restrained. In the circumstances, it would not have been surprising if Margaret had suggested a fairly prompt retiral; but in fact it was now Malcolm who was for off and Margaret who seemed to wish to linger on, moving around and making herself pleasant. None, of course, might retire from the hall before the monarch, and the Princesses Agatha and Christina were soon adding their pressure to the bride and groom to make a move — although Edgar was too drunk to care. Presently Margaret could no longer decently delay, and she turned to cast a last and almost panic-stricken look around the hall as her husband grasped her arm strongly. Her eye caught Maldred's and for a moment he almost believed that there was a kind of appeal in it. Then she was led away, with all sober enough to do so rising in valedictory salute.

As they disappeared, Maldred slammed down on the table the beaker he had been drinking from, and without a word to any swung about and marched out of the other doorway with a slightly unsteady gait. He was, in fact, just a little drunk himself. Magda, at least, noted his departure.

Next day Margaret Atheling was calm, poised and contained, if rather more reserved, less outgoing than she had been recently. Apparently she had been very early at her devotions, despite all the circumstances. Malcolm, for his part, was more forthcoming than usual, almost genial, with something of a proprietary air. He seldom let his new wife out of his sight.

The feasting and celebrations went on — as indeed they were to do for the rest of that week in one form or another, not all at Dunfermline, with the royal couple honouring the houses and tables of such of the nation's great ones as lay within a half-day's journey; for Malcolm was not so besotted with his new acquisition as to forget the threat from England. He kept his armies mustered — and a great trial they were to their various assembly areas — and was ready, with his lords, to join them at short notice.

The Queen gave no outward sign that she found the married state any ordeal — unless an actual increase in religious exercises could be so construed. These had to be held early in the morning, in view of the full day's activities, and were performed alone or in the company of the monk Turgot — who clearly had made a major impression on Margaret — her husband certainly not co-operating. Magda, who still did duty as principal lady-in-waiting, even though less closely than heretofore, said that her mistress was apt to emerge from these devotional sessions showing signs of tears — although whether from religious ecstasy or otherwise, who could tell? Hitherto her orisons had not produced such reactions.

Malcolm, it seemed, developed his own views on this matter, for at the end of that first week he sent the man Turgot packing, back to Durham. The next day, Low Sunday, the Queen kept to her room. But thereafter she appeared to be more or less herself again, another marriage-hurdle over.

There were those at Court who hoped that it would not be so very long before the other Athelings themselves, and their hangers-on, likewise got their marching orders. Magda, commenting on this, suggested that Margaret might indeed be less affected by such eventuality.

8

MALCOLM FRETTED, AND his lords with him. He had been very patient, none could assert otherwise. But at this rate they would not reach Kilrymont for many hours yet, perhaps not even by nightfall. Yesterday they had not covered a score of miles. He had accepted, when he agreed to take Margaret and her women with him, that the journey would take longer. Alone, he could have covered the forty miles from Dunfermline in a day, easily enough. But here they were, nearly at noon on the second day, not yet at Corn Ceres. Not because the women could ride no faster, but because of this everlasting and time-wasting concern for the most useless folk in his kingdom, beggars, cripples, lepers, vagabonds, even slaves, on all of whom his new wife seemed to dote. Where such were concerned time and trouble — and his own royal wishes, seemingly — were of no account. Nor his money. Already practically all of the silver coin he had brought with him had been expended — not in defraying expenses and rewarding suitable subjects, but handed out like some priest's broadcast benedictions on all the riff-raff of Fife. It was not to be borne.

"My dear," he said loudly, interrupting Margaret's interrogation of the half-naked slut with two bairns at heel. "A mercy — enough! You desired to see Kilrymont — St. Andrews. We shall never win there if we stop for all this land's scum and trash. Your soft heart does you credit, no doubt. But we require wits as well as hearts. I have a realm to rule. Affairs await me. We could have been at St. Andrews by now — and we are not yet at Corn Ceres. Mount, lass — and let us be on our way, in God's good name."

There were murmurs from most of the illustrious company, not actually spoken agreement, for the Queen was the Queen, but leaving no doubt as to how they felt. Even Maldred nodded his head.

Margaret looked up, but kept a hand on one of the children's doubtless louse-ridden tangle of hair.

"To be sure, my lord — if that is your command," she said mildly. "But is God's good name not as well served by cherishing His lambs, as the Lord Christ commanded, as in hastening to this council? And these unhappy folk are part of your realm, are they not?"

"As fleas are part of the hound-dog, perhaps!" the King jerked. "Come, I say."

She sighed, but inclined her head dutifully, and turned back to her horse. Maldred, who had aided her to dismount, stepped over to help her up to the saddle again. But on an impulse, Margaret turned back, and sweeping off the fur-lined travelling-cloak she wore, draped it round the part-bare and unwashed shoulders of the other young woman — who shrank within it almost as though it had burned her.

Malcolm snorted and heeled his beast into movement, not waiting for his bride of two weeks to mount. That cloak had been a present from himself.

As they rode on, Maldred reined over to his chosen place at Magda's side. "Foolishness," he said, low-voiced.

"On whose part?" she wondered.

He raised his brows. "Her's — the Queen's. To offend the King unnecessarily is never wise. *This* King in especial. Ingebiorg discovered that!"

"Your King does not know what he has taken in hand!" the girl said briefly. She spurred forward, to offer her own less handsome cloak to Margaret — and had it refused, but with a smile.

They were riding over the higher ground of Craigrothie towards the Howe of Fife, perhaps one hundred strong; and although the April sun penetrated thin high cloud to give a noonday brightness, an easterly breeze off the sea made it cool enough for cloaks to be welcome. Malcolm was leading at a spanking pace now, but the Queen at least was having no difficulty in keeping up, for she was an excellent horsewoman. It was old Duncan, Earl of Fife, who was protesting, gross and bumping about in his saddle like a basket of peats. Gradually he fell behind, with only a group of his own thanes lingering to escort him.

Presently MacDuff caught up with the Queen nevertheless, if not his monarch and one-time companion-in-arms, just short of Baltilly. It was a scene of rural industry which had halted Margaret, late-spring ploughing proceeding on the rigs of Baltilly township. There were four teams at work on the gentle slope, three of them stolid plodding oxen pulling the heavy wooden ploughs, with small boys goading the brutes on with pointed sticks and thin skirling cries, these last all but drowned in the screechings of the wheeling, swooping flocks of seagulls which followed each team to snatch up the worms and grubs from the new-turned soil. Two stooping men steered each massive plough. It made an inspiriting, timeless picture. But it was not at these that Margaret was looking, but at the fourth team. Instead of eight oxen, this plough had still more numerous haulers, double the number indeed, although making no faster headway. But these were men and women, who dragged, bent almost double in their harness, stumbling, staggering, whilst the boys attendant used not goads here but whips to improve the pace. Even at a hundred yards or so of range it was noticeable how fair was the hair of most of these plough-pullers.

As MacDuff came up, puffing, the Queen, tight-lipped, halted him with an uplifted hand, and then pointed.

"My lord of Fife — these!" she exclaimed, her voice uneven for once. "This, in your Fife! Must I believe what I see?"

The Earl glanced at her sidelong from small pig-like eyes. "Hech, hech — they are but slaves, lady," he panted. "Saxon slaves."

"*I* am Saxon, my lord! Have you forgot?"

MacDuff moistened his lips. "Prisoners. Taken in the fighting. Better drawing a plough than slain, are they not . . . ?"

"Are they yours?"

"No, no. Not mine." He turned in his saddle. "Machan, these are your lands, are they not? Machan here, Highness, is Thane of Ceres."

"Then, my lord of Ceres, is this your doing? Treating my countrymen — aye, and women too, God forgive you — worse than brute-beasts!"

The youngish dark man looked more surprised than embarrassed. "I bought many slaves, lady. Paid my lord King well for them, too. These no doubt are some of them."

"And this is how you treat fellow-Christians?"

"They are but prisoners, Highness. Won fairly in war. What would you have? Bought with good money. Honest work will not hurt them."

"How much did you pay for them, sir. These country-men of mine?"

"I bought forty, men and women. And I paid forty silver pieces for them."

"I would have thought thirty more apt! What our blessed Lord was valued at! You shall have the thirty for these, my lord. There are . . . how many? Sixteen, there. You have a good bargain, do you not? Three-quarters of your purchase-price for less than half your goods! I buy them. You shall have your money, never fear. Now — go and release those unhappy people. Loose them. And tell them that they are free."

"But, Highness . . . now?"

"Now, sir. They are mine now. Buy you oxen for your ploughing. You shall have your thirty pieces of silver in good time, I promise you. Maldred — aid you my lord of Ceres in this. And see that these poor Saxons understand that they are free. Come, my friends." And she touched up her mount.

When Maldred and Ceres rejoined the Queen's party it was within the place of Corn Ceres itself, a pleasant and quite large township on the banks of a sizeable stream in a shallow wooded valley, presided over by the thane's rath on one knoll and a cashel of hutments within a wall on another. Margaret was dismounted again, and in the midst of a small crowd, mainly women and children and the aged. It was astonishing how such folk seemed to flock to her as by some instinct. When these saw their own lord ride up, they began to move back warily, and disperse; but the Queen halted that, beckoning them closer again. She was holding by the hand a small boy who had great running sores on cheek and neck and arm. She looked up.

"How then, Maldred? You saw those poor folk released?"

"Yes, Highness. They thank you. They were very grateful. But . . ."

"But, Maldred?"

"They did not know what they should do. Do now. Where to go. Prisoners still . . ."

"They are not prisoners now, but freed. Did you not tell them so?"

"Yes. But — *where* are they to go? What to do? They are still strangers here, if not enemies. At least, as slaves, they were housed after a fashion, and fed. Now . . . ?"

"We must see to this, Maldred. They should return home. To Northumbria. I shall speak with the King's Highness on this. Meantime, my lord of Ceres here, must see that they lack neither food nor shelter, until they can be sent back. No doubt they will work, decently, honestly, not like cattle but as free men. You hear, my lord . . . ?"

As though not only Ceres but Malcolm himself had heard, at this juncture a horseman arrived from eastwards, none other than Maldred's brother Madach. He rubbed his chin over what he saw there by the burnside.

"Highness — my lord King sent me," he said. "To see what's to do. He is at Pitscottie — beyond there. Five miles on, from here. He is . . . concerned at the delay."

"Indeed, my Lord Madach? I am humbly sorry for that," Margaret returned — and actually sounded so. "As you see, we are detained. So much requiring attention. Here we await heated water and salve brought from the monastery. This child suffers grievously. My noble husband and lord would not have a child to suffer needlessly, I vow, if *I* can aid. Go tell him, Madach, since His Highness has important matters to see to at St. Andrews, to press on. Not to wait for me. I shall come after, in my own time. Maldred here will attend on us women. That is best."

Madach looked doubtful, but Maldred nodded to him, briefly.

The Queen turned to the huffing and puffing MacDuff of Fife and his impatient-looking party. "My lords — go on, all of you. Join the King. I shall do very well, never fear. All who would be on their way to St. Andrews, go."

With ill-concealed relief practically all the men of the company reined forwards, with the old Earl. Madach saluted and went with them, leaving only Maldred, the Benedictine Oswald and one or two servitors with the Queen and her ladies.

As they went, a group of monks arrived from the cashel of St. Cyr, two bearing a steaming cauldron of water. One, older, introduced himself as the Abbot Cormac and declared that God would assuredly bless the Queen's Highness for her works of mercy.

"Would He not more conveniently bless *you*, my friend, and yours, had the mercies been done rather by His Holy Church?" Margaret asked.

The Abbot looked a little put out, but rallied. "Noble daughter — Holy Church never ceases in its work of ministering and prayer for sinful and distressed mankind. But there are so many . . ."

"To be sure, so many." She did not pause in her sponging of the boy's sores with one hand while she held him tightly with the other, as he wriggled to escape; but she gestured with her fair head around at the watching crowd, now grown the larger, so many of them underclad, thin, wasted, diseased. "All these, at your monastery door!"

"We do what we can, Highness. But we have no great resources. Our cashel is poor, save in the spirit. But we pray continually. Prayer is above all necessary, efficacious, my daughter."

"Yes, Father. *I* pray also. And shall pray for you, my

friend, that your works ⬚⬚⬚⬚
made . . . manifest, more ⬚⬚⬚
salve now, please — ointment.

"There are more folk here than ⬚⬚⬚⬚
asserted, defensively. "Many of thes⬚
Not our own folk. It is the Feast o⬚
prepare to go in procession to bless the ⬚⬚⬚
There are five of them. Very sacred, very cu⬚⬚
praised."

"Indeed. This boy and his mother have not ⬚⬚ ⬚⬚
them, it seems! Now — clean cloth to bind this up. ⬚ne
looked round. Clearly the monks had nothing such with
them. Nor the bystanders.

Magda sighed, knowing what must be. Yesterday
Margaret herself had cut away part of her own shift for
bandaging. Grimacing, she anticipated the Queen's plea,
and turning to Maldred, raised the front of her skirt.

"Your opportunity, Maldred mac Melmore!" she murmured. "Your dirk, man. Not your stares!"

"Thank you, my dear," Margaret said, smiling.

Flushing, Maldred drew his dirk, and stooping, made a
distinctly bungled job of cutting away a fair proportion of
the white linen underskirt, seeming to take an inordinate
time about it. There were exclamations and some laughter
from the crowd, even the monks much interested. Magda
turned her eyes heavenwards.

"Cut it in two parts, Maldred," Margaret instructed.
"And hold this child." She took the material and plunged
it into the cauldron, to wash it. Wringing it as dry as
possible, she bound the boy's arm and neck efficiently.

While she worked, she spoke. "This of the Feast of St.
Donnan — that is the name? I am glad to hear of it, my
friends. No doubt, as well as the procession you spoke of,
there will be some true feasting, as is suitable?"

The Abbot cleared his throat. "Some, some modest
provender, Highness. For a few of the faithful."

"For all, surely — *all*, sir. Is your saint interested only
in a few? Christ died for all, did He not?"

"To feed many would cost more than we possess, lady.
You must understand. We are not rich . . ."

Margaret turned. "Magda — have we *any* money left?"

"No, Highness."

"Maldred — you?"

"None. We gave it all away yesterday."

andaging, tipping lips with pink
nodded, to herself. "Brother Oswald,"
wo gold pieces from the satchel you carry."
Benedictine all but choked. "Princess! Highness —
no! That, that is not for giving away. That is Maundy
Money. Especial gold. Not for, not for . . ."

"But two pieces, Oswald."

"It is being taken to the Bishop of St. Andrews. Left
over from the King's distribution. To be kept until next
Maundy Thursday. You cannot give it to these, these . . .
people."

"These coins you carry, Oswald, were minted
especially, yes. From gold taken from Northumbrian
churches. Crucifixes, pattens and the like. By my
husband. Melted down. I say that this is none so ill a use
for some of it."

"But it has been especially blest. The Bishop? And the
King? He gave it to me to carry. Trusting me, the only
churchman in his train."

"Which was fortunate. I shall speak to the King. And to
Bishop Fothad. It was, after all, *my* suggestion that this
Maundy Money should be minted and distributed. Two
pieces, Oswald."

Unhappily the monk opened his satchel slung from a
shoulder, extracted a leather bag and picked out from it two
shiny coins. They were very small and roughly stamped as
with a seal, but gleamed authentically yellow gold.

"Give them to the good Abbot. That will more than pay
for your provision, will it not, my friend?"

Cormac took the money almost gingerly, turning the
pieces this way and that. Almost certainly he had never
handled a gold piece before. Even silver coins were
seldom seen in a Celtic cashel.

"You are very good, Highness. Most kind . . ."

"Then see that the kindness extends to all these, sir,
this feast-day. Food for empty bellies. So long as the
money lasts. I shall remember you and your monastery in
my prayers. And seek news as to how you fare. See you, of
your goodness, to this boy hereafter. These sores require
dressing daily." She rose, the lad released at last. "Now, if
you will give us your blessing, Father Abbot? I, and all
here, I fear, need it!"

Only the Benedictine did not bow the head for that
sudden and hurried benediction, he undoubtedly con-

sidering non-Romish blessings as invalid if not positively blasphemous. Margaret possibly felt a little the same way, but recognised the uses of tact to sweeten determination.

They mounted and rode on.

Needless to say they never caught up with MacDuff, much less the King; and it was almost dark when eventually they crossed the wide Muir of Muckross to enter the curious community of Kilrymont or St. Andrews, weary and hungry, having eaten nothing substantial since setting out from Balgonie in the morning — such minor provision as had been carried, gone with Malcolm's party. By that time, the little bag of Maundy Money was barely half-full, for they had come across other scenes and situations which wrung the Queen's heart; and having once made a start upon the gold pieces, she was not to be restrained. Gold, to be sure, was of no use to common poor folk, however needy. So she had exchanged some of the pieces at the hospices of Blebo and Strathkinness, for lesser coins, not without some difficulty and even suspicion on the part of the clergy. She paid for more food distributions, handed out largesse and ransomed more slaves. When Maldred, and even Magda, suggested that this might be over-doing it and that there might well be major trouble with the King hereafter, Margaret quietly assured them that this was how it must be. She must start as she intended to carry on. When she had agreed to wed Malcolm, at his continual urging, she had told him that she would marry not only the man but the realm; that she had no desire to interfere in his rule and governance but that the people, the ordinary folk, the poor and needy, would be her especial care. Malcolm perforce had accepted that. He must learn that she had meant what she said.

None of her party, even Maldred, had ever before been at St. Andrews. Arriving in semi-darkness, they gained but little notion of the town, save that it was extensive and very evidently on the rocky edge of the sea. It was a strange place altogether, in name and character as in the comparative isolation and remoteness of its situation, stuck out near the very tip of the thrusting horn of Fife. Its name apparently was not really St. Andrews at all, but Kilrymont-in-Muckross, and the saint's appellation referred only to the bishopric. Yet the Bishop's own church was not called that but St. Mary's on the Rock; and the large abbey was named after St. Regulus or Rule, not Andrew. There were no fewer than seven churches here, although some were very small and none stone-built — save for the tall tower of St. Regulus, built as a place of defence rather than worship. Not one was dedicated to St. Andrew.

They found their way to Bishop Fothad's house without difficulty, even in the gloom, for it was much the biggest building in the town, a fine hall-house in gardens and orchards, at the neck of a rocky little headland on which stood St. Mary's. It was in fact bigger and finer than Malcolm's palace at Dunfermline, the Ard Episcops, or King's Bishops, obviously taking their position seriously. The newcomers discovered that Malcolm, with the Bishop as Chancellor, was now in conference in the main hall. So they settled down to eat in the lesser hall. And while they ate, Margaret asked the Abbot Nechtan of St. Regulus to explain the peculiar situation of this church-city, which she had never fully understood, which was not the Primate's seat, nor yet the true centre of authority, these being at Dunkeld and Iona respectively.

According to Abbot Nechtan it had all started when Bishop Regulus of Patras, in Greece, was driven ashore here after his long voyage, bringing with him three fingers, part of an arm, the knee-cap and one tooth of the blessed St. Andrew, Simon Peter's brother. He had been fleeing from the invading Emperor Constantine and brought the precious relics with him, warned in a dream that wherever his vessel was forced ashore, there should he set up a church and shrine to contain them. Hence St. Regulus Abbey. In due course the name of St. Andrew had become as much used as Kilrymont. Himself, he would have preferred his abbey to be called St. Andrews instead of St. Regulus, who was after all the lesser saint. But the King's Bishops had adopted the style of St. Andrews for themselves, ten of them before this Fothad the Second.

Margaret, sensing a certain hostility creeping into the Abbot's voice and recognising possible rivalry, with abbots being in some ways superior to bishops in this Columban Church, steered the subject elsewhere. When did this happen, she wondered? According to her understanding of history, Constantine the Great reigned in the late third and early fourth centuries. She had not heard that Christianity even came to Scotland as early as that. Or was it another Constantine?

The Abbot coughed and declared that it was most certainly Constantine the Great. They were greatly favoured, here in Fife, in the blessed light of the Gospel reaching this hallowed spot before all others.

Maldred opened his mouth to speak — for this was not the story his father, the Primate, told — but closed it again when a younger keen-eyed Keledei further down the table, who had been introduced to them as the priest of St. Peter's here, raised his voice.

"Your Highness's doubts are well founded," he said, clearly. "For all this is but an old contrived tale. There was no St. Regulus. Or if there was, he did not come to Kilrymont. That story was concocted three centuries ago, about the year of our Lord 750, in order to make the bishopric of St. Andrews seem to pre-date the blessed Columba's coming to Iona. And so to deny Iona's superiority."

Maldred broke into the Abbot Nechtan's angry intake of breath. "That is how my father explained the matter to me," he agreed.

"Wrong!" the Abbot cried. "All wrong. Lies! Do not heed them, Highness."

"The good Abbot cannot dispute the facts of history," the Keledei insisted. "The Emperor Constantine lived in the fourth century. This Regulus is said to have come to Scotland, or Pictland, in the reign of Hungus, or Angus mac Fergus, King of Picts. And he reigned in the eighth century! The large lands around Kilrymont owned by the Abbey were gifted by Hungus. Each year the Abbot thanks God for his gifts."

Nechtan puffed and waved a dismissive hand.

Margaret looked from one to another thoughtfully. "And the relics?"

"Sadly they have been amissing for long," the Abbot said. "Some evil men stole them. Probably Norsemen, Vikings. They made many raids on this coast."

It was the Keledei's turn to snort.

"And St. Regulus himself? Surely it is possible to learn just when he lived? If he was indeed Bishop of Patras."

"He came in the year 347, Highness," the Abbot declared flatly.

"Then, unless he was over four hundred years old, he never met Hungus, and you have been praising God for the wrong king and your lands!" the younger man asserted. "I say that St. Regulus of Patras never came here. But in the sixth century the Irish missionary St. Caineath did. From Iona, one of the Brethren of Columba. And he founded the first church here, and dedicated it to his old abbot in Ireland, St. Riagull of Muckinsh. That is where the name Rule comes from, not Regulus. The names are spoken much alike, Riagull and Rule — but never Regulus."

"From all such scoffers and unbelievers, God in His mercy deliver us!" the Abbot announced piously. "You disgrace your Order and calling, young man."

"I was taught by the Keledei to seek and discern truth . . ."

"This matter much interests me," the Queen said soothingly, and looked kindly on them both. "I am sorry to hear that the blessed Andrew's relics are lost . . ."

Further discussion was cut short by the noisy entry of the King and his companions, conference adjourned. Malcolm appeared to be in a good humour, so presumably the decisions had gone as he desired. It had been a debate to try to thrash out the conflicting interests of the bishopric, the earldom of Fife and the Crown, in this East Neuk of Fife. That the King had agreed to come here at all, to hear it, instead of summoning all concerned to Dunfermline, said a lot for the famous boar-hunting facilities of this area — the name Muckross of course, meant the promontory of the boar, and these scrub-covered moorlands had always been notable for the creatures. In the morning, Malcolm would be able to indulge in what had really brought him here, his favourite activity after raiding.

He greeted his wife with a sort of grim joviality, ponderously pretending to be surprised to see her having got this far, with so much to delay her, and wondering how much more of her wardrobe she had parted with on the way.

Margaret kissed his cheek and assured him that she had profitably drawn not a few of his subjects closer to his person and Crown that day.

The Benedictine chaplain looked agitated.

Malcolm sat down, calling for drink. Bishop Fothad came, as host, to greet the Queen. He seemed less cheerful than either the King or MacDuff, so it might be inferred that he had come least well out of the conference.

"How good to see you, my very good friend — whom I have not seen to thank sufficiently since you wed us," Margaret said. "I do thank you. And much admire your house. I could wish that we had as good at Dunfermline."

The Bishop looked somewhat wary at that, despite the warm tone. "It is none so fine a place — but all at your service and disposal, Highness."

"How kind! We have already dined well of your excellent provision. We must consider well how best to show our approval and appreciation, Bishop."

Fothad's look changed from the wary to the sceptical, but he murmured civilities.

"Do I take it, my friend, that your talking today has not been entirely to your advantage?"

"In some respects, perhaps not, lady."

At her other side, Malcolm hooted. "What Fothad lost as Bishop he gained as Chancellor, it might be said! Should churchmen be so concerned with lands and worldly gear?"

"We require goods in order that we may *do* good with them, Highness."

"Well said, Bishop! So say I," Margaret supported. "That is the only destination for Holy Church's worldly riches." She looked down the table at the Benedictine. "Oswald — bring Bishop Fothad what remains of the Maundy gold. I distributed some small portion of it on our way here, Bishop, to your monasteries and hospices and poor sorry folk. But there is still some left."

At her left Malcolm gulped over his ale. "You did what?" he demanded.

"Used some of the gold pieces you minted, my lord, for their proper purpose — God's work and the relief of need."

"You did? That gold was mine. Stamped with my seal."

"To be sure. So I esteemed. And gave it the more gladly. That my husband's name should be the more blessed, also. Better than it lying in some coffer here waiting until next Eastertide, is it not? Bishop Fothad would have preferred so to use it, anyway — would you not, my friend?"

Fothad began to speak, then thought better of it. He turned to take the leather bag Oswald was holding out, weighed it in his hand, pursed his lips, and laying it unopened on the table, said nothing.

"I am very happy," the Queen informed them. "So much Christian charity and caring. I was saying, my lord Malcolm, that we must take thought how to assist the good Bishop in his important work, in the Church and realm both. Much could be done, I am certain."

Neither of her neighbours made encouraging noises.

"I think that I see opportunity," she went on, undeterred. "I have been talking with the excellent Abbot of St. Regulus, and the young priest there, whose name I have not heard. From them I learned much. Which could, I think, be important. It seems that there are grave doubts as to the beginnings of this St. Andrews bishopric, doubts of age and founding. Which can only be to the detriment of its authority."

"Ha!" Fothad exclaimed. "So you have been listening to our Brother Ciaran, Highness? That young man is very earnest, godly — but perhaps suffers, like many of our Keledei Order, from presumption of the mind. Overmuch learning, it may be, and too little simple faith."

"Could it be that, Bishop? Perhaps. But he appears to know his history. And it is in the history, is it not, that your St. Andrews is . . . doubtful? And it seems, from the Lord Maldred here, that the Primate his father agrees with the young man's doubts."

Maldred, across the table, was no more eager to be brought into whatever Margaret was up to than was Fothad to welcome him.

"My uncle Melmore is an ass!" the King observed, yawning. "He lives in books and papers — I swear he eats them! I never trust such folk. The past is the past — leave it so."

"It is the future I am more concerned with here, my lord," his bride suggested, with due modesty. "Does there not appear to be a notable gap in this Church in your realm? Between authorities — Iona, Dunkeld and this St. Andrews. Is there not — or do I mistake, in my ignorance? With Iona claiming the supremacy. As perhaps is right and proper. But Iona is far away, in the distant Hebrides, and authority should surely be where the people are? Lest error grows."

She had at least Fothad's attention now. Malcolm refilled his beaker from a flagon.

"The Bishop here is also Chancellor," she went on. "He knows what is necessary for the Church's better witness and service, as well as for the realm's good. In such way as the Abbot of Iona cannot know, on his island in the sea. Would it not be wise, therefore, to seek to increase the authority and influence of St. Andrews in matters spiritual? To no hurt of Iona."

"How could this be achieved, Highness?" the Bishop asked.

"What are you at?" Malcolm said, more bluntly.

"It came to me while we were discussing the matter of the missing relics of St. Andrew. That they *are* missing is a weakness, none can deny. And since we shall not find them now, it might be wise to forget them. And to erect some different shrine of veneration. Which could turn all eyes to St. Andrews."

"*All* eyes? And shrines!" the King asked, grinning.

"In time, yes. For men and women all, at some time, require to think on things eternal. If only when in trouble, or death approaches. Let them turn their eyes, then, to St. Andrews here. Rather than to far-away Iona which they do not know and will never see."

"There is much wisdom in what Her Highness says," Fothad acceded. "But how is such advantage to be achieved?"

"Replace the emptied shrine of St. Andrew," she replied. "Since we have no sufficiently important other relics that I know of, build not on such but on faith itself. The simple, essential, every-day faith of ordinary men and women. At Corn Ceres there was a lesson taught us. Wells. There they cherish five wells, no less. Healing wells, each for its own ill. You must have wells here at St. Andrews? And who is, above all saints, beloved of ordinary folk? Not Andrew. Not even the blessed Peter his brother. But Mary, the Mother of God Himself. Replace Andrew with Mary, then, my friend. Your own bishop's church here is St. Mary's on the Rock, I am told? Make it what St. Regulus has ceased to be, a place of pilgrimage, to which all eyes turn. Many more will turn to the Blessed Virgin than ever would to poor Andrew and his sad cross, however deserving. Women in especial. You need no bones and teeth, relics, for the Virgin Mary. Only a shrine, a stable, a manger. Beside a well."

"Yes. Yes — it could be. I see it. But . . . it would be difficult to establish. The pilgrimages. For folk to come, to make the journey. If it was to be, shall we say efficacious, many must come. From near and far."

"To be sure. I would help," she told him simply. "I would rejoice to do so. For I venerate the Mother of God with all my heart. Almost I intended . . ." She let that go. "I will make the pilgrimage. Each year. And bring many with me. Perhaps even my lord the King will accompany me, on occasion?" She did not wait for Malcolm's reaction. "There ought, surely, to be a shrine for Mary, here in Scotland? An especial shrine."

"Some might think that a Romish notion," Maldred spoke up, from across the board.

"Does our Lord's Mother belong only to Rome?"

"No. But . . ."

"What service will all this do Fothad? Or my kingdom?" Malcolm demanded yawning again.

"If your people turn towards St. Andrews, in times of doubt or peril, then the Bishop of St. Andrews must greatly gain, in esteem, in spiritual authority. Fill a gap which Iona fails to do. You must see it, my lord? And the whole kingdom gains, if King and Church are seen to be at one and the stronger."

"This is greatly to be thought on," Fothad nodded. "Your Highness gives me, gives us all, food for deep thought. There could be great advancement here — which I confess I have never considered . . ."

"Then consider it at some other time, man!" the King declared. "Enough of such chatter, in God's good name! If we are to be up at cock-crow in the morning, to seek out those boars of yours, time it is we sought our couches." He rose, and stooped to raise Margaret with him, less than gently. "Come, lass — there is more than religion and holy talk to living — as I shall prove to you! Come — and a good night to you all! We ride for Boarhills so soon after sun-up as we may."

They all rose. Magda went hurrying after the departing royal pair. Maldred scratched his chin, and frowned.

Part Two

9

IT WAS A summer of alarms and rumours and questions, mainly emanating from England, which kept Scotland in a ferment and the armies mustered — or at least their nuclei, since the hosts consisted of the levies, tenants and clansmen of the earls, thanes and chiefs, and these could by no means afford to keep them standing idle for long, with the hay to cut, the sheep to shear, the peats to dig and the harvest to win. William the Norman, they heard, was doing this, doing that, threatening the other. Some tidings were more reliable than others. For instance, it seemed fairly certain that he had given his niece Judith to the Earl Waldeve of Deira, as wife, bringing him her earldom of Northampton and confirming him also in that of Northumbria, no doubt to bind him to him indissolubly — this news coming from other sources besides the outraged Waltheof of Cumbria. Likewise, it seemed to be accepted that he had promised his ten-year-old daughter Gundred to Edwin, Earl of Mercia, another Saxon, when she should be old enough to marry. Again, there seemed no good reason to doubt that the usurper had put down the latest Welsh rising with his usual bloody ruthlessness and appointed his second son, William the Red, or Rufus, to be viceroy there and to institute a reign of terror which ought to ensure no further risings. And it seemed to be verified that the Conqueror had brought over the Channel his other son, Robert, now being named Duke of Normandy in his stead, with a further host of Norman knights and foreign adventurers from all over Christendom, and was giving these incomers Saxon heiresses to wed, there being many such available after the dire slaughters of Stamford and Hastings and the subsequent campaigns of extermination. And with these he had brought a Cluniac monk, Lanfranc, whom he had persuaded the Pope to appoint as Archbishop of Canterbury, displacing old Saxon Stigand. Less well authenticated stories were legion, but all tended to lead to the same conclusion, that the self-styled Conqueror was making a comprehensive effort to build up his strength, and securing his base for some new and major campaign. Few in Scotland had any doubts as to what the target would be.

In all this, Malcolm was not so preoccupied with domestic bliss that he failed to take precautions and some counter-measures. He commanded all his nobles, great and small, to put in hand and practise speedy mobilisation of their very largest man-power, and to ensure a high level of training. He sent out a further selection of the Atheling's Saxon refugees, to earn their keep by secretly moving amongst their kind in England and seeking to stir up a spirit of revolt. After all, the great majority of the landholders there were still Saxons, or Danish-Saxons, the Normans thinly spread. And the continuing savageries, the heavy taxations and burdensome conditions imposed by the usurpers, should be causing even worms to turn. All that ought to be needed was leadership, information, unity of purpose and a planned strategy. These Malcolm and Edgar proposed to supply. There were already patches of revolt here and there, notably that of one Hereward in the fen country of the Isle of Ely; but nothing like a unified insurrection.

The two flash-points for military adventures were, of course, always the late spring — when the rivers had sunk sufficiently after the winter rains and snows to be fordable — and the early autumn when the harvests were gathered in and labour freed. Malcolm had sent off the secret Saxon emissaries in good time, whilst the grain was still ripening; and by the beginning of harvest-time reports were filtering back. The season had been reasonably good and by mid-August cutting had started in favoured areas. One day, Cospatrick arrived from Dunbar in Lothian, summoned by the King. Quite soon thereafter Maldred himself was sent for from the orchard where he had been helping the Queen and her ladies to pick plums.

He found his two cousins closeted in an upper room of the stone tower.

"Ha — the fruit-picker!" Malcolm greeted. "I must ensure that you confine your picking to fruit not already spoken for!" He turned to Cospatrick. "This young kinsman of ours is over-partial to women's company. *My* woman in particular! There are times when, I vow, I have my doubts about him!"

"Old men married to young wives ever so doubt!" the Earl observed, a pleasantry not well received. Malcolm's sense of humour had not been highly developed.

"I have been of good use to you, Highness. With the said ladies," Maldred returned shortly.

"And shall be again, perhaps. But not with these, this time. I have a task for you. A *man's* task! You and Cospatrick did well together, in Galloway and Cumbria. You make a pair, I think. A rogue and an innocent! Those who do not trust the one, might trust the other?"

The Earl hooted, nowise offended.

"You will go south into England again. But further, a deal further. A small company, fast and secret. As before. Down into Deira. Near to York. Perhaps further still. And you will take Edgar Atheling with you."

"Edgar . . . !" That was Maldred, in protest.

"Edgar, yes. He has eaten my bread uselessly for sufficiently long. Now he can be of some use. But he needs to be watched, guided, led. Made to act the king, for once."

"Even we cannot work miracles!" Cospatrick said.

"You will make him *seem* to act. That is all. See you, I have gleaned much word from England. From our spies. This Hereward of Bourne is doing well, in the east. The whole Isle of Ely is now barred to the Norman. Edwin, Earl of Mercia, despite the promise of William's daughter Gundred, is disposed to rebel, and his brother Morkar with him. They see the Saxon cause going down for ever, otherwise. Better still, old Eldred, Archbishop of York, he who crowned the Bastard at Westminster, has suffered a change of heart. He returned to York with a rich train, booty gained at the expense of Canterbury when Stigand was deposed — and the Norman governor of York took it all from him. Claimed it was all King William's. Nor will William give it back. He does not need Eldred, any more. Now that he has this Frenchman Lanfranc in Canterbury instead of Stigand. So most of the Church is now against him — and the Church's gold!"

"And we are to do what?" Cospatrick wondered.

"Go to see these Saxons, with Edgar. Treating him as their King. When in their presence, at least. Have them to rise. Together. Arrange it — since it seems that they cannot do so themselves. See Eldred first. Over the gold. He is at Durham, in Deira. Waldeve is not there. He is at Winchester, with William, with his new wife Judith.

Then see Edwin of Mercia. He is holed up in his hill country, at Haddon-in-Peak, near to Derby. Coax him, with promises of Eldred's money. Then, if you can reach him, this Hereward. Who seems to be the best fighter they have got. In any rising, Edwin of Mercia will have to seem to lead it, under Edgar. He was King Harold's good-brother and commander. But in truth, the Fenman Hereward should lead, I think. You must contrive it."

"Contrive is a notable word, cousin! And you? What will you be doing, while we contrive all this?"

"I shall have a fleet ready. To sail a host south when I hear of the first Saxon success in arms," the King said levelly.

"Aye!" Cospatrick commented grimly. "But, only then?"

"Only then."

They were to ride two days later. The next morning it was the Queen who sent for Maldred. She was at her now daily task of washing the feet of six poor pilgrims, sent down from the cashel, before feeding them and despatching them on their way to the veneration of St. Serf's relics at Loch Leven. He waited while she finished, frowning his distaste, although unwittingly.

"You do not approve, by your looks, of what I do, Maldred?" she put to him when the pilgrims were sat down to eat at the table she had provided nearby, Magda supervising.

"No," he agreed bluntly.

"You see it as lacking in dignity? As does Malcolm. As it is, indeed. But that is why I do it. To shed dignity. Do you not see? I am endangered always with this dignity, of being a queen, of power and wealth and men bowing down to me. There is deadly danger in this. To me, Margaret. That I forget that I am but a mortal sinner, like all others. So I do this, for my soul's good. To remind me, and others."

He shook his head. "I say that it is too much, Highness. Overdone, you might say. Unsuitable. In such as yourself. Almost pride, of another sort!"

"Spiritual pride? Surely not, Maldred? That I am on the watch for, always. If it was not unsuitable for our Blessed Lord, is it so for me?"

He shrugged, unable to answer her. "Your Highness sent for me?"

She sighed. "Yes. I learn that you are leaving us tomorrow. On a mission into England. With my brother. It is my hope that you will do some small mission for me also, on your way?"

"To be sure. If I can."

"I am greatly concerned, Maldred, for all the poor Saxon captives in this land, brought from Northumbria and sold into slavery here. That I, a Saxon princess, should sit on the Scots throne and yet these my countrymen be in hard bondage here, is grievous. I would have them all released, but Malcolm says that is not possible. They all have been sold, moneys paid for them. To free them it would be necessary to repay the buyers. So — I need money, much money. None other is concerned for them — so I must be."

"But . . ."

"You will be visiting Saxon lords in England, Maldred. Ask them for help. From me. Say that you are my envoy. That I ask, beg them to help their fellow-Saxons in distress. Go to the churchmen in especial. Go to Walchere, the new Bishop of Durham. He is a friend. Or was, when he was Prior of Hexham. And ask Eldred, Archbishop of York. You have to see him, Malcolm says. At Durham. He is very rich. You will do this, my friend — for my sake?"

"If it is your command, Highness . . ."

"It is *not* my command. It is my humble request. The plea of Margaret Atheling to her good friend Maldred mac Melmore. That only."

He was moved. "I shall do what I can."

"I thank you. Here is my ring. Take it. As sign that you speak for me. And . . . God bless you, Maldred. And, and aid Him by taking some care of yourself . . . !"

*   *   *

They rode the following morning, early, to a warm send-off from the ladies — for with Edgar going, all the Athelings were involved — Maldred receiving an unexpected and full-on-the-lips kiss from Magdalen at the last moment, which sent him on his way distinctly bemused. Although with only the same size of escort as before, some two hundred helmeted and leather-jerkined horsemen, they made a much more distinguished company. For with the Prince Edgar was a group of his own nobles, almost all that were left of the original refugee party, including Merleswegen, Siward Barn or Beorn the Dane, Archil, Edric Spur and Bartoloméo Leleszi, or Leslie, a Hungarian. Like Edgar himself, none of these approved of Cospatrick, indeed none had any real enthusiasm for the venture at all. As a result, they tended to ride apart, to the rear of the column, with Cospatrick and Maldred ahead — which suited the latter very well.

Conditions otherwise were very different, also. Instead of harsh winds and rain, snow-streaked hills, rivers in spate, flooded ground and bogs everywhere, they rode pleasantly through a smiling land of bracken just beginning to turn to gold and heather to purple, of waving yellow corn, not yet ready to cut in these central uplands, of blue lochs and sparkling rivers, and the young folk of the country up with the herds of cattle, sheep and garrons in the idyllic summer life of the high pastures. In consequence they made much better time, for Cospatrick was not disposed to linger, whatever the others would have preferred — and from the beginning he made it entirely clear who was in command, as indeed had Malcolm before they started. They followed approximately the same route as in February, although saving some time by not having to follow the more secret ways, since no trouble from Galloway was looked for. They managed to reach the head of Annandale by the first night, resting at a lonely hospice dedicated to St. Patrick, the Saxons, not in the best of training after their enforced idleness, quite exhausted. The next day was less demanding, down Annan, to cross Esk into Cumbria, to pass the second night at Caer-luel.

Unfortunately the Earl Waltheof was not present, being up in the fells of Geltsdale hunting deer. Nothing would do, however, but that fast messengers should ride forthwith, night or none, to bring Waltheof back without delay, no excuses to be countenanced.

So they had a restful day following until a grumbling Waltheof turned up in the afternoon — to grumble still more vehemently when he was told by Cospatrick to prepare for an immediate journey of some duration. Protests were unavailing — he was to come with them, on the orders not only of his strong-willed elder brother but of the King of Scots his liege-lord. His knowledge of

Cumbria, and his authority as governor, would be helpful.

Waltheof was only a little less unpopular with the Saxons than was Cospatrick; he had never actually taken sides against Edgar in the past, but he had refused to support him.

So the great riding was resumed, and little the more harmoniously for Waltheof's sulky presence. They had little expectation of involving any of the Cumbrian lords in their project, for though these might hate and fear the Normans, they almost equally disliked the Saxons, from whom they had suffered much in the past, themselves being of Celtic blood, similar to the Welsh. Cumbria indeed was à strange land politically, ostensibly paying allegiance to the Scots throne but in fact all but independent, and remaining so mainly on account of its remote situation and awkward hilly and waterlogged terrain. That it would not long remain clear of the Conqueror's clutches was the message the visitors sought to put over, to the one or two distinctly suspicious chiefs they made contact with. But their main concern was to ensure that their presence and progress was not reported to the Normans in the south. They made a strong enough company to have little fear of actual attack from local levies. And Waltheof's presence helped.

They followed the Eden valley south-eastwards for forty miles, up through ever-rising moorish hills, by Lazonby and Kirby Thore and Appleby, to Stainmore under the high fells of Warcop and Lune. They were near the Deira border here, but in these lofty and little-populated moorlands, cattle and sheep pasture, there was little or nothing to mark divisions, save occasional cairns of stones. Nevertheless, from here onwards they would have to go more warily, less speedily. There were no hospices for travellers in such empty Pennine uplands, and for the first time the lordly ones, as well as the escort, camped under the open sky, by the now narrowing Eden at Musgrave.

The further south and east they had come, so had grown the aura of fear, the preoccupation with oppression, the tales of slaughter and rapine and terror, the weight of it beginning to loom like a pall over the land ahead. And, inevitably, the sullen wariness of the local people. Anyone who had campaigned with King Malcolm knew well about slaughter and pillage; and this whole land had suffered terribly for centuries previously under the assaults of the

Danes and Vikings. But these, more or less haphazard, episodic, almost casual, however grievous for the victims, were not to be compared with the Norman terror ahead, which was an expression of deliberate policy, systematic, comprehensive, merciless. Entire areas, it seemed, were turned into smoking deserts, whole towns wiped out, populations butchered, not as acts of war or reprisals but merely as warnings to others, or to create wide buffer zones around particular spheres of influence. Here, the steel-clad Norman knight, the so-efficient fighting machine and alleged symbol of chivalry, was looked upon as the Devil Incarnate, a scourge worse than the Black Death. The travellers could not but be affected, in some measure, the need for caution and secrecy borne in on them.

They reached the Deira border actually on the wide, high anonymity of Bowes Moor. The lower lands of upper Teesdale lay ahead of them, and they swung away north-eastwards to avoid that more populous area, especially the vicinity of the abbey of Egglestone, which might well be Norman-held, keeping to the heathland pastures of Hamsterley Common until they came to the Wear. That river would have led them winding down to Durham, their immediate goal, but again through populated lands. So they forded Wear near Witton and kept to the high ground by Brancepeth and Langley Moors until, with the sunset, they could look down into the deep shadow-filled valley out of which rose the steep, hog-backed ridge, almost encircled by the Wear, whereon stood the large and handsome church of St. Cuthbert, shrine for the bones of that great missionary and also of the Venerable Bede, humble luminary of all knowledge — but, for their purposes, more importantly the seat of Bishop Walchere of Durham. It was as much fort as church, on a strong site, with semi-monastic buildings attached, and massive construction work appeared to be going on alongside, in stone, further on the ridge's crest. The town, quite large, nestled in the gut of the valley below on both sides of the river, a bridge linking.

Cospatrick sent Maldred to announce the arrival of Edgar, rightful King of England, and of the Earls of Dunbar and Northumbria and of Cumberland, to see the Archbishop of York, with greetings from the King of Scots. This resounding announcement quickly won him into the presence of Walchere, a tall, ruddy-cheeked man of middle years with shrewd eyes, who had succeeded old Ethelwin in the see whom Maldred had last seen on that ship in Wearmouth Bay. It was this Walchere who had sent the monk Turgot to attend the royal wedding at Dunfermline. He was known to be of independent mind and incensed at the Conqueror's scornful treatment of Holy Church, especially the deposition of Archbishop Stigand and the maltreatment of his own superior Eldred of York. He was cautious, however, and declared that he would welcome the distinguished visitors provided that they came in peace and goodwill. But that, sadly, Archbishop Eldred was gravely ill, and that he feared for his life.

This last was a blow to the party from Scotland, for Eldred might have been the key to much, the most senior and notable churchman in England now that Stigand was imprisoned and the unknown Lanfranc in his place at Canterbury. Walchere was sympathetic, but not a great deal of use to them. His position was complicated by the fact that his territorial lord here, the Earl Waldeve of Deira, was also his close friend and was now apparently firmly in William's camp; indeed it had been part of the Earl Waldeve's bargain with the Conqueror that his friend Walchere of Hexham should get the bishopric. The ambitious new building which was going up nearby was in fact a great Norman-style castle-palace which the pair of them would occupy, so oddly close was the relationship. So that there was not much that Walchere might do to encourage the visitors. But he did not seek to prevent them having an interview with the sick Archbishop.

Edgar now suddenly asserted himself. He declared that he was the rightful king of this realm and that Eldred was his subject and friend. Admittedly he had failed him, and crowned the hated Norman; but he had repented of that folly, and he, Edgar, would forgive him. He would therefore interview him alone, as was suitable. This he insisted upon, with Walchere confirming that it was inadvisable for numbers to enter the sickroom, or for any controversy to take place, for the Archbishop was very frail. Cospatrick cursed below his breath, but was outmanoeuvred this once, being anxious not to seem to devalue Edgar's authority here in England.

However when presently Edgar rejoined them, he was in sour mood. The old man was doddering, he announced, all but senile, hardly had recognised him, seemed scarcely aware of what was going on, what was at stake. There was nothing to be gained there, nothing.

Cospatrick started up, asserting that they had not come all this way for *that*. He would go up and see what *he* could do. But Walchere firmly put his foot down. The Archbishop was in *his* house and care, as were they all. He was responsible. One interview with the invalid was sufficient for the present. In the morning, perhaps . . .

In the early morning, an unheard-of thing, Cospatrick attended Lauds, the cock-crow service of the Romish Church to start the day — whilst the others still slept. Walchere was impressed, and permitted the Earl thereafter to go up and see the sick man — who was apparently at his poor best first thing in the morning. Maldred, arisen by then, went with him.

The emaciated old man in the great bed looked frail indeed, a shrunken shadow of a tall and powerful figure, with a gaunt tonsured head and eyes deep in hollow sockets. But the eyes themselves were bright enough, almost fevered, far from dulled in senility. The Bishop introduced them, and left.

After their greetings, jerky and a little difficult, there was silence whilst the haggard prelate eyed them searchingly. At length he spoke, thinly, tremorously, but with no lack of certainty.

"You have come from that coxcomb Edgar?"

Cospatrick did not fail to note the tone, however weak. "No, my lord Archbishop. He is but in our company. We are from the King of Scots. Cousins of His Highness, both."

"You, Cospatrick, I . . . have heard of. Not always . . . to your credit!"

"I would have been surprised otherwise," the Earl admitted, smiling. "Folk only spoken well of are, I swear, exceeding dull! Yourself, my lord, I have heard, are not *all* saint!"

A momentary twitch, which might have been a hint of amusement, flickered across the wasted features. "Bold!" he acknowledged. "Malcolm your King . . . is no saint. But is now . . . wed to one . . . I hear."

"She, the Queen, sends you her greetings and remembrances, my lord," Maldred put in.

"She was . . . ever the best of that family. Likest her

grandsire Edmund. I never could abide . . . his sainted brother Edward!"

This whispered outburst seemed to exhaust Eldred and he lay for a little, eyes closed, breathing heavily, while his visitors glanced at each other.

Then they found the sunken gaze on them again. "What does your Malcolm . . . want of me? A done man," he got out.

Cospatrick judged his man. "Money," he said baldly.

"Aye. You are frank."

"Would you have me otherwise? Your Edmund Ironside was *my* grandmother's brother, see you."

"Ha! Yes — Elgiva. I had . . . forgot. So you are . . . some kin . . . to Edgar."

"To my sorrow."

"He, he wanted money also."

"For a different purpose."

"Eh . . . ?"

"He wants it to gain a throne for himself."

"And you?"

"I seek it to fight Norman William. There is a difference."

"Aye. That is true." There was a sudden and distinct strengthening of that faint voice. "William the Bastard — hell receive him!"

"As you say, my lord. But — hell requires some assistance! King Malcolm seeks to provide that. But it is a costly business. He seeks to unite your Saxon lords, in armed rising. To assist this Hereward. To rouse Edwin, Morkar, Engelwine and the rest. Money, gold is required — of which Malcolm is short. Your earls and lords here have all been sorely impoverished by William's taxes and burdens. You know it all. To bring them to arms, we need treasure."

"Such treasure as I hold . . . is not mine. Belongs to Holy Church."

"No doubt, my lord. But in this, it will be used for Holy Church's benefit. The Norman tramples on Holy Church. None knows that better than you. He puts his own men wrongfully into your benefices. What use your treasure to the Church you serve if William lays his bloody hands on it?"

The old man lay silent.

Cospatrick came a step nearer to the bed, leaning

forward. "I hear that William has named a new man, a Norman, to take *your* place, my lord. One Thomas. You know of him?"

The broken prelate seemed to convulse with a spasm of sheer fury, shocking to see. He could speak no words.

"So — your treasure will be Thomas's treasure! Or William's. If you let it lie, do not use it aright. Now. Do you wish that, my lord Archbishop?"

The croak emitted from those blue lips was less than intelligible — but entirely eloquent and negative.

There was a pregnant pause, all waiting. Then the words came.

"How can . . . I trust you . . . Cospatrick? Trust any?" That was agonised.

"I too hate William," the Earl said simply. "Whom *you* crowned!"

There was a long, gulping sigh from the bed.

Maldred spoke. "I swear, my lord, that all is truth, honest. That this is King Malcolm's purpose. That our mission is to seek to lead the Saxon lords in revolt. Forthwith. That this is what the gold is for — not for Edgar. Or for any other."

Eldred gave his almost imperceptible nod. "When do you ride?"

"So soon as we may. Time is short."

"So be it. Leave me now. I am weary. But send Walchere to me."

As Cospatrick raised a hand in salute, Maldred again intervened.

"My lord Archbishop — the Queen. Margaret Atheling asks, begs your charity. To help her. She seeks to free the Saxon slaves, taken by the Scots. There are many. Their owners must be paid. She is gathering moneys for this. Believes that you will help. I am to speak for her. Here is her ring. She is good, kind. Will you aid her? And them?" That came out in something of an embarrassed rush.

Again the hint of a nod. "Give her . . . an old man's . . . blessing." Two trembling fingers were raised, as much seemingly to point to the door as in benediction.

They left him, a little doubtfully, to seek Bishop Walchere.

It was after they had breakfasted that the Bishop came, to draw them apart from their companions and take them to a small chamber nearby.

"I do not know what you have said, or done," he declared. "But the Archbishop has been more openhanded than I have ever known him." He pointed to two leather bags on a table, one large, one small. "This is for King Malcolm's use. This for Queen Margaret."

Even Cospatrick was affected when he opened his weighty bag and saw what it contained. Eldred had indeed been generous. As well as hundreds of gold and silver coins, there were jewels, chains, rings, bracelets, chalices and other vessels, mainly gold, even an earl's sword-belt, far more than either of them had hoped for, a breath-taking treasure. And in the small bag there was sufficient to ransom many slaves, coins, brooches, medallions, trinkets and the like, but above all, a most splendid golden crucifix encrusted with rubies, priceless.

The Bishop eyed them curiously. "This is what you came for?"

"Yes," Cospatrick admitted. "But we need more than gold to defeat the Norman. You will thank the Archbishop for us . . . ?"

Before they rode, Walchere added his own contribution to Maldred's bag, but nothing to the Earl's.

"The wages of hate and the wages of love!" Cospatrick commented cynically. "And hate will ever win!"

"Not in the end," Maldred said doggedly.

*   *   *

Thereafter they rode cautiously indeed, not slowly but by unfrequented ways and high moorlands, due southwards now but making many detours and always with scouts out ahead, guided by one of Walchere's men. They had basically about one hundred and forty miles to go, but half as far again by the routes they took, partly to avoid populous and strategic areas in an increasingly Norman-dominated land, and partly to visit certain Saxon chiefs thought to be prepared to do more than curse the Normans. So they went by the North and West Riding moors and dales, and Haworth, to the Hebden Water by the Forest of Trawden, and then began the long climb into Peakland and the Derwent, making brief but high-pressure visits to ealds and thanes and lords on the way, Edgar playing the king, his Saxon friends persuasive, Cospatrick the paymaster. They had some limited success, with gold eloquent and word of Hereward's Anglian successes encouraging. But it became ever more evident that major military co-operation would depend on the active participation of their natural leaders, the Saxon earls, most of whose attitudes to the Conqueror had been equivocal, to say the least. Waldeve of Deira and Northumbria was in William's pocket now, although he was really a Dane, of course; Edwin, their own lord, talked but did nothing; Ulfwin of Kent was a mere boy; Edmund of Essex was married to a Norman, as was Ecgbert of Sussex. Wessex, greatest of all, was now wholly a prisoner of William, who had taken over his capital, Winchester, as his own favourite seat. So the visitors could not judge the extent of their success or otherwise, until they had made an impact on Earl Edwin of Mercia. Maldred, however, did rather better, on Margaret's behalf, managing to extract small but useful sums from men who found that a deal easier than to commit themselves finally to armed intervention.

Mercia, once an independent kingdom under the mighty Offa and Penda, was now much shrunken to a Midlands territory of something over one thousand square miles comprising much of the spine of England, its perimeters now largely occupied by the Normans who had carved whole new earldoms out of it. In consequence, Edwin and his brother Morkar ought to have been in the forefront of any opposition to the invaders, as their father Alfgar had been, their sister Eldgyth married to the late King Harold. But, although fighters, they were not of the same calibre and stuff of leadership. It was the Saxons' great misfortune that in their major hour of need, the generation of leaders seemed to have sunk to the second-rate. The cream of the race, of course, had fallen at Stamford Bridge and Hastings.

The travellers came, on the fifth day, into the high Peak area of Derby-in-Mercia, above the Derwent valley, where Edwin now roosted in a hilltop eyrie, once the site of a British fort, now little more than a robber's hold and a poor establishment for the successor of the ancient Kings of Mercia, once the most powerful in England. Their great castle of Tamworth, thirty-five miles to the south, was now the seat of an arrogant Angevin baron. Always on the watch for trouble, Edwin's guards intercepted the newcomers miles before they reached their goal, and so they were escorted up the steep corkscrewing track to the fort in fine style, the royal banner of the Athelings, specially sewn by the princesses at Dunfermline, flying bravely at their head.

The effect, however, was somewhat wasted, for although it was not much after mid-day, both Edwin and his brother Morkar were so drunk as barely to be able to greet the visitors coherently. This, of course, was the great weakness of the Saxons, and undoubtedly the reason for many a sad defeat. The Scots were hard drinkers too, but not to rival these. The Saxons drank ale, mead and cider with a sort of unquenchable enthusiasm, the more so since troubles had descended upon them.

Edgar was considerably offended at receiving little in the way of royal welcome. After all, he had once gone through a ceremony of proclamation as king, at which Edwin had been present. The consequent sulks perhaps helped to explain the less than white-hot Saxon enthusiasm for his cause.

There was nothing that they could usefully achieve that day, for the brothers were not quite so inebriated that they could not give orders for the visitors to be feasted — and plied with drink, naturally, of which it would have been unmannerly for the hosts themselves not to partake. As a result they were carried to bed eventually drunker than ever. Cospatrick and Maldred decided that they must circumvent this process somehow, and perhaps use the same tactics as at Durham — without the unfortunate necessity for early-morning religious exercises.

So at least two of the visitors were up betimes next day and awaiting the Saxon earls in what passed as their hall when eventually they came down for breakfast, both within a few moments. They were both big shaggy men, with full beards and shoulder-length fair hair. The Saxons, unlike the Normans, did not much go in for hair-cutting and shaving. Edwin, in his early thirties, was stocky and inclining to corpulence; Morkar, two years younger, was less heavily-built, less hearty. Now, they looked at their early-risen guests a little doubtfully. They knew Cospatrick sufficiently well, after all, his quality and repute; Morkar indeed had been one of the many who had for a little been Earl of Northumbria, in its recent troubled story — hardly a matter for congratulation with the representative of the original displaced line.

"A good day to you, friends," Cospatrick called out genially, for all that. "You are the better for a night's sleep, I vow!"

Uncertain how to take that, the brothers exchanged glances, muttering something vague.

Retaining the initiative, their formidable visitor went on almost without pause, "Have you thought further? To improve on what we spoke of last night?"

Again the blank stares. Clearly last night was something of a closed book for the Alfgarsons.

"Can you not commit *more* men? And more swiftly? We — or at least King Malcolm — can find the money."

"Men . . . ?" Edwin wondered.

"Money . . . ?" Morkar said.

"To be sure. You can do better than a mere three thousand, I swear. You could double that, God's Blood! And, who knows, we might double the gold."

Bewildered, the others eyed each other. "What three thousand? And what gold?" Edwin demanded. "Are you out of your wits, man?"

"Do not say that you have forgotten? Or would resile from your promises? In the sacred cause of England! And Mercia. The downfall of Norman William?"

Edwin sat down heavily at the board, calling for meats. And for ale, of course. He gestured mutely to his guests to sit.

Maldred took a hand. "My lord Earl — how many men *can* you muster? In short time. And how many later? In a few more days."

"Muster for what?"

"For battle, what else? You will not defeat the Norman sitting here." That was Cospatrick again.

"I have not many men. Since York. Aye, and Stamford and Senlac . . ."

"Your earldom is still large, widespread. With many men on it. Do not tell us that Mercia has lost all its fighters? Or its will to fight!"

"We have fought all too much. And with little but sorrow to show for it."

"*We* could give you something to show for it, man. Or do you want it all to go to this Hereward?"

"A plague on Hereward! In his fenland mud!"

"William also has reason to say a plague on Hereward and his mud!" Maldred reminded.

Morkar spoke. "This of gold, money? What do you mean?"

"I mean that King Malcolm — and King Edgar, to be sure — know well that the Saxons are prevented from putting their full strength on the field, having lost so much treasure as well as blood, by robbery, by taxations and long warring. So we have collected much treasure. The Archbishop Eldred has been generous. We can pay for men. Help to feed the fires of war!"

"So-o-o! This payment? How much?" Morkar was evidently a man concerned with things economic.

"Sufficient."

"To raise and feed and arm many men requires much money."

"Even when the fight is your own? The enemy your oppressor? The cause yours, not ours?"

"What is your, or your King Malcolm's, interest in this?" Edwin asked. "Why are *you* seeking to have us fight?"

"We also hate William. He threatens Cumbria, in Scots Strathclyde. Malcolm is now wed to Edgar's sister. He believes that we must act together."

"But with *my* men!"

"And others. Many others. Malcolm prepares a fleet, has a great army mustered. We have been winning promises from Saxon lords. Many are ready to march. But look to you, my lords, as leaders."

"You offered them moneys also?"

"Some. The greater part of it had to be kept for you. Who can field most men, should lead." Cospatrick shrugged. "And of course, for this Hereward."

There was a pause. "He is a small man. Of no importance. With a band of cut-throat fenmen. What need has he of moneys?"

"He has taken William's measure. Fought him for more than a year. Made the Isle of Ely a refuge for many. Broken men, yes — but men who are fighting. Are not these better than earls' men who will not, my friends?"

Another pause as, angrily, they chewed and gulped. There was a hostility between the Mercian brothers and Hereward of Bourne. There was even a tale that he was of illegitimate kin to themselves, possibly because of nothing more than that the fathers of both were named Leofricson.

"A thousand armed men, well led, are worth much gold," Morkar observed.

"Two thousand are worth more. Three thousand, more still!"

Again silence.

"Maldred — shall we say a chalice with one hundred gold pieces for these good lords? How think you?"

Nodding, Maldred went back up to their chamber, where two of Cospatrick's own men kept guard on their treasure. He counted out the coins into a suitable large golden cup.

Back at the hall the brothers' eyes gleamed when they saw the chalice, itself worth more than the pieces which filled it.

"Yours," Cospatrick said, pushing it across the table. "And more, much more. If you will find the men."

"How much more?" Morkar insisted.

"How many men can you raise . . . ?"

Gulping down his ale and taking a rib of beef with him — since he could hardly carry away eel-pie — Maldred left them to their unsavoury bargaining.

By mid-day Cospatrick was satisfied — or as nearly so as was possible, with inebriation setting in again for their hosts. They had the promise of three thousand men within the week — and no more gold to change hands until these were mustered and ready to march. He and Maldred left Edgar, Waltheof and the others of their party to keep the Alfgarsons up to scratch and to help marshal the assembly. Also to send out messengers to the thanes and lords they had visited on their way, to tell these that the Earls Edwin and Morkar had joined King Edgar in armed uprising, and to bring or send their contingents to the muster in the Peakland heights forthwith. With a mere dozen horsemen as escort now — for this was to be a *very* secret expedition — they set out, with two Mercians as guides. They took their treasure with them.

They had almost as much country to traverse as they had had from Durham to the Peak — one hundred and thirty miles or so. But this was very different country, low-lying, fertile, once populous and almost wholly Norman-occupied — save for the devastated areas. In fact, it was these dire stretches of man-made desert which made the journey a practical proposition, for by using their grim reaches for route, however circuitous, linked together by night-marches and detours to avoid danger-spots, they were able to accomplish a large part of their difficult travelling unobserved, or at least unaccosted.

But it made grievous and terrible riding, through what should have been a good and lovely land. Most of the burning and sacking and killing had been done during the previous two years, so that green growth had sprung up partly to hide the fire-blackened desolation. But it was still all there beneath, the sour acrid dust of it rising around them only partially to overcome the stench of rotting carcases of man and beast. Out of the growth rose the charred skeletons of roof-timbers and door-posts and trees, from all too many of which the grisly fruit of flesh-tattered and shrunken bodies still hung, amidst flocks of obscene birds. They rode through many dead villages and small towns, and unnumbered farmsteads, with the only life the rooting swine and half-wild poultry. And rats. The rats were everywhere, legion. Maldred for one felt sickened to the heart of him.

They went east by south, avoiding Alfreton and Derby, to cross Erewash near Codnor and so into the welcome fastnesses of Sherwood Forest. Southwards now, giving Nottingham a wide circuit to the Vale of Witham and Ermine Street into the levels of Kesteven, with water becoming ever more of a problem, standing, seeping, flooding water. To avoid the marshes they turned more and more into the south, through the worst devastated areas, to cross Welland near Stamford. Now Peterborough lay ahead, and here they were particularly circumspect, for it was known to be an armed camp, the headquarters of the Norman forces arrayed against Hereward, its great monastery the late Canute's favourite retreat when he had turned religious.

Now they felt their way heedfully into the no-man's-land where the scouting parties of both forces might be operating. It quickly became real fenland, waterlogged with meres and pools and ditches everywhere, appalling country to fight over unless born to it, and disastrous for cavalry — hence the Norman failure here. Their Mercian guides were useless in this extraordinary terrain. All they knew was that somewhere ahead was the Isle of Ely, a great tract of firmer ground in the quaking watery wilderness, twenty-five miles across no less, almost the last quite unconquered corner of all England. Horses were a positive hindrance here. Landmarks were almost non-existent, any sort of straight course impossible. Soon the travellers were utterly lost, floundering in more than their footsteps.

Happily they were not long in being picked up by a patrol of Hereward's fenmen, in what proved to be Wimblington Fen, before they had wandered too far, with a seemingly impassable water-barrier ahead — and not over-gently treated by their rescuers, who were predictably suspicious of all strangers. These took them, by devious ways, and eventually by flat-bottomed scows, used apparently for cattle transport, across a wide open channel above which an early-autumn haze obscured the further prospect, until there rose above it all the roofs and spires of St. Etheldreda's Abbey of Ely itself, an unlooked-for sight in those endless flats.

There proved to be quite a sizeable town around the abbey, with whole streets of clay houses and hovels, warehouses and barns and brewhouses, even windmills — for this had to be very much a self-sufficient community, capital indeed of a self-contained land — if land anything so excessively watery could be described. The catching, farming, fattening, drying and smoking of eels appeared to be the principal occupation. But sheep and cattle seemed to thrive in these marshes, and spinning and weaving and tanning were much in evidence; also cider-presses, for there were orchards, like leafy islands, everywhere that the ground was sufficiently firm. The visitors were surprised and impressed.

They were conveyed to the abbey, and received by the Abbot Thurstan, a lean and muscular Benedictine of middle years, known to be much more than any mere spiritual adviser and useful provider of food and shelter to the outlawed Hereward, in effect his second-in-command. He was, indeed, also his landlord, for Hereward was a tenant of the abbey, with the former Abbot Brand, now dead, his uncle. Hereward himself was off on some venture. Thurstan knew of Cospatrick, of course, and when he heard that they had come to aid in the fight against the Normans, his welcome grew the warmer.

Waiting for Hereward, they discussed strategy. It quickly became evident that, cleric or none, their host had a full and swift grasp of things military and something of a flair for tactics. By the time the leader himself arrived, in the late evening, they had in fact worked out quite a possible plan of action.

Hereward Leofricson was a large, a huge, man, of a stature to match his achievements. Heavily bearded, with a shock of long fair hair, he had twinkling blue eyes and a ready smile to counter his distinctly fearsome appearance. He was mud-spattered, as were all who travelled the fens, and vastly hungry.

He talked as he ate, through mouthfuls of food. "The Norman can be beat, yes. If *we* choose the field. Not he. He can beat us with armour and cavalry and bowmen. Aye, and with discipline. But we can use the land to fight for us. So we draw him to where his horses are of no use to him, where on foot his heavy plate-armour drags him down, where there is no mass target for his arrows. Into our marshes. Or in dense scrub-forest."

"Yes. The pity that so little of England is such," Cospatrick commented.

"It need not be. So long as there is sufficient to defeat him on."

"If you *can* draw him there."

"Aye, there is the rub. He is wary. Will not commit himself here. In large force. When we can coax him in, we beat him. Now, he will not be drawn much east of Peterborough. This devil-spawn Turold seeks now only to *contain* us."

"Turold . . . ?"

"An accursed Norman priest, whom William has appointed Abbot of Peterborough. He ravens like any wolf, a man of blood. They say that William sent him here saying that since he behaved like a soldier rather than a monk, he would provide him with someone to fight! Us. So the Normans here have a priest as leader." He looked over and grinned at Thurstan. "We answer him as best we can!"

"How many men do you have?"

"Of my own, some two thousand. But many broken men have flocked here, to the fens. Not all are of the best. But some are good. And learning how to be marshmen. Enough to double my force. I have never brought them all to battle, yet, for the Norman will not come for us in force. If only I could coax them in . . ."

"I think that I know how you might. With the good Abbot, and Maldred of Atholl, I have been discussing this.

I say that if you muster your full strength near enough to Peterborough to be an open threat. And then another force, as large, say four thousand men, comes eastwards to join you, as openly — at least for the last part. Then the Normans will be forced to move. In strength. To prevent the junction of so large an army."

"Who would raise so large a force?"

"It is being raised now. The Earls Edwin and Morkar, with Edgar the Atheling, are mustering now. In Peakland. With other Saxon lords."

"Those! They will do nothing. Or do little and badly. These are but straw-men!"

"They may not have to do so much. Their part is to draw the enemy — for *you* to slaughter in your marshes."

The big man chewed reflectively. "You believe they would attempt this?"

"We are paying them well to do it."

"They would require to be skilfully led. I have no faith in these Saxons." The men of the fens were not really of Saxon origin, but Angles with a strong admixture of Danish blood. This was, after all, East Anglia and formerly part of the Danelaw.

"Send of your own folk, to lead them. Send the good Abbot, here."

"The problem will be to get the Saxons down into the marshes before the Normans can reach them," Thurstan said. "Else there could be a massacre. But on the wrong side!"

"It will have to be carefully planned, yes. The place well chosen. So that the Normans will be tempted to follow, almost *forced* to follow. Into ground where they will be trapped and your fenmen can descend upon them. Ground which the Saxons can reach from the north-west. Yet in your Ely marshes. You can think of such?"

"How long until this Saxon host appears?" Hereward asked.

"This is our fourth day gone. Three days more, to win back. Then four more. A week. Can you have your people ready in a week?"

"Yes." There was no debate, no temporising, no bargaining, about Hereward.

Maldred actually brought up the subject of money. "Do you need gold?" he asked. "To aid you in this?"

"Gold? Why should I need gold? All men love gold, yes.

But need it? No. We do not fight for gold, my lords, but for our freedom, our homes and land. Our hatred of the usurper."

"To your credit, friend." Cospatrick smiled. "But have I not heard that you, on occasion, have found considerable treasure for your taking? Was it not from Peterborough Abbey?"

"That! That was *Norman* gold. Stolen from our churches. By that evil man Turold. We but took it back. Brought it here, for Thurstan. But then, the Danes stole it from us! Such is gold — a stone for stumbling."

"If you have gold and to spare, my lord Earl, give some small part to Holy Church here," the Abbot put in. "We have lost much through the Danish raids."

"Very well," Cospatrick agreed. "Suitable that some of Eldred's treasure should come back to the Church . . ."

And so, thus easily, it was settled. Cospatrick, Maldred and Abbot Thurstan would go back to Peakland, and bring on the Saxon host. A rendezvous was selected, in the area between March and Chatteris, using the River Nene's flood-plain as tactical field, for ten days hence — a week would probably be too soon, with the Saxons mainly on foot. The thing was worked out in fair detail, with contingency plans in case of a variety of major hitches. These two were easy men to work with.

10

MALDRED FRETTED AS he rode. He berated himself for his impatience and irritation with these slow-moving Saxons, telling himself that they could not help it, that it was not in their nature to hurry or to be amenable to discipline or even to greatly enthuse. They were friendly, cheerful and courageous, which probably should have been enough. Moreover he was assured, even by Thurstan, that it did not greatly matter that they were already a day late for the link-up with Hereward's force — which would not evaporate into the hazy marshland air. In a way, the delay might be all to the good, giving more time for the Normans to become aware of the situation and to summon reinforcements — for the whole idea was that this should be a major defeat and disaster for the invaders, with large numbers trapped; it was even hoped that all of East Anglia might thereafter be recovered and used as a base area for an expanded English uprising and campaigning, its ports available for the looked-for Scottish ship-borne army, with possibly even Danish aid — although the fenmen, understandably, were less than keen on that.

Looking behind him at the vast straggling host, spread out in groups and parties — nothing so orderly as companies — over a great area, in no least haste and almost holiday mood, Maldred wondered how effective they were going to be. Perhaps they all, leaders included, were taking too literally the suggestion that they were to be the bait rather than the trap itself? If the Normans were to descend upon them now . . .

This was their sixth day out from the Peak, a large enough force not to have to hide themselves from any or to make tactical detours — save for reasons of terrain — and so able to follow the shortest route, by Alfreton and Sherwood Forest and Grantham and Bourne. No doubt, all the way, messages would have streamed away to inform the Norman authorities of their existence, numbers and progress. But that was the intention. Thurstan and Cospatrick had in hand the screen of mounted Scots acting as scouts well ahead of the column, to give warning of any trouble.

They were nearing the chosen strategic area here, just east of March, where the sluggish Nene wound its way into the wettest marshland and there spread itself into a vast shapeless network of channels and pools and meres, and so continued, forming a corridor perhaps eight miles by three, an all but impassable maze which ended eventually in the open water around Ely itself. Hereward and Thurstan had agreed that this was the most hopeful scene for the attempt, almost midway between Peterborough and Ely. The Fens army was to be massed to the south of this barrier, threatening Peterborough from the south-east, in the Ramsey and Tick Fen vicinity; the Saxon array to approach from the north-east, in what would appear to be a joint attack on the Norman-held city. It was not in the Norman nature to wait to be assailed by the despised, conquered and rebellious English, and it could be assumed that they would choose to descend upon the advancing Saxons, on firm ground, rather than on the amphibious fenmen in their own swamps. The main project was based on this assumption, but contingency plans were made for varying eventualities.

Maldred would have preferred to ride with the scouts, but Cospatrick was anxious that one or other of them should always be in the company of Edgar and the Saxon earls, to try to make sure that any urgent messages sent back were promptly and properly attended to — no sinecure of a task. Actually Edgar and the earls now were scarcely on speaking terms. They had never loved each other, and now Edgar accused the brothers of being in Cospatrick's pocket, and only in this venture out of love of gold not of loyalty to himself. There was some truth in this, to be sure — which did not help. So the Saxon leadership rode in two companies, Edgar, Waltheof, Siward Biorn, Merleswegen and others from Scotland, with a few unfriends of the earls; and Edwin and Morkar, with old Bishop Ethelwin who had joined them, and their own ealds and thanes. Maldred tended to ride with the earls rather than with Edgar — who did not love him either.

It was in the early afternoon that Cospatrick rode back at speed to announce that the Normans had indeed issued from Peterborough in force and were heading this way roughly parallel with the course of the Nene, in the Whittlesey area. Thurstan was keeping them under observation meantime. There were about five hundred knights and cavalry and possibly two thousand spearmen and archers. Thurstan advised that the Saxon army halted meanwhile, to give time for Hereward to be informed and to bring his fenmen south-east-about by intricate routes through the marshes, with a view to a final trapping of the Normans in the Langwood and Wimblington Fens northeast of Chatteris.

There was no objection to a halt being made; but when the Earl Edwin heard that the new-suggested combat area was still some five miles off, and in the swamps, and moreover learned that the total Norman force was only about two thousand five hundred, he argued that this projected programme was ridiculous. He had nearly five thousand men and this Hereward four thousand, more than three times the Norman numbers. To suggest that nine thousand should scurry and hide and flounder about in bogs in order to achieve the destruction of two thousand five hundred was absurd, humiliating. They would choose a good tactical position, here on firm ground, where the Saxons could fight like honest men, not bog-trotters; and if they had not defeated the Normans before Hereward and his savages crawled up out of their fens, in the rear, they could finish off the task between them.

Cospatrick pointed out that the entire strategy was based on forcing the Normans to fight, out of their element and depth, *away* from firm ground, where horses and armour would be a drawback, their famed discipline nullified. Maldred reminded that the Saxons all along had been considering themselves the bait rather than the trap. But the earls insisted that the numbers situation changed all. The five thousand Saxons under their command were not going to play the partridge with the broken wing just to coax half that number of the enemy into the arms of these mud-walloping Angles. It was unthinkable.

Unfortunately Edgar, when he came up, agreed with his fellow-Saxons rather than with the Scots — not having forgiven Cospatrick over the Archbishop's gold.

Cospatrick was furiously angry, but could make no headway with the obdurate Saxons. They had had their gold and he could by no means take it back. Malcolm's fiat that he, Cospatrick, was to be in overall command did not impress the other earls, particularly with Edgar now calling himself their King and siding with them. The only faint compromise achieved was that they agreed to move forward meantime in the required direction until a better battleground was found, the present position scarcely suitable.

Maldred was sent on to inform Abbot Thurstan. He had some difficulty in finding him, not unnaturally in the circumstances; indeed he glimpsed and had to avoid two Norman scouting parties, all gleaming steel and banners, before he ran the Abbot's group to earth in thorn scrub just north of Chatteris, with the van of the enemy force just visible a couple of miles away.

Thurstan was upset by the situation. But, an eminently practical man, he adjusted quickly. Questioning Maldred closely as to the attitudes, position and direction of the Saxons, he sent messengers by different routes to inform

Hereward. Then he accompanied Maldred back to the earls' column, leaving the rest of his party to watch and report.

If the Abbot thought that he could convince the Saxons, where Cospatrick and Maldred had failed, he was disappointed. He found them, in a fairly strong position admittedly, where two streams joined — or wide drains might better describe them at this dry season with practically no flow in the water. They had protection on two sides, therefore; and on the third side of the triangle they were busy erecting a barrier of thorn-trees and stakes and willows to hold up horses. Most of the force was to remain within this redoubt, but two companies of five hundred or so were to be detached to threaten the enemy flanks. Movable gangways were being constructed to span the ditches when required for sallying out.

Cospatrick was far from happy with all this, pointing out that despite the Saxons' aggressive intentions, these represented purely defensive tactics. Also, the archery risk was being underestimated. Thurstan added that to change to the attack from here would be very difficult. Likewise, that Hereward's strategy was being wasted, made void.

All to no effect. Pride was involved now, no sound basis for military decisions.

Cospatrick, Thurstan and Maldred drew apart, to confer. Could they still rescue their plan, or some part or alternative of it? Could they even yet entice the Normans into a trap? If Hereward could move up on their left, eastwards, into Pymore Fen, then perhaps later they could prevail on the Saxon host, or some part of it, to withdraw down into that, in seeming disorder, and the Normans after them, or some of them? They must achieve some gain out of it all, somehow . . . Messengers were sent off.

Scouts reported the enemy only two miles away now, and coming directly towards them. There was no word of Hereward. The barriers were almost finished. The two flanking companies had improved their positions, defensively.

The Normans appeared in sight. They might be only half of the Saxons' numbers, but they looked a sufficiently daunting array, with the massed cavalry in front, long lines of fluttering banners and pennons, steel glittering everywhere, especially on the tips of a forest of spearheads, formation upon formation of these, massed, controlled, disciplined. The Saxons raised a great shout of challenge and defiance.

The enemy drew up less than half-a-mile away, and a small party under a white flag rode forward to within hailing distance.

"In the name of William, King of England, your liege-lord, the Lord Abbot Turold of Peterborough declares that any large gathering of armed subjects is contrary to the law and the King's express command," a colourfully-dressed herald shouted. "The Lord Abbot should take steps to break up this assembly by force. And hang such as lead it. But he is merciful, and declares that if all will disperse quietly, in companies, and return whence they have come, he will hold his hand. He will overlook the offence. In the name of King William. How say you?"

There was a roar of scorn and hate.

"What does the fool think we are? Children?" the Earl Edwin demanded. "To run at resounding words? Belly-wind!"

"Scarcely a fool, I think," Cospatrick commented. "This is to gain time. While he considers your situation. Plans his attack. Disposes his force . . ."

"Look!" Thurstan was pointing. "There is the size of his folly!" A sizeable portion of the Norman strength was moving off to its right, slantwise, eastwards. "You see — down towards the fen . . ."

"Where you want him to go, do you not?" Edgar put in. "Is not that your intent?"

"Why should he go there now, my lord Prince? *We* are not coaxing him. He must know of Hereward's force, and sends out this screen to keep us from joining him. These will not go down into the marshes, but stay on the firm ground at the edge, to keep *us* from doing so."

"At least it divides his forces, gives us even greater advantage of numbers," Morkar said.

The herald's hail came again, demanding what message to take back.

Edwin raised his voice. "Tell your insolent cleric that I, Edwin of Mercia, have come to hang him! Just as the true King of England, the Prince Edgar, here at my side, will in due course hang your bastard master, William of Normandy! Tell him . . ." The rest was lost in bellowed approval from all the Saxon rank-and-file within hearing.

The white-flag party turned to trot back.

There was little delay thereafter. Two long columns of spearmen came marching forward from the Norman front, some four hundred yards apart, four or five deep, on and on, fully a thousand strong, the greater number on the west side. When the front ranks of these came near to the Saxon barricade, they halted, and thereafter both ranks turned to face outwards in drilled fashion, there to set their spears at different heights and angles to form a lengthy, bristling frieze of sharp steel. The very orderliness and precision of this obviously practised manoeuvre was alarming to men whose battle tactics tended to be a yelling charge with sword and battle-axe.

"They are countering our flanking companies," Cospatrick declared. "Few will penetrate that fence."

No sooner were the spearmen in position than troops of horsemen rode out, some within the corridor of spears, some outside it. As these drew closer, it could be seen that each rider carried another man behind him.

"Archers!" Thurstan cried. "Now may the good Lord preserve us!"

"We are out of their range. Behind the barricade," Edwin asserted.

"From direct shooting, yes. But if they shoot into the air, dropping shots, these will reach you. I have seen it done. It all but doubles the range."

The Abbot's fears were justified. The horsemen set down their burdens before the barrier, and were then seen to be carrying extra supplies of arrows also. Swiftly the bowmen formed themselves into kneeling companies close behind the barricade of trees and stakes, where they could not themselves be shot at. Not that they need have taken such precautions, for the Saxons, like the Scots and the Norsemen, had no tradition of using archery for anything but hunting. From this protected stance they proceeded to shoot up showers of arrows at such an angle that they curved over and fell on to the heads and shoulders of the Saxon host. It was indiscriminate work, but since the targets were inevitably close-packed, lethal. Screams and yells began to proclaim casualties. Although the Saxon lords had helmets, few of their men were so equipped. Most of them had shields, but these were of the small, round, leather targe variety, useful in close swordery but less than effective for holding above the head to deflect dropping arrows.

Back and back the Saxon ranks pressed, away from that barrier — and, as inevitably, closer and closer to the two ditches or stream-sides. And promptly here too the archers moved up, protected by their flanking cavalry screens—and from across these drains they were not so distant that they might not aim directly at individual targets. The casualties mounted.

It was, of course, grievously bad for morale. It did not take long for the Saxon leadership to recognise the fact and to propose distractions, sallies, counter-attacks. The trouble was that despite all the advantages in numbers, they were hemmed in here in this so-strong defensive site. They could break out, but it would be at the cost of heavy losses. And if they did, they would be exposed to the dreaded Norman cavalry.

Presently, waiting idly for arrows to rain down on them, and worse, to be aimed at from across the ditches, with no means of hitting back, the situation became intolerable. Many were already dead and dying, more were wounded, even some of the lords — whom the marksmen beyond the drains especially aimed at. There was little point in the Scots and Thurstan saying I-told-you-so. Something had to be done, most evidently.

Any break-out had to be on one or more of three sides. To demolish and push through the barricade itself would involve desperate losses. To cross the west ditch, using gangways, might produce the fewer casualties, but would lead to little betterment. The east side was the obvious one, to make for Pymore Fen nearly a mile away. Unfortunately that would be equally obvious to the enemy; and the strong Norman detachment was already positioned and waiting to intercept such a move.

Nevertheless, it was decided to make the attempt. At Cospatrick's suggestion, a feint display at pulling down the barricade should be enacted, to distract the Normans on that side, with the men crouching low to drag at the material, so that the archers could not reach them. Meanwhile, all the gangways to be assembled, hidden in the crowd, on the east side. Then, over with all possible speed, the best armoured first.

It was probably the best that could be devised, at this stage, but it became little short of a shambles nevertheless. Not all the gangways, thrown across, held firmly on the slimy mud banks, precipitating those crossing into the stream. The water was not deep but the bed was soft silt into which men sank; and the steep slippery bank made climbing out extremely difficult. Many in the front ranks who did cross safely, fell back, pierced by close-range archery, hampering those who followed. Some of the gangways collapsed under sheer weight of numbers. With five thousand men to get across, under the hail of arrows, in no more than a minute or two the entire stream-channel became filled, jammed, choked with dead and dying, wounded and merely fallen, as more and more were pushed on from behind, a dire sight. Nevertheless, this in the end enabled the greater numbers to stream over, trampling their fallen comrades, using them as filling material. Even the massed archers could not cope with the thousands before them. And the ranked spearmen to the south, formations broken, had the river to cross before they could take part. Sheer numbers did prevail after a fashion — but at a fearful price.

Cospatrick and Maldred, with Thurstan and a little group of Scots, burdened with what was left of their treasure — for horses now had to be left behind — waited until the exodus was half-over before moving, and had to trample on bodies like the rest. Indeed they were all but trampled on themselves, when a party of young Saxon lords, escorting Edgar and the Earl Waltheof, came plunging over on horseback, careless of all beneath, cursing and being cursed.

But beyond that ghastly ditch's horrors was the true killing-ground where, past the archers, who in the end were in fact swept away by the weight of the Saxon rush, the detachment of Norman cavalry awaited them. There-after it was sheer massacre, fairly firm ground on which the armoured knights could wheel and quarter at will, swords and maces slashing, themselves all but invulnerable, their mounts protected by heavy leather trappings. There was almost a mile of this to cover before the blessed soft ground and reeds of the first fen.

That Maldred's group — or most of them — eventually made it, across that blood-soaked plain, when most did not, was largely thanks to Cospatrick — and possibly to Abbot Thurstan's prayers. The Earl demonstrated a drastic but effective method of dealing with individual horsemen, demanding a strong nerve, a quick eye and much control of muscle. The intended victim took off and held his tunic or jerkin in one hand, his dirk in the other. When the cavalryman bore down, the attacked actually ran towards the horse. Just a yard or two in front of it he flapped his tunic up under the brute's nose, at the same moment leaping aside, to whichever side was opposite the rider's sword-hand. Nine times out of ten the horse reared high on its hind legs — when the dirkman darted in with his dagger and ripped up the exposed and unprotected belly of the animal whilst the rider was seeking to adjust his seat and sword-wielding. Sometimes the horse only sidled away, when the target had to react differently but as swiftly, ducking down double and leaping off at a tangent to avoid the down-sweeping blade. Usually it worked, if messily; and if it did not, the horseman got a fright and tended to seek alternative victims.

At any rate, breathless and blood-spattered, Maldred grazed by a mace on one shoulder, Cospatrick limping from a hoof-kick, they eventually reached the haven of the wetlands and could pause and look back — with personal thankfulness but no least satisfaction. Whatever happened hereafter, it was all a major disaster by any standards. However many might survive, the Saxon army was destroyed as a fighting force, without any real battle having been fought. Men were fleeing in all directions, not all into the safety of the fens, the main force of the Norman cavalry and knights now reorganised and hunting them down efficiently. Edgar Atheling and the Earls Morkar and Waltheof were there, the first wounded, the latter, his horse killed under him, much shaken. Of Edwin of Mercia there was no sign, nor of most of his thanes and leaders.

It was while they were pantingly assessing the grim situation that a fenman, so plastered in mud as to seem barely human, found his way to Thurstan's side. He had come from Hereward, he said, and had been trying to reach them for long, but could not in the circumstances. He brought sore news. Hereward had moved northwards, as the Abbot had requested. He had reached the south end of this Pymore Fen, waiting for the Saxons to move. Then he had received the word. There was a second Norman army. Come up from the south, from the Cambridge area. Under the hated banner of Bishop Odo of Bayeux, William's fierce and notorious half-brother. It was clearly aiming at Ely itself, evidently to capture the fenmen's base.

"Odo!" Thurstan cried. "The greatest savage of them all! Bishop or none, an affront to Christ's Church . . . !"

"How many?" Cospatrick demanded.

"I do not know, lord. But the Lord Hereward thinks as many as has Abbot Turold. And all horsed."

"Come from Essex," Thurstan amplified. "William has given Odo Kent for earldom and Essex to govern. What now, then?"

"Hereward has gone back to Ely. Says you, my lords, should find your way there. To him. Through the fens. You my lord Abbot will know ways. As do I."

They eyed each other bleakly. Join Hereward in Ely? What else was there to do? If they could. Save as many as they might. For the moment . . .

Hereward at least knew how to fight.

* * *

Somehow the reeling, exhausted remnants of the Saxon host found their way to Ely, by devious, secret and wearisome paths and no paths, covering round-about miles to gain a furlong — and once there found little to their comfort. Bishop Odo had the place all but surrounded — that is, his forces had occupied all the half-moon of firmish land bordering on the belt of open water on west and south, for Ely was in fact completely islanded. And to add to the menace, a fleet of shallow-draught boats, laden with armed men, had come from the north-east, the Wash area, using one or more of the Ouse channels from salt water, some twenty miles. Indeed the refugees from Pymore Fen were only just in time; the motley collection of small craft which Hereward sent to ferry them over the final half-mile of water would have been intercepted an hour later.

Hereward could offer the newcomers little cheer. Odo was actually building a causeway out across the water, of thorn and willow branches, scrub, turfs, anything which came to hand. The water was shallow, even though muddy beneath, and the belt only about five hundred yards wide where he had chosen to build. He had plenty of men for his task. If they continued to work by night — it was sundown now — the chances were that it would be completed by next forenoon. A simultaneous attack, then, along the causeway and by boat at a number of points

175

around the perimeter, and nothing could prevent a landing. He, Hereward, had not sufficient men to beat back any concentrated assault, especially when Odo's army was reinforced by Turold's force. He foresaw Ely being occupied before very many hours had elapsed.

His hearers listened, angry and depressed — Edgar, Waltheof, Merleswegen, Siward Biorn, Bishop Ethelwin and one or two others besides Cospatrick's group. Edwin was not there — indeed there was a story that survivors had actually seen the Earl being struck down by his own men, during the later shambles at Pymore, presumably blamed for that debacle. None, not even Cospatrick, had suggestions to make to deal hopefully with the situation — other than to ensure that they sold their lives dearly.

Hereward declared, then, that he had not defied the Conqueror for all these months by hanging on in hopeless entrenched positions. He was going to move out, before it was too late, before dawn indeed. His fenmen would melt away into their marshes, to reassemble in due course somewhere else. There were sufficient boats available around the Ely island to carry away most of those who might wish to flee. But they would have to go in ones and twos, to infiltrate in the darkness. No mass exodus would get through.

There was little enthusiasm for this course, much disagreement. Many of the Saxons declared that they were not going to scuttle off again like water-rats, into the unknown fens. They had had enough of fleeing cravenly. They would fight here, where they had at least some advantage, fight and die if need be, repelling the invaders. Also many were wounded and in poor state to face hurried and hazardous journeying in boats. Presenting a strong front, if they repulsed the first assault, they might well win not unfavourable terms from the Normans — so said Morkar, and most concurred.

Hereward was adamant. They could do as they would. *He* was for off. Already they had caused him much trouble and loss. And he advised against any bargaining with Odo, who would renege on any terms.

Thurstan agreed with his friend, and advised flight. He himself must remain with his abbey here, his simple duty before God.

Cospatrick, brows raised towards Maldred, nodded.

Hereward had the rights of it, he maintained. This was a campaign, not one battle. They must save what they could, to fight another day in better circumstances. The Scots would accept Hereward's offer to get them out of Ely as quickly as possible.

Surprisingly perhaps, Edgar, who was not good at making up his mind, came to a decision and threw in his lot with Cospatrick without being asked. No doubt the security of far-away Scotland beckoned him, however much he might deplore the company he must keep to get there. None of the Saxons sought to dissuade him.

So it was settled. Hereward reserved a few boats for his own use and then sent word that his people should disperse as best they could, in small numbers, to reassemble when they could, in the Wisbech area to the north. He, and those who wished to accompany him, would move off at midnight.

In the end, only Bartoloméo Leslie, the Hungarian, Merleswegen and the Thane Archil, chose to accompany Edgar, with the dozen or so surviving Scots. Farewells were brief, and save with Thurstan, with few regrets on either side. Defeat and disaster make for simplification of relationships.

Hereward led his little string of boats out on to the dark waters soon after the abbey bells had tolled twelve. Torches were glowing along the line of the building causeway, and campfires by the score gleamed all along the western shore. No doubt many of the Norman seaborne crews had landed by now to east and south, but in darkness on strange ground these were unlikely to mount any attack until daylight.

Hereward held close inshore for a while, waiting until he calculated that he was opposite a waterway to the north through Burnt Fen, actually one of the many channels of the Great Ouse. A quiet but steady row across half-a-mile of water brought them to this without challenge — or so their guides assured the visitors, for these could make out little or nothing in the gloom.

A little way up what was presumably the Ouse, however, they ran into trouble when the leading craft was suddenly confronted by a line of boats stretched across the river, only a few yards ahead. Hereward, as the shouts rang out, waved up his other craft on either side of him and drove straight in at the barrier, standing in the bows, sword swinging and yelling his own slogan. In a few hectic and confused moments of slashing and rocking and flailing, they cut their way through — for the barrier was only one boat thick — and rowed on little the worse. Hereward declared that here was something the Normans did *not* know how to do. Had the enemy boats been linked together by ropes, and held broadside on, and double-ranked, it would have been very difficult to get through. They had probably been alerted by previous escapers from Ely using these Ouse channels.

After that there were no further incidents, as they crept and crawled their way through the maze of nightbound waterways, reaches and channels which constituted the River Ouse's ultimate approach to salt water. Moving almost due north now, dawn did not seem greatly to expedite their progress for white mists now rose from the marshlands, to no improvement. Nevertheless, when at last the sun rose and dispersed the mists, Hereward assured that they had made good progress. This was St. Mary Magdalen Fen near Watlington, and they had covered some twenty-five miles — perhaps sixteen as the crow flew. This was all part of his own unconquered terrain and there was little chance of them being pursued now.

They rested and refreshed themselves at the village of Wiggenhall, where Hereward was received as a hero even if the others were eyed with suspicion. Quite a number of his men from Ely were already here. He was leading them, he told his passengers, as he left all but one of the accompanying boats there, to the port of Lynn, where they ought to be able to find a deep-sea fishing-vessel to put them at least some of the way back to Scotland. They would have to go carefully, for Lynn was probably where the Norman boat-fleet had started from — although it was not normally in Norman hands — and they might have left some of their people there. He would go on ahead and do what he could to find them a ship. But such would cost money. However, that was the one thing that they had sufficient of, was it not?

Hereward was as good as his word, and presently he came back to escort them into Lynn's west shore, where, with no sign of Normans about, he presented the fugitives to a surly East Anglian skipper, two-thirds Dane, who would take them as far north as Whitby Eskmouth, no further — for a price. They did not haggle, even though Cospatrick grumbled that they were not *buying* the ugly, smelly craft, only hiring it.

Gratefully they said goodbye to Hereward, telling him that he was the finest Englishman they had encountered, and wishing that there were more like him. Wishing him well in his warfare, they pressed on him a substantial contribution from their treasure, declaring that it could not be in better hands. Even so, that man was doubtful about accepting. He seemed to have a suspicion of gold, a rare affliction.

He was going back to continue the struggle, he said — and the travellers felt somehow shamed as they waved him farewell from the smack's deck.

They put to sea almost immediately.

11

MALCOLM CANMORE DID not like failures, and made the fact sufficiently clear as he stamped up and down his hall-floor at Dunfermline, glaring at the three returned travellers before him.

"I tell you, the Saxons' weakness and folly are no excuse for your own," he berated them. "You knew what to expect. You, Cospatrick, I set in command. You, Edgar, claim their obedience. You both knew my wishes, my *orders*. As did you, Maldred. Yet you allowed prideful half-wits and wilful dullards to over-rule you. To the ruination of all."

"I protest!" Edgar rose at the table. "I will not be spoken to so. Like some scullion . . . !"

"Sit down, man. Back to the board from which you are fed! Under this my roof in which you and yours are housed. Have you any other? Board or roof? Then think well before you lose these! In this realm I speak as I will — and do more than speak." He turned. "You grin, Cospatrick — you grin! I could make you grin much otherwise — and *should*, by God!"

"No doubt, Highness. I but relish your humour — you who speak so loud here, but scarce so-loud in Saxon-land! They scarce hear you, there, I fear. Even the prince, here, had difficulty in making his voice heard. Those Saxons have deaf ears and a loud pride. Have you ever tried to lead a Saxon army, cousin?"

"From all I hear *none* led the Saxons. They were like the swine in Holy Writ."

Maldred blinked at that. To hear Malcolm quoting Holy Writ was new. So much for marriage.

"I am no swineherd," Cospatrick observed. "But we carried out your commands as best we could, lacking your royal presence. Which *might* have worked miracles! And if it had been a Scots fleet and host which sailed to Lynn and Ely instead of a Norman one, all might have been otherwise."

The King eyed him levelly. "No such Scots fleet was to be sent before I had word of some success."

"I sent word of the gold. And we have seen no sign of any fleet, any number of ships, assembled here in the Scottish Sea or the Firth. I fear that you were not anticipating that word of success!"

Malcolm switched his attack. "With the gold and siller you gained from that archbishop — who is now dead, I learn — you ought to have been able to buy half the men in England, man!"

"Men gold will buy — but not wits, leadership, in their masters."

"Who got the moneys?"

"Many. But chiefly the Earl Edwin, now slain. And his brother Morkar."

"And what is left?"

"That." Cospatrick whipped a single gold crucifix on a chain out from within his tunic and tossed it over the table in front of the King. "It will serve for your lady-wife, the Queen, perhaps." He spoke casually, but his glance caught Maldred's in the by-going, with its message.

That young man swallowed. Was his silence being bought? Blatantly? A contribution to the Queen's cause, which he had made so much his own. And in return he was not to reveal that he knew that there was a great deal more treasure left than that. Edgar would not know of it, never having been informed of the extent of the hoard. Cospatrick, it seemed, was aiming to keep the gold.

Malcolm picked up the handsome crucifix, shrugged, and set it down on the table again. "She shall have it, when she returns. And no doubt will thank you. A pity that there was not more." But that was as casually said. To do him justice, the King had never been greatly concerned with money and material wealth.

Maldred did not speak.

"It was Saxon gold. Given for the Saxon cause," Edgar mentioned — and was ignored.

"Tell me of this battle. Of Ely?" Malcolm said. "How it went. The Norman's methods for victory."

"It was no battle, cousin. The Normans used their forces skilfully, yes. But the Saxons defeated themselves. Would not heed us. That was at this Pymore Fen. A slaughter. Later, what happened at Ely itself, after Hereward won some of us clear, we know not . . ."

"*I* know. Morkar, your brother Waltheof, and the other fools attempted a fight of sorts. Then yielded to the man Odo, the Bastard's bastard brother. On terms. Whereafter, he hanged some of them and sent the others marching in chains, at horses' tails, to William at Winchester!"

"In chains? Hanged? Who? Which? Do you know?"

"Morkar and Waltheof, the earls — that I know. In the chains. Siward Biorn. Even Bishop Ethelwin — another churchman . . ."

"Ethelwin! The good Ethelwin!" Edgar wrung his hands.

"Waltheof would rather have died, I say, than walk in chains," Cospatrick said harshly.

"And Thurstan? The Abbot Thurstan?" Maldred demanded.

"I know not. No abbot was named to me. I had the word through a ship-master two days back. Into Dysart. From the Humber. Who travelled more quickly than you, it seems."

"We were much delayed. Had no little difficulty," Edgar said. "At the hands of rogues and scoundrels."

"Your Saxon subjects!" Malcolm observed unkindly.

"So that is Odo of Bayeux!" Cospatrick exclaimed. "Chief Justice of England! My foolish brother! At least they were warned. Hereward told them how it would be. I urged Wattie to come with us . . ."

"These are weak men. They will talk," the King interrupted, almost accusingly. "When William questions, they will talk — nothing surer. They will tell him of *you*, Cospatrick. And the Scots part in this mismanagement folly. So — we may look for trouble, in due course. From William. He will not forget it."

"Are you blaming that on me?"

"If it had been a victory, you would have taken the credit, would you not?"

The cousins stared at each other.

"So I am to be the scapegoat? I will not thole it, Malcolm, I tell you — I will not thole it!"

"You will thole whatever I put upon you, cousin. You are one of my earls, now. Remember it, always. And now — begone. All of you. Out of my presence. God help me, I have sufficient to trouble me . . . !"

Thankfully Maldred made his escape.

He discovered that the Queen was not presently at Dunfermline. She was, in fact, at Malcolm's summer palace, the Ward of the Stormounth, up between Gowrie and Atholl. She was pregnant, now six months gone, it seemed; and the palace gossip was that since she would no longer allow the King to lie with her, he found it more tolerable to have her out of his sight. So he had sent her to the Ward for the interim. Another version was that he had found himself to be so badly in need of a rest from religious devotions and family piety that some such device had been essential. Also he could no longer stand the presence of the Princesses Agatha and Christina, and all had been packed off. Magda, of course, had gone with them.

Maldred, next morning, sought permission to go visit the Queen, and received curt dispensation.

*   *   *

The Ward of the Stormounth was a pleasant smiling place, even for almost November — for it was as late as that in the year, the fugitives from Ely having taken over a month to win their way back to Scotland. The Ward, just over thirty miles due north of Dunfermline, as the crow flies, was almost twenty more by the shortest road Maldred could ride, round the Cleish Hills, past Loch Leven, through the Ochils, across Tay at St. John's Town of Perth, and up to the junction of Tay and Isla thereafter, into the fair land of the Stormounth, which comprised the foothill country of the Highland Line between Blair-in-Gowrie and Dunkeld. Maldred covered it in seven hours of hard riding however, thankful to be off on his own, free of difficult companions, outwith the oppressive atmosphere of Malcolm's palace — and feminine company ahead. Occasionally he sang as he rode, albeit tunelessly.

The sight of the great rock-and-heather mountains ahead of him always gave him a lift of the heart, anyway — he was, after all, an Athollman and these were the hills of home to him. They drew him on now, blue slashed with deep purple shadow, above the russets and sepias of the autumn woodlands. The Ward was set amongst those coloured woodlands, on the crest of a grassy ridge of the rolling foothills to the west of the Loch of Clunie. Although called a palace it was nothing of the sort, no more than one more extensive hall-house, with clustered outbuildings, set like so many another within the circular turf-and-stone ramparts of an early Pictish fort. The Picts had always an eye for a fine site, with scenic as well as defensive advantages, for they were an artistic people with a great sense of beauty and form. This site was particularly lovely, not grand or impressive but gentle, sylvan, retired, really now a hunting-lodge in the lap of the mountains yet not difficult of access, lying between Dunsinane and Dunkeld.

The sun was sinking behind the forested Birnam hills to the west when Maldred rode up and into the courtyard. He was hardly dismounted, and shouting for a groom, when Margaret herself came running out to greet him, Queen, pregnant or none, laughing, calling out, arms wide. And she was heart-breakingly lovely, despite her prominent belly, flushed, sparkling-eyed, the picture of health, like some harvest-goddess indeed, rather than any demure Bride of Christ.

"Maldred — my good and dear Maldred!" she cried, clasping him to her and kissing him on one cheek and then the other. "You are safe back. Thank God! It has been long, long. Oh, it is good to see you. We feared for you — for you all."

Somewhat overwhelmed, and very aware of that belly pressing against him, he made incoherent noises and stirred a little within her grasp. He was, after all, in only his twentieth year and had never before been embraced by another man's pregnant wife, much less that of his dread monarch — greatly as he admired the embracer.

Perhaps she perceived his slight embarrassment. She drew back, but still held him, at arm's length now, to examine him frankly.

"Are you well?" she demanded. "You look more thin — as *I* do not! But . . . none so ill. I praise the dear Lord." She recollected. "And Edgar? Is my brother well? Returned also?"

"Well," he nodded. "Scarce content, but well enough."

"You were not successful, then?"

"No. Leastways, not in the main. In the prince's business, it was a sore disappointment. But . . . in other matters we did none so ill." He turned to his horse, which a groom was now beginning to lead away, and from the saddlebag extracted an obviously heavy leather satchel. He held it out to her. "You laid a mission upon me, lady. Here is the result. See — you will require both hands, for it is weighty."

"Maldred — you did not forget! Oh, my dear, I thank you. So good, so kind." She tried to open the bag but could not, finding that it took her all her strength to hold it. She set it down on the courtyard cobblestones then found that she could not stoop to open it because of her great stomach.

Smiling, he opened it for her.

Margaret gasped, her eyes widening at what she saw. For moments she could not find words. With trembling fingers she picked out the large gold-and-ruby cross which lay on top. Speechless, she held it out between them.

"That will ransom many Saxon slaves," he said. "It came, like much of the rest, from the Archbishop Eldred. With his blessing. Many others gave also."

She flung her arms around him again, and actually shed a tear or two, so moved was she.

This time it was the sight of the Princess Agatha, watching them disapprovingly from the hall-house doorway, which made the man release himself.

Margaret cared nothing. "Mother — I am so happy," she exclaimed. "See — look what Maldred has brought me. From the good Archbishop. And other kind friends. For my slaves. All this. See this splendid crucifix . . ."

Her mother came over, to take the extended cross, her brows clearing. She had a healthy judgement in matters of this sort.

"This is quite magnificent," she pronounced. "Far too good for ransom-money. You must keep this, Margaret. Is there more as fine as this?"

"Maldred did not bring this treasure for *me*, Mother. He besought it, on my behalf, for our Saxon people in distress. Besides, I do not need it. I have the Black Rood. More than sufficient."

"Nevertheless, child, this is not for handing over to hucksters or whoever will pay the most. It is a superb symbol of our Blessed Lord's sacrifice . . ."

"Our Blessed Lord sacrificed Himself, His very life, for the poor and needy, did He not? Shall *I* hold back gold and rubies, in His name?" That was no question but a stated decision, and sufficiently queenly. She took back the crucifix and returned it to the bag. "Bring it all within, Maldred and we shall see what there is. And I thank Almighty God, and all who enabled you to bring it . . ."

It was not long before Maldred asked for Magdalen, since she was nowhere to be seen.

"She has gone on an errand for me," the Queen said. "There is an aged hermit, one of your Keledei from Dunkeld they say, who dwells in a cave in the hills to the north. Custodian of a sacred well, the water a specific against blindness. Or so it is claimed . . ."

"The blindness of superstition!" her mother interjected.

"No doubt. But the common folk here believe it. And some waters do have healing qualities. There is a child in the village going blind. She is a poor sorry thing, crippled from birth also — but with a quick mind. Her mother, a widow, believes that this water will save her sight. It may be folly, but she longs for it. The child is too weakly to travel to the well. They think that if I, the Queen, send to this hermit, he will send some of the water to her, with his blessing. It seems that he will not leave the well. I cannot now ride far in my present state. So Magda has gone, with a message from me to the holy man. I had expected her back before this."

"Where is this cave and well? She has not gone alone?"

"No. One of the men here, a shepherd, has gone with her. The place is some miles into the hills. Across a waste called Gormack . . ."

"I know it, the Muir of Gormack. I have hunted there,

from Dunkeld. A wild place. This side of the Lornty's glen."

"That is the name, the Lornty Burn. The hermit lives there, beyond this valley. Near some dykes or walls, they say . . ."

"The Buzzart Dykes. It is a deer-dyke. As they have at Kincardine. The King Kenneth MacAlpine, who built this hunting-palace, made it. For driving the deer. It is a sunk-fence, very long, and angled. Once the deer are driven in behind it, they cannot leap out again. More readily hunted."

"No doubt. That is where this cave and well are. I had thought that Magda would have been back by this. It is dusk now." The candles being lit in the hall set all the treasure gleaming and glittering. There was just the hint of anxiety in Margaret's voice.

"She will be well enough," the Princess Agatha said. "That Magdalen is well able to look after herself."

"Yes. And she has this shepherd with her. But I do not like to think of her out there, in the darkening hills . . ."

Neither did Maldred. As he ate the meal put before him, and the evening grew darker, with the girl still not back, he grew the more concerned — as clearly did the Queen. At length he could stand it no longer.

"I am going to look for her," he announced.

"But — will that serve anything, Maldred?" Margaret asked. "In the darkness. How can you hope to find her, at night?"

"Foolishness," her mother agreed. "If she, with a guide, cannot find her way here, how shall you find *her*?"

"It is not more than five miles to the Buzzart Dykes, I think. Less probably. You say that she went well before noon? Even with the Muir of Gormack to cross she should have been there in less than two hours. The same back. Something is wrong."

"What can you do, Maldred?"

"I know the country. Not closely, but well enough to find my way. There is a half-moon rising. I shall take some man from the village. Take torches. And horns to blow. In only five miles, we should find her. Better than sitting here, idle."

Margaret nodded, only wishing that she might go with him.

In these conditions horses would be only a handicap.

Torches and hunting-horns were readily provided. Maldred could have had half-a-dozen falconers or foresters, but saw little advantage in numbers and the organising they would entail. He collected one of the royal foresters, a middle-aged man, Donald by name, who knew the hills well, and set off without further delay.

There was a horned moon and little cloud, so that once their eyes accustomed themselves, it was less dark than it seemed at first. They did not light the torches yet, recognising that this would injure their night vision. There was only the one road to go, a little to the west of north, by a track up through the foothills to the villagers' summer pastures in the Braes of Logie. No one could have got lost here, surely. They climbed steadily, Maldred questioning his companion's local knowledge. The man agreed that if there was anywhere between here and the Buzzart Dykes where anyone might go astray, it was while crossing the Muir of Gormack. But even there, the track over to the Lornty was clear, and marked with cairns of stones. The shepherd with the lady knew it like the palm of his hand. So where were they? There were wolves in these hills, to be sure — but it was much too early in the winter for these to be of any danger to humans.

As far as the sheilings, up on the western spine of the moor, the route remained perfectly clear, even in semi-darkness, for up here the people cut their peats and dragged them down by pony-sled on a well-defined track. The two men had blown their horns at intervals, and then waited, listening for any answering call. After the peat-cuttings however, although there were many paths across the slanting waste, cattle, sheep, deer and human, these were apt to be a confusion. The true path northwards to the Lornty valley was marked with heaps of stones at intervals, these to project through winter snows and mark the way. They were not so effective in the darkness.

Nevertheless, winding their horns as they went, the pair found no real difficulty in following the track, downwards now over the long slope to the Lornty, a full mile of it. They crossed the stream, almost a river but shallow here, by stepping-stones alongside a ford.

The Buzzart deer-dyke came down to the Lornty on the other side, climbing for half-a-mile northwards thereafter before making a right-angled turn eastwards to run for many miles, a quite major construction. It was part of this

Donald's duty to help keep it in repair, so he knew all the vicinity notably well, and exactly the position of St. Ethernan's Well and the hermit's cave — which proved to be about a quarter-mile up from the river and under a little escarpment of rocky outcrops. There was an ancient stone-circle nearby also, so that it seemed likely that, as so frequently, the original Celtic saint had only taken over some holy well of the Druids.

As the standing stones loomed up, a voice, surprisingly robust, hailed them before ever they reached the cave-mouth, demanding to know who, in the name of the Blessed Ethernan, walked the hills at this ill hour, forby making the night hideous with horn-blowing? The forester called back that it was Donald from Cluniemore, with the Lord Maldred of Atholl, come seeking the Sassunach lady.

The hermit proved to be a sturdy, almost burly character who smelled strongly, and scarcely the frail old recluse the Queen had imagined. He declared that the fair young Sassunach female had indeed been there, some hours ago, with the new Queen's message and offering, and had duly obtained her flagon of the precious water, additionally blessed by himself, for the unfortunate child — although he stressed that he did not really approve of this sort of second-hand, long-range use of the water's healing qualities, which ought to be applied by himself personally. This Donald, or others, could have carried the child to him, in a litter if need be, in Christian charity, instead of involving the English Queen and her lady. And more to that effect.

Maldred, whilst agreeing that this was no doubt so, pointed out that the Queen was kind-hearted and much addicted to good works. However, the point was that the Lady Magdalen had not returned to the palace, and the Queen's Highness had become anxious. They had been blowing the horns to try to attract attention, on the way here, in case she was lost. But without result. When had she left? Was all well with her then?

The Friend of God did not seem too greatly concerned. The young female, who had appeared to be as sensible and rational as such were ever likely to be, had gone off about the third hour after noon, or a little later, with the shepherd Moirdach. They had taken two other poor sufferers with them, to assist them on their way, cripples who had limped here to wash themselves in the sacred waters — for the holy Ethernan's well was effective, in God's providence, for more than blindness. Indeed these two pilgrims were sitting on the young female's garron and herself walking.

"They went burdened with two cripples, then?" Maldred exclaimed. "This could have made some difference. After three in the afternoon? They would go much more slowly. But — not so long a delay in only five miles, surely? And we would have passed them . . ."

"Where were these pilgrims bound?" the man Donald asked.

"They were from Blair-in-Gowrie, they said. And were making for Kinloch of Drumellie, this night."

"Drumellie — that is some miles east of Clunie," Maldred pointed out. "Is it possible — could she have taken them there? Gone on to Drumellie, and from there returned to the Ward, along the Blair road?"

"Who knows what Sassunach females might elect to do?" the hermit asked.

"It would be a charitable act . . ."

They left, with a blessing of a sort, torches lit now for possibly wandered folk to see.

Across the Lornty they climbed the long slope towards the spine of the Muir of Gormack again, their flaring, smoky torches actually making it more difficult to see. Maldred, leading, was following a wrong track when the other called him back.

"Wrong track?" he wondered. "But, see — there are cairns along it."

"Cairns yes, lord. But it is the track to Drumellie, not Clunie. The roads part here."

"Ha! Then, if they did think to take these cripples further on their way, this is the track they would go?"

"Yes. But we do not know that they did, whatever."

"No. But it is a thing that Magda, this lady, might do. Since we saw no signs of them on the Clunie track. I say that we should follow this track now. See if there are any traces. How long would it have taken them to get to this Kinloch of Drumellie? From here?"

"It is some three miles. As it is by the other, to Clunie."

"An hour, no more. Even so they should have been back to the Ward by the time we left. Nevertheless, we should try this new track . . ."

"Lord, is it wise? If they went to Kinloch, the lady may be back now. If so, will not the Queen's Highness send out a messenger to inform you? Such would come by this *Clunie* track. If we take the other, we would miss him. Then it is *you* who would seem to be lost! More men sent to search . . ."

"M'mm." Maldred saw the point of that. They decided, therefore, that one should go some way along each track meantime, looking for signs. Their torches should at least help for close inspection. If one found a clear indication he should blow three quick blasts on the horn. If not, after half-a-mile perhaps, they should both return to the track-junction.

Maldred chose the Kinloch path, as the more hopeful. Unfortunately there had been no rain for a day or two and there were few suitably muddy patches, the granite grit not showing up footprints, not in the smoky torchlight at any rate. Then, presently, round a bend, was sufficient evidence — a pile of horse-droppings, fresh, only hours old. He was reaching for his horn when, plain from the north-west, wailed three unmistakable blasts.

At something of a loss, he paused. It would be absurd to both start hooting at each other. When the three notes sounded again, he decided to go to see what Donald had discovered.

It was, in fact, a more significant find than his own, where an apron of surface-water had made a wet area on the path — the imprints of a woman's shoes, too small to be a man's. Facing south-west, towards Clunie, and recently-made, the possibility of them being other than Magda's was remote for women did not frequent the moor at such time of the year, and anyway, the local women usually went barefoot.

So what did it mean? With dung on the other track? And only the woman's footprints here? They must have separated. Magda must have sent the pilgrims on direct to Kinloch, on the garron, with the shepherd, and herself chosen to walk the three miles back to the Ward alone. And presumably somehow got lost.

What to do now, then? They had come this way, and seen nothing — not that they had been able to see any distance in the darkness. So clearly she must have strayed off the path. But where, when, why?

As darkness fell, they concluded, she must have

followed by mistake one of the deer or cattle trails which criss-crossed the main track, and then been unable to find her way back. They decided therefore to split up, and to move parallel well above and below the main track. Maldred chose the lower side. Magda was no fool, however unused to such terrain, and would surely realise that climbing uphill was unlikely to aid her. Although there was the possibility that she might likewise realise that the lower ground was more apt to be boggy and difficult going. The slantwise moor was about three miles wide here, so there was plenty of room to get lost.

They parted, after searching another wet apron of track and finding no footprints. They had their second torches lit now, and blew their horns regularly. If anyone *was* sent from the Ward to intercept them, they ought to see the lights or hear the noise.

Quickly Maldred found the going becoming very much more difficult, even though he tried to stick to animal-tracks, winding and uncertain as these were. Tripping and stumbling he pushed on, blowing, listening and hearing Donald's horn growing ever fainter. Was he being a fool, he wondered? This seemed a quite profitless venture, highly unlikely to achieve anything but discomfort and humiliation . . .

He was blowing one of his blasts, and consequently not looking down at his feet, when he tripped over a heather-clump into a peat-hole and fell all his length into black slime. Cursing explosively, he was struggling to rise when he stopped, both the rising and the cursing. Had he heard something? A call? A high-pitched, thin calling? Not a curlew . . .

Listening, he heard it again, faintly but distinctly now, coming from some distance down on his left, still lower ground, a woman's cry.

"Magda!" he yelled. "Magda!" And thereafter, he was up and running, actually running, stumbling inevitably but caring nothing for peat-mud or clutching heather or outcrops, last torch left flaring on the ground. Every now and again he panted out a shout, and gained an answering call to aid his direction.

He came to her, where she sat on an ancient whitening skeleton of bog-pine root, a throat-catchingly lonely figure in the desolation. She started up as she saw him, but sat back again quickly.

"Thank God!" she called. "Oh, I am sorry. A fool! My ankle. I lost myself. My ankle . . ."

"Magda!" he bellowed. "Magda, lass! Saints be praised, I've found you!"

"Maldred? Dear Lord — can it be . . . ? Is it . . . is it . . . ? Oh, Maldred, my dearest, my beloved, my heart's darling!" And ankle or none she was on her feet again and limping towards him, to fling herself into his arms, gulping incoherences.

Fiercely he took her, to clutch her tightly to him, kissing her brow, her hair, her eyes, her lips, in an ecstasy of joy, love, relief.

Laughing chokingly, she clung to him.

* * *

The first outburst of emotion over, but still holding on to each other as though afraid that they might somehow be parted again, they panted out words and phrases and half-formed questions and explanations and wonder and delight — frequently interrupting to kiss again, to stroke each other, to pat or just to grin joyously in the pale moonlight. Magda's was the major surprise, of course, for she had not known even that he was back from the English war, and his appearance out of the night in this wild and lonely place, to her deliverance, was like a miracle. But he had his own surprise singing within him — surprise at the sudden and blinding clarification of his understanding and emotions, as at her frank, spontaneous and enthusiastic response to his kissing and embracing. Nevertheless, he felt disinclined to possibly precipitate any return to normal and conventional behaviour by any injudicious comment on the subject. It might be only relief, excitement, a temporary reaction, on her part at least.

"Your ankle?" he said, instead. "You are hurt, Magda?"

"Yes. I fell . . . Oh, I have been a fool. I must have strayed from the road, the track. As it got dark. I did not realise it at first. But when I did, I turned back. But must have taken the wrong path. Hurrying, when I realised that I was lost in this wilderness, I fell over some stone in the heather. Turned my ankle. So I could not walk. I tried to limp, with the aid of a stick I found. But could not . . ."

"My dear, my dear. You would be afraid. Frightened. And in pain . . ."

"Not really afraid. More angry with myself. I was not frightened — until I heard a sort of howling. In the distance. I feared that it might be wolves. I realise now that it was your horn, only — such a witless dolt!"

"No! No — do not say it. Lost, and in pain . . . See." He pointed to a large heather-bed nearby. "There — you must sit. No — I shall carry you." It was an excellent opportunity to gather her up in his arms. She was a well-made creature and no light-weight. So he panted a little as he strode with her. "You must sit . . . rest . . . no more trying to . . . walk."

"Dear Maldred!" she said.

Sitting in the heather, his arm about her, she alean against him, they talked — but scarcely listened, so preoccupied were they both with each the other, their sheer physical presence and proximity. He explained that he knew of her errand for the healing water, that he had been as far as the hermit, knew of the crippled pilgrims and her sending of them on on her garron. She asked about his activities in England and when he had got back. But answering her in some measure, he was much more aware of the disturbing rise and fall of her swelling bosom under his arm and against his side; and when his hand somehow came to rest on that conveniently projecting shelf, she did not appear to notice — or at least did not push it away.

Gradually they fell silent.

It was the man who spoke, at length, his voice different, a little husky. "You are happy, Magda?"

"Yes."

He digested that, turned it this way and that, and decided that it was satisfactory, even encouraging, especially as she had not stirred in his arms, save for the pleasing rhythmic motion of her breathing.

"You are . . . content?" he pressed.

"Content, Maldred? No — I scarce think that is the word I would use."

"What I mean is . . . we are here . . . just you and I. None other. It does not displease you?"

"Should it? After all, you have come to my rescue, found me. Should I not be pleased, be grateful?"

"It is not gratitude I want."

"What, then?"

"You, yourself."

She said nothing.

"We kissed each other."

"Yes."

"Was that . . . gratitude?"

"Who knows? It might have been."

"You named me your beloved, your, your heart's darling."

"Did I . . . ?"

"Yes." His breath came out almost in a snort. "That is what you said. I would have an honest answer out of you!"

"This of question and answer. Is it . . . necessary?"

"Yes it is. I want to know where I stand."

"I thought that you, Maldred mac Melmore, were a man of deeds. Rather than words!"

"Deeds? What do you mean — deeds?"

"I mean, have done with all these words and questions. My dear, you kissed me roundly enough before, without talk! Should you not put it to the test again — and discover your answers, honestly? Like a, a good knight . . ."

She got no further words enunciated for some time.

But he was back to his words again, presently, if somewhat breathlessly. "Does this mean . . . that you care for me? Love me? Would be mine? Mine only . . . ?"

"Dear Mary Mother — must it be I who make the avowals? When you, when *you* have always mooned after Margaret Atheling, doting calf-eyed!"

"Me? Margaret — the Queen? Not so. How can you say it? Nothing of the sort. I admire her, yes. Esteem her greatly. And find her . . . kind. But that is all."

"I wonder. For she is beautiful, much more beautiful than am I. And notably attractive to men. And clever. Moreover she is fond of you . . ."

"And you? You are all these things, and more. *You* are beautiful. And fine. And strong. And good — but not *too* good, I think! You it is I love . . ."

"So! You have said it, at last! I despaired that ever you would . . ."

"Save us — why do you think I came searching for you, here? Near out of my wits!"

"Margaret might have sent you."

He actually shook her. Then he recollected belatedly. "The forester! The man Donald," he exclaimed. "He will still be searching for you. Up on the higher ground . . ."

He moved her — but only a little, not so drastically that

he could not retain his arm round her — to blow loudly on his horn, three short blasts and again three. They listened, but heard no response.

"He could be far away. Beyond hearing. Perhaps I should go back up to the track? Call him from there."

"Why so eager? Let him be. We are very well here, are we not?"

"How think you I am going to get you back to the Ward? We need him to go and bring back a garron. If he does not come, I shall have to go my own self . . ."

"No. You will not. You will not leave me now. We can bide here, very well. Keep each other warm."

"But . . . Margaret? The Queen. She will be anxious."

"For you? Or for me?" But she smiled as she said it. "She will survive the night. As shall we."

"Your ankle? Does it not pain you greatly?"

"Not when I do not move it."

"You must not get cold."

"I shall not — if you hold me sufficiently close."

"To be sure . . ."

Nevertheless, he blew on his horn again. And after the third attempt they heard a faint but distinct reply. Thereafter with regular blowings, he guided the forester down across the slanting moorland to them. Presently they saw the red gleam of his torch.

"At least we shall have a fire to warm us, while he is gone," Maldred said. "This old bog-pine burns fiercely. Full of pitch."

"I am none so ill as we are," she assured him.

Donald arrived, part congratulating, part commiserating. He helped Maldred gather a collection of bog-pine roots and splinters, with some dry old heather-stems for tinder, and they lit a fire from his torch, before he departed again for the Ward.

Thereafter, they reckoned, they had about two hours to wait — and envisaged no weariness or boredom in the interim. They did not actually tell the man not to hurry back, but Maldred urged that he should be very careful in his selection of a suitable garron to carry the sufferer home, a notably canny beast required, and not to rush his choice. Two hours, after all, was not a great deal for all the necessary private concerns they had to cope with.

Keeping that fire going developed into something of a distraction.

12

THEY CHOSE TO have a Yuletide wedding. It was not all
natural and healthy impatience. The Queen's lying-in was
due for late January, and Magda, as principal lady-in-
waiting, was expected to be involved. For Maldred, too, an
early marriage was advisable, since the nation was on
continuous alert militarily, and few expected the coming
spring campaigning season to be a peaceful one. King
William was over in Normandy at the moment, teaching
his eldest son, Duke Robert Roundlegs, a lesson in
keeping his place, with his usual heavy hand; but he was
expected back in England before long — and he was
reported as having sworn to teach the Scots a lesson
likewise when he returned. So all men who could bear
arms were under notice to hold themselves in readiness
for war, the leadership ranks in especial.

So the wedding was held, in the midst of the now much
muted Yuletide celebrations, on Holy Innocents' Day —
which the wags found entirely suitable — 28th December.
Maldred would have liked the ceremony to be performed
quietly at his old home of Dunkeld, and Magda in agreement. But the Queen saw it otherwise. The union of her
two true friends must be no hole-in-corner affair, she
insisted — and she was certainly going to be present
personally; after her return to Dunfermline at the end of
November, there was to be no more riding the country for
her until after her delivery. So Dunfermline must be the
venue, the abbey where she and Malcolm had been wed.
She herself would see to all — since Magdalen had no
kinsfolk in Scotland to arrange and pay for what was
necessary. She, Margaret, might be handicapped physically meantime, but certainly was not otherwise. This
would give her something absorbing to attend to, during
the last weary weeks of waiting for her time. Magda
confided in her husband-to-be that this was the Queen's
way of purging her conscience over her initial resentment
at the couple's announcement of betrothal — which

Maldred had scarcely been aware of in his elation but which the young woman declared had been entirely evident although sternly swallowed. Be that as it might, most of the preparations were taken out of their hands, with all the expense. It was to be no quiet wedding therefore, with all the Court attending, the celebrant again to be Bishop Fothad of St. Andrews, the Chancellor, assisted by the Benedictine Oswald — since Malcolm would by no means have the monk Turgot back.

In the presence of the King and Queen and a large and distinguished company, they were joined together, Magda looking quite lovely in a lively, spirited way, with little hint of the blushing and demure bride. Prince Edgar, in theory her monarch, took her father's place, if less than enthusiastically, and Madach acted groomsman, with Kerald assisting the Bishop. Their father, the Primate, graced the occasion but did not officiate. Once again the Romish addition was longer and much more high-flown than the main Celtic service; but with the bride nominally of that persuasion this fell to be accepted.

Thereafter the banquet was almost as lavish as had been the royal one, the entertainment judicious, and once again the populace were well provided for, indoors this time in the abbey domestic premises. Also the poor, the crippled and the freed slaves fed, with the Queen herself going to serve them, taking the bride and groom with her. Malcolm perforce paid for all; and if he did not appear the soul of mirth and hospitality personally, at least he did not deliberately prevent others from enjoying themselves — save in the one respect, for the royal command now was that drinking should be in moderation only, the King himself showing an extraordinary abstinence compared with former days, however painful a process he appeared to find it. There were grumbles, naturally. Surely a wedding, his nobles and guests complained, was no occasion for this excessive holiness? Also, to be sure, there was none of the traditional and much-appreciated bridal-bedding ritual and high jinks, wherein the happy pair were publicly disrobed, the groom by the women guests, his partner by the men, amidst much practical advice and admonition, and thrown on to the nuptial bed together, there to demonstrate their fitness and aptitudes for the married state. Margaret would not hear of anything of the sort — and for this the couple were not ungrateful, however disappointed their friends. To ensure that no enterprise of a more private nature was perpetrated, Maldred had arranged that they should slip away during the waiting on the poor folk, and ride to Kerald's abbey at Culross six miles off, for the first night. The Celtic Church authorities were not difficult about such things. Thereafter they would go to the house and property of Bothargask, which was to have been Maldred's inheritance on coming of full age but which his father had presented to him now as wedding-present. Bothargask was in the Stormounth, not so far west of the Ward, and had been his mother's dowry.

It took them two days to reach that pleasant place, in the difficult, flood-water winter conditions; but they were in no hurry any more, all they saw and experienced holding a new significance for them. At Bothargask, a smiling house of moderate size set on a shelf of the birchwoods above Botharstone Loch, they settled in to the magic, intriguing, timeless business of learning more about each other, all about each other. The weather was consistently bad, cold, with gales, driving rain-squalls and sleet. But they cared nothing, more than content with what they had, blazing fires, a sufficiency of food and drink, a discreet housekeeper and her woodman husband, who kept largely out-of-sight — and themselves. To make love on skin rugs before an aromatic birch-log fire, listening to the distant howling of the wolves, the whine of the wind round the house and the blatter of rain, was something never to be forgotten.

With both hands and full hearts they grasped their happiness and felicity.

All too soon it was time to return to Dunfermline. The Queen expected to be delivered about the Feast of Candlemas and it was felt advisable for Magda to be available at least two weeks earlier.

They were back only just in time. The child came early, after a short but fierce labour — which Margaret bore a lot better than did her husband, who stamped the palace like a man distracted, and all but throttled a servant who was so injudicious as to grin in the royal presence. He had not behaved like this at Ingebiorg's two deliveries. An hour after midnight, on the Eve of St. Agnes, a lusty squalling boy was born — and by the hour of Lauds thereafter, Margaret was giving thanks in divine service at her bedside, attended by her mother, brother, sister and Magda. But not the happy father, who was quite drunk, for the first time for months. When the monk Oswald finished, the Queen announced that the child would be named Edward — although Malcolm had talked about calling him after himself if it was a boy. It would be the first time that a Scottish prince had borne a Saxon name.

Bells rang that day in every abbey, monastery and church possessing such, which the royal command could reach in time.

Margaret made a notably swift recovery, the child throve and the King doted on both in his rough and abrupt fashion. He was for ever taking the infant up out of its cradle and marching around the house with it, showing it to all he encountered, behaving like any youthful father with a first-born — which, considering he had the two princes, Donald and Duncan, bestowed away out of sight with his half-brother Donald Ban in remote Mamlorn, and had fathered innumerable bastards up and down the land, was unexpected to say the least. Margaret herself, although the fond mother, was entirely sensible about the matter, and indeed not infrequently requested the monarch to leave the child alone, in less than subservient tones.

Malcolm declared that this was the son who should one day succeed to his throne — a statement which raised eyebrows and caused sundry wise heads to shake.

Margaret, however, was not above making good and effective use of her curious husband's post-natal euphoria, as had many a wife before her. She impressed on him that thanksgiving should be practical as well as verbal, outgoing not self-centred. God had been markedly good to them, and there was much that they ought to do to demonstrate their gratitude in the way of thank-offerings. For instance, there was the matter of the Saxon slaves. Thanks to Maldred's efforts, she had been able to purchase the freedom of a great many. But there were as many more still held captive. It was surely unsuitable that with a Saxon queen and a half-Saxon prince, Scotland should hold Saxons as bondmen, like dumb beasts? Could he, the King, not decree their freedom from slavery, at least? If they could not be sent home, let them remain as honest servants, freed men?

Malcolm promised to think about it.

More far-reaching, if less expensive, a suggestion concerned some reform in religious matters and observances, she pressed. The Columban Church was strong in some ways, sincere, with certain virtues. But it was inadequate for its task, mistaken in some respects, gravely erring in others. Detached from the rest of Christendom, it had ceased to grow and burgeon, like a branch torn from a great tree. It required to be grafted on anew — or in time it would wither and die. To Scotland's sore hurt and Almighty God's grief.

The King, who had little interest in the subject, found it easier to accede that this might possibly be so. But what could be done about it?

A conference, she declared. A great council of churchmen. And others. The Keledei in especial. To discuss the entire issue. To debate what reforms could and should be made, to establish the eternal verities, standards, excellencies. Malcolm was doubtful but did not say her nay. And that was sufficient for Margaret Atheling.

Maldred was quickly drawn into the business. He must help the Queen to arrange such a council. It should be held during Lent, before Easter — for the mistiming of Easter was one of the major errors of the Scots Church. It would be best if the assembly was called by the Primate rather than the King. Maldred must get his father to allow the summons to be sent out in his name. Supported by Bishop Fothad's. All abbots and bishops invited to attend, with representatives of the Keledei and priesthood. They would hold it here at Dunfermline, in the eating-hall of St. Ternan's — she called it the refectory.

Maldred was as doubtful as was Malcolm, more so probably. Where was the need, he wondered? The Church was none so ill. It could look after its own affairs, surely? Would the churchmen come, indeed?

They would come, she asserted confidently. Especially if the Earl Melmore asked them. The Church, reformed, could be endowed with broad lands.

*   *   *

The first Council of Dunfermline was held on St. Duthac's Day, 8th March 1072, well-attended as Margaret had prophesied. Earl Melmore of Atholl opened the proceedings formally in the presence of the King and Queen, but

Bishop Fothad presided. There were some dozen abbots attending, twice that number of bishops — for in the monastic Celtic Church abbots were the senior, some having as many as half-a-dozen bishops under them — although the bishops performed certain sacramental rites which the abbots did not. There were some thirty senior Keledei and an equal number of priests and monks of various categories. The Keledei or Friends of God were a special order within the Church, in theory more strict, more learned, more authoritative in matters of doctrine. Many of the abbots and bishops were of that order. As well as the clergy there were a few secular folk present, but apart from Margaret, only three women — her mother, sister and Magda. The Athelings' confessor, Oswald, sat behind the Queen, for consultation if need be. Oddly enough, Cospatrick of Dunbar had elected to attend, little of a churchman as he was.

After a brief prayer for God's guidance on their deliberations, Fothad the Chancellor made an opening speech explaining something of the reasons and need for this conference, and the benefits which could accrue to their land and people from certain reforms and adjustments in their ancient Church, even possible amendment of mistaken doctrines. He added that last rather hurriedly, and sat down.

All waited, then, for a fine-looking man of middle years, who sat inconspicuously amongst the others, dressed in the simple black robe with leather belt worn by all the Celtic clergy irrespective of position — the Abbot Dunchad of Iona, St. Columba's successor and true leader of the Church, as senior abbot, even though not the Primate. He had arrived only that morning, having had a long way to travel; but without him the council would have been to little effect.

"My friend," he said, deep-voiced. "It is right and proper that our humble and unworthy part of Christ's Body the Church should recognise its sins, shortcomings and backslidings. Likewise seek to improve itself in God's service. To this end, I say, all here ought to be agreed. But you speak of reforms and mistaken doctrines. Will you enlighten us on whether we are here to acknowledge failures in practice or to debate alleged mistaken doctrines? There is, you will agree, a distinct difference."

"I suggest both, Brother Dunchad," the Bishop

answered carefully. "We should not limit ourselves, I think, in this council."

"To be sure. But that implies that there *are* mistaken doctrines, Brother Fothad. Doctrines common to us all, not only to individuals who may personally err. If that is your contention, we ought to know where you conceive these mistakes and errors to lie. It is a grave matter to accept that our Church is mistaken in its doctrines. I am only a humble and ignorant servant of the Church, and know not of these errors. But I am prepared to receive instruction."

There was a noticeable pause, with Fothad understandably hesitant. He was suddenly in a very difficult position, thus early. Although St. Andrews was the most prominent bishopric, as it was the wealthiest, and he was the Chancellor of the realm, he was in no position to instruct his senior, the Abbot of Iona, in doctrine or anything else — except perhaps finance — as all there realised very well. He coughed.

"The alleged errors are . . . various," he said, rather feebly. And glanced over at the Queen.

"So there are a number of them? Which we in our frailty have missed? Now, in God's providence, and in the fullness of time, revealed? To *you*, Brother?"

Holy mirth was discreetly manifested.

"There is the matter of Lent. And of Easter, Brother Dunchad, on which we differ from the rest of Christendom. For a start."

"Differ from the Romish communion, my friend," the Abbot reminded gently. "Which is *not* the rest of Christendom. Have you forgot the great Eastern Church in all its many branches? But . . . how are we mistaken in the observance of Lent?"

"It is suggested that we have always calculated the time of it awry."

"Who suggests it, friend? You? Only now? After you have been bishop for a score of years?"

Unhappily Fothad looked again at the Queen.

Margaret was only too eager to come to his rescue. She leaned forward in her throne-like chair. "My lord Abbot," she said. "If I said that *I* suggested it, that would be but vanity, presumptuousness, unsuitable in a mere woman. But when I remind you that a thousand bishops and archbishops of Holy Church assert it, led by the Holy Father,

St. Peter's successor in Rome, himself, then the matter calls for some consideration, does it not?" She spoke simply, clearly, modestly.

Dunchad bowed towards her. "Highness — you are right to remind us whence come these assertions of error. Rome we all respect. But do not seek slavishly to emulate."

"Not even when Rome is demonstrably right, my lord?"

"Lady — of your forbearance, lord is a title we in our Church reserve only for One. In matters secular it is different. The Primate here, is the lord Earl or Mormaor. But as Abbot of Dunkeld he is but our brother in Christ. Forgive us, of your charity, *our* little foibles and distinctions. But . . . you said *demonstrably* right, Highness?"

"Yes, Abbot Dunchad — and I regret my error over the honorific. I do applaud your distinction in that respect. As to Lent. It is a simple calculation, is it not? Lent is the forty days fast of Our Lord. You commence your Lent, not on Ash Wednesday as do others, but on the Monday after the following Sunday?"

"From that Monday to Easter Sunday is forty days, is it not?"

"Forty days, less six Sundays. Which are not fast-days, never fast-days. So you fast only thirty-four days."

'Did Our Lord's forty days in the wilderness not include Sundays? Or Sabbaths, lady?"

"Perhaps. But the injunction put upon us as Christians, by the holy apostles, is to fast *forty* days. Your Church fails in that."

"Is Almighty God so concerned with such calculations, Highness?"

"He has given us, made in His own image, the wits to calculate *aright*, Abbot. If we are going to obey the injunction to fast forty days, we should surely do it accurately."

"As I see it, the issue is unimportant, depending upon whether forty days' fasting means a period of six weeks less two days, or forty different and distinct days, not necessarily consecutive. Scarcely a sufficient issue to divide Christendom!"

"So say I, Abbot Dunchad — so say I! Not sufficient. But since it is you, the small Columban Church, which calculates differently from all the rest, for the sake of the unity of Christ's Body, should you not accept the alteration?"

"If that was all that divided us, I might say yes, lady. But — how say others?"

Most there clearly esteemed the matter of too little importance to argue over.

"The next issue I have noted," Bishop Fothad announced, "is that of the Holy Eucharist on Easter Sunday. It is our custom not to celebrate it on that day. As a sign of our penitence. Acknowledgement that we are all guilty of the shameful death of our risen Lord. The Queen considers this in error . . ."

"It is not the *Queen*, Bishop Fothad, who so considers. But all the rest of Holy Church," Margaret intervened strongly. "Of all days to commemorate Christ's Body and blood, surely the festival of the Resurrection is the greatest?"

"Is that not a matter of judgement?" another abbot asked, Gillibride of Restenneth, a dark, intense-seeming youngish man. "If we judge Good Friday the most grievous day in the Church's year, with the greatest weight of blood-guiltiness upon us all, should all be forgotten two days later? Should not our shame and repentance at least cause us to deny ourselves the benefits of the sacrament the following Sunday?"

"If that Sunday, sir, is the most joyous of the year, the celebration of mankind's hope and certainty of everlasting life, the resurrection from the dead, should not of all days this be the most worthy of participation? Abstain the Sunday before, if you will. But not on Easter Day."

"Can any true sense of guilt be so swiftly banished, lady? If it is a real abasement on the Friday can it be so completely gone by Sunday? And, if not, recollect what the blessed apostle enjoined. 'He that eateth and drinketh unworthily, eateth and drinketh damnation unto himself.'"

"What, then? Shall all who are sinners refuse to partake of the holy mysteries? Always? For that is where your reasoning leads, sir — since we are always utterly unworthy. Or would you have advised Almighty God to retain Our Saviour longer in the tomb, if three days does not suffice you?" She paused, on a sudden intake of breath, and gazing about her, shook her lovely head. "Oh, I am sorry!"she exclaimed. "I should not have said such a thing. God forgive me! And you, sir. My foolish tongue outran me. It often does. I crave the pardon of all."

Everywhere men cried out. But it was not condemnation nor offence. Quite the reverse. Abruptly, she had almost all that assembly, whatever they thought of her theology, approving of her heartily. By that one spontaneous, so-human apology, so utterly unexpected in a queen, she gained more than all the arguments of doctrine or conviction. Women might have been less affected, but there were only three other women present, and they were mere spectators, on her side anyway. Even the Abbot of Iona was moved to reassure her.

"Never fear, Highness — it was none so ill said. Such talk is no doubt good for our souls, at times! And you may be right, in the wider issue — this of Easter communion. We shall consider it . . ."

But even all this acclaim and goodwill did not suffice to make her next point acceptable — for now all there recognised that, whatever the nominal authority and whoever presided, this was Queen Margaret's conference, called at her instigation. Bishop Fothad announced the subject of communion in both kinds, Bread and Wine — and immediately there was a stir of concern, a stiffening of the ranks. Sensing it, Margaret advisedly held her tongue meantime.

"This is an old story," Abbot Dunchad said. "We know that the Romish Church proffers only the Bread to the faithful, with only the priest sipping the Wine. Why this should be I have never learned. It seems unreasonable, even somewhat arrogant. The good Lord said 'This is my Blood. Drink ye all of it.' He did not say '. . . only the Body to the people, the Blood to you, the apostles'. But . . . there is a Romish priest present." He turned to look at Oswald the Benedictine. "Perhaps he will explain it to us?" Undoubtedly the Abbot was seeking to spare the Queen in what he conceived to be a lost cause.

Embarrassed, the Saxon monk rose, after a glance at Margaret. Obviously he had not expected to have to speak. In somewhat bull-like and jerky fashion he did his best.

"It is the teaching of Holy Church," he began. And then, perhaps realising that might sound a shade dogmatic in present circumstances, added, "The Holy See has always instructed that the Whole Person of Christ is contained in the consecrated Bread. The Blood is naturally contained *within* the body, is it not?"

"Then why did Our Lord bless the Wine also? And say again 'Drink ye all of this'?"

"The priest *does* bless the Wine also. And sips of it. But it is not essential to give to the people."

"So then, Sir Priest, there is a distinction? Between celebrant and people? Two sorts. Discrimination. The one worthy to receive Christ's Blood, the others not?"

"No, it is not that. I do not say that. But it is . . . convenient thus. Since all good is contained in the Bread, the Body. It *prevents* discrimination indeed, not fosters it. Between rich and poor, between great and small. To provide wine for all would cost poor churches dear. Holy Church can use its treasure to better ends . . ."

"Then this question is not one of doctrine at all, but only of convenience?" Abbot Gillibride interrupted. "Of . . . an economy, a frugality?"

Oswald moistened his lips. "Not so. The Doctrine is that the consecrated Bread is enough, sufficient."

"You are inconsistent, friend."

The Benedictine shook his head, less than happy. "There is added benefit in this," he plunged on. "No sickness nor plague may be transmitted from the chalice. No evilly-disposed person can hurt the many by poisoning the cup, as has been done . . ."

A sort of groan went up from the assembly. Cospatrick actually hooted. Margaret stirred restlessly. That would have been better left unsaid.

Abbot Dunchad spoke gently. "I see no reason here why we should alter our rite and custom. Is God's good love not sufficient to protect faithful participants from poison or plague? We thank Him that we have had no such here, forby. And our treasure, although very modest, will suffice to continue to purchase the wine — even the best wine, from Italy!" He smiled faintly.

Margaret lacked nothing in practicality, and knew when to adjust her stance. "This, I think, is a case where the unity of Christ's Church should be the principal guide," she said. "I pray you to consider it in that light."

They left it at that.

There were two more points at issue — Sunday work and marriage within prohibited degrees. The Queen, much aware of the poor showing over the last matter, moved in strongly over what she described as the Celtic Church's failure to preserve the sanctity of the Seventh Day as a day of rest and worship only. She pointed out that in Scotland, after only divine service in the morning, the folk were free to spend their time as they would, and apt to treat the day as one for amusement, great eating and even drinking and work — different perhaps from the earning of the daily bread, but still labour of a sort. Did not all Scripture enjoin otherwise? Rest and worship only?

A Keledei bishop spoke up. Was not the Queen in danger of confusing her authorities here? Confusing the Old and New Testaments? The Jews were enjoined to keep the Sabbath, the Seventh Day, as a day of rest, in the Old Testament. The Saturday, indeed, not the Sunday. But here they were not Jews. Christ's injunction was different, for worship rather than rest. Worship could be other than only divine service. Such should always be held, and attended, on the Lord's Day. But not *all* the day. The human frame and mind were not normally capable of such constraint — even priests and monks. So worship could become mere repetition, form, not substance, if over-prolonged. Better the briefer and more effective worship. And some joy instead of the daily toil, thereafter. The Church, with joy its true message, could be insufficiently joyful.

Margaret conceded much of that. But asserted that a deal of the so-called joy on Sunday, after service, was no more than licence, much trading and huckstering and immorality went on, defiling a day which had started with the Holy Eucharist. Could any deny it?

Actually she was partly supported in this instance by Abbot Dunchad and others of the Keledei who had been long concerned at the progressive erosion of the Lord's Day. It was generally agreed that some improvement was called for.

The last of the Queen's charges, for this session, concerning marriage, she was less certain about — but the monk Turgot of Durham had impressed upon her how obnoxious to God's will was the union for instance of step-mother and step-son, or of a man and his brother's widow, as allowed by the Columban Church. She merely stated this assertion, without arguing the case. There was some inconclusive discussion. But she did not pursue the issue, partly lacking any great conviction, partly because King Malcolm, who had not opened his mouth throughout, was growing distinctly restive. When she whispered to him that it might be enough for one day, he was on his feet the next moment — and so perforce was everyone else.

Later, and the next day, the clergy would meet again, in private, to debate the points raised, and report thereafter on any decisions reached.

As they filed out after the royal couple, Cospatrick spoke to Maldred. "That young woman will have us all kissing the Pope's toe before she is done! Malcolm is as clay in her hands. That old fool Fothad likewise. It even seems that she may win over the man from Iona. We will have to watch her, lad, or she will bring down this realm!"

"Scarcely that!" Maldred protested. "She could change much, yes. But it could be for the better."

"If she destroys ancient tradition, changes ways of thought, she could do great harm. I am no clerk — but the Church is guardian of much. She is making a strong play for the Church — for her own ends."

"She has her methods. I say that she seems to be playing *against* the Church, rather."

"In time, yes. But not now. She will seek to draw that Dunchad into her net, you will see. One way or another, with him, and with Fothad — aye, and with that father of yours — she will have the Church as she has the realm, with Malcolm. You will see. She will have Dunchad — if she can."

Maldred was not greatly concerned by all this. But he began to take Cospatrick more seriously when, presently, Margaret sent for him and asked him to go tell the Abbot Dunchad that she would be glad if he would come and see her hereafter. She wished to discuss with him how she and Malcolm might assist in the restoration and rehabilitation of the Abbey of Iona, burned and badly damaged in Viking raids a few years before.

After the private assembly next day, Bishop Fothad came to report. The council had reached the following conclusions. It was recommended that Lent would in future commence on Ash Wednesday. The Eucharist could be celebrated and dispensed on Easter Sundays at the discretion of individual bishops. Communion would continue to be administered in both kinds. Strong steps would be taken to improve the keeping of the Lord's Day. And a further conference would consider more fully the question of marriage between degrees of relationship.

Margaret Atheling praised Almighty God.

13

LONG-FEARED AND prepared-for as it had been, Norman William's assault took Scotland by surprise. Word had barely reached them, in late April, that the Conqueror had returned from France, before reports began to flood in of fleets heading north from the Wash, the Humber, the Tees, even the Thames, concentrations of ships which had been known about but which had been alleged to be assembled for reinforcement of an enlarged French campaign against King Philip. Almost the entire Norman army, of four thousand mounted knights alone, with unnumbered spearmen and archers, was being moved up, accounts said, directly from the Channel ports, having come over from Normandy, by sea and land, with no breathing-space between campaigns.

Cospatrick, who had been given the Dunbar and March earldoms specifically to take responsibility for the initial defence of the Border marches, was despatched at once to organise a first line of opposition to any land-based invasion — and Maldred, who now seemed to have become established as his lieutenant, was sent with him. They left hurriedly, at the same time as the Queen and infant prince, with Magda, the Athelings and much of the Court, were packing up to head north for Dunsinane in Fortrenn. Dunfermline, almost on the shore of the Scottish Sea, could be vulnerable, a target for any sea-borne assault. Malcolm did not like Dunsinane because it had been MacBeth's seat — but it was certainly a much stronger position.

The newly-weds had had four months together.

Cospatrick and Maldred found the Borderland alive with rumours. There was talk of armies assembling all over the English North. Most seemed to be heading for the Tyne's mouth area, whether to embark in one or other of the aforementioned fleets, or to concentrate for a march on the Tweed crossings, was not clear. But one host was said to be hastening up from the Welsh marches, through Cumbria, not so far swinging across country to the east; so it·looked as though the assault was to be made on both sides of the land — if credence was to be given to these reports. What would be the reaction of the Orkney earls, and Galloway, to such a west-coast advance, remained to be seen. Cospatrick was much less than his usual confident self. Nor did Maldred perceive any cause for optimism.

Nevertheless, they set to work with all speed and endeavour to mobilise and position the maximum manpower of Tweeddale, Teviotdale, Jed, Rule and Ale Waters, Lauderdale, Ettrick and Yarrow, Gala Water and the rest, a large area in and around the skirts of the vast Ettrick Forest. Most of this Maldred had to cover, with local assistance, for Cospatrick himself was dealing with the more populous country of the fertile Merse, where larger numbers could be raised and handled much more swiftly.

So they were separated for four days, during which Maldred was responsible for sending a steady stream of hard-riding, hard-bitten Border dalesmen, reivers and fighters, some of the toughest horsemen in the land, down to Cospatrick in the Merse — a useful contribution.

Thereby, however, he missed such action as this peculiar campaign produced. For on the fifth day, at Ersildoune in Lauderdale, a courier from the Earl reached him, recalling him immediately, with all haste and with whatever company he had at hand. He got back the score or so of miles to Birgham-on-Tweed in the Merse, at almost exactly the same time as messengers from the King arrived from the north — to find the crisis over for the moment. A Northumbrian host under Earl Waldeve had come up by the Till valley and made a concerted attack on the three Tweed fords of Coldstream, Wark and Carham. The first two Cospatrick had driven back without too much difficulty, but the third assault had won across in strength at Carham, and the enemy had only been halted and then driven back likewise after hard fighting, with heavy losses on both sides. Waldeve had withdrawn up the Till valley again, presumably to lick his wounds and await reinforcements.

Cospatrick, who was no tame waiter-on-events, was planning to cross Tweed in turn and go teach Waldeve a lesson, before he could recover — after all, he had personal scores to settle with that character to whom the Norman had handed over *his* Northumbria. But Malcolm's messengers put a stop to that. Cospatrick was to return northwards at once, to join the King at Abernethy-on-Tay.

Despite the Earl's curses, there was no doubt about the situation. All or any hostilities were to cease, forthwith. William himself was now on Scots soil behind them, and in overwhelming strength, armies landed on the Forth, Tay, Clyde and Mearns coasts, possibly elsewhere also. Any unified resistance was impossible, pointless. Malcolm was seeking negotiations with the invader, and had been left in no doubt that such would not be considered unless there was an immediate cession of hostilities in the interim.

Frustrated, alarmed, suspicious, scarcely even believing it all, they had no option but to obey. They did not disperse the Border array, however, but left it guarding the fords of Tweed under local commanders. Then they turned their horses' heads for Fortrenn, with only some two-score men as escort.

Hostilities might have ceased, but much of Lothian seemed to be on fire as they skirted its lovely plain on their northward journey.

At the Stirling crossing of Forth they found the vital bridge and causeway under strong Norman guard. Indeed, they had much difficulty in being allowed to proceed, the haughty knight in command arrogantly hostile. The Earl Cospatrick's name and repute did not advantage them, and in fact it was only the private passing over of a handsome jewelled clasp, part of the Archbishop's treasure, that opened the way for them — although even so they went on with a convoy of Norman cavalry. Cospatrick confided to Maldred that most of these Norman knights, although so proud and lofty-seeming, were in fact nothing more than adventurers, often of quite humble origin, and little more than robbers at heart. Even some of the men now boasting English earldoms had started out as ordinary horsed bandits. The breed could seldom resist gold.

They rode on through the green Ochil passes to Glen Farg and the opening vale of the Tay. It proved to be as well that they had their Norman escort now, for almost every strategic position they came to was occupied by invading troops, who were obviously well-informed as to Scots geography, and who were in strength sufficiently to hold up even quite large hosts. There was no doubt that King William knew the business of war.

Emerging on to the Tay plain near the confluence of the Earn, where MacBeth had fought his great battle with Waldeve's father Earl Siward the Strong, it was as though battle was again imminent. The entire riparian level was an armed camp — or rather two, with the winding River Earn dividing them, Scots to the west, English to the east, endless lines of waiting men and horses, pavilions, tents, camp-fires, colourful banners, and everywhere the glint of sun on steel. How many thousands filled that plain there was no calculating; but it was very apparent that there were far more English than Scots. Also that the former were in strength on the north side of Tay likewise; while the estuary itself was full of their shipping. Since there had been enemy forces all the way north, and there were no doubt more up Strathearn westwards, as their Norman escort asserted, the hopelessness of the Scots position was all too evident.

Malcolm's instructions had been to come to him at Abernethy, a couple of miles to the east; but their Norman knight conducted the newcomers down the side of the River Farg to near its junction with the Earn, this in turn only a mile or so to the latter's confluence with great Tay. Here, at the farmstead of Culfargie, Malcolm was based, with the Earls of Fife, Angus, Lennox and other leaders. Cospatrick's and Maldred's arrival produced no notable elation in a gloomy and humiliated company.

It transpired that Malcolm, High King of Scots, was actually waiting here, on his own Scots soil, for permission to approach William the Bastard of Normandy at Abernethy, and that permission was being withheld until he could produce Edgar Atheling with him before the Conqueror. Edgar had gone to Dunsinane with Margaret and the others. Until he came, no appearance could be made, no terms discussed.

"What terms, man!" Cospatrick demanded bluntly. "He

has you in his grip. You are in no position to seek *any* terms. Nor is William the man to grant any. Instead of waiting here, on his pleasure, you should surely be cutting your way back through these English to the west, into the Highland mountains? Where William could not follow you, not with his heavy chivalry. Even with a small company you could hold out in the hills for long."

"Fool! Think you I have not considered that? He could blockade me into those mountains — as his ships are blockading my seaboard now. I would be like a treed cat, an outlaw in my own land! I have a wife and child to think of. Better to make what terms I can. Get him away out of my realm, whatever the cost — since he cannot bide here for long, with so much else to hold down, the Saxons, the Welsh, the Irish, the Cornish, even his own Normandy and French possessions. Get him away — and then we shall see how his terms will hold!"

"You will have to pay dear to get that one away, cousin!"

"Perhaps. But all the cost may never be paid. Invaders often swallow more than their bellies can digest!"

Soon after this Edgar was brought in, from Dunsinane, looking highly alarmed and protesting strongly. And with him, unexpectedly, came his sister the Queen.

Malcolm was upset, concerned — especially when Margaret insisted that she should accompany them to the interview with William. At least she had left the infant prince back at Dunsinane.

The King put on the best display possible for his humiliating meeting, taking with him a large and high-born company, decked out in their finest, under a score of banners, played on by a dozen pipers. Edgar Atheling went most reluctantly — and Margaret was moved to remind her husband that whatever transpired, Edgar was still his guest, with responsibility remaining for his well-being.

They had to ride through the seemingly endless English camp, objects of much interest but little respect from the soldiery, with some hooting and jeering. The Conqueror had taken over the ancient Abbey of St. Brigit of Abernethy for his quarters, summarily ejecting the monks. All around that pleasant place on its shelf of the green slope of the Ochil foothills, with its pencil-shaped round tower, small church, spreading monastic buildings and related township, was now the special encampment of the thousands of Norman knights, William's main and dreaded arbitrament of war, the scourge of Christendom, their magnificent horses tethered in long, regular lines, their armour stacked in gleaming piles crowned by painted shields, their pennons, flags and emblems a colourful riot, the abbey furnishings fuelling their camp-fires. In the midst of these the Scots had to wait, at the abbey gates, until William deigned to allow them entry — which was some considerable time — Malcolm fuming, Margaret calmly urging patience. The ignominy of it all was made worse for the monarch, undoubtedly by the Norman's deliberate choice, in that this Abernethy had been the ancient capital of the Picts, taken over by Kenneth MacAlpine of the Scots, Malcolm's own ancestor.

At length the ranked spearmen at the gates received orders to permit the Scots to enter the monastic precincts. They were ordered to dismount, however, and flanked by soldiers like any file of prisoners, they were marched in — although deliberately they dawdled.

Outside the abbot's house they found a group of Norman notables awaiting them, these proffering no greetings. With their short hair, clean-shaven chins, chain-mail tunics and colourful linen surcoats, they were very distinct in appearance from both the Scots and Saxons.

"William is not there," Cospatrick murmured, at Malcolm's back. He and Edgar Atheling were the only ones present who had seen the Conqueror before.

"There is one of his bastard brothers, Count Robert of Mortain," Edgar amplified. "A scoundrel!"

"Are not they all?" Malcolm said. He raised his voice. "I am Malcolm of Scotland. We have come to see William of Normandy, calling himself King of England. Acquaint him of our royal presence."

"He is well enough acquaint, never fear, sirrah!" the Count Robert, a stocky, grim-looking individual with a cast in one eye, returned gruffly. "Since he summoned you — Malcolm, calling yourself King of Scotland! My brother will come when he is ready. He is, I think, having his hair trimmed. As others might emulate!"

There was laughter from the assembled Normans.

Malcolm glared. He was about to reply, angrily, when Margaret touched his wrist.

"You must be the Count Robert?" she called, easily,

pleasantly. "Since I do not think that you are the Bishop Odo of Bayeux."

The Norman barked a laugh of a sort. "No, Christ be praised — I am not Odo!" He pointed a finger. "Who is this woman?"

"I am Margaret. Wife to the King. However unworthy."

"So! And sister to *him*!" The finger changed direction, to jab towards Edgar. "The trouble-maker."

"The undoubted heir of King Edmund and King Edward, sir, nevertheless," she amended quietly. "That you will not deny?"

"God's Blood — heir of hairy poltroons, fumblers . . . !" the other was exclaiming, when a stir behind him turned all heads. Another man of almost exactly similar build and appearance, save that he had no eye-cast and he wore a gold circlet round his crop-haired brows, had emerged from the abbot's lodging and was eyeing all keenly. The Normans all bowed, even Count Robert ducking his bullet-head.

The Scots remained silent, unmoving.

"The King Malcolm whom you sent for, Sire," Robert said, in a different tone. "And the Lady Margaret, his queen."

"Ah." William came down the two steps. He scarcely glanced at Malcolm, his keen, narrow eyes on Margaret. A man of forty-five years, he was well-known to be much interested in women. "We are unexpectedly honoured, cousin," he said. Their cousinship was very distant; he had indeed been Edward the Confessor's cousin, hence his claim to the English throne.

Margaret bowed, but left the first speaking to her husband.

Malcolm spoke heavily. "If you are William of Normandy, then I would ask why you are on Scottish soil lacking my invitation or permission, sir?"

The other did not so much as glance in his direction. "To what are we indebted for this . . . felicity, lady?" he went on, conversationally, his voice unexpectedly light, very different from his brother's. "Do not tell me that my poor presence so prevailed upon you? Intrigued you, perhaps?"

"Why yes, my lord Duke. How could it be otherwise? Your renown is great."

"My lord *King*!" William corrected gently.

215

"How may *I* call you King, my lord, in the presence of my own brother, the rightful King of England? Would that be sisterly?"

"It would be *wise*!" he said briefly.

"You must forgive my lack of wisdom, my lord — as much else, I fear."

"We shall see what we can forgive you, lady." He emphasised that 'you'. "Since I admire fair women greatly — am but clay, indeed, in their soft hands!" Then abruptly he swung on Malcolm. "But I am less forgiving towards rebels, bond-breakers, robbers and mischief-makers!" he added.

Malcolm was not quick of speech, but he did his best. "Should you come to my realm of Scotland seeking such?" he demanded. "Any rebels *you* have you would require to seek in Normandy, I think?"

"In Normandy, in England, in Wales, in Ireland, I seek out and punish rebels. As Lord Paramount of Scotland, I have come to do the same here."

"Lord Paramount? What is that, sir? I know of no such title. I am *Ard Righ*, High King of Scots. And save God Almighty, there is none higher."

"Then you are ignorant. As any child could tell you. Ask your lady, here. Always the Kings of England have been Lords Paramount of Scotland. You know it. Your own great-grandsire, Malcolm the Second, swore fealty and duty to my predecessor, King Canute of England, forty years ago."

"Not so. Malcolm, of honoured memory, made fealty only for lands he held in England, Canute's England. Another usurper. No more than that. Myself, I would be prepared to do the same. As I would expect *you* to do, sir — if so be it you held any lands in Scotland."

"I can hold all Scotland! You are an obdurate man, wilfully blind. But if you will not accept the assured truth, you must needs accept the hard fact that has brought you here today. I hold your realm in the palm of this my hand. And can do as I will with it."

"As to that, by armed invasion you may presently hold a part of Fortrenn. But this is only a small corner of my kingdom. Near to your ships. You will not find the rest easy to take. Still less to hold."

"You think so? I have forty thousand men into Scotland. I can double that, if need be. How then?"

Even Malcolm Canmore's breath caught at those figures. Never had such numbers of armed men been heard of in Scotland. For the moment he was speechless.

The Count Robert laughed. "Be not so gentle, brother!" he urged. "Teach him the price of rebellion. And the other two, likewise."

"To be sure. Edward Atheling and Cospatrick of Bamburgh. Rebels indeed."

"Can I be rebel? Against myself?" Edgar demanded. "Could *you* be rebel, in Normandy?"

William ignored him. "That Cospatrick! Turncoat as well as rebel. Betrayor!"

"It is a fool, Highness, who does not know how to change, when he has made a mistake!" the Earl said, shrugging.

"You have made over-many mistakes. And changes! That is folly also. Now is the hour of reckoning. For all of you."

Malcolm had recovered his voice. "What do you want?" he asked. "I have come here to negotiate. Let us do so, and be done."

"Negotiate? What have you got to negotiate? You have come here because I summoned you. To hear my terms. Nothing more."

"You think that? In your overweening pride! Without a blow struck? You may call yourself Conqueror. But you have not yet conquered Scotland!"

Margaret intervened. "If a mere woman may speak — I say that since you are all men of reason and experience, as well as renown, reason and good sense must prevail. To the best benefit of all. Talk of conquering and blows struck and rebellion will serve only to prolong disagreement. And you have met here to agree something, have you not? Else why meet?"

William actually smiled at that, something that went oddly with his thin lips and traplike mouth. "How wise!" he declared, part-mockingly. "The voice of reason. Let us heed it, indeed — and save much unprofitable talk. I know what I require. And no doubt your husband knows what he has to concede. So let us come to agreement, yes!"

Malcolm's already prominent chin thrust forward. He drew a deep breath. But before he could translate his anger into words, Margaret spoke again.

"Before you commence, my lords, and my weak voice may be lost in greater talking, permit that I say a word, if you will. I pray, my lord William, that you will carry a letter from me to the good father-in-God Lanfranc, Lord Archbishop of Canterbury."

"Lanfranc? You know Lanfranc, lady?"

"By repute only. That he is a noble and learned priest. Whom you are to be congratulated on bringing to the primacy, my lord."

"That is as may be. And this letter?"

"I seek the Archbishop's good offices. With King Malcolm's agreement, I intend to erect a fine stone church at Dunfermline, in the name of the Holy Trinity. As thank-offering for our marriage and the birth of our child. In this land, God-fearing as it is, churches are small, not stone-built, much worship done in the open air. All unworthy as I am, I plan to build a great church, something not seen here ere this, a sanctuary to house the precious relic, the Black Rood, my fragment of the True Cross of Calvary. To God's glory. And I seek the holy Lanfranc's aid and blessing. As head of Holy Church, the Holy *Roman* Church, in these lands."

"Ha!" said William.

"Clever!" muttered Cospatrick, nudging Maldred.

That young man, like most others there, looked uncomprehendingly, perceiving no point in this, clever or otherwise, where the Norman was concerned.

"You will understand, my lord," Margaret went on, "that we require aid. There is no custom and practice of fine building in stone here. Wood, yes — but not stone. You Normans build strong castles and great churches. The abbots and bishops here have no experience of the sort of church we seek to erect, its style or its plenishing. So this letter seeks the good Archbishop's aid, and his benediction on our endeavour." She drew out a folded and sealed paper from her cloak and offered it to the Conqueror.

He took it distinctly doubtfully. "A . . . a noble and worthy project, cousin," he said. "To your credit — yes, to your credit." He turned the letter over, for once that most potent character at something of a loss.

"You see?" Cospatrick whispered. "By that single stroke she has cramped him, given him pause. Sown a seed of question in him. Aye, clever!"

Maldred could only see one more blow struck against his father's Celtic Church.

The Queen spread her hands. "We all seek to be better Christians, do we not? However great our failures."

"H'rr'mm." William cleared his throat and looked at Malcolm, just a little uncomfortable.

The other looked blank, as little assured. Clearly this all was unanticipated on his part.

Count Robert of Mortain snorted. "Enough of this play-acting!" he jerked.

His brother looked at him thoughtfully, then turned back to Margaret. "Yes," he said. "I shall give the letter to Lanfranc. And consider what has been said." He waved a hand. "Now — to business. Here are my terms. If you would have me to leave Scotland. You, Malcolm, swear oath of fealty to me, William. We agree no hostilities between our realms. You harbour no more of my rebels. This Edgar Atheling leaves your borders forthwith. Also this Earl Cospatrick. I had intended that they should become my prisoners, but I will content myself with banishment." This with a glance at the Queen. "Lastly, as token and promise that our agreement will be kept, I require your eldest son as hostage at my Court."

There was more than one sharp intake of breath at that last, including Margaret's and her husband's. No word was spoken for moments on end.

"Well, man — well?" the Norman demanded. "What is it to be?"

"Time," Malcolm got out. "I require time. To consider."

"What will time serve you? There is nothing to consider. Either you accept, or I occupy your kingdom with my forces. And raise up a viceroy to rule it for me. That is all there is to consider. I have modified my demands — for which you have to thank this lady. What need of time?"

"Time I require, nevertheless."

William shrugged. "As you will. A little time I grant you. There is the chapel — it is scarce a church. Go there. Consider — if you must. But . . . my terms are light. And the alternative . . . ?" He left the rest unsaid.

So the Scots filed into the little church of St. Brigit's, Malcolm and Margaret equally silent, tense. Oddly enough it was Cospatrick who led what discussion there was, sounding almost cheerful.

"Look not so black, cousin," he said, in the dim half-light, when the door was shut. "It is none so ill. Better than I had looked for, I swear. For *you*. Myself, it seems that I must needs go wandering again! But — I am a man of itching feet, anyhow . . ."

"None so ill, fool? When I must swear to be that French bastard's man — I, Malcolm!"

"His bastardy is scarce the worst of him — it happens to many!" That was as far as even Cospatrick would go in reminding Malcolm that he too was a bastard. "Just as this swearing of fealty is not the worst of the present matter. After all, it is but words spoken. Under duress. Words are but words — deeds a deal more weighty! Once the Norman is gone back to his own place, the words will mean . . . only what you wish them to mean. You said yourself, before — get William away, and then see how his terms will hold!"

"Fealty, man — *fealty* makes ill swearing."

"There is fealty and fealty, cousin. You have no lands in England, I think? But *I* have. My mother, the Lady Aldgitha of Northumbria, heired lands in England from her mother, the Princess Elgiva, daughter to Ethelred the Unready. Lands in three provinces. Those lands, in name, are mine. I have not set foot on a yard of them since these Normans came. Nor shall I, now. So — I, in my love for you, give them to you, my father's brother's son! Here, before witnesses. Thus, you may make that sort of fealty to William, since you must — for those lands in his England. Only that. Although, perhaps you need not say as much, aloud!"

"M'mm." Malcolm peered at him, in the gloom, doubtfully.

"In return, to be sure, I would expect you to keep my earldoms of Dunbar and March reserved for me, during my enforced absence abroad. And have their revenues transmitted to me on my travels. Young cousin Maldred, here, no doubt would serve as my deputy, meantime?"

"You have it all designed!" the King accused. "This you have not just thought of, now, I swear!"

"Agreed. It behoves a man responsible to think on his future. As must you, now. When I heard that Norman William was come, I knew what it would be. But — that is no matter. You must decide, for your realm. Do as I say — or else, seek excuse to get out of William's hands here, now, and once out, flee into the Highlands. And fight the invaders from their fastnesses."

"Aye — that is talking!" the Earl of Angus declared. And there was a murmur of support from other lords.

"That way would lie disaster for all Lowland Scotland," Malcolm declared. "William would treat it as he has treated so much of England. Turn it into a smoking desert . . ."

"Yes — oh, yes!" Margaret put in. "Never that. The land destroyed. The innocent paying. Never that. Better as Cospatrick says . . ."

"And what of me?" Edgar interrupted. "All this — but what of me? What am *I* to do? Where am I to go?"

Malcolm dismissed his brother-in-law's problems with a flick of the hand. "Go where you were going when that storm drove you into Wearmouth Bay, man. Go to Hungary. Or your kinsman the Emperor. You will be as well there as in Scotland."

"But . . ."

"This of the Church," Cospatrick interrupted. "It was well thought of, Highness. Quick wits. It gave William pause. Caused him to think anew. If he believes that he has *you* to aid him. Through the English Church. He will hope to gain the more, at little cost. And so act the more mildly meantime. He requires the Pope's support for what he plans in France. This of Lanfranc was shrewd thinking . . ."

"It was *honest* thinking, my lord. I have had this resolve in my mind since the day of my marriage. When we were wed in that small chapel, without, without . . . with most left outside. A great church, to the greater glory of God. I but mentioned it to William that he might be more . . . clement. Lanfranc is his close friend and spiritual guide. I wrote the letter yesterday, not knowing what today would bring . . ."

"That one seeks no spiritual guide!" MacDuff of Fife snorted. "Satan himself guides him."

"Nevertheless, it was sound thinking. And hit its mark," Cospatrick insisted. "And may serve well hereafter, I think."

Malcolm was not interested in talk of churches and clerics. "If I make this fealty. For lands in England, it might serve. What else does he ask? To shelter no more of his rebels. That is easily promised, less easily ensured. No further hostilities between the realms. None so ill, that. If I am strong enough to invade England, I am strong enough to forget such agreement!"

"War is to the benefit of none, moreover," the Queen contended. "This, of all, is the least sore requirement, surely?"

Politely, none actually controverted her.

It was left to Maldred to raise the issue of the last conditon. "The hostage? Your Highness's son."

Malcolm grunted. "Aye. God be praised, he does not understand! He said my *eldest* son. That is Duncan."

There was a pause in that dim, candle-smelling place, less than comfortable.

The King emphasised the position, that there be no mistake. "He does not know. That our Edward is to be my heir. He conceives it to be Duncan, because he is eldest. Let him so believe."

A number of those present were less than happy with this statement. Admittedly the Celtic monarchy was not wholly concerned with primogeniture, succession often going to the most able of the royal house, as in the clan polity, sometimes even a nephew taking preference over an inadequate son. But this was a decision for later, when young people could be judged, and for the realm's high council of *righ*, or lesser kings, to take. That Malcolm should have already chosen this infant and set aside the two princes by Ingebiorg, was contrary to both nature and tradition.

"He could never have taken Edward, my baby!" Margaret cried. "He, he would have had to have taken me also!"

"Never fear," her husband said, "that he would *not*." He looked round them all. "So be it. We accept his terms. In name. It will be necessary to produce young Duncan. From my brother's house in Mamlorn. Maldred, you had better go fetch him. He knows you."

"It will be a sore matter for him, Highness. A boy of eleven years . . ."

"None so sore. It will be something new. As well in England as in the wilds of Mamlorn."

Margaret bit her lip but said nothing.

So they moved out, and William saw them again — although once more they had a considerable wait.

"I have decided that I must accept your terms," Malcolm declared bluntly.

"Wise." The Norman was equally brief. "You will take the oath? Fealty?"

"Yes."

"The rebels and trouble-makers will be banished?"

"Yes."

"And the prince? Your son."

"I shall send for him. He is at my brother Donald's house, in Mamlorn. In the Highlands. A long day's journey."

"Then have him here without delay. My forty thousand are a charge on your realm until I have him! And meantime I will supply you with a guard of my best knights. It would be a pity if you, and this fair lady, were to suffer the attentions of my unruly soldiery! Whilst you wait."

"That will not be necessary. I have ample guards of my own."

"It will, however, be my pleasure. And duty. *You* know how invading troops may behave! Say no more." All knew that it was only a precaution lest Malcolm should indeed have second thoughts and seek to bolt behind the Highland Line.

So under large escort they were conducted back to Culfargie. And from there, that same late afternoon, Maldred set out on his long ride to Mamlorn.

He went up Strathearn, using the old Roman road, by Gask and Strowan, to Loch Earn. Then climbed steep Glen Ogle to the head of Loch Tay, and so over the high pass of the Lairig nan Lochan at the west shoulder of great Beinn Lawers to Glen Lyon. And there, off that lovely wooded valley winding through the lofty mountains, up a little side-glen, was Loch Deabhra, really only a flooded valley-floor, at the head of which, on an artificial crannog, or island, built of stones and logs and turf, rose the hall-house of Donald Ban mac Duncan, lawful son of the King Duncan whom MacBeth had slain. It was an extraordinary place for a king's son to live, hidden away in these remote fastnesses. It had been a hunting-seat and fort combined of the Scots Kings of Dalriada, or Dalar, remaining royal property and in occasional use after the union of the Picts and Scots. MacBeth had given it to his stepson Lulach, who succeeded MacBeth as King for five months until Malcolm slew him also. Donald Ban and Lulach had been close friends, too close some unkind folk suggested; and had dwelt here together. Having little love for his half-brother Malcolm, and few ambitions as to power and the life of the Court, he had stayed on at Deabhra, content with the simple life. Unlike the King in so many ways, he was something of a scholar, as had been Lulach — fit only for the Church, in Malcolm's estimation. They had gathered together a notable library in this sequestered spot; and Donald, when he left it, usually did so to visit other scholars of the Celtic Church, occasionally his uncle Melmore of Atholl. So Maldred knew him fairly well. Now Malcolm had at last found some use for his awkward brother, as keeper and tutor of his unwanted sons Duncan and Donald Beg.

As it transpired, Malcolm was right, and Prince Duncan showed no distress at the news of his sudden summons into the outer world. Donald Ban, a quiet, withdrawn man, notably fair of hair and beard — hence his by-name of Ban — seemed only mildly concerned at losing one of his charges. Only the young Donald Beg, ten years old, was at all upset, and that because he too would have liked to have gone adventuring.

Maldred was no more than twelve hours at Deabhra, the King having impressed on him the need for haste, the urgency of getting the English away and off their necks at the earliest moment. The boy Duncan would not be able to ride so fast and far as he had done on the outward journey, so going back would take longer. They were up with the dawn, therefore, and with fresh horses set off for Fortrenn just after sunrise, Donald Beg tearful, his brother scornful, bright-eyed, eager. Maldred did not know whether to warn the boy that what lay ahead of him was not likely to be all excitement and adventure. On the other hand, hostages for lofty folk often did quite well at an enemy Court. Young Duncan was a fairly tough character anyway, much less sensitive than his brother. Apart from explaining what a hostage was, then, he added little.

They covered the ground well, in poorish weather, and got as far as St. Fillan's monastery at the tail-end of Loch Earn that evening, and rode down the Earn to reach its junction with the opening estuary of Tay next day, by noon.

The royal party at Culfargie awaited them impatiently, only the Queen showing any concern for the young prince. No time was lost in making a move over to Abernethy, in their company of arrogant Norman knights.

This time they were received promptly enough, without any of the infuriating waiting. Presumably William himself had had enough of waiting around. He was curt — except to Margaret — and businesslike. Actually he greeted young Duncan more civilly than his father had done.

It was a day of intermittent rain-showers, and William elected to hold such ceremony as there was indoors, in the eating-hall of the abbey. One king swearing fealty to another was a very major event, and was not to be conducted in any hole-and-corner fashion. And there had to be sufficient witnesses. On the other hand, no lengthy procedure had to be involved — and neither William nor Malcolm were men much inclined to ceremonial.

In the centre of the crowded refectory, then, the Conqueror produced his chaplain and clerk, William de Poictiers, a foxy-faced individual with a shirt-of-mail showing under his monk's habit, a gospel scroll held in his hand. He instructed Malcolm to kneel before William.

"No, clerk," the King said flatly. "The King of Scots kneels only before Almighty God."

"But . . . it is necessary, Your Grace."

"Not so. I do not kneel."

"The oath of fealty, my lord King, must be taken kneeling . . ."

"*Mon Dieu* — let it be!" William jerked. "So long as he takes it, head bowed, it will serve."

"As you say, Sire." The monk looked sour. "King Malcolm — take King William's hand in both your own. Then rest them on this Holy Writ."

The Conqueror held out his right hand, palm vertical. Grimly, distastefully, the other placed his own hands on either side of it.

"Now, repeat after me, head bowed, 'I, Malcolm, King of Scotland . . .'"

"I, Malcolm, King of *Scots* . . ." the other amended — and if his head was bowed, it was so little as to be unnoticeable.

". . . do hereby take you, William, King of England and Lord Paramount of Scotland . . ."

". . . do hereby take you, William, King of England . . ."

". . . Lord Paramount of Scotland!"

"King of England, *styled* Lord Paramount of Scotland."

The priest glanced at the Conqueror — who, expressionless, gave the merest nod.

". . . to be my lord of life and limb and I your man, for the land I hold under God . . ."

". . . to be my lord of life and limb for the lands I hold under God . . ." Malcolm's lips continued to move for a moment thereafter, but soundlessly. And probably few noticed that he had said lands instead of land.

"Moreover, I swear to support and uphold you, William, with all the strength of my land . . ."

". . . I swear to support and uphold you, William, with all the strength of my lands . . ." Again the lips moved.

". . . and to adjudge all your enemies as my enemies — so help me God!"

". . . and to adjudge all your enemies as my enemies — so help me God!"

Malcolm released the other's hand as though it was burning him, William looking grimly amused. They stared at each other for a long moment, two bastards, the miller of Forteviot's daughter's son, and the tanner of Falaise's daughter's son.

"It will serve," William said. "No doubt but you will keep your solemn vows — for it will be my concern to see that you do! And, to be sure, I will have your son further to ensure it!"

"You will treat the boy well?"

"As well as any son of my own — for so long as you abide by your oaths." He looked around him. "Now — Edgar Atheling and the Earl Cospatrick? They leave this realm? All other Saxons likewise. Before the Day of St. John the Evangelist."

"Yes."

"Then our business is done, I think."

Stiffly Malcolm inclined his head.

"Your lady-wife has been a joy to meet." William bowed to Margaret. "I shall not forget her, nor her . . . good works. I shall give your letter to the good Lanfranc, lady, and tell him of your excellent purposes. Any assistance I may give, call on me."

"Your kindness I shall not forget, my lord."

"Nor I your beauty."

Margaret went over to the now rather forlorn-looking small boy, and spoke kindly. But he turned away — as well he might. Malcolm was making for the door, without further remark, when Maldred went to touch his arm.

"Highness — the boy," he said.

"Ah, yes." The King turned and went to Duncan. He looked down at him for a moment. "Aye, lad," he said, at length. "I am sorry. This is how it had to be." He swung about and strode out.

The rest of the Scots followed, a few thinking to bow towards William.

Maldred eyed Margaret, who was looking at young Duncan still, biting her lip, pain in her eyes. He went over to her.

"Come," he said. "Come, Highness. It was not your doing. And there is nothing that you may do now. Come now." He clapped the boy on the shoulder, and led the Queen away. He had never seen her less sure of herself.

14

MALDRED SPENT LITTLE of that summer at Court. After Cospatrick left for Flanders, he took seriously his new duties of keeping an eye on the Earl's Border lands of Dunbar and March — a task in which the King encouraged him, for of course the territory was vital for Scotland's security, especially in present circumstances — for although William and his hosts had gone, without battle, the climate and attitude prevailing thereafter was more or less that Scotland had suffered a grievous defeat, and was therefore more or less open to enterprising raiders and freebooters. The Orkney earls were not long in displaying that sort of initiative both in Cumbria and

Strathclyde north of Galloway; and Waldeve of Northumbria, with old scores to settle, might be expected to seek to improve upon the situation. So Maldred spent much of his time at the two new Norman-style stone castles Cospatrick had begun to build at Dunbar, by the Lothian coast, and Ersildoune in Lauderdale, Magda usually with him — although the Queen required her presence at Dunfermline frequently. Maldred devised quite an elaborate system of defensive arrangements, along the Tweed and Teviot rivers, based on the various fords, with a rota of men on guard at all times, and plans for swift muster and reinforcement locally, in the event of any major assault. Fortunately the area was fairly populous and the people warlike — indeed only too eager for military exercises, which were apt to be worked off amongst themselves if no more suitable target offered — so that manpower was little problem, however much the maintaining of discipline was otherwise. Maldred's preoccupations were more with keeping rival petty chiefs and their bands from each others' throats, and acting the judge in altercations, than in actually repelling enemy raids. He was, in fact, doing an earl's work without an earl's authority. But his royal connections helped, and it was excellent experience for a young noble, almost everyone assured him. Sometimes his brother Madach came to aid him; but he was now largely managing Atholl for their father, who preferred bookish pursuits. So the two brothers were kept busy, controlling three major earldoms. Maldred's duties were not all military and judicial, of course; the productiveness of Cospatrick's great domains, especially in Lothian and the Merse, had to be maintained, and the revenues despatched to Flanders — less what was required for the upkeep of the properties and the support of the Earl's three young sons, Dolfin, Waltheof and Cospatrick, and the daughter Ethelreda, at Ersildoune.

Cospatrick himself had sailed from Dysart for Sluys, in company with the Athelings, mother, son and daughter, and most of the remaining Saxon refugees. Count Robert of Flanders, who had recently succeeded his father Baldwin, although his sister was William's Queen Matilda, had little love for his brother-in-law — indeed Duke Robert of Normandy, the Conqueror's eldest son, whose revolt his sire had been so recently and bloodily putting down, was known to have taken refuge with his uncle Robert of Flanders. Cospatrick believed that he could sell his sword to the Count meantime — himself a notable warrior, with many private wars always in hand in the Low Countries. Nothing was more certain than that once he had deposited the Athelings in Flanders, Cospatrick would not be long in disengaging himself and leaving them to their own devices.

The departure of the Athelings occasioned little distress at Dunfermline, even Margaret accepting their loss with equanimity. They had made little attempt to adjust to the Scottish scene and ethos, and in the circumstances had overstayed their welcome. Where they would go from Flanders would depend on circumstances. Edgar had hopes of King Philip of France.

Malcolm, who was not of course an eloquent or talkative man, said little about his humiliation at the hands of William; but undoubtedly he brooded on it, felt it keenly. Save towards Margaret, he was ill-natured, cross-grained, moody, and wise men were concerned to keep their distance. He lashed out, on a larger scale, where he safely could — for instance, at the Orkney brothers who had been making their inroads into Strathclyde, and at the Earl Somerled in the Hebrides who was given to raiding into Lochaber in Dalar — these efforts more to salve the King's pride than anything else.

Margaret remained his consolation and joy — if so essentially stern and harsh a man could be said to know joy. With her he could forget his troubles, sink his pride and dominance in her beauty and goodness. He doted on her. Nothing was too good for her, nothing to be denied her. His humbling before William only made him the more determined to shine in her eyes.

Although there were stones for stumbling in even that marital path, as Maldred was witness on one of his brief spells at Court in high summer. The King came to his bedchamber one night, as he was preparing for sleep.

"You know Margaret passing well," he jerked, without preamble, almost accusingly. "Is she . . . has she . . . how true is she to me?"

"True? The Queen? Save us — you ask that? You jest, surely?"

"God's Blood, I do not jest! Answer me, man."

"But . . . to be sure she is true, Highness. None could be truer. You know that . . ."

"I do not know it. I believe that she is deceiving me."

"No, no — I swear not! You misjudge. How could that be? In what would she ever deceive you?"

"With another man, it may be. Aye, another man. I am old enough to be her father, see you."

Maldred stared. "You, you cannot mean that, believe that! Margaret?"

"You, boy — I might have known! You are besotted on her, your own self! Despite being wed to that Magda. You are of no use to me!"

The younger man stiffened. "My lord King — you have no call to say that. I have always served you well, and honestly. Just as you have no call to think ill of the Queen, I vow."

"Why, then, does she steal out from my bed? Early in the morning. Seeking not to awake me. Does not tell me where she goes, who she has gone to?"

"She goes to her early devotions . . ."

"No. Earlier than that. This morning I rose after she had gone. She had not gone to the chapel. I went to that monk Oswald's chamber. He was still snoring in his bed. I could not find her in the house. She had slipped outside. Later, much later, I heard the chanting of the orisons from the chapel. Who had she gone to meet, earlier?"

"It would be some good works, some kindness to the poor . . ."

"At that hour? Before even the poorest are out of their beds?"

"I do not know, Highness. But — it can be nothing ill, amiss. That is certain."

"We shall see. In the morning," Malcolm said grimly. "You will rise, at the hour of four. No later. It is soon after that she goes. Go out, and hide you between the kitchen-door of this hall and the postern-gate. Amongst the apple-trees. She will not use the great door and the gate-house entrance, where guards are always on watch, day and night. Wait there, then follow her unseen. Discover where she goes. Then come tell me."

"But — a mercy, why me? I am her friend . . ."

"And are you not mine?"

"Yes. To be sure. But . . . why not your own self?"

"Fool! If I seem to be awake when she leaves, she will not go. I must let her go, then dress, before I can follow. By which time she has gone. Too late."

Maldred looked unhappy, but saw no way out. He wished that Magda was here with him, but he had left her at their new home of Bothargask, at her own urging. He could have done with her counsel now.

So, at an ungodly hour indeed next morning, he dragged himself out of bed and went glowering out, to station himself behind a tree on the dew-soaked grass of the orchard, feeling both fool and rogue. To be spying on Margaret like this was repugnant to him. But what could he do against a royal command?

It was chilly thus early, everything damp, the entire affair ridiculous. He was quite prepared for all to come to nothing, prove a mere figment of the King's imagination — although admittedly he was anything but an imaginative man — when the small rear door from the palace kitchens opened quietly, and was as quietly closed. The Queen, wrapped in a long, hooded cloak, had emerged and now hurried across the narrow belt of orchard to the postern-gate set in the high enclosing wall. She passed through, and closed it as quietly as the other.

Maldred gave her a few moments. He moved over to the gate, and peered through, in time to see her disappearing down the palace-hill in a north-easterly direction into the wooded gut of the Pittencrieff Glen. Once she was over the brow of the slope, he could hurry after.

Further down, the trees gave him cover and he was able to keep her in sight. She went for about three hundred yards along the valley-floor, and then, where a little side-burn came cascading down to join the main stream, a rocky bluff rose within the angle. To the foot of this Margaret turned, and round its shoulder disappeared from sight.

Cautiously he moved after her — and was surprised to discover that under an overhang at the west side was the opening of a cave of sorts. It had been provided with a door, but this now stood open. He had never had occasion to be round here before, although it was not a quarter-mile from the palace, with nothing to bring him.

He paused, hesitant. He heard a faint murmuring from within. He did not go closer. The last thing that he desired was to have Margaret find him hanging about, eavesdropping. He turned and hurried back to the palace.

The King was just emerging from the kitchens door as he came up.

"You have her? You have not lost her?" Malcolm cried. "Where is she?"

"She, she went to a cave. A small cave, under a rock. Not far . . ."

"A cave? God's Name — a cave! Is she with a man? Meeting him there?"

"No, no. Not that, I swear . . ."

"What, then?"

"I do not know."

"Take me there, man. Quickly."

Hating himself, Maldred led the way back.

At the cave-mouth they halted. There was silence, but the door was still open. It seemed to be no large cavern, between six and seven feet high, perhaps eight feet wide, how deep was not to be seen, for there was a bend in it after a few feet.

The men eyed each other doubtfully. Then the murmuring sounded again, from within. With an oath, the King strode inside. Maldred paused, and then followed reluctantly.

Round the bend in the cave it took moments to see what was there, to accustom the eyes to the gloom. Maldred in fact bumped into his monarch's back. A single candle flickered ahead, and by its pale uncertain light Margaret was to be discerned crouching at the far end of the place — which seemed to be no more than some twelve feet deep. She had turned to gaze back in something like alarm. She appeared to be alone and on her knees. Behind the candle, the diamond-studded shape of the crucifix known as the Black Rood cast its shadow on the damp stone walling.

As vision improved, Maldred could distinguish that candle and cross stood on a stone shelf of the wall, natural or artificial. There was another shelf, bench-like, lower and to the side, on which lay parchment scrolls apparently. Apart from some kind of skin rug on the wet floor, that was all that the cave contained. Obviously the place was an improvised chapel or oratory. And, oddly enough, the improved vision revealed something else — what looked very like guilt sharing the alarm on the Queen's face.

Malcolm was gulping, swallowing audibly. "Lass!" he got out. "Margaret lass! I am sorry. I did not know. I thought . . . how could I know? Christ God — why? Why here?"

She rose from her knees. "Forgive me, Malcolm. It is folly, I know well. Only folly, I hope and pray — not grievous sin. But . . . but . . ." She spread her hands. "How can I tell you? And Maldred — is that Maldred too? I am sorry."

"But why, lass — *why*? Why this cave in the rock? Running with water. Is your chapel in the palace not good enough for you? It is a deal better than this, I swear!"

"It is not that, Malcolm. It, it is Oswald. Oh, I am sinful, I know — for he is a good man. And God's servant. But . . . I have come to find him trying. It is my fault, no doubt — but I am more and more at odds with him. He is stiff, correct, unyielding. Righteous, yes, but unyielding. He does not approve of what I seek to do. I have felt this for long. But, of late, it has become too much for me . . ."

"God's Blood, woman — then send him off! Away with him — like the other Saxons . . ."

"No, no, husband — not that. He is God's good minister. And must not suffer for *my* failure. Do not send him away."

"Highness — why come to this damp hole?" Maldred put in. "If your confessor displeases, why not worship in your own chapel without him?"

"Then he would know. That I was, was spurning him. This way he does not know. I go back, to hear Lauds with him, afterwards. In the palace."

"You mean that you worship *twice*, of a morning?"

"God forgive me if it is a deceit before Him — yes. I find that I cannot worship fully, properly, with my whole heart, while I have these wrong thoughts in my heart and mind, on Oswald. Can you not understand? It has come between me and my Saviour, in some evil fashion. So I have made this little oratory, set up the Black Rood in it. After an hour's confession and prayer here, with God's help, I can face Lauds with Oswald. Is it sin? Tell me, is it grievous sin?"

The men looked at each other helplessly.

"If this is sin," Maldred said, "then God and all His saints help the rest of us!"

"You will not tell Oswald . . . ?"

They left her there, for she had not finished her devotions, and would return to the chapel for Lauds later, anyway.

Two days later, without a word to the Queen, Malcolm

despatched the monk Oswald off back to Wearmouth in a
Flemish trader sailing from Culross. Announcing the fact
thereafter, he told her that she could find another confessor of her choice; and that he, the King, would pay for
all the cost of building her the finest church north of York,
to replace her dripping cave, if she would forgive him for
doubting her.

*　　*　　*

Maldred did not lack for activities and responsibilities that
year of 1072, for in addition to his preoccupations with
Dunbar and March and his establishing of their new home
at Bothargask, Magda announced herself to be pregnant
and that he should prepare himself to assume the duties of
fatherhood in the early spring.

In these circumstances, Magda was not so often called to
Dunfermline, and Maldred in turn was there less frequently, although they both remained part of the royal
household. So that, when they were indeed both called to
Court, for the Vigil of All Hallows, a Romish observance
which Margaret was seeking to establish in place of the
all-but-pagan celebrations of Nutcrack Night, it was to
discover not a few developments. For one thing, the monk
Turgot was back, and now Margaret's personal confessor,
Malcolm having been cajoled to allow it, despite his sus-
picions. Turgot was a very different man from Oswald,
strong but pliant, able, shrewd. Margaret had always
thought the world of him — which perhaps was why
Malcolm was less than enthusiastic. For that matter,
Maldred himself found the man rather much. And
undoubtedly he would much encourage the Queen in her
Romanising endeavours.

She had not allowed the grass to grow under her feet in
the matter of the great church or minster. Although no
master-builders or masons had yet arrived from the south,
so that actual building could not be started, masses of
stone and timber, and sand and oyster-shells for mortar,
were being collected and readied. The site chosen was on a
sort of plateau of level ground east of the palace and west
of the abbey, nearer the latter — indeed all the material
being assembled from far and near, to keep the actual site
clear, had to be stacked and piled meantime in the
precincts of the abbey itself — producing a certain lack of

enthusiasm amongst the monks there. But Maldred discovered that such mild resentment seemed to stem only from the inconvenience and mess, not because of the forthcoming erection of a large temple of an alien faith alongside their ancient establishment. He was a little surprised at this acquiescence, as he had been at the comparative ease with which Margaret had won her doctrinal and procedural encounters with the Celtic Church council. He had a word with his brother Kerald about this, who told him that there was no real animosity or fear about the Queen's reforming zeal amongst the churchmen. They recognised her sincerity and innate goodness, and few asserted that improvement and rededication were not possible and indeed desirable. Besides, the Queen was putting the entire Columban Church in her debt by her efforts in the restoration of the Abbey of Iona, ravaged heart of that Church.

Then, the day before Maldred and Magda were due to leave for Dunbar, in early November, an English vessel arrived at Dysart haven bringing three monks and a letter from Lanfranc, Archbishop of Canterbury. The senior of this trio, Godwin by name, was a Saxon strangely enough, but an experienced architect, who had studied his craft in Normandy and the Low Countries and had had a hand in building many fine churches. The other two, both Normans, were a master-mason and a skilled wood-carver.

Margaret was overjoyed with this response to her appeal; especially when she read the Archbishop's letter. Indeed so pleased was she that she had to show it to somebody. It was written in Latin, and Malcolm, whose schooling had been of the scantiest, could speak only Gaelic and English. But Maldred had a scholar for father and knew his Latin. The Queen showed him the letter, with Magda, in a strange mixture of pride and humility.

It was lengthy and, he thought, effusive, although Margaret did not see it so. He read it out, for Magda was no Latinist either.

Lanfranc, unworthy bishop of the holy church of Canterbury to the glorious queen of the Scots, Margaret, greeting and benediction:

The brief space of a letter cannot unfold the great gladness with which thou has filled my heart, when I have read thy letter . . . queen beloved of God. With what delight glow the words which proceed by inspiration of the Divine Spirit. For I believe that the things thou hast written were said not by thee but through thee. Truly He has spoken with thy mouth, who says to His Disciples "Learn from me because I am gentle and humble of heart." From this teaching of Christ it has come that thou, born of royal stock, royally brought up, nobly united to a noble king, hast chosen as father me, a stranger, worthless, ignoble, entangled in sin; and dost beg me to regard thee as a spiritual daughter. I am not such as thou thinkest; but may I be such, because thou thinkest it! Pray for me that I may be worthy as a father to pray to the Lord for thee . . . let there be traffic of prayers and benefits between us. Henceforth let me be thy father and thou my daughter.

According to thy request, I send to thy glorious husband and thee our dearest brother Sir Godwine; also two other brothers, because he could not fulfil in himself alone all that ought to be done in God's service and yours. I ask earnestly that you should endeavour resolutely to complete what you have begun for God and for your souls. And if you can, or wish to, fulfil your work through others, we would greatly desire that these our brothers should return to us; because they were very necessary to our Church in their services. But let it be according to your will; and we desire in everything to obey you.

"Is not that a wonder and a joy?" Margaret demanded. "So kind, noble, generous — and I so sinfully unworthy."

Maldred cleared his throat. "Most . . . flattering," he said. "For a Norman. This of being your father in the Lord, you his daughter — what means that? Which he makes so much of."

"What but that he takes me under his especial loving care and authority."

"Authority, yes, Highness. That is where I might think to tread carefully. These Normans are cunning. And this man is William's close friend — or he would not have him Archbishop of Canterbury. He put Stigand away, for him. As Archbishop, I have heard that he claims authority over all the Romish Church north of the archbishopric of Normandy. That could include Scotland, could it not?

Church authority over Scotland! And over you, Scotland's Queen. Certainly over this new church which he is aiding you to build."

"Maldred — what do you mean?"

"I mean that William the Norman now claims to be Lord Paramount of Scotland. Temporal Lord Paramount. Perhaps Lanfranc the Norman intends to be *spiritual* Lord Paramount of Scotland! The Normans to have us in the grip of both fists!"

Both young women looked at him blankly.

"Unkind, Maldred," the Queen reproved. "To take such thing out of so kind and good a letter."

"Perhaps. But King William said that he had made more modest his terms, at Abernethy, because of your intervention and letter to this Lanfranc. I do not think that man would do so just because of your fair face, Highness. Some might — but not William!"

Disturbed and a little hurt, the Queen took her letter and left them.

Next day, however, she had forgiven him, for she came to see them off to the Borderland, as friendly and kind as ever. She kissed them both farewell — and then drew Magda back for a moment, to murmur in her ear.

Later that young woman revealed to her husband that Margaret was pregnant again.

15

MAGDA GAVE BIRTH to a daughter, at Bothargask, on the Eve of St. Duthac, in early March, and they called her Marsala, a family name, also Margaret after her godmother. And Margaret herself was delivered of another son two months later, and named him Edmund, another Saxon name for a Scots prince.

Maldred was greatly taken with his daughter — indeed he esteemed her unique. She was a sturdy, healthy, uncomplicated child, who gave her parents a minimum of trouble. Her cousin-at-a-remove, Edmund, however, was a sickly infant, puny and wailing, such as *his* father had no use for at all — which made his mother the more protective.

Maldred could not remain at Bothargask, playing the proud father, of course, with the affairs of the Border earldoms demanding ever more of his time and attention. The Border folk, with all their toughness and military virtues, required a strong hand and a visible presence to keep them under control — which was why Malcolm had appointed Cospatrick thereto in the first place. So now Maldred could never be away for long. Fortunately, serious and sustained raiding from Northumbria had not developed, as feared — this almost certainly because King William, driven by whatever devil of urgency possessed him, had once again sailed with his armies across the Channel and was now involved in a double campaign, against Flanders in the north-east and the French province of Maine to the south; and the Earl Waldeve of Northumbria with his manpower had perforce to go with him. The Duke Robert of Normandy was once again in revolt against his father it seemed, and this time he had his brother William Rufus assisting him and acting as King Philip of France's lieutenant in Maine. The Conqueror appeared to be able to impose his will on almost everybody except his own family.

When, in early June, Maldred reached Dunbar, alone but with arrangements for Magda to follow with the baby in due course, he was astonished to find installed in the half-built castle there none other than its owner and builder himself, secretly but as large as life. Or not quite as large as he had been, for Cospatrick had been seriously wounded in the early stages of the Flanders campaign, fighting for Duke Robert against William, and had lost a lot of blood and weight. His right shoulder had, in fact, been shattered by a mace-blow, through his shirt-of-mail, and a muscle and blood-vessel of his neck affected at that same side. So now that shoulder sagged badly and he had something of a twist to his head. This made his raffish good looks more sardonic than ever but appeared to have by no means quenched his spirit.

"So, like an old wounded dog I have limped home to die, Maldred!" he told his cousin cheerfully. "Look not so glum, man! It all might be a deal worse."

"But . . . how are you to do? What is to become of you? Hidden, a fugitive in your own house. You cannot remain so . . ."

"We shall see. I have a notion or two about that. Drastic situations demand drastic cures!"

"Yes. But — have you thought this out? Malcolm cannot permit that you remain in Scotland. It was one of the terms of his agreement with William that you should be banished from his realm. You have been gone barely a year. William will hear of your presence, never doubt it. He is a master of spies. The King will have to put you away — he can do no other without defying William openly and all that that means. You cannot go over into England, where you would be hunted down as an outlaw . . ."

"William, God destroy him, is still in France, where he is like to remain for some time. Waldeve also. The odious Odo is ruling England for his bastard brother. I cannot think that he will have much time for northern adventures, chasing such as myself."

"Not meantime perhaps. But presently. And then Malcolm will stand accused of harbouring you. Laying himself open to reprisals. You know the King. Will he be prepared to suffer it, for you?"

"Probably not. Our royal cousin is scarcely a long-suffering man. But I have a little time, see you. I said that, like a wounded dog I had limped home to die. I have no intention of dying just yet. But I might *seem* to die. And my young son reign here in my stead — under your good direction."

"Do you mean that?"

"To be sure. Why not? Stranger things have been done. It would relieve Malcolm of his responsibility. Give the Normans no cause to come poking their long noses into my lands and affairs . . ."

"But what of *you*? Where would you be? What doing? You, a man all know, kenspeckle indeed. You would be recognised. People would talk . . ."

"True. I had thought of Holy Church!" Cospatrick put his hands together piously. "What more appropriate? It looks as though I shall never wield a sword again, with any satisfaction. Suitable that I should retire discreetly into the arms of the faithful, become Brother Anselm or something such — of not too strict an order, see you — and come and go as some wandering friar."

Maldred wagged his head helplessly. "You! A *church-man*!"

"Of a sort, lad — of a sort! And until times improved, shall we say? When I might re-emerge, none the worse. Or improved! And who knows what Brother Anselm might achieve, in the bygoing? Heigho — do you still say that I have not thought it out, cousin?"

It took Maldred a little time to digest. "Who would know of this?" he demanded, at length. "How would you contrive it?"

"Few indeed should know. At first, none save yourself. And some secure priest, to effect the business. I shall seem to grow sadly sick, and fade fast. *You* shall take me away to some monastery. To die. In the care of Mother Church. Suitably. Then the Earl Cospatrick will be buried, and the monk Anselm born. Twisted as I am now, with my face shaven and head tonsured, none will know me — because none will look to see me. But . . . enough of that, Maldred. Tell me of your stewardship here. And what has happened in Scotland this past year? You are now a father, I hear . . . ?"

All worked out very much as Cospatrick had visualised. Only a few of the Earl's house-servants knew that he was back at Dunbar — he had come by sea from Flanders and landed by night in a small boat — and those who knew had been left in small doubt as to what their fate would be if they revealed his presence. Now he kept to his room, and Maldred gave it out that he was gravely ill. Then, after a few days, a horse-litter was prepared, and Maldred and a couple of his own huscarls took the Earl, well wrapped and hidden, and rode off south-westwards into Lammermuir.

The story was that they were making for the small Abbey of St. Bathans, in the green hills which overlooked the Merse on the north, where a man might die in holy peace. But in fact, once they were well away from all the haunts of men, Cospatrick rose from his litter to sit his horse properly, and they swung away due southwards into the fertile levels of the Merse itself, going at a good spanking pace now. They were heading for the Tweed, for it and across it, having come to the conclusion that the Earl's reincarnation had better be as a friar of the Roman Church rather than any Celtic monk. The Romans went in for wandering and mendicant friars much more than did the Columbans. Also this would enable Cospatrick to roam about in England too, where a Celtic monk would have stood out notably and his ignorance be exposed. Moreover, his hair already beginning to thin a little on top, he was more prepared to sacrifice an incipient bald patch to the Roman crown tonsure than to shave his brow and head frontal in the Celtic fashion. Lastly, it might be wise, for Malcolm's sake, not to die on Scottish soil. So they were making for the nearest and most modest English monastery — which in fact was that of the small house of Ubbanford, of mendicant friars, just across Tweed from Horndean in the Norham area, founded incidentally by Cospatrick's own grandfather-maternal, the Earl Uchtred of Northumbria, in an access of remorse for some unspecified sin.

The Horndean ford led them into Northumbria, and after some persuasion and slightly-veiled threats, the extremely doubtful Prior Horulf of Ubbanford received them and took reluctant charge of his new novitiate, very much aware of how vulnerable he and his priory were to pressure from Scotland, across the river, in the event of non-co-operation.

Maldred left his cousin there. Cospatrick said that he would stay at Ubbanford for a week or two, possibly, learning the basis of his new identity, having his head tonsured and generally turning himself into a convincing mendicant friar. Then there would be a quiet funeral for the erstwhile fugitive Earl Cospatrick; and thereafter he would set out on his wanderings. Just what these wanderings were to consist of, he did not detail. He said that he had various enquiries and discreet visitations he wanted to make in North Northumbria and elsewhere, then he would make his way back to Ersildoune in Lauderdale, where he proposed to settle down near his family and his own March earldom's castle. He would send for Maldred there in due course. Clearly the mendicant friar had no intention of becoming any less the autocrat, in essence, because of his change of habit.

It was a full month later, in high summer, with Magda and the baby settled in at Dunbar and enjoying the seaside life, when Maldred got his summons to Lauderdale. On this occasion he did not take his wife. The message was brought by a so-called serving-brother, in reality a body-servant of Cospatrick's own, whom Maldred had previously known as Patie's Dod, still with something of the clash of steel about him, monk's habit notwithstanding.

At the Earl's Town of Ersildoune, four miles up the River Leader from its junction with Tweed, his guide brought Maldred to a cot-house built some way apart from the other houses and hovels of the community which served the new castle, under the green cone known as the White Hill of Ersildoune. This proved to be no ordinary cottage, normal as it looked from the front. For one thing, it was much larger than it seemed, with a quite long rear extension consisting of cowhouse, stable and other domestic quarters. The front part was in fact fitted up as a simple chapel, with altar, candles, piscina, aumbry and lectern, in the Romish fashion. But behind this a vestry door led into a large and comfortable chamber for living and sleeping in, with a stone-built fireplace and flue, a couch of skins, a paved floor with rugs of deer-skin and sheep, a table, benches, coffers and plenishings. Patie's Dod — or Brother Ulfric as he was now to be called — revealed that this was his lord's new dwelling-place. He himself had a shakedown off the cowshed nearby.

Cospatrick was not present at the moment — no doubt up at the castle with the children, Dod said. The Earl had now assumed the character of chaplain and confessor to his own family, it was explained — which seemed to Maldred a distinctly risky development, however tempting and convenient. Nevertheless, when Cospatrick turned up presently, he was indeed hardly to be recognised as his former dashing self. Clean-shaven of his little forked beard and thin down-turning moustaches, with his twisted head and sagging shoulder, short-cut hair — to say nothing of the tonsure — and grey, long monkish habit, it would have taken a keen eye to suspect that this was the celebrated earl of heretofore.

"Ha, my son — greetings, in the name of God the One in Three and Three in One!" he intoned, and sketched the sign of the cross over Maldred, grinning — a grin that at least was no more sanctimonious than formerly. "Welcome to my lowly retreat and poor eremitage. Ulfric, man — wine! A beaker for each of us. And full, man — full! It is plaguey thirsty work, this holiness!"

"So — it is all as you proposed and forecast," Maldred said. "Friar Anselm, indeed!"

"Ah, no. Anselm, I decided, did not suit me. So I am Friar Eadwulf, a notable healer of diseases of the skin. I do not actually cure leprosy — but anything else, come to me — with a suitable offering — and I shall see what can be done! Ah — drink up, cousin. Thank God I had a good supply of Burgundian wine laid in at the castle, whilst I had opportunity."

"I thank you. But — is this wise, Cospatrick? This of the castle. And your children. So close . . ."

"Eadwulf, man — not Cospatrick! Never that. Cospatrick is dead. Did you not hear?"

"To be sure. All Lothian and the Merse rang with it. But — your family. Are the children not bound to talk?"

"Not them. Think you that I have not warned them sufficiently? And you would not have me to abandon my own bairns? They need a father. Now they will have a better, closer one, than they ever had. Holier, too! Forby, the castle has its advantages." And he gestured with his wine-beaker.

"I can see that. But . . ." Maldred shrugged. "You always were sure of yourself."

"And with reason," the other agreed. "Have I ever failed you, myself, or my friends?"

"Some might say so. You are namely for, for changing sides!"

"Only a fool does not change when his wits tell him to. Dealing with kings and rulers, a man changes — or suffers! Mind you that, young Maldred. Especially rulers such as Malcolm and William, bastards in more than their birth! Either would sacrifice you, or me, at a snap of their fingers. But — sit, man. It is Malcolm I sent for you to speak on. Ulfric, oaf — bring food. Meats, do you hear? For the Lord Maldred . . ."

With his cousin settled at the table eating, and eating well, Cospatrick went on,

"I want you to go to Dunfermline, to see Malcolm for me. Tell him, in closest secrecy, that I am alive. Tell him that I can be of much use to him. That I want my son Cospatrick, young Pate, made Earl of Dunbar and March in my room. And tell him . . ."

"Pate? But Pate is your *third* son. What of Dolfin? And Waldeve? Dolfin, I have heard, was born bastard. But Waldeve . . . ?"

"Aye. Waldeve, shall we say, had some doubt about his

birth, also! It happens, now and again! Besides, young Pate has the wits of them all. Waldeve is like his unfortunate uncle of the same name, a little weak. He will do for the Church, belike. So — Cospatrick to succeed me as Earl here. As for Dolfin, have Malcolm create him Earl of Cumbria in the room of his uncle . . ."

"The Earl Waltheof? Is he dead?"

"My foolish brother is William's prisoner, in some Normandy castle, and like to remain so. As is Morkar. As would be Bishop Ethelwin — but he died."

"Dear God! But, see you — how can *I* have the King create earls of these boys? Think you he will heed me, in so great a matter . . . ?"

"Perhaps not. But he will heed *me*. Or the message you bring him from me. He has all but lost Cumbria. Galloway too. All of Strathclyde is at risk. Tell him that — although he knows it well enough. I will make it my business to watch over Cumbria. Secretly, to be sure. I will move about therein, unknown. I have lands there. Unknown — but *knowing* all. I know all the lords and the churchmen. My father, to be sure, was Maldred, Prince of Cumbria, Duncan's brother. So, I will keep Malcolm informed, and more than that. Let him appoint a governor for me to work through, meantime. But my Dolfin to be Earl there. He is twelve years now. In a few years he will be able to rule there. That is my price. If Malcolm wants to save Cumbria for his realm."

Maldred stared. "For a dead man, you speak strongly!" he said.

"As I have reason to do. And am able to perform. I am not yet forty. Think you that I am going to spend the rest of my days doing nothing, playing only the friar? Norman William will not live for ever. When he goes, there will be changes, large changes, with those weak sons of his. Who knows, there may be a resurrection from the dead! That Waldeve Siwardson — who is also cousin, see you — will come to a bad end, that I swear! So Northumbria could lose its earl again. And I will be waiting. Duke Robert and William Rufus think none so ill of me — I have fought at their sides. So — one day, Maldred, you may see Cospatrick, Earl of Dunbar and March again, Earl of Northumbria again and Earl of Cumbria also! A territory half as large as Scotland itself."

His cousin had no words.

"Tell Malcolm that, man. Tell him that I could put Scotland's Border at Tyne and Ribble instead of Tweed and Esk. Tell him. You have it?"

"I, I hear you, yes." Maldred shook his head. "Whether Malcolm, or any other, will believe you . . . ?"

"I do not ask him to believe it. Only to wish it! The wish will do. He needs such wishing, see you. I will provide it." Cospatrick rose. "Now — if you are sufficiently fed and refreshed, cousin, we shall ride."

"Ride? You . . . ?"

"Both. A servant of God so sore distressed in the body as I am, may surely ride, on occasion, as well as tramp the land? I have a suitable fat palfrey, which was my daughter Ethelreda's pad . . ."

So, side-by-side, the cousins rode off, sedately, down the Leader in its fair wooded valley, the four miles to its confluence with great Tweed, Cospatrick bestowing casually sketched benedictions upon any individual they happened to pass on the way, in seemingly absent-minded benevolence, Maldred seeking to school his expression.

Where the two rivers joined, a quite large promontory of suddenly higher land had been formed in the loop, not liable to flooding, the *meall rhos* of the name Melross, whereon had been one of the earliest and most famous Columban monasteries in southern Scotland, or Bernicia as it then had been. Founded by St. Aidan, as an offshoot of Lindisfarne, in the mid-seventh century, here St. Boisil and St. Cuthbert had been successive priors. But, like its parent-house, in time it swung over to the Romish adherence; and in 859 the heavy-handed King Kenneth MacAlpine had sacked and burned it for such apostasy. In the intervening two centuries, although used intermittently as a hospice for travellers and as a settlement for Saxon slaves, it had never been restored as a monastery. Its farmery and mill on the low ground, remained intact however, and these were run by tenants of Cospatrick. This proved to be their destination.

It was not the farmhouse they made for, nor yet the mill, but higher, for the ruins of the old monastic enclosure itself. Here one of the low-browed buildings had been rethatched and made habitable, clearly recently, and another, on which four monks were working, was in process of being restored, evidently as a church of sorts. Something familiar about one of the men attracted

Maldred — and when he got closer he was astonished to recognise the monk Turgot, Margaret's confessor. One of the others was a fine-looking older man, with the hot eyes of a fanatic, the others ordinary serving-brothers.

Cospatrick smiled. "I perceive that you recognise our friend from Dunfermline. In changed circumstances — like myself! Such is the lot of man, God's will being done! And this is the Prior Aldwin, lately of Jarrow. And Winchcombe, was it? An even more notable churchman, I am assured."

The two priests greeted Maldred distinctly warily, Turgot acknowledging him by name as the Lord Maldred, but referring to Cospatrick as Brother Eadwulf.

"What brings you here?" Maldred demanded. "Working with your hands. In this sorry place. How come you . . . ?"

"None so sorry, man," Cospatrick intervened. "One of the most sacred fanes in the land, once. And may be again — who knows?"

"Perhaps. But Brother Turgot was the Queen's chaplain a month back, no more."

"The King's Highness has never thought well of me," Turgot said. "He ever suspects me. Of over-much weight with the Queen. He has banished me, for the second time."

"Then what do you here?"

"Friend Turgot was making south down Lauderdale when he came to rest for the night at Ersildoune," Cospatrick explained. "Someone told him of my humble self, and he came to me. Earlier, while I was at Ubbanford, our friend Prior Aldwin here arrived there, a fugitive from his priory of Jarrow-on-Tyne, whence he had been ejected by a Norman nominee of the new Archbishop Thomas of York, who has succeeded old Eldred. This is happening all over England. He was at a loss where to go, what to do. So, in all due humility, I proposed that he and Turgot should come here to ancient Melross. Form a community here again. And, who knows, perhaps build it up to what it was before?"

Maldred was almost beyond being surprised by Cospatrick mac Maldred. But to accept him as a founder of monasteries and protector of ousted priests, demanded considerable mental adjustment.

"Why?" he demanded, baldly.

The other shrugged. "Now that I have embraced God's cause and service, you would not have me slack in it? Or turn my back on my fellow-servants in their need?"

That from the greatest cynic it had ever been his lot to meet, left Maldred little the wiser. "These, then, know who . . . that you are . . . ?"

"That I am Eadwulf, who has been other. Come to God late in life perhaps — but with the more need to make up for time past! But still with some small sway in this land, it may be. On both sides of Tweed."

"We greatly admire and give thanks to God for what Brother Eadwulf in his goodness permits us to attempt, in the cause of Holy Mother Church," Prior Aldwin declared carefully.

"No doubt. But . . . this church or community, which you seek to establish here, will be a *Romish* one, I think? Not Columban."

"To be sure, my lord. It could not be other. We are all good adherents of the Holy Father at the Vatican, however unworthy . . ."

"It was Romish before, Maldred," Cospatrick pointed out. "The Celtic Church has shown no interest in Melross. And as a daughter-house of Lindisfarne, under Bishop Walchere of Durham, it would have to be." That mention of Bishop Walchere was distinctly emphasised — and set Maldred's mind speculating on a new course. As it was no doubt meant to do.

"Yet this is Scotland," he said. "Where the Church is not Roman."

"It would not be the first such," Turgot put in. "Are not the King and Queen building a great new church at Dunfermline, of our Roman faith?"

There was no answer to that, of course. But though Maldred held his peace, he eyed Cospatrick the more thoughtfully.

Leaving the two serving-brothers to continue with the building efforts, the other pair led the visitors into the restored house, which proved to be a tiny, makeshift sanctuary combined with living-quarters, severely functional but clean and adequate, if much less comfortable than Cospatrick's little establishment under the White Hill of Ersildoune. They did not produce Burgundian wines, either.

It did not take long for that man to make it clear why he

had brought his cousin here. "The Lord Maldred is going to Dunfermline in a day or two," he said. "I wish him to be able to inform King Malcolm as to the situation in the North of England now prevailing, so far as you know it. You are both Bishop Walchere's men, and have no reason to love the Normans. You may speak freely. My cousin approves of that Bishop."

The Prior Aldwin needed little encouragement. With his burning eyes, intense expression and pale leanness, Maldred judged him to be of the stuff of martyrs and prophets, no carefully discreet cleric — although Turgot was of a different sort.

"The land simmers in near revolt," he said. "The man Odo — I will not call him bishop, for he disgraces his mitre — is worse hated than even King William. Everywhere his hand is heavy, the folk groaning under his oppressions . . ."

"That we know, friend," Cospatrick interrupted. "It is details that we want. The state of Northumbria, Cumbria, Durham, Deira, even Mercia, or what is left of it. Of Hereward the Wake in his fens . . ."

"Hereward is captured. Betrayed. William has taken him to Normandy. What to do with him, only God knows. Or Satan! The Abbot Thurstan was forced to surrender. To Odo. What is become of *him*, none can tell. I fear the worst. The fenland revolt is crushed. But other revolt is stirring. Even amongst the Normans themselves."

"Ha! Which Normans?"

"Roger fitz Osbern, for one, Earl of Hereford. And Ralph Guader, the Breton, Earl of Norfolk. Others less lofty but still powerful. Even some of the Norman bishops . . ." He began to say something else, but thought better of it. "Odo has offended them. Now that King William spends most of his time in France, Odo rules all as viceroy and Chief Justice. Even William's youngest son, Henry, is at odds with his uncle. There will be trouble, nothing more sure."

"Hereford, you say? One of the Norman Marcher earls! This could mean much. If Hereford rebelled, the Welsh would rise again, for sure. Especially as, I am told, the other Marchers, Chester, Shrewsbury, Gloucester, are with William in France. Aye — what, then, of the North?"

"The North seethes. With the Earl Waldeve absent,

Edwin of Mercia dead and Morkar prisoner, the North is leaderless. But it seethes . . ."

They discussed the situation in greater detail, Cospatrick putting shrewd questions, not all of which the churchmen could answer. During the Earl Waldeve's absence with William, his friend Bishop Walchere of Durham was acting his deputy — and since no other major leaders remained, he could be said to be ruling the North. But, to be sure, he was no warrior, however capable; and one Ligulf, a thane descended from the ancient line of the Earls of Bernicia, was acting as his right hand in matters secular and military. Cospatrick knew this Ligulf, in fact could claim distant relationship, and was keen to have relevant information. It was clear, to Maldred at least, that his cousin was not going to be content with any passive role, friar or none.

For his own part, when Cospatrick had got all he could, for the present, out of Prior Aldwin, Maldred sought information from Turgot as to affairs at Dunfermline. The Benedictine was no gossip, but he was at least an enthusiast over Margaret and her activities, obviously no less smitten by the Queen's attractions and excellences than were others — but of course confined his panegyrics to her piety, saintliness and good works generally. The handsome new church to the Holy Trinity was going up apace, he said — although one gathered that if *he* had been the architect instead of the monk, Godwin, sent up by Archbishop Lanfranc, there could have been improvements to the design. The Queen had persuaded the King to endow the new foundation with broad lands and properties, some taken from the forfeited MacBeth family — lands in Fortrenn, that is, for even Malcolm was not sufficiently strong to take lands from the late King's heirs up in Moray and the North, where they still remained powerful. Moreover, of course, now the Queen was much concerned with increasing the power and prestige of the See of St. Andrews, so that it might give a lead to all Scotland in matters religious . . .

"See is a word we do not use in Scotland," Maldred interrupted flatly. "We have no sees."

"The see is the diocese of a bishop, my lord."

"I know what the word means, sir. But we have no dioceses or sees in our Church. Our bishoprics are otherwise. Bishops are with us a kind of priest distinct from

249

abbots, as both are from lesser ministers. Equal to them in certain functions, inferior to them only in rule. And . . . I do not think that we require being given a lead in religion, as you say."

The other pursed his lips. "No doubt you best know the peculiarities of your faith, my lord. But — that is scarcely my concern. I but say that the Queen seeks to enhance the position and status of St. Andrews. Endow and improve it, that it may be in a position to give lead to others. You will not deny that conditions cannot but be improved in matters of religion, in this land? Or in any land?"

"I urge that you watch where you tread, Brother Turgot!" Cospatrick said, grinning. "Recollect that the Lord Maldred's father is Primate of the Columban Church. And so where leads are to be given, *he* falls to be consulted!"

The monk said nothing to that.

"I knew that Her Highness advised Bishop Fothad of St. Andrews to change matters at St. Andrews. I heard her tell him so two years ago. But this you speak of — raising the position of his bishopric, you said? How shall this be done? His is but one of the bishoprics, if the richest, under the Abbey of St. Serf of Loch Leven."

"But the seat of the most eminent of the bishops. Fothad."

"Eminent as Chancellor of the realm and King's Bishop. Not otherwise. What can the Queen do?"

"Endow with lands, moneys. Improve the places of worship. Contrive fine vestments for the St. Andrews clergy, as she is doing for those of Holy Trinity to be, she and her ladies working these with their own fair hands. So, in God's service, may a minster or a bishopric be built up."

"Perhaps so. But all this of raising up and adoration is foreign to our Celtic ways."

"You have your own saints. Many of them. Of which Holy Church has never so much as heard! This Serf you speak of. Ternan. Others. You would not deny that Christ's own Mother and His apostles are more worthy of reverence?"

"No. But our saints were missionaries. The Brethren of Columba. The churches named after them they established. We do not adore them — only commemorate their work in our land . . ."

Cospatrick yawned openly, bored. "I say, leave the Queen to it. No harm in it. What interests me is where she intends to find the siller for all this endowing and bestowings and building of churches? Malcolm was never one for gathering moneys. Where is it to come from? I do not see our Scots lords dipping deep into their coffers. Which are scarcely full, forby!"

"The Queen is full of projects to increase and multiply treasure," Turgot assured. "And not only in God's service but for the prosperity of this kingdom and people. She is seeking to encourage more trade and manufacture, greater produce of the country. Many distant lands, she says, would purchase Scottish goods — in especial wool and woollen cloths. Hides. Salted fish. Spirits. Skins of deer, wolves, seals, martens. To set up guilds, as in the Low Countries and Hungary. To foster craftsmen. Ports and havens to be improved, enlarged with piers and jetties. Burghs to have rights of tax and custom — of which the Crown gets some part. Other like enterprises . . ."

"Lord — once I told Malcolm that he had wed a queen of some commerce!" Cospatrick exclaimed. "It seems that I was right. And does the King swallow all this? Malcolm, who ever lived by and for the sword! Trade, huckstering and chaffering! Salted fish and beeswax! You conceive of Malcolm Big Head setting his hand to this?"

"He is already doing so. Or aiding the Queen to do so. And . . . it is how Holy Church gains much of her revenues." There was reproof in that.

"I stand corrected, Brother! I have much to learn, it seems. But — not today! We must take the road. Maldred has far to ride." He rose. "Blessings on the good work here. I shall see you again . . ."

As they rode off, back to Ersildoune, Maldred eyed his companion consideringly. "You *want* a Romish church there, cousin, do you not? This is no chance matter. Why? You care not a snap of the fingers for either Church, I swear. Why, then?"

"For sufficient reason, man — and you much miscall a sinner but newly repented and enrolled in holy orders! I want a Popish church here because a Columban one would be of no least use to me. To sustain my part as friar, I require a parent house to which, if need be, I can seem to belong. And since I am a Romish friar, it must needs be a Romish one . . ."

"You could belong to Ubbanford — as I thought that you did. There is more to it than that."

"There is, yes. Can you not see? You heard — Bishop Walchere is ruling Northumbria and Deira for Waldeve. Waldeve is now part of William's own household, wed to his niece Judith. And with Northampton and Huntingdon, richer, softer, earldoms than his northern ones — and he is a soft man. As I see it, Walchere and his new friend Ligulf — Walchere is a great one for friends! — will continue to control Northumbria, Durham, and probably much of Cumbria, for some time to come. So, for my purposes — which are also Scotland's purposes — Walchere will be a useful friend for me! Although a different kind of friend!"

"I see that. But . . ."

"So I set up a monastery at Melross in Scotland — or encourage these others to do so. Under Walchere's bishoply rule and authority. Will he not thank me? And trust me? Aldwin is his friend — another of them! Both are therefore in my debt. There can be much coming and going between Melross and Durham — to my much information and comfort! I will have a sure and secret road to the man who rules the North of England. And who thinks well of me. He is no danger to Scotland, Walchere, no warrior like that Odo. Forby, he will not rule there *always*. When the time is ripe — Walchere goes! And . . ."

"And Cospatrick, alive again, rules in his stead!"

"You said it, Maldred — I did not! But it behoves a wise man to be prepared for changes, does it not? For our Scots realm's sake, as well as our own."

"Between you, cousin, and Margaret Atheling, I say — God help the Scots realm! And that realm's Church . . ."

16

MALDRED AND MAGDA stared about them at the transformed servants' hall of the palace — as they had stared at almost everything, indeed, since they had arrived at Dunfermline after a longer than usual absence. Change was everywhere — and only a churl would have failed to admit that it was almost all for the better. This lesser hall, for instance, was no longer for servants but was a splendid and indeed delightful apartment, well-lit, tapestry-hung, handsomely furnished, actually carpeted with a sort of heavy plaiding, even provided with instruments of music in a little gallery — from which now a young woman was strumming tunefully on a clarsach or harp. It was now the Queen's hall, the servants banished elsewhere; and Margaret, laying down her needlework, rose and came to embrace them both warmly.

"My dears, my very dear friends!" she exclaimed. "It has been so long. I declare, I thought that I would have myself to travel to your Borderland for a sight of you. Magda — you look so well. Comely. He must be treating you passing well, I think! And you, Maldred, are more handsome each time I see you — which is insufficiently often."

They made due acknowledgement of this flattering welcome, Maldred at least embarrassingly aware of the interested and amused glances of the bevy of the Queen's ladies, another new feature — all now standing because she was on her feet — all so attractively-dressed and turned-out, all clutching their colourful sewnwork, Romish church-vestments most evidently. Margaret herself was superbly gowned, the fine embroidered silken fabric seeded with Tay pearls, and looking her most beautiful — even though neither of her visitors mentioned the fact that evidently she was pregnant once more.

Perhaps she perceived their quick glances, for she smiled. "*My* husband is equally attentive, Magda, you will see! In all matters!" She raised one shoulder in an incipient shrug. "God blesses me."

"Yes. How are the princes, Highness?" Magda asked.

"Edward thrives, and is unruly. His father greatly spoils him. Edmund remains less than strong. I pray daily that he will gain in vigour. And — your Marsala?"

"Sufficiently well for me to be jealous of her! She has her father as plaything! I come second."

"She is not to be believed," Maldred asserted. "Highness — you have made great changes. Since last we were here. It is, to be sure, some months. All this . . ." He gestured around.

"You like it? You, who prefer things to be left as they are!"

"Some things. It is very fine. All that we have seen, all much to be admired."

"I think that I hear doubt behind your words, my friend? You reserve your approval of what I do?"

"No. Leastways, not altogether. It is only that it all seems . . . foreign. Not in our own Scots style and custom."

"And you conceive that to be wrong, Maldred?"

"If overmuch, it could be, Highness, I think."

"But — I do all only for Scotland's betterment. Nothing to the realm's or the people's hurt. Surely you know that?"

"I know that is what you intend, yes. But . . ."

"Do not heed him," Magda said. "He would have us all back in the days of barbarism. He will have no advancement."

"Advancement I welcome. But not all English, *Saxon*, advancement . . ."

The palace-steward — now being called chamberlain — appeared in the doorway behind them, and thumped on the floor with his staff-of-office. "Silence for the King's Highness!" he cried.

Malcolm stalked in and all bowed low. He was dressed in rich clothing such as Maldred had never before seen him to wear, cloth-of-gold, velvet and a jewelled belt. He did not really suit it, being a man more apt for armour and the harness of war; indeed he gave the impression of wearing it with some unease.

"Ha! I heard that you were here," he jerked, without preamble. "Should not you have come seeking me, instead of I you?"

"I was told that you were not in the palace, Highness," Maldred said. "We greet you well."

"Aye, no doubt. You have news for me?"

"Some, yes."

"Of moment?"

"That is for Your Highness to judge. I but carry it."

"Be not so prickly, man! Come, then. Where we shall be free of the clatter of women's tongues." He cleared his throat. "If Her Highness will excuse us?" Malcolm mac Duncan had a long way to go before he was all that his wife would make of him.

The two men went into a small ante-room, dark and unembellished.

"What are Cospatrick's tidings for me, then?" Malcolm demanded at once.

"He has learned much, this time. But how much will be new to you I do not know. There is great upheaval in England. William is still in France. There has been revolt in the South. And along the Welsh marches. Led by William's own people — Normans. But it has failed. Been betrayed to Odo. It was mainly against him, rather than William himself, it is said."

"Roger fitz Osbern was it? And Ralph Guader of Norfolk? As your last messenger foretold?"

"Yes. The Earls of Hereford and Norfolk. And sundry others. But the Earl Waldeve has fallen also . . ."

"Waldeve? Of Northumbria? Waldeve fallen? William's man. How, man — how?"

"It seems that he threw in his lot with these others. Why, I know not. He had come back from France — Cospatrick learned of that months ago. It may have been only against Odo that he turned, not really William. But he is ruined now. And a new situation in Northumbria and Cumbria and Deira."

"You say all has failed? How was that? Was there battle?"

"No real battle. All had been planned for long. Hereford was to rouse the marches and the West. The Welsh to rise, as usual. He was also to bring over a large force of his Bretons. No — that was Ralph Guader. *He* is the Breton. He, Ralph, was to raise Norfolk and East Anglia, and the fenmen again. Also, a Danish fleet to come, under the new Danish king's brother Knud. Great plans. All was to be concerted at a notable occasion, a marriage celebration, to hide the plotters assembling, so that they might gather from all over the land without arousing Odo's suspicion.

It was held at Norfolk's castle of Thetford. Norfolk was marrying Hereford's sister Emma. There were hundreds there, many of them Norman barons and knights. Waldeve came, and took part. No doubt he was to raise the North. But — he was the weak link, the cause of the disaster. For his wife, the Countess Judith, betrayed all to Odo, her uncle. She was not at the wedding, but Waldeve must have told her . . ."

"The fool! To let a woman lead him by the nose!"

Maldred swallowed. "Yes, Highness. So all was lost before it ever started. Odo descended upon Norfolk while he was still only mustering, and waiting for the Danes to arrive. At Cambridge. He shattered the rebels. Norfolk fled overseas. Hereford has fled into Wales. And Waldeve — Waldeve cravenly yielded himself up to Odo, confessing all, and claiming that he was pressed only unwillingly into it. Odo has sent him to Normandy, to plead for mercy with William himself. The Danes came late, into the Humber again. They sallied as far as York only, sacked the minster and much else, then sailed back to Denmark."

"God's Grace!" the King exclaimed. "The folly of it! To trust that Waldeve — and he to trust his wife! William's kin. So the Bastard survives another attempt — the fiend take him! But — what of Northumbria?"

"That is the heart of Cospatrick's tidings. Odo has appointed Bishop Walchere to rule the North. He was doing so before, in Waldeve's name. Now he has all the powers of a great earl. In King William's name. It is even better than Cospatrick hoped for."

"Aye. And Cumbria?"

"The situation in Cumbria is the more improved. Walchere has more than he can handle, without Cumbria. So, although Odo expects that he governs there also, the Bishop will not attempt to do so. He has an understanding with Cospatrick. He will not interfere in Cumbria. And Cospatrick will not interfere in Northumbria — meantime. So, with Hereford and the Norman West, like Wales, lying low, Madach has little to fear in Cumbria. The Orkney earls will not make any move, out of Galloway, in such situation. Thus your realm is secure, Highness, down to Lancaster and the Ribble."

"Aye. For the moment."

Malcolm had, the previous year, doubtfully agreed to

Cospatrick's urgings, through Maldred. He had created his cousin's eldest though illegitimate son, Dolfin, Earl of Cumbria; and his third son Cospatrick, Earl of Dunbar and March. The former was a purely nominal title, and the boy stayed at home at Ersildoune. But the King had sent Madach mac Melmore, Maldred's brother, to be governor of Cumbria and the West March of the Border, at Caer-Luel; whilst Maldred himself remained in practical control of the East March. With, of course, Cospatrick senior secretly manipulating all. All were cousins of the King.

"This mummery of Cospatrick's has served none so ill," Malcolm went on — and it was not often that man admitted to satisfaction, save with his second wife. "Fool's play as it seemed. He is a cunning fox. But I would never trust him far."

"He is serving your cause well, in this at least. And Madach says that he could not govern Cumbria without him. He comes and goes at will."

"Many must now know that he is alive?"

"Some few, no doubt. But only, I think, those in whose interest it is to keep the secret. He will see to that."

"As to Cumbria, when William returns, or the man Odo recovers himself after this failed revolt, he will not be content to leave Cumbria in this Walchere's feeble grip."

"Perhaps not, Highness. But — Cospatrick has other tidings for you. Which could affect this. Lanfranc the Archbishop is at odds with the new Archbishop of York, Thomas — indeed, he refuses to consecrate him as such. Until Thomas accepts subservience to Canterbury — which he does not do. They put the issue to the Pope, in Rome. And he has sent a Cardinal named Hubert to England, to consider and decide on the matter, in council. This Cardinal has found and proclaimed that York is indeed subject to Canterbury, and Lanfranc undoubtedly Primate of England. But — it does not stop there. It is declared that the archdiocese of York is only to control its own see, that of Durham, and such bishoprics as shall or will exist in *Scotland*!"

"Christ God! Scotland?"

"Yes. Cospatrick urges that you should take heed of this. It is the overlordship claim again. In religion, as in all else. I would counsel Your Highness to remember this when, when these new Romish churches and practices are established here!"

The King eyed him levelly for a moment, but said nothing.

"As to the quarrel between Lanfranc and this Thomas," Maldred went on, "there could be advantages in it, also, Cospatrick says. For Thomas was appointed at *Odo's* bidding. They are friends. So now Odo quarrels with Lanfranc. He, Lanfranc, has complained indeed to William in France that Odo is encroaching on his Canterbury lands. So, with bad blood between William's friend the Primate and William's half-brother the viceroy, there is likely to be little adventuring in the English North for some time."

"The saints be praised that these Normans must so quarrel amongst themselves! And so save more honest men greater trouble. This will please Edgar, I swear."

"Edgar . . . ? Edgar Atheling? Why?"

"Do you not know, man? Edgar is here again — a plague on him! He came on St. Grimbald's Day, a week back. I thank God he had not brought his mother and sister with him! The Queen loads him with gifts . . ."

"Why? Why has he come back? When it is against your agreement with William."

"He comes as from Philip of France. He has been at his Court these many months. Philip has offered him the countship of Montreuil-sur-Mer, in the Pas de Calais. On condition that he uses it to assail William's eastern flank in Normandy. For this he seeks my aid — as does Philip. In men and treasure. He says the more attacks on William in France, the less will he be seen in England! To my advantage. Philip sees France and Scotland uniting to contain him. Edgar is but a pawn in this game."

"This is something Cospatrick has *not* heard, I think! And — are you going to give Prince Edgar this aid?"

"In money and gear and arms, yes. Margaret is as good as a mint for moneys, these days! All she touches seems to turn to gold. But — no men. Not one man from Scotland will I entrust to Edgar Atheling! Gold I care little for — but men are different. All my men I can use here! Edgar may go hire him his own Saxon men. If he can."

A knock at the door revealed Margaret. "I am going to take Magda to see how the new church grows," she announced. "Will Maldred come on after, when you have finished your talking? Perhaps yourself, Malcolm?"

"Take him, if you will. Now. We have spoken sufficient, meantime. Myself, I pray to be excused, my love. I have seen the church times uncounted. I cannot think that it will look so different for having a few more stones added."

"As you will, my lord."

Attended by her personal almoner, without whom apparently she seldom moved abroad, to distribute bounty and relief to the needy and afflicted as she went, Margaret led her visitors through the township surrounding the palace and up the hill to the abbey precincts — and as they went folk came to bow and smile and wave, from cottage doorways, lane-ends and garden plots, with children actually running up to greet and even touch the Queen, as a sure friend. Every now and again she paused or stepped aside to speak with the aged or the crippled; and once she disappeared within a dark, low-doored hovel, and, when she emerged, sent her almoner in after her. Clearly she was greatly beloved by the common people — as well she might be. And as clearly her affection and sympathy for them was no mere assumption nor act of charity, but came from the heart. This was something new in queens.

At the abbey gates quite a crowd was waiting. This was normal, it transpired, for here the daily feeding of vagrants and indigent folk had been transferred from the palace premises, on the King's insistence; now the monks of St. Ternan's dispensed the royal provision, though often with the Queen's personal assistance, sometimes as many as ten-score of the needy — and the greedy, no doubt — applying. Margaret moved amongst this patiently-waiting, ragged and strong-smelling throng, with no least hint of embarrassment or condescension, Maldred at least somewhat out-of-his-depth.

The new church construction was very evident to all comers, both on account of its size and prominence and of the noise of the hammering, stone-chipping and general clatter which accompanied the work — and which helped to account for the lack of enthusiasm on the part of the abbey denizens. Magda and Maldred had seen it, of course, as they passed by on their arrival — they could scarcely do otherwise; but they had not paused to consider details. Now Margaret, with infectious eagerness, demonstrated all.

There was no doubt that it was going to be a large and fine place. No other church building in Scotland was half as large, well over one hundred feet long by sixty or seventy in width. So far the walling had risen to only about two-thirds of its full height, to the eaves-course, at some thirty feet, with seven pointed-arched windows on each lateral wall, and the beginnings of seven smaller clerestory windows above, flat pilasters rising between. The gables to east and west rose considerably higher, with the great main doorway to the west, arched and surmounted by tiers of semi-circular carving, above it a large many-lighted window with stone astragals. Although the most elaborate construction appeared to be here, the work was in fact further ahead at the east end. Margaret explained that this was normal building practice, that the east end, with the chancel or choir, and the altar, should be finished first, so that the building could be consecrated and used, at least partially, with the uncompleted western or nave end walled off temporarily. Internally, two rows each of seven great pillars — seven being the godly or perfect number — rose for the support of the eventual groined stone roof, which would be twice as high as any hall roof at nearly one hundred feet, the pillars alternately carved with spirals or zigzags. All was at present enclosed and part-veiled within a spidery scaffolding of poles lashed together, with ladders and gangways for the busy masons, masking the effect of all the expert and ambitious stone-work and ornamentation. But even so, the visitors were impressed, Maldred especially. This Holy Trinity was not going to be so large as the cathedral at Durham, but it was bigger and finer than any other church he had ever seen. And he could not but admit — if only to himself — that it made the little timber, turf and thatch Celtic churches seem very modest, if not mean, by comparison. Even though, he reminded himself, they had very different ideas behind them, as well as different functions.

Margaret led them into the chancel to see the high altar, already in position, built of polished pink granite with a slab-top of the most lovely green-veined Iona marble — this, the Queen revealed proudly, a gift from the Abbot of Iona himself. Which was thought-provoking. Then she showed them the underground crypt being excavated beneath the chancel-floor — for this, she declared, was to be the place of royal sepulture hereafter, where, God permitting, she and her husband and their descendants would lie when their due time came.

"Pray that will be far hence indeed!" Magda said hurriedly.

Her husband cleared his throat. "To be sure. But . . . sixty Scots, Pictish and Dalar kings lie buried on Iona, Highness. All of the most ancient line in Christendom. Have you forgot?"

She looked at him, her lovely eyes untroubled. "No, Maldred, I have not forgot," she said. "But there is a time and a tide for all things. For standing still and for moving on. For holding fast and for pointing forward and renewal. I believe that God, in His wisdom, sent that great storm to bring me to this northern land for a purpose. *His* purpose. In all humility I say it. For myself, I am nothing. Only, I truly believe, the most unworthy and humble instrument of God's purpose here. How else has all fallen out so wonderfully? Perhaps because I bore here the Black Rood, part of Christ's True Cross, to Scotland — who knows? But . . . it is a time for going forward, not for standing still, dear Maldred. Do you not see it?"

He inclined his head, but said nothing.

Sighing, she turned, to lead the way out.

The Queen conducted them then to a small chamber of the abbey itself, with Abbot Ivo in attendance now. And here, the door unlocked, they were all but dazzled, ill-lit as the place was. The room was, in fact, a treasure-house, full of gleaming gold and silver and jewels, of magnificent coloured vestments, of rich tapestries and hangings, of priceless church plenishings. In pride of place was the splendid crucifix Maldred had brought from Archbishop Eldred.

"To furnish the church when it shall be finished," Margaret said, the sight of it all beginning to recover her enthusiasm. "Will it not be glorious? See — these Gospel-books. These I had in my cave — you remember, Maldred?" She produced a quick, almost conspiratorial little smile. "Malcolm had them covered in gold for me. Is he not good?"

"Very kind, yes." Maldred took one of the four beautifully-illuminated if well-thumbed manuscript books, now encased within boards plated with hammered gold and set with rubies and pearls. "Handsome. Costly. Your lady-mother would approve."

Closely she looked at him in that dim light. "Why do you say that?" she demanded.

"I but remember the day, at the Ward of the Stormounth. The day Magda was lost on the Muir of Gormack. When I handed over to you the treasure. From Archbishop Eldred. The Princess Agatha said that you must keep that crucifix. And other things of great worth. Too good, she said, to sell for the poor and your slaves. And you said no, Christ did not require gold and jewels to be held back for Him. But the poor, for whom He gave His life, did. Or words of that sort. I see that you have come round to the way your mother thought."

"No. It is not that, Maldred — why do you ever misjudge what I seek to do? Have me in the wrong? Much I give to the poor. Always they are in my heart and prayers. But God's house must be furnished. Surely of the best that we can give?"

"Must it? Because you build this great church, Highness — must God dwell in it? Does He require men to build Him His house? And fill it with *their* treasures? These may not be *His* treasures . . ."

"Hush, Maldred!" Magda exclaimed. "This is no way to speak. And to the Queen."

"No — let him speak," Margaret said. "I must hear him, at least. I must never turn my friends away unheard. Or even my enemies. Say on."

"I am no churchman, Highness. But I have heard my father talk. And others. Abbot Ivo, here, would be the better man to speak. But — is this not one of the great gulfs between your Romish and our Columban Churches? You seek for God oftenest in a *building*. A building made by man. We do not. We seek everywhere that he made — out in His world, under His heaven, in the open, in woods and trees and springs. On hilltops where the ancients worshipped. Are you and yours not in danger of worshipping your great buildings, and the gold and silver within them, instead of the God-Child born in a stable?"

There was silence in that treasure-store for a moment or two, Magda and Abbot Ivo in major discomfort, the other two staring at each other.

"Oh, you are wrong, Maldred, wrong!" the Queen said, at length. "Worship God out in the open, yes — in the woods and hills. When you remember to do so! But surely men should offer to God, in worship, what is precious to them, the finest work of their hands and skills. God gave them these skills, to develop and use in His service. Gold and treasure men seek after — so should they not offer of it to God? Worship should *cost* something, surely? This church we build will stand for untold generations, a witness that we worshipped God, a thing of beauty and peace."

"Could you not say that of the simplest stone-circle up on the moor? Which may last the longer, who knows?"

"These were set up by pagans, to worship the sun. Only that."

"But still for worship. The best they knew. Until Christ's Gospel was brought to them. By simple Columban missionaries, preaching in their stone-circles. By brave words only — no gold-and-jewelled books." Maldred stopped, and shook his head. "I am sorry," he muttered. "I should not have said so much. I know that you are good, better than any of us. And I am not. I should not speak so. But . . . I think that you are mistaken, in some of the things that you do. Here in Scotland. In especial, this of seeking to turn our native Church to Rome."

"But I do not, Maldred. Only to bring it into *harmony* with Rome. And with the rest of Christendom. That surely is not mistaken?"

"This great church you build is to be a Romish one?"

"Yes. But it is only one."

"What of St. Andrews? From what Turgot says, you would turn that into a Roman bishopric. As example for others."

"No. You do not understand. I only seek to improve, to help, to encourage . . ." It was her turn to stop and sigh. "I will never convince you, Maldred, I know — you, who I would wish above others to understand. I am sorry, also." She turned, and moved outside. "Abbot Ivo, I think, even Abbot Dunchad of Iona, do not think so ill of me as you do, Maldred."

"I do not think ill of you, Highness — God knows I do not! Only that in this matter you could be mistaken."

They left it at that. And thankfully Abbot Ivo, non-controversialist, made his escape.

On their way back to the palace, Magda chattering somewhat fervently for her, the Queen presently interrupted.

"You spoke of Turgot, Maldred. Do you know how it goes with him? Where he is now. Since, since . . ."

It had come eventually to King Malcolm's ears that the monk Turgot, whom he had expelled, had in fact gone no further than Melross in the mouth of Lauderdale, and there, with Prior Aldwin, started this new monastery. Whatever his lack of concern about the Romanisation of his realm's Church, the King was sufficiently displeased — and jealous, presumably — to send command for Turgot to be gone, right out of Scotland. Malcolm had had enough of Turgot. Because Melross was in fact Cospatrick's monastery, and that man, in the guise of Brother Eadwulf, was proving to be a very useful tool and source of information, the King had had to dress up his expulsion order in less bald style. He declared that the incumbents of any religious establishment, as of any other in Scotland, must take oath of allegiance to himself, as monarch — or else go. Turgot, a member of the Durham community, could scarcely do that: Aldwin the more so, as Prior. So they had both had to leave the country, a few months ago. The monastery at Melross was consequently reduced to only eight or nine serving-brothers of Scots extraction, under the supervision of the Prior at Ubbanford, across Tweed. It was still, of course, sufficient for Cospatrick's purposes, as excuse and screen.

"He is gone to Bishop Wearmouth, Highness. Near where we first all met. Bishop Walchere has withdrawn him there, with Prior Aldwin. They are to build up that monastery. It has been run from Jarrow, it seems, and had fallen into decline. They are there now . . ."

"Wearmouth! That unhappy place! Although, perhaps I should not say that, since God sent me there, to meet Malcolm. And so brought me to Scotland. Poor Turgot. Malcolm bears hardly on him. Is he . . . bitter?"

"I think not. He is a very shrewd and careful cleric, that one."

"He is a good man. A, a stout pillar of God's house!" Her smile was brief. "I grieve that Malcolm distrusts him.

The Queen recognised the situation, and referred no more to it.

Outside the palace a commotion was in progress, evidently marking the return of Prince Edgar from a hawking party on the tidelands of Forth. Margaret revealed no enthusiasm for conversation with her brother, and did not press Magda and Maldred to stay when they made prompt suggestions that they should be on their way to Bothargask — which, with little Marsala to consider, had to be journeyed to in shorter stages. They would rest for the night at the St. Serf's hospice on the shore of Loch Leven. Neither had any desire to renew their acquaintance with the rightful King of England.

As, presently, they rode away from Dunfermline, Magda berated her husband. "That was unkindly done," she accused. "You much hurt Margaret. Since when have you become so strong a churchman? I never noted it previously. You were unkind, and scarcely wise, I think. Since she *is* the Queen."

"Perhaps," he admitted — for he was himself somewhat troubled. "I would not wish to hurt her, or to be unkind. Wisdom does not come into it. But — what I said had to be said. By someone."

"If so, I do not see why it should have to be you. There is a sufficiency of your Columban clerics to say it, is there not? If it is so important."

"But they are not saying it! They are tied in their tongues. Because she *is* Queen. And is so good. So kind. And buys their sufferance with her generosity and gifts. This restoring of the harried Abbey of Iona. And the like. Lands for Loch Leven. Indeed, I think that they do not perceive the danger. To their Church and traditions. Aye, and to the realm itself."

"And you do! Whose concern it is not. If your precious Church is in so much danger from the doings and kindnesses of one woman, then I hardly think that it is worth all the trouble!"

"When the one woman is the Queen, strong of mind and determined, with the King caring nothing either way but doting on her — and no body of churchmen united to combat her — then the danger is real. This is, as I see it now, one of the weaknesses of our Church. It is not as your Romish one, with a strong authority at the head. It is not concerned with any hierarchy. It is the Church of the people. So there is no body at the centre to fight its cause. It has never had to fight such assault before. This is not its purpose. Those who should be taking the lead do not, it seems. My father, the Primate, is no fighter, a gentle man lost in his books. Abbot Dunchad of Iona is strong, but he is so tied up with the rebuilding of his ruined abbey

— and so grateful to the Queen — that his hands are bound. And the King's Bishop, Fothad, is also bound. His St. Andrews she is putting in her great debt. And he rises in influence. I tell you, she is clever, far-sighted, as Cospatrick says . . ."

"Cospatrick! There it is, I think. It is that Cospatrick who has put you up to this, Maldred. He is a snake, that man! Oh yes, diverting and excellent company. But cunning as he is devious. And a despoiler at heart. He has too much ascendancy over you, Maldred. I have felt this for long."

"That is foolishness, girl!" he exclaimed. "You do not know what you say. Of course I see much of him. And heed him in many things. It could not be otherwise, since I am administering his earldoms for him. And he is as clever as she is, and sees things very clearly. But — I remain my own man. What I said came from *myself*, not Cospatrick. And, I tell you, *had* to be said. By someone." His chin out-thrust, subconsciously he was urging his horse to greater speed, so that he drew ahead a little.

She did not attempt to keep up with him.

After a little, he threw back over his shoulder, "I shall go speak with my father. Before we return to Dunbar. Warn him. Urge him to act."

She shrugged. "And to think that I once feared that you were too fond of Margaret Atheling!"

He looked back, frowning. "I am fond of her," he said. "I esteem her greatly. She is, she is good as she is beautiful. That, God's mercy, is a large part of the trouble!"

They rode on in silence.

17

MALDRED ARRIVED BACK at Dunbar Castle on an evening in
the following early summer to find that they had a most
unexpected visitor, none other than the Queen herself.
She had arrived unheralded, alone save for a small escort,
having crossed the Scottish Sea by the Earl of Fife's ferry
to North Berwick on the Lothian shore. Malcolm, it
seemed, was off on a visit to Dalar, to old Gilliadamnan,
Lord of Argyll, where, at Dunstaffnage, he was holding a
conference of West Highland chiefs, in an attempt to
present a more unified front against the incursions of
miscellaneous raiders who terrorised the entire Hebridean
seaboard, Norse, Orkneymen, Manx and Irish, and simple
pirates. It had not been considered a suitable occasion for
his wife to be introduced to those barbarian parts of his
realm; so she had felt free to make this more modest
journey on her own. She wished to visit her friend and
former confessor, Turgot of Durham — and of course to
give herself the pleasure of seeing Magda, Maldred and
her infant god-daughter Marsala, once more.

Margaret seemed in excellent spirits, pregnant again but
only by three months and not yet showing it. At Dunbar
she could put off almost entirely the trappings and attitudes
of royalty, and clearly rejoiced so to do. Girlish laughter,
even giggles and baby-talk, enlivened that rather grim
stronghold, with Maldred acting the fond, indulgent and
slightly superior male.

The Queen had a problem, however. While she wanted
to see Turgot, she did not wish to see Cospatrick. She had
always been very doubtful about that man and his
methods; and this present elaborate deceit as to his
supposed death went much against her principles. To
countenance the fraud by personally meeting the Earl and
then prejudicing her conscience by pretending that she
did not know that he still lived, she would find
distressing. Maldred was able to assure her that Cospatrick
had gone to Caer-luel. But it was a long way to Wearmouth . . .

Margaret was determined, however, and indeed seemed to look upon the whole episode as something of a holiday. Magda announced that she was going to come too. It would be only some one hundred and forty miles, less than three days' journey and over level coastal country. So next morning the three of them, with a small escort, rode southwards to Berwick-on-Tweed and then on through the Northumbrian coastlands, past Lindisfarne and Bamburgh, to Alnwick, a long day's ride but pleasant enough, in fine weather. The following day they did even better, fording the shallows of Coquet and Lyne and Wansbeck and Blyth, and a host of lesser streams, on their way to the Tyne. They were at the Wear by the next noon-day, tired but well-pleased with their progress.

To say that Turgot, and his superior Aldwin, were glad to see the Queen, however surprised, would be a major understatement. Aldwin was the more effusive, but Turgot's satisfaction was sufficiently manifest. This royal condescension and effort was flattering; but there was more to it than that, a personal and mutual admiration and a meeting of minds — Rome-oriented minds, to be sure. Maldred found himself out-on-a-limb, Magda too, to some extent, for she was a deal less religiously-inclined than was her mistress and friend.

Nevertheless they both remained at the Queen's side, after they had been shown round the establishment, situated at the farther side of the river-mouth from where they had all first met those years before. It was a somewhat decayed monastery now, but the two monks had plans for its improvement, and the visitors had all explained to them. Maldred was more interested to know just what had brought Margaret all this way — surely more than just a desire to see her former confessor?

In the refectory, regaled with simple fare suitable to the Cluniac ascetic reforms which these two Benedictines supported, the Queen unburdened herself.

"You travel the land at times, I believe, my friends? To your parent-house, at Durham. Even to York? And still further afield?" It was really Turgot whom she addressed. "When you do so hereafter, or go elsewhere in the English North, I would be much in your debt if you would do me a service — a service to God's cause also, surely. I require much church furniture and plenishing which I cannot find in Scotland. Much ornament, decoration, holy vessels, missals, books, pictures. Of such necessary aids to true worship there is a great dearth here. I desire you, of your goodness, to find these for me. For the furtherance of Christ's good purpose. Will you do this, my friends?"

"To be sure, Highness. How noble, how godly a quest!" Prior Aldwin enthused. "It shall be our joy."

"I hope that it may prove so. But you may find it something of a weariness, too. For I need much. I have set my hand to great labours. Although I shall not call them that, since they are *my* joy also. At Dunfermline and St. Andrews both the work proceeds. Of beautifying God's houses, of bringing the people into more fulfilling worship, in setting up shrines for pilgrimage, in strengthening the hands of the clergy who will work for the fuller witness for Christ in His One Church, Holy, Catholic and Apostolic."

"Most excellent, Highness! God reward you — most admirable. It shall be done."

"Admirable — but costly," Turgot mentioned. "Where shall we find the moneys for all this, Highness?"

"I have brought some gold pieces with me, for you. A token only. For a start. But all the articles you gain for me will be paid for, never fear. I do not ask you to beg, for me. The Lord Maldred here, of his goodness, did that for me once, to my undying gratitude. *I* do not mind begging, in Christ's cause — but I do not ask you to do that. Only to purchase. Money, mere money, is now little problem. My merchanting ventures are almost everywhere proving successful. Trade increases and taxes with it. The ship-men bring back much wealth from foreign lands. The Fife havens grow rich. I have set officers in each, customars they are called, to collect a tithe on all the wealth brought in. Our Hungarian shipmaster, Maurice, I have put in charge of all this revenue-making. Maldred, you will remember him. He mastered our ship which brought us from Wearmouth to Scotland, those years ago. He is now rich himself, with wide lands in Lennox — but unlike your Scots lords, not too proud to soil his hands with trade. As nor am I! So the money is there. Spend it for me."

"The King? He does not look on this with disfavour?" Turgot wondered, carefully.

"The King leaves such matters to me, of his goodness. I regret that he commanded you to leave Dunfermline, my good friend. He misjudged. But he will not hinder in this. He, indeed, is not much concerned with moneys and wealth, as with goods or even trade."

"These items we may purchase for you, Highness — how are they to be sent to you?" Turgot asked.

"Send them to Dunbar. Maldred here can have them shipped from there to my new haven of Inverkeithing, only four miles from Dunfermline. You will do that, Maldred?"

He could not do other than nod.

"I would ask also that you find for me, if you can, a man, more than one, skilled in woodwork, in wood-carving. Carving for church furniture. The good Archbishop Lanfranc sent one, Arnold, with the two master-masons who are building Holy Trinity minster at Dunfermline. But he has had to return to Canterbury."

"Are there not sufficient skilled wood-carvers in Scotland?" Maldred put to her. "Our ancient Celtic tradition is rich in fine and intricate carving, both in wood and stone."

"To be sure. But it is not in church carving that these are skilled. Their work is decorative, but scarcely religious. Strange animals and dragons, serpents and the like. I would set up a school of carving, to train such people in truly Christian design. If you had seen the great minsters of England, Maldred . . ."

"I have seen Durham. And Ely. From where I brought you . . . tokens!"

"Yes. Forgive me. I become carried away. But a school of craftsmen is much needed. For there is so much to do. Also, I plan that there should be a manufactory. At St Andrews, to start with. To make crucifixes and the like, in great numbers. For the pilgrims, first. Then for all the land. I have my Black Rood. I would have all households, even the poorest, to have each their crucifix."

"This we shall see to, also," Aldwin promised.

"Bishop Walchere will help, perhaps? Maldred — you found him kindly disposed to us, did you not?"

"To *us*, the Scots? That I know not, Highness. We found him against the Norman invaders, rather. Welcomed our armed aid against them. As to more than that, who knows?"

"He is a good man, one of God's chosen vessels," the Prior declared. "He will help in this, I feel sure."

"He gave his blessing to the establishment of the monastery of Melross, in Scotland," Turgot reminded. "Your h'm, friend, my Lord Maldred, Brother Eadwulf, esteems him. And he Eadwulf. They are close."

This was part of what worried Maldred. Cospatrick would use Walchere, as he would use anyone and everyone else, in his efforts to win back Northumbria for himself. And so long as he won it, care little the price others might pay. If the See of Durham sought spiritual hegemony over Scotland, or part of it — as all this might well lead to — Cospatrick, who cared little more for such things than did Malcolm, would not stand in the way. He, Maldred, therefore did not wish to see Walchere, or any English bishop, encouraged to play any part on the Scottish scene. But he could scarcely say so in present company.

"His superior, the Archbishop Thomas of York, is a Norman," he contented himself with pointing out. "Odo's man. Walchere may have to walk warily."

That was not disputed, and they left it there.

Presently Margaret retired with Turgot to the monastery chapel for a short session of prayer and confession — he was still, evidently, her choice as confessor — whilst Aldwin took the other two down to see the great new fish-ponds, fresh-water and salt, near the shore, of which the monks were very proud; for from these they could have a selection of salmon, sea-trout, burn-trout, carp, perch, lampreys and eels, from the fresh pools, and many sea-fish from the salt, caught and put alive in these to keep and take out as necessary, providing a great variety of dishes during Lent. The piscator-monk rejoiced to show them his ponds, tanks and hatcheries. Even Maldred conceded that here was something the Romans might teach the Scots.

Margaret was cheerful, happy, as they made their long return journey, going out of her way to display her friendliness towards Maldred, clearly sensing his reservations. He, for his part, was not the man to repulse such attentions, nor to fail to respond to them, from any attractive woman, queen or other. Magda, in consequence, was as relieved as she was amused. The sun smiled on them, still.

18

MOST CERTAINLY NONE of the three brothers mac Melmore
could have foretold that they would be riding *northwards* together from Dunkeld the following summer, at
the head of five hundred Athollmen, on warfare bent. For
years, all eyes had been turned southwards, as far as
possible hostilities were concerned — indeed as far as
almost everything went; because of the Normans' appearance on the scene and the opportunities for raid and
spoliation in troubled England. Despite — or possibly
partly because of — the fact that the late MacBeth's
kingdom had been largely based on the north of the
country, Malcolm Canmore had always turned his back on
the north and the Highlands, tending to look upon these
regions as barbarous and beyond the pale. MacBeth had
come of the northern branch of the royal house and had
been Mormaor of Ross and Moray before he ascended the
throne. Now, unexpectedly, out of the blue, almost
without warning, there was trouble in the north, danger,
revolt.

Oddly enough, such warning as there had been, had
come from the *south*, or at least the south-west, via the
useful Cospatrick. He had arrived seemingly from
nowhere, at Caer-luel some ten days earlier, to inform
Madach, acting governor of Cumbria there, that the Earl
Erland of Orkney, governing Galloway, had set sail from
the Dee estuary of Solway, northwards, with a large fleet
of longships, including a sizeable contingent under
Godfrey Crovan, King of Man. The rumour in Galloway
was that they were bound for the Dalar coast in the
Lochaber area, there to support a rising against King
Malcolm of Scots — whom the Orkney brothers had
evidently not forgiven for their sister's shame and death.
Cospatrick had learned no details of this rising itself, but
declared that Malcolm must be warned; and Madach, to
emphasise the urgency of the matter, had himself brought
the tidings to the King.

In the event, his arrival at Dunfermline had coincided

with news brought by Maldred's old fellow-standard-bearer Cathail, son of Lachlan, Mormaor of Buchan, to the effect that a large army under Malsnechtan of Moray was on the march southwards, allegedly with the object of unseating Malcolm and restoring to the throne the northern line of the royal house. Malsnechtan was the only son of King Lulach, who for five months had succeeded MacBeth on the throne until Malcolm had slain him. So Malsnechtan had both a prior right to the crown and good reason to hate Malcolm. Why he had waited until now to make his bid was not evident — but the King took it entirely seriously, especially when he heard of the Galloway and Man expedition. Clearly there was to be an attack on two fronts.

So the royal army was mustered fast, or such of it as could be, at short notice. Maldred, amongst others, was summoned and ordered to bring with him as many Border and Merse horsemen as he could spare without weakening the essential watch on Tweed, Teviot and Esk. On arrival at Dunfermline, he had been sent off after Madach, who had gone on to Dunkeld to raise the Atholl manpower and lead it northwards. And Maldred had been surprised and pleased to find his other brother Kerald accompanying him, monk though he was. *He* was being sent to collect and bring on the celebrated Brecbennoch of St. Columba, the holy casket containing a bone and relics of Columba himself, which traditionally should be carried before the King of Scots in battle — failure to produce which many blamed for the humiliating climb-down forced on Malcolm by Norman William at Abernethy. The reliquary was normally kept at Dunkeld, and should of course be carried by the Primate-Abbot himself. But the Earl Melmore was no man for battle-going, and Malcolm had ordered Kerald his son to act bearer instead. Indeed he had been appointed Abbot for the occasion, of the small and admittedly not important Abbey of Meigle in Strathmore — but it was a step on the ladder to greater things.

So the three brothers raced northwards with their twenty-five-score garron-mounted Athollmen — although with mixed feelings. It was one thing to ride gallantly to war at the head of a goodly company, and bearing the most cherished talisman in the land after the Stone of Destiny; but altogether another to be riding against their own fellow-countrymen, indeed their distant kinsman. But they had all sworn allegiance to Malcolm, so this was their simple duty.

They went up Tay and then Garry to the Pass of Killiecrankie, then swung north-eastwards at Blair-in-Atholl to follow up the long valley of the rushing Tilt to its source in remote Loch Tilt; and then through the Bynack Pass and down to the upper Dee's pine forests at Linn of Dee, in Brae Mar. The King's information was that Malsnechtan had moved out of Moray itself into Mar; and he was bringing his main royal army up over the Mounth passes to the mid-Dee at Banchory St. Ternan, where he had arranged a rendezvous, not only with the Athollmen but with Lachlan of Buchan, Gillibride of Angus and such force as his officers had been able to raise in the Mearns — whose Mormaor Colin was unfriendly. The Mormaor of Mar, Martacus by name, who also like Colin had been a close friend of MacBeth, was more likely to support Malsnechtan than the King and would have to be watched. Hence this rendezvous in his territory.

The Atholl contingent, which had had furthest to come — forty miles down Dee itself — found almost all the rest assembled at this, the only bridge over that wide and swift-running river for nearly a score of miles in either direction. With their arrival, the royal host numbered about five thousand, and made a brave show. But Malcolm was far from satisfied, saying that reports put the rebels at four thousand at least, not counting any aid from Galloway and Man. And if Martacus of Mar threw in his lot actively with the Moraymen, he could raise as many as two thousand more from his wide and fertile lands. Madach told him that another six hundred Atholl foot were following on, but these would take at least another two days to reach the Dee. The King snarled that he had no time to wait on such laggards.

He was pleased to see the Brecbennoch, however, seemingly confident that it would bring him luck — for it was in that light that he saw it rather than any religious persuasion. It was a rather lovely thing, a triumph of seventh-century Celtic workmanship, quite small and easily carried by one man, shaped like a tiny gable-roofed cottage. Its box was hollowed out of a single block of wood, but it was plated all over with silver and bronze, and adorned with enamelled panels, oblong and circular, in red and gold, these and its peculiar baton-like handle being decorated with typical interlaced Celtic design. It was, however, distinctly battered with much carrying in battle.

A council-of-war was held that evening in the monastery founded by the same Ternan whose abbey was at Dunfermline, and whose monks here kept the important bridge in repair. Malcolm detailed the situation. His scouts reported the enemy advancing down the Don, having come over the Rhynie heights from Strathbogie, latest word placing them in the Alford area, only some twenty miles to the north-west — so time was short. Kildrummy, Martacus of Mar's main seat, was some ten miles further west and being watched heedfully — but there was no sign of any major mustering of forces there meantime. Although the Marmen might be assembling secretly elsewhere. The questions were these. To await reinforcements here — and possibly to allow the rebels to be reinforced likewise? Remembering the threat from the west — the Galloway force presumably marching across Drumalban from Lochaber — to divide their host and send part of it to counter that danger? Or to use their full strength at once, move up fast to confront Malsnechtan and seek to choose the best battle-ground?

There was some discussion, but clearly the majority there were in favour of the last course.

"Malsnechtan — has he any skill at war?" Maldred asked. "He is young, is he not? And can have little experience, save perhaps at small feuding."

"Older than yourself!" Malcolm rejoined. "Although a babe at war, I would say. But he may have more experienced friends. I am told that Farquhar of Ross is joining him in rebellion — a curse on him! And *he* saw much of war with his father."

Farquhar, Mormaor of Ross, was MacBeth's eldest son, and who might, of course, have himself laid claim to the throne. But he was known to be a man of little ambition — proved by the fact that he had yielded the great mortuath of Moray, the largest in the kingdom, to his nephew Malsnechtan, and retained only the lesser inheritance of Ross, vast in size but much the less rich. He was, however, a veteran fighter.

"Is Farquhar with Malsnechtan now?"

"That I do not know, more is the pity. The word was that he was following on, with a force from Ross. But that was two days ago. He may have joined Malsnechtan by now."

"It could change all if he has. If Farquhar directs the battle, then it could mean much harder fighting. Is there any way by which we could learn of this? You say that Malsnechtan has come down through Strathbogie? Could you send a fast-riding party there, by round-about route? To enquire if Farquhar was with him, with his Rossmen?"

"Not to be thought of. Strathbogie is thirty-five or forty miles north. In this country, that would take at least three days to bring us news."

"I do not mean that we should sit idle meantime . . ."

"Maldred mac Melmore will win all our wars for us — if we but heed him!" Dufagan MacDuff interrupted mockingly. "How fortunate that we have him with us!" A darkly handsome youngish man with a hatchet-face and long chin, he was son and heir to MacDuff, Earl of Fife; and, since his father, senior noble of the realm, was now too heavy and gross for war, the son led Clan MacDuff and so was entitled to claim to be the King's right hand, second in command of the royal army and to have control of the right wing in battle. There was no love lost between him and the Atholl brothers.

Strangely, the monarch did not seem to be grateful for this support. "Quiet!" he barked. For so able a warrior-king he was not good at councils-of-war. "What would *you* do, cousin, instead of sitting? You, who know it all?"

Maldred glanced sidelong at his elder brother, who as heir to Atholl had the right to speak first. But at that quiet and solid character's brief nod, he went on.

"As I see it, Highness, we have few advantages here. We do not know the country, as does the enemy. The folk are hostile, and so will keep Malsnechtan better informed. He can draw on ever more local support whilst we cannot. Time, thus, is on his side, rather than ours. But we *could* have the advantage of surprise. He will know our position and strength, nothing surer. But — he will not expect a night march."

"*Night* march? Through country we do not know? Hill country, such as this Mar? With a host of this size?"

"That is why Malsnechtan will not expect it. Would you? Or any? The unexpected could be as good as another thousand men to us, and more."

"Well, man — well? Out with it."

"I do not know this Mar any more than you do, sir. But I see ahead of us this great hill. It is six or seven miles long at least, east and west, and high. The Hill of Fare it is called, I am told. So it is like to be little less in width, north and south. No army could go over that — so we must go round it, east or west about. The Don lies to the north, a dozen or so miles, all know. On the west side, this Hill of Fare sinks into lesser hills and valleys. But on the east, it is fairly level land, we can see. So Malsnechtan will expect any large army to come by the east, from here. A night march by the *west* side, then, could put us, by dawn tomorrow, where he would never look for us — and only a few miles in front of him."

"Aye — and weary with night marching! If we were not bogged in the hills," MacDuff commented.

"It has been a notably dry summer, thus far. The bogs will be none so bad. The burns are low."

"There is much in what he says," Gillibride, Earl of Angus said — who was not usually Maldred's friend, anyone's friend — but who especially did not love MacDuff. "Hear him."

"I have finished, my lord," Maldred said. "Save only to say that we might gain twelve hours. And so perhaps be able to choose the field of battle. Even, it may be, to force the fight before Farquhar of Ross comes up."

Madach spoke, at last. "My brother speaks sense. The unexpected is our opportunity. These nights, it is never truly dark. Let us march."

Presumably the King found himself in agreement for he slammed down his palm on the monks' table, and rose to his feet. The project was accepted.

They marched as soon as the great host could be marshalled into disciplined movement, north-by-west into the nightbound hills.

It proved, from every point of view, a difficult proceeding, trying to man and beast. And slow as it was exhausting, threading narrow, winding valleys, ploutering through marshland, climbing steep braes, negotiating rock-falls, struggling through slantwise woodlands, circling fallen trees. Before long, the royal army was strung out over miles, men cursing whoever it was who had thought of this nightmare journeying. Admittedly it was never wholly dark, being early July, but the half-light could be as confusing as darkness, green slime could look like firm turf, a hole seem no more than a shadow, a burn appear narrower than it was. With a local guide, pressed unwillingly into service, Maldred pushed ahead — and kept well away from the monarch's immediate vicinity.

Nevertheless, well before dawn, at least the van of the host was round the mighty western shoulder of the Hill of Fare, into the Tillenhilt area, with the land beginning to fall away perceptibly before them, their guide agreed, towards the valley of the Don.

Presently, when the King caught up with the path-finders, he was in fact in fair spirits — for whatever else he lacked, Malcolm did not lack energy and drive, and could not have cared less for the complaints of his men. He accepted that they had indeed stolen a march of ten miles or so on the rebels, and were almost certainly in a position where they would not be looked for. They would press on until sun-up before halting.

The lie of the land now took them first north-by-east and then north-by-west, to avoid the Black Hill of Tillycairn. Then, depressingly for this late stage of their exhausting march, a great detour westwards again was necessary to circuit the Moss of Cluny, a large expanse of marshland and lochans which heightened and firmed only gradually into the Muir of Balvack. By the time, wearily indeed, the vanguard was crossing this last, the sun was rising behind the low hills to the east, its yellow, level rays illuminating another vast and more pointed hill directly ahead of them, rising like a cone above wooded heights, blocking all vistas to the north — Beinn a' Chie, the Mountain of the Maiden's Breast, their guide mentioned. He added that around its base, west-about, the Don flowed.

From a slight escarpment bounding the north side of the Muir of Balvack, Maldred and his brothers drew rein and waited for the King, the light now sufficient to show them all this reach of the Don valley, the great coiling river, still dark, in its floor. Immediately below them lay the small monastery and associated township of Mony-musk, at a bend of the river, a daughter-house of the great Abbey of Deer, in Buchan. To the west, the Don emerged from the jaws of a deep wooded cleft between Beinn a' Chie and another steep but lower hill which their infor-mant called Pitfichie. To the east it flowed on through an ever widening vale, fair and green with cornlands and hay. There was no sign of an armed host or even a scouting party in all that noble prospect.

Malcolm, when he came up, had no doubts. "They are not yet come so far," he declared. "If they were past, they would have left some trace, followers, stragglers. So we are first. And can choose the field. If there is one here to choose."

"That great cleft, sir," Madach pointed. "From which the river flows. If they are coming down Don, they must come through there. An ambuscade. Could we have better place?"

"What will an ambuscade serve us, man?"

"Surprise, Highness. Trap them in that narrow gulf. Between river and steep. A great slaughter."

"You think so? How say you, Maldred?"

"No. Not that. Not an ambuscade. This is not a small company but a great army of thousands. Ambush them, and a hundred or two of us might slay a hundred or two of them. But that is all. The rest would retire, undefeated, the full numbers of neither side engaged. We seek a victory, not just to turn them back for a little."

"Aye — you have the wits of your family, as I have ever said." Maldred had never heard the King say it, but he inclined his head in acknowledgement — although with an apologetic glance at his brother.

"So we look for a battlefield not a deer-trap!" Malcolm went on. "See you that haugh? The one below the monastery of Monymusk. The bend in the river much narrows it. To three or four hundred yards, no more. With the road running through. West of that is that lochan and marshy ground. There, I say. That should serve. The host hidden. Behind the monastery and the village. And in the scattered woodland around the lochan. We shall split into two. Let them come on, unsuspecting. Then an assault, at the front first, from the monastery. When this has them fully engaged, strike behind, from the lochan woods. That should damage them, on a narrow field, pressed against the river."

"If they have scouts forward, they could discover us, sir," MacDuff said. "Warn them. No surprise."

"They will have scouts, yes — if they are not fools. But early in the day — if early they come — they will be for pressing on. Not searching woods and monasteries back from their road. They will hold to the road, after coming out of that ravine, I think. We let the scouts past."

"You cannot hide five thousand men, Highness. And hundreds of horses," the Earl of Strathearn objected. "In a monastery, a village and a wood!"

"Can I not, man? You were not with me that day, twenty years back, when I hid more than that! At Dunsinane. When I brought Birnam Wood to MacBeth's Dunsinane! Hidden thousands under branches and boughs. There are birches here in plenty. We shall cut leafage. Most horses to be sent back, behind this wooded brae. A few hidden in the monastery. At a quarter-mile, they will not perceive the deception. So — two arrays. Or three. You, MacDuff, with Angus, will take the left, at the lochan. I will command at the monastery. Strathearn — you will hold a reserve, to aid where needed. And all must remain hidden."

"Another, smaller force, Highness," Maldred suggested. "To move over into that defile, where the river issues. The ambuscade place. To hold up any reinforcement of the enemy. And to prevent his escape from the field."

"As you say. That is wise. Not too many — I cannot spare many. Take you half of your Athollmen, then. But — remain well hidden until the fray starts, see you. No — you place them, then come back to my side. Madach can command there. Meanwhile, our scouts will probe ahead . . ."

This was Malcolm Canmore in his own element, at his decisive best.

So all went forward as the King commanded, weary men not consulted. Maldred and Madach, with some two hundred of the Athollmen, moved forward, mounted still, to the deep wooded cleft between Beinn a' Chie and Pitfichie Hill — and were surprised to discover it much longer than they had anticipated, winding away north-westwards seemingly for at least two constricted miles. But they were concerned only with this bottom end, and there was no lack of suitable, narrow, gorge-like locations where a few men could hold up hundreds. There proved to be a track on both sides of the river; but that on this western side was obviously the main one, a drove-road, and almost certainly to be used by an advancing host. Which was as well for Malcolm's plans.

The brothers were placing their men to best effect when one of the forward scouts hurried back. In passing, on his way to the King, he shouted that the enemy van was in fact less than three miles ahead, on the move and entering these narrows at a place called the Mill of Tillyfoure, scouting party in front. It seemed to be a great host, but much strung-out in this close country.

Maldred saw Madach installed at a vantage-point where he could control his own ambuscade and also see down towards the chosen battle-area around Monymusk, and be in a position to observe the course of the engagement and react accordingly. Then he hastened back to the monastery.

He found there a scene of great activity. The village's inhabitants had been rounded up and placed under guard in the eating-hall of the monastery, with most of the monks likewise, in case, voluntarily or otherwise, they might give warning to the enemy. The horses, save for the leaders' own beasts, hidden in the village cow-byres, had disappeared. Most of the army was engaged in cutting down birch-boughs and greenery in the scattered wood-land of the surrounding slopes. The King and his lords were plotting out tactics on the ground. All this move-ment must be stilled very shortly, for they calculated that the enemy scouts would be emerging from the pass in no more than half-an-hour.

Presently, with all activity ceased, or screened, and the royal army in its three great sections crouched down under the canopy of leafage, they waited. Maldred, had he not known, would not have suspected that so much of the birchwood and fern was in fact false and that men hid there in their thousands.

Malcolm, sniffing battle, was almost genial, patient now.

After what seemed an inordinate delay, they saw what they looked for — movement in the mouth of the wooded defile. Out, two by two, trotted a score of horsemen, in the plaids, calfskin jerkins and blue bonnets of the North, Malsnechtan's scouts. Down into the open haughs flanking the Don they came, most evidently unconcerned and keeping in their formation.

"The fortunate ones, this day!" Malcolm almost whispered. "Since they pass unscathed."

Despite the King's confidence, Maldred at least tended to hold his breath as the party rode down the track midway between the riverside and the village. One man's foolish move amongst the thousands hiding there could ruin all.

But no alarm was raised and the scouts trotted on down-stream and were soon lost to sight behind trees. No doubt they conceived the royal army as still in the Banchory area this fine morning, all those miles ahead.

Now there was more waiting — but the atmosphere had changed, as men tensed themselves for battle. Many might not be alive in an hour or two.

At last they came, flooding out of that dark cleft in the hills, a great and gallant throng, all colour and gleaming steel, the leaders under a dozen flags, topped by the great blue-and-white banner of Moray.

"The red-and-white of Ross is not there," Maldred observed. "Unless it comes in the rear."

There was over a mile between the monastery and the mouth of the defile. The head of the Moray column came about one-third of that way into the wide haughland, and there halted — clearly to await the consolidation of its force behind it after the long, stringing-out process of threading the narrows.

"He has the wits for that, at least," the King commented. "Although it is to *our* advantage, even so. I do not want to engage only a portion of his strength."

When the enemy came on again, in close order now, they made an impressive sight. Only the leadership was mounted — for despite the late MacBeth's efforts to copy the highly successful cavalry tactics of the Normans, the Scots still preferred to fight on foot, even mounted bodies like the Atholl contingent only using their garrons to bring them swiftly to the scene, then dismounting to face the foe. Seen thus, it looked fully as large a host as the royal one, and as well equipped.

There was still no sign of any large red-and-white Ross banner.

"We wait until he is level with yonder trees. Some way past this monastery. Before we strike," Malcolm announced to his lieutenants. "So that he has to turn his van back. A further confusion . . ."

Something had been niggling at the back of Maldred's mind since arriving at this place, something perhaps relevant. Suddenly it came to him.

"This monastery of Monymusk!" he exclaimed. "It belongs to Deer. The Abbey of Deer. Malsnechtan is pious. I have often heard my father say so. He has granted large lands in Moray to the Abbey of Deer. It was King

MacBeth's favourite house. So — he might come here. Come to the monastery. To pray. Or make an offering. Since he is so close . . ."

"A curse on you, man! Why did you not say so sooner?" Malcolm cried.

"I but now recollected . . ."

But the King went on. "Yet — it could be to our good. Aye, it could so. This is a small house. He would not bring any large company up to it. See you, if he comes, he will leave his host down there. Come up with only some few of his close friends. So, for a space, his army will be all but leaderless. Praise God, I say, if the man does come to pray!"

There were some grins at that — but Kerald, with the precious reliquary in his arms at Maldred's side, moved closer.

"I do not like this, Mal," he muttered. "It is ill-done. If this Malsnechtan is a man of God and supporter of the Church. And we use this house of God to lure him to ruin. Carrying this sacred shrine of Columba against the son of a King of Scots who is a better follower of the saint than . . ."

When he choked on the rest, Maldred nodded grimly but said nothing.

Perhaps Malcolm heard some of that, for suddenly he cried out, making for him a surprising gesture. "If God gives me the victory this day, I swear to give this monastery and the lands here to St. Andrew. Who once gave my forebear victory. And to increase this house in wealth, strength."

The brothers were not the only ones who stared, at that — although probably Maldred was the only one who paused to think why the dedication was to be to St. Andrew and not St. Columba, significant in the circumstances.

There was no time for further talk. The enemy van was almost level now, some three hundred yards away. Without the column halting, suddenly a small mounted group spurred away from the banners-party and came trotting towards them.

"Wait!" Malcolm said. "Let them come almost to us. Glamis — your troop to deal with them. The rest, heed them not. Follow me down. To the middle of their van. Maldred, raise you my banner. Kerald, at his side with the

Brecbennoch. Wait, I say! Every moment will tell. Hugh, sound . . . now!"

High and clear the bull's horn ululated, its wailing notes echoing from the hill-slopes, to be drowned in a great shout from two thousand throats as the King's array leapt up out of hiding and went surging down into the haugh after the monarch, yelling, swords, maces and battle-axes upraised.

Maldred had no opportunity to observe what happened to Malsnechtan — presuming it was he — and his mounted party. On foot, without the support of the saddle-socket, holding up the large royal banner of Scotland, the silver hump-backed boar on blue, was no light task, especially when he had to keep up with the bounding Malcolm. He could not wield sword himself, requiring both hands for the staff; but he managed to draw and clutch his dirk, for some measure of self-defence. At his side Kerald, monkish robe hitched high, scorned anything of that sort, reliquary clutched tight.

So they led a tide of shouting, blood-lusting humanity down upon their shocked and utterly unprepared fellow-countrymen, doubts and scruples for the moment forgotten in a fierce and savage upsurge of elation and naked aggression.

What followed was not really a battle at all, even though individually the Moraymen fought bravely enough. But individual fighting does not make a battle, and seldom makes any major effect on the issue. They were in column-of-route, not in any defensive formation; their senior leadership was separated from their men; the host was mentally and emotionally unready. Moreover, Malcolm's tactics were sound. His first furious impact struck some way down the column, so that the head of it was forced to turn back on itself in major confusion. Thus a large part of the front half of the Moray army was largely invalidated for the moment, ineffective. And as the rear portion came hastening to its aid, the second array of the royal force, under MacDuff and Angus, launched itself down upon them from the woodland. When the reserve thousand under Strathearn, uncertain as to where if at all it might be needed, showed itself in further menace, the thing was all but over, defeat accepted, conceded. All who could of the enemy turned and fled, back towards the defile, where Madach waited.

Maldred himself saw very little of it all, being fully occupied in maintaining his position at the King's back and in keeping the boar banner approximately upright above the royal head. In fact, he did not strike a single blow throughout. Malcolm himself did all that was necessary in that respect, smiting his way forward into the tightest press with unflagging energy and complete disregard for personal safety. He favoured the battle-axe to the sword for such close combat, and wielded it with a methodical and tireless figure-of-eight rhythm which succeeded in cutting a lane of bloody ruin through the opposing throng, along which the Atholl brothers were his closest followers.

But if Maldred saw little and contributed less, save as standard-bearer, he experienced sufficient in that brief encounter to imprint the Battle of Monymusk on his mind's eye and memory for ever after. For, with Malcolm having driven almost right through the Moray column, and swinging round to seek a new series of victims, there was an inevitable brief pause in the process for those immediately behind. And in that moment or two of panting lull a small wiry Highlander who had ducked agilely under the sweep of the royal axe, darted in behind and slashed his sword up and clean across Kerald's unprotected throat. In a sudden and dreadful fountaining of blood, that inoffensive young man staggered a couple of steps onward and then collapsed in choking, ungainly death, the Brecbennoch of Columba flung out of his nerveless grasp on to the trampled, slippery grass.

Appalled, for the moment paralysed in horror, Maldred stared down at his brother, the royal banner wavering in his grip. Croakingly he found his voice, to call out, to Kerald, to God, to the King. God may have heard him, but the others did not. Malcolm was already plunging back into the thick of the fighting, shouting. And Kerald mac Melmore would hear no more until he would hear better things than this in a better place.

Maldred had seen enough of war and sudden death to know that there was nothing to be done for his brother; also to know his own duty as standard-bearer and knight. As well as demonstrating to all, friend and foe, where the monarch fought, to ensure that the realm's colours remained flying high, it was his part to protect the King's back with his own person. He could not stop, therefore, could not kneel to Kerald's jerking, ghastly body, must press on to fill again the gap which had opened behind Malcolm — the hardest thing ever he had had to do in his life. What he did do, although with a grievous swaying and dipping of the boar flag, was to stoop in his striding and snatch up the precious Brecbennoch, dropping his dirk in the process, and, clutching the reliquary to him also, in Kerald's stead, lurch on after their liege-lord.

He had no sense of time or detail, after that, nor of danger nor anything else, save the one requirement of keeping his place close at the King's back. In fact, it was all over in only a few further minutes, and his immediate duty over. It was Madach's turn now, holding that bottle-neck of a defile against the fleeing Moraymen, and, with the pursuing pressure from the haughland, turning defeat into rout. But the King left that task and slaughter to others, and Maldred did not require to be involved. Stricken, he went back for Kerald.

Because of the brevity of the engagement and the total surprise, casualties were not really heavy, in relation to the numbers present, even on the enemy side. In fact the worst killing took place in the mouth of the cleft itself, with MacDuff and Strathearn pressing the fleeing foemen against the barrier of the narrows blocked by Madach's Athollmen. But even so, most of the Moraymen escaped, thanks to the wooded and broken nature of the terrain. Many flung themselves into the Don and, lightly clad in short kilts and little else, were able to swim across safely. Some broke away downstream, southwards. Others got away by the tree-clad slopes of Pitfichie Hill.

Malcolm was less fervent in pursuit and punishment than might have been expected. Not in any spirit of clemency towards his misguided subjects but because there was still no sign of the Mormaor Farquhar of Ross, who might well be fairly close behind the Moray host. He respected Farquhar's military abilities and reckoned that the Ross army might well be a large one. He did not want his own strength to be caught dispersed and chasing fugitives. So he forbade any major pursuit, and ordered his force to concentrate again at Monymusk.

Strangely enough, to the King's wrath, Malsnechtan himself had escaped. Piety, in this instance, had paid off, and he and his small group heading for the monastery, had evidently at once recognised the hopelessness of the

Moray frontal position when the royal array made its charge, and bolted without delay before young Glamis could reach them — they being mounted, he not. Because of Malcolm's stringent orders to keep their people hidden at this early'stage, MacDuff and Angus likewise had not revealed their position to the mass of the enemy by rising to intercept Malsnechtan. So he and his leaders had got clean if ingloriously away — and the Thane of Glamis was left in no doubt as to what his sovereign thought of him.

But if this was an odd circumstance of the fight, there was another even more so when, presently, Madach arrived with a group of distinguished prisoners, amongst whom was none other than Malsnechtan's mother, the Lady Malvina, Lulach's widow and for a few months Queen. What she was doing with her son's rebel army she did not divulge. Madach's people had found her, with the baggage-train coming along a discreet distance behind.

She was, to be sure, something of an embarrass-ment — Malcolm had, after all, slain her husband. But she might be useful to hold as a hostage against her son's future activities, possibly even against Farquhar of Ross, whose sister-in-law she was. So, after the briefest of cold greetings, she was placed in the care of Dufagan MacDuff — she was a kinswoman of his — who was told that the monarch did not wish to set eyes on her again.

They spent that night — a night which Maldred and Madach passed in sad vigil in the monastery's little timber church with the body of their brother — and much of the next day, waiting for Farquhar at Monymusk. But though their forward scouts probed a dozen miles and more north-wards, they discovered no sign of him. Whether he was delayed, not coming at all, or warned of the defeat and turned back, they knew not. But there seemed to be no point in waiting in hostile country — the King was still concerned about the intentions of Martacus of Mar, so comparatively near at hand, who likewise so far had not put in an appearance but who could raise the whole country against them. He was in no position to attempt the lengthy process of full conquest of the North, with his English preoccupations ever with him. He decided that, having had a cheap victory, he would be content meantime. There were also the Orkney earls to consider.

The Atholl brothers saw the victory as less cheap.

So they left Monymusk and the Don to return

southwards, Malcolm assuring the Abbot that he would not forget his vow to raise the status of the monastery, along with its change of dedication from St. Drostan, Columba's nephew, to St. Andrew. What he thought of this, and his transference to St. Andrew's bishopric instead of the Abbey of Deer, he did not announce. As well, which may have affected his attitude, they left behind a long and specially-erected gallows bearing a row of dangling corpses, senior prisoners taken in the rout, as demonstration of how Malcolm, High King of Scots, looked upon rebellion. They did not leave behind Malsnechtan's baggage-train, which proved to be unexpectedly rich; whether this had been for possible bribing of support further south, or an indication of supreme confidence in the result, was not known.

Not left behind, either, was the Church's newest abbot, Kerald mac Melmore, wrapped in plaids and slung between two garrons, for burial at Dunkeld, the Brecbennoch of Columba with him.

19

MALDRED HAD NEVER looked to see Wearmouth again, nor hoped to. That he should be riding there dressed in his oldest clothing — not that he was any sort of stylish dresser — and in the company of only two false friars, Cospatrick and his man Patie's Dod, seemed unlikely to say the least. His reluctance to be doing anything of the kind had been pronounced. But Cospatrick had been pressing, if not peremptory. And he had come to respect that man's assessments and urgencies as usually valid, however much his motives might sometimes be suspect. The Earl had insisted that it was expedient for Maldred to make this surreptitious, indeed secret, journey into Northumbria — and when the younger man had demanded for whom or what it was expedient, he had merely been told that Prior Aldwin, and to a lesser extent the monk Turgot, had especially sought his presence. Why, was not forthcoming — although Cospatrick almost certainly knew more than he was telling — and suggestions that the monks could have come to Dunbar or Ersildoune if they were so anxious to see him, had met with the reply that they were afraid to venture into Scotland contrary to Malcolm's express commands since they had refused to take the oath of allegiance to him. All of which, whilst not satisfying Maldred, was superficially reasonable. And, of course, while Cospatrick was not actually his master, as a sort of steward of his two earldoms, Maldred had to take the older man's wishes very much into account.

So here the three of them were, riding unobtrusively through dangerous, lawless and ungoverned Northumbria, a year less a month after the defeat of the Moray rising, a friar on a jennet, a serving-brother on a heavy garron and a nondescript traveller on the most broken-down nag in the Ersildoune stables.

They had had to make a wide detour, increasing by half again the length of their journey, in order to avoid the Tyneside area where, at the first possible crossing of the river, after the estuary, the Normans were laying the foundations of a great new stone castle, at Monkchester, site of a one-time Roman fort, and wherein was their only permanent presence north of Tees — meantime at least. So the travellers had come south from Teviotdale over Carter Fell into Redesdale, and down Rede to cross Tyne eventually at Corbridge, near the great Roman Wall, before turning eastwards by Gateshead and Boldon. Cospatrick rode throughout with an easy confidence and familiarity, bestowing blessings now and again as the notion took him. Clearly this was all well-trodden ground for him, and he entirely at home in his role — remarkable considering that he had once been undisputed lord of all here.

They came down to the estuary and bay of the Wear, ten miles south of that of Tyne, on the third afternoon — for clerics apparently did not hurry on the road — unchallenged and without having seen a single Norman. Wearmouth, on this sunny June afternoon, looked very different from the day nine years before when Maldred had first seen it, in storm and war. Moreover, coming to it on the other side of the estuary, at Monk Wearmouth where was the original settlement from Lindisfarne, the Scots army had never reached this south side, where at Bishop's Wearmouth was the monastery of St. Michael to which they were now headed. This did not at all seem to be the place where, in stress and bloodshed, he had first met Magda — and Margaret.

St. Michael's, a Benedictine priory, was likewise a notable contrast to the establishment their monkish hosts had been seeking to build up at Melross, a settled, extensive, stone-built place founded in 930, with a fair church; not so venerable as the St. Peter's church across the water in Monk Wearmouth where Malcolm had taken up his quarters that evening of 1069, and which had been in fact originally a Columban foundation, where the Venerable Bede had lived and written.

The visitors were well received. Aldwin was Prior here and Turgot his assistant, so that the hospitality of a quite large establishment was available. Nevertheless their masquerade was maintained in front of the ordinary monks — which seemed to emphasise the seriousness of this alleged need for secrecy. It was not until, fed and refreshed, the four of them were closeted in the Prior's own chamber, that Maldred learned the reasons for his being there.

He could scarcely believe his ears, in fact. It appeared that what he was being involved in was little less than a plot to detach Northumbria from England and incorporate it into Scotland. Linked to this astonishing project was a scheme for consolidating South Strathclyde, or Cumbria, much more positively within the Scots realm — and so making the Scots-English border to run effectively, not at Tweed and Esk but at Tees and Ribble.

"But, but . . ." Maldred floundered. "How could this be? It is beyond all possibility. For Scotland to be taking part of England! After Malcolm having to submit to William . . ."

"It is none so impossible, my lord," Aldwin asserted. "Matters are not what they were, with the Norman. His affairs are in disarray. He has been defeated in the field, for the first time for many years. At Dol, in Brittany. By the King of France. A notable battle . . ."

"Defeated? William . . . !"

"Yes, God be praised! He is in retreat. At last. The Count Robert of Flanders has risen against him, again. And his own son, Duke Robert of Normandy, with him.

William Rufus, it is thought, will join with his brother against their father, once more."

"This is stirring news. But that is France, not England. Here we would have Bishop Odo to face. And strong Norman arms."

"Not so strong as they were. Not united now, as they were before Hereford's and Norfolk's rising. There is much trouble in England. In especial, since the Earl Waldeve was executed . . ."

"Waldeve executed! The Earl of Northumbria . . . ?"

"You have not heard? Yes, Waldeve of Northumbria is dead. Beheaded at Winchester. William made a sore mistake there. To execute a Saxon earl."

"The man was a Dane!" Cospatrick interpolated. "And a fool. But — William should not have cut off his head. After keeping him in custody for almost two years."

"Why did he do it?"

"None know for sure," Aldwin said. "And it was ill done. As Almighty God Himself chose to demonstrate."

"How so?"

"On the scaffold, at Winchester, before thousands, the Earl was repeating Our Lord's Prayer, before his death. He had turned much to the consolations of religion in his long captivity. He daily recited the entire Psalter. Asked to be allowed to become monk. But, no. On the scaffold, reciting, he got no further than '. . . lead us not into temptation', when he choked with tears and could say no more. So the headman's sword struck and the Earl's head was severed from his neck and fell to the ground. And there his lips continued the prayer '. . . but deliver us from evil'!"

Cospatrick snorted. "A likely tale. For bairns!"

"You may scoff, Brother Eadwulf. But thousands do not. All over England the thing is spoken of, believed. To William's hurt. The people are stirred as seldom before. To execute a Saxon earl — and then this! There is unrest everywhere."

"We shall need more than unrest to take Northumbria. And hold it!"

"Yes. But there *is* more," Turgot intervened. "Bishop Walchere is now given sole authority in Northumbria. He has been the Earl's deputy for long — but now he rules, as the King's lieutenant. Perhaps not for long. But meantime he is supreme. So — there is need for haste, it may be."

"Haste for what?" Maldred demanded. "Do you say that the Bishop of Durham is prepared to give Northumbria to King Malcolm?"

The two monks exchanged glances. "Scarcely that, perhaps," Aldwin said. "But . . . he might well go some way along that road. The Earl Waldeve was his close friend . . ."

"We know of that. But he is a Norman, is he not?"

"No, he is not. He is a Lorrainer, of ancient Celtic stock. He mislikes the Normans, almost as much as do we Saxons — although he supports Lanfranc. Hates them more than ever now, since Waldeve. As Brother Eadwulf knows well."

Cospatrick nodded. "Say that the good Walchere is at present more kindly disposed towards Malcolm — or perhaps his Queen — than towards William!"

So Margaret came into this. Maldred might have known, or guessed, with Turgot involved.

"What is the purpose, then? Remembering that Bishop Odo is still viceroy in England."

"Odo — I prefer to name him Earl of Kent, since he is a disgrace to the calling of bishop—is also in trouble, God be praised!" This Prior was not one of the cautious-speaking clerics. "He is at odds with Archbishop Lanfranc. And Lanfranc is William's friend. It was Odo who gained Archbishop Thomas the appointment of York. And now he supports him against Lanfranc. Odo has taken Canterbury lands, arrested Lanfranc's revenues . . ."

"What has this squabble amongst Normans to do with Northumbria? Or Odo's ability to bring a great army northwards?"

"Not a little, my lord. Odo has his hands full, in the south. With the unrest over Earl Waldeve and the hatred for his wife — for all believe that it was the Countess Judith who prevailed with her uncles to have her husband executed, in order that she might marry again. His enmity with Lanfranc has already resulted in fighting. And the Welsh are stirring again, as ever. William, in France, is demanding ever more men and moneys, to be sent there, for his wars. Odo is at his weakest."

"So you urge armed revolt? War?"

Again Turgot intervened. "We are churchmen, not soldiers," he said carefully. "You must understand, my lord, we do not seek war. Only say that now is a great opportunity for a change to be made — a change, pray God, for the better. A change through Holy Church. We Saxons of Northumbria are grievously unhappy under King William and the Normans. But Prince Edgar, who should be our king, has now made his peace with William. He will, I fear, never lead England out of her sorrows. So we must needs look elsewhere."

Maldred accepted that, at least. Edgar Atheling was one of the world's unfortunates. He had left Scotland again, those two years ago, with his fine retinue, his ships, arms and treasure, to go take up his barony of Montreuil-sur-Mer, which King Philip had given him on the condition that he assailed William's flank in Normandy. He had got nearly to his destination in the Pas de Calais when typical ill-luck struck again. A fierce gale drove his ships ashore and he lost all, many of his men, his treasure and all his spirit. After months of wandering and skulking on foot, he had found his unhappy way back to Scotland and his sister Margaret — why, when his mother and other sister were much closer, in Philip's Paris, Malcolm for one did not know. At any rate, his welcome this time was less than warm. The King had bluntly told him that he could help him no more, and advised him to go make his peace with William on the best terms he could get — Margaret presumably concurring, but she had found him more moneys, so that he could present himself to William in some style and in comparative dignity. Actually the Conqueror had found it convenient to receive him in less humiliating fashion than he might have done, to detach him from Philip for good; but imposed on him terms in which once and for all he renounced any claim to the English throne and accepted that the Saxon cause was dead — a sorry business.

"You look to Scotland?"

"Yes. England, the *South* of England, is firmly in William's grip. But the North has never been so. The Saxon North, at least, might throw off the Norman yoke. And, who knows, perhaps give a lead to the rest. Cumbria, in name, adheres to Scotland. Down to the Ribble. If Northumbria could be in the same state, then William's writ would run only as far north as Tees and Ribble. To be sure, this was all Bernicia none so long ago, up to the Scottish Sea — Lothian, the Merse, Teviotdale and Northumberland, all in Bernicia. It could be again, and adhering to the Scots realm. And, in this change, the Church could lead the way."

"How that?"

"Do you not see it, my lord? Queen Margaret makes it possible. Placed in Scotland by God Himself, I do believe. Holy Church has now a presence in Scotland — which it did not have before. I mean the Church of Rome. The Archbishop Lanfranc thinks highly of the Queen of Scots, conceives her to be his daughter in God. The archepiscopal see of York has been declared by the Papal Legate Hubert to include Scotland. Bishop Walchere is Lanfranc's man. The Church could lead all Bernicia back to Scotland. And be a deal happier than under William and Odo."

"And the Romish Church triumph in Scotland!" Maldred commented grimly.

"Not so. No triumph. Nothing of conquest. Only harmony. The Queen does not seek to incorporate your Scottish Church in Rome, my lord — only to bring it into harmony. To the benefit of all. What harm for Scotland in that?"

"If the Archbishops of England claim spiritual sway over Scotland, as they will — as it seems they do — how long before the *King* of England claims a like sway?"

"He does so now, man," Cospatrick pointed out. "Did not William make Malcolm swear allegiance to him at Abernethy, as Lord Paramount? Are we going to be any the worse off? And gain all Northumbria at no cost. Strengthen hold on Cumbria also."

And Cospatrick, resurrected, the lord of all between Forth and Tees, Clyde and Ribble, Maldred almost added. He saw it all now — what his cousin had been working for. "The cost is St. Columba's Church!" he said flatly.

"Nonsense, Maldred! The Keledei are well able to look after themselves. They will not be swallowed up. A few reforms, that is all. Some they have already agreed."

"All? Our birthright sold for *your* Northumbria!"

"See you, lad — there are a thousand and more Keledei in Scotland. Two-score and more ruling abbots. Thrice that of bishops. Leave that to them, whose business it is, not yours."

"What *is* my business here, then? Why did you bring me?"

"We desire you to go to King Malcolm, my lord,"

294

Aldwin said. "To explain all to him. To seek his . . . adherence."

There was silence in the Prior's room for a little, as Maldred pondered.

"Whether this is for good or ill, I would have to consider more," he said at length. "But . . . it seems to me that much depends on Bishop Walchere. Since he rules Northumbria now, for the realm as well as the Church. You are his friends. Is this his will? Does he favour it all?"

There was a momentary hesitation.

"The good Bishop is a man pulled two ways," Aldwin said. "He wears, as it were, both mitre and helmet. The mitre favours this move. The helmet is yet fully to be convinced."

"That I can believe."

"He can, and will be convinced, we believe," Turgot said. "For the man who advises him in matters of state, his lieutenant in the rule of Northumbria, is for this great project. Indeed much of it is his planning. With Brother Eadwulf, here. The Thane Ligulf. He will convince the Bishop, we have no doubt. For he much relies on Ligulf."

"And even if he does not, Walchere will not oppose Malcolm with armed force, I swear!" Cospatrick added.

"Oppose . . . ? Then you look for Malcolm to *invade* Northumbria? Bring an army here?"

"To be sure. That is what you are to tell him. For Walchere's name and repute, we must *seem* to constrain him. By armed force. Then the churchmen, Lanfranc, Thomas and the rest, have to accept the situation with a good grace. That is how it goes, man. This Ligulf will lead Walchere's army, see you. The thing is well thought out, never fear."

"That I do not doubt. What I doubt is the cost. And who gains?"

"Let Malcolm decide that, cousin. The decision is not for you. Maldred mac Melmore is only the messenger — but the *informed* messenger. We would have you ride tomorrow . . ."

*　　*　　*

Whatever his doubts, Maldred could scarcely refuse to carry the tidings to the King. Whatever else these might be, they were important enough; and it was not his business to choose which messages the monarch should receive and which not. Cospatrick himself, of course, could not appear at the Scots Court; otherwise he could, no doubt, have acted courier himself and used his persuasive powers on Malcolm. Maldred was left in no doubt that he was expected to support the scheme before the King — but that *was* his own business and he reserved his judgement.

So with Patie's Dod, no longer dressed as serving-brother, to act as escort as far as the Border, and both better mounted than on the journey south, Maldred headed northwards next day, making for Tweed and the Scottish Sea.

They rode much more swiftly now, and he reached Dunbar in two long days. There he collected Magda, who always enjoyed a visit to Court — or at least to see Margaret. She was pregnant again, but only in her third month and able to ride well enough.

Along the Lothian shore that late afternoon, they were making for the monastery of St. Wilfred at Abercorn, a Keledei place, to pass the night when, making up on a foot party of travellers, men and women carrying bundles, poor folk, Maldred was asked if they were on the right road for Queen Margaret's new ferry. Having to admit that he did not know, he asked in turn what and where this was that they spoke of?

"Och, sir, it is the good Queen, bless her," one of the men answered. "She has set up fine ferry-boats. At Ardgarvie. To carry folk across the water to Fothrif. To make the pilgrimage to her great new church at Dunfermline. Aye, and on to St. Andrew's shrine at Kilrymont too. Have you not heard tell of it?"

"No. We are from the Merse. And Dunbar. This is new?"

"Aye, new. All may use this ferry. To save the long road round. By Stirling's bridge. At no cost, mind. All at the Queen's own charges. She is a right good woman, that, English as she is."

"To be sure. Free, you say? And at Ardgarvie?"

"Aye. It is just across the water from Dunfermline, sir. Saving four long days' walking, and more, praise God. But we are not sure of the way . . ."

"The road to Ardgarvie I know. In another mile, near to Dalmeny, there is a stone-circle. This road divides there.

Straight on to Abercorn and Stirling. Right to Ardgarvie. Then another mile, no more."

"We thank you, sir. May the blessed St. Colm and St. Serf and all others, smile on you and your lady . . ."

"I think that you will soon have to be changing your saints, friend!" Maldred commented, as they rode on.

"Think of that," Magda said. "Free ferries for the poor. Who would have thought of that, but Margaret? Even you will not deny her goodness, kindness!"

"I have never denied that, lass. But her thoughtfulness extends to more than the poor, I think!"

Nevertheless, when presently they reached the stone-circle near Dalmeny, he suggested that they too took the right-hand track to the Ardgarvie shore. If a ferry-boat was indeed there, it would save them fifty miles of riding.

Sure enough, down at a new jetty where a shingly small headland jutted out towards the rocky islet of Inchgarvie, and a larger point, Cult Ness, projected on the other side, narrowing the Scottish Sea to the Firth of Forth, a large flat-bottomed scow was just drawing in, with a load of travellers, some with pack-ponies. They did not all look like returning pilgrims, by any means, some seeming to be packmen and merchants. The scow had a single square sail and a crew of four men dressed in the dark habits of serving-brothers of the Roman Church, with long sweeps to manoeuvre the vessel and propel it when the wind was contrary.

They joined a group of waiting passengers, to lead their doubtful horses aboard by a gang-plank. When Maldred told the ferrymen that there was another party coming, just a mile behind, he was informed that there was no need to wait as another scow would be across from the Fothrif side in a short time. It was only a mile across at these narrows. In fact, they passed the companion ferry as they neared Cult Ness.

So, with only four miles to ride thereafter, they reached Dunfermline half-an-hour after landing, and a full day earlier than they had anticipated, even Maldred prepared to bless the Queen for this provision, at least.

Margaret received them warmly, as ever, laughing about her now normal state of pregnancy — and delighted to hear that Magda was in the same condition, however far behind in the reproductive race. The Queen now had four sons, Edward, Edmund, Ethelred and Edgar — and was praying for a daughter next. She seemed in no way concerned by all this child-bearing, apparently throve on it, for she was the picture of radiant health, a lovely and mature young matron of thirty-three years. She made use of the fosterage system, of course, as did almost all noblewomen, so that much of the burden of suckling and child-rearing was spared her. But she kept her sons with her in the royal apartments, not farming them out with foster-parents as was so often done, so that the small palace, being constantly added to as it was — mainly upwards on account of the restricted hilltop site — rang with children's voices. But not to the discomfort of adults and guests, for though a fond mother, Margaret was proving to be a strict one, with strong views on discipline and manners — and of course, on piety. Any infringement of her rules met with prompt and condign punishment, and the palace chamberlain had firm instructions as to dealing with excess of spirits, even to whipping the young princes when necessary. For all that, the youngsters clearly adored their mother — who was also their tutor, it transpired, educating them as no Scots princes had ever before been educated. It was not only in their Saxon names that they were different from all their predecessors.

Malcolm was absent at a council at Scone when the visitors arrived, so that they had Margaret to themselves for that evening and most of the following day — and much relished her good company and unaffected friendship, Maldred being careful, for once, not to introduce controversial topics, and Margaret herself only once or twice coming out with remarks which he felt it incumbent upon him to indicate had another point of view — despite the warning glances, even glares, of his wife. It was difficult not to embark on the subject which had brought them, especially as the Queen was eager to hear if Maldred had seen her friend Turgot and to learn about his doings. But he felt bound to reserve his business for the King's ears first, and Margaret no doubt recognised this and did not press him.

In the end, however, the Queen heard of the Northumbrian proposals just as soon as did her husband, for on Malcolm's return he joined them at once, unannounced, the three of them and the children, under the apple-trees of the tiny, slantwise orchard. There, dismissing the boys almost immediately, without preamble, he wanted to know what had brought his cousin to Court this time, unsummoned — since he had not come for love of seeing him, the King, that he swore. This whilst standing chewing at a leg of roe venison and drinking from a beaker of ale. Margaret's preoccupation with good manners and the civilities, for her sons, did not seem to have rubbed off at all on her lord and master. At Maldred's hint that it was all a matter of some moment and perhaps should be discussed in a more private place, the monarch jerked to be out with it, and not to play the self-important popinjay.

"Very well, Highness — if so you wish. I come, as usual, from Cospatrick. But this time also from others whom you know of — and indeed ejected from your borders for failing to take the oath of allegiance! The Prior Aldwin and the monk Turgot, friends of the Bishop of Durham."

"Ha!" the King said, and glanced at his wife. "Go on."

"They, all three, have a proposal to make to Your Highness. I am but the carrier of their proposals. For I doubt their wisdom and worth . . ."

"I am not interested in your doubts, man. What do they propose, these beauties?"

"They propose that Northumbria should become part of Scotland. To the same extent that Cumbria is. And that the Church, the Romish Church, should lead the way."

"God Almighty!" Malcolm exclaimed — and recollecting, shrugged apologetically towards his queen.

"Yes, sir. It is no small matter."

"Well, man — well? What dizzard notion is this?"

"It comes in two parts, sir — the Church's and the realm's. Bishop Walchere now rules Northumbria wholly. As lieutenant as well as bishop. Did you know that the Earl Waldeve is dead? No? William — or Odo — has had him executed. There is a great anger in England, it seems. Never before have the Normans in fact executed a Saxon earl, however many they have imprisoned or slain in battle . . ."

"No doubt. The man was weak and a fool. What of it?"

"There is near revolt, especially in Deira and Northumbria. And Walchere is appointed to rule in his place. But the Bishop was Waldeve's friend — closer than brothers they were." Maldred's eyes flickered towards the women. "So Walchere hates. He is not a Norman but a Lorrainer. He aided us, you will mind, in the matter of Hereward and the Mercian earls. It must be that Odo, and King William, do not know of this hate — or they would not have appointed him. But however that may be, he is now prepared to put his see of Durham under you, sir. Under Scotland."

"Why, in God's name? What advantage to him, in that? And what good an English bishopric to me?"

"These monks see it as a way of getting out of the intolerable rule of Odo of Bayeux, the viceroy. Of throwing off the hated Norman yoke. They say that the Archbishop Lanfranc, who is Walchere's friend, and is at odds with Odo and the Archbishop Thomas of York, will approve. He admires Queen Margaret, we know . . ."

"He is my good friend and father-in-God," she agreed.

"And *my* advantage in this?" the King asked again.

"Since the Bishop rules Northumbria as lord now, there would be no opposition to your army, sir, if it marched in and took possession."

Malcolm stared, and Margaret caught her breath.

"They want me to do that?" the King demanded, almost incredulous.

"That is why they have sent me, Highness."

"But, Christ God — a bishop! A mere snivelling clerk dreams thus! Because his catamite is beheaded! What proof have I that all this is not the maunderings of a deranged dizzard?"

"I said, sir, that I doubted the worth of these proposals. But . . . I must remind you that Cospatrick is behind it, has been working towards it, I think, for long. He has been much in touch with Walchere. He sees himself as Earl of Northumbria again, no doubt. But *he* is no fool or dizzard. And there is more to it. The Thane Ligulf is the Bishop's right hand, in the rule of Northumbria. Leader of his forces as well as adviser. And he is deep in this . . ."

"Ligulf I know. I knew him when I was a lad, at Bamburgh. He will be old-getting now. But a sound man and soldier. He is far-out kin to me, indeed — descended from the old Earls of Bernicia, as was my mother." Oddly, Malcolm appeared to be more impressed with this mention of Ligulf than with anything that had gone before. "If Ligulf is in it, there may be some sense to it."

"The way it was put to me, sir, was that with Ligulf commanding the Bishop's army, you could count on the Northumbrians not only not to oppose you, but to *join* you. And aid in repelling any assault by Odo thereafter."

"Aye. There is that. But — Cospatrick! He is clever — oh, yes. But I do not trust him. He would have me to win Northumbria back for him. And he had me make one son Earl of Cumbria, the other Dunbar and March. So — he could rule over a territory half as large as all Scotland! Who knows, the clever Cospatrick might think to topple me from my throne, one day — since he too is of the blood-royal." The King did not add that Cospatrick was the legitimate great-grandson of Malcolm the Second, whereas he was a bastard.

Maldred swallowed but said nothing.

"Husband — you should not harbour such ill thoughts of Cospatrick," Margaret rebuked, gently. "He has served you well these years past. Myself, I am not happy about armed invasion. But if it could be achieved without war, for Durham and the Northumbrian Church to come under Scotland would be a joyous thing."

"Once it was so, Highness. But it was the Columban Church then," Maldred reminded. "From Lindisfarne."

"Which clutch of churchmen is no matter," the King said, dismissing that aspect of the question. "What is important is whether, afterwards, I could defend the Tees to Ribble border. And what William would do."

"You have heard, sir, that William has suffered defeat? In France."

"Yes. But William is a better soldier than that Philip of France, a curse on him! He will not remain defeated for long. Odo I could deal with, I believe. But William is a different matter."

None actually reminded him of his oath of allegiance to the Norman.

"The monks Aldwin and Turgot believe that the Saxons of the South are so hot against Odo that they might well rise if Northumbria did. The Welsh are, as ever, stirring. Odo is fighting Lanfranc. So it could be that William, heavily engaged in France, and with his sons and Flanders against him, would not be in any state to march against the North for many a day." Maldred said that without any great conviction, for he had no wish to persuade the King to this course. "But one day, William would have to be faced, my lord King."

"Aye, so say I. Only . . . if the Welsh could be made best use of, properly led . . . They are bonnie fighters.

Cumbria stretches down almost to Wales. Speaks the same language. Cospatrick covets Cumbria also. Does he think that he can raise a Cumbrian army? With your brother Madach? They have not fought, as a folk, for a century. If they could be brought to it also . . ."

"I know not, sir. Cospatrick did not speak of that. But . . ."

"Four armies — the Scots, the Northumbrians, the Cumbrians and the Welsh — all facing south and east together. Would that not cause the wretched Saxons to rise? Then together to throw the Normans into the sea! Before William could return from France." Malcolm took a pace or two back and forth beneath the apple-trees. "I have to think on this. Consider well. I shall tell you tomorrow what I have decided."

And abruptly as he had come, he left them there.

Margaret was looking troubled now. "Does this mean war, Maldred?" she asked.

"It could," he allowed. "But may not. He may refuse to do it."

"I think not. You have baited your hook too well!"

"Not I!" he protested. "I am against the project. I but brought the word. From Cospatrick and your friends."

"You think that it will not succeed?"

"I do not say that. Cospatrick believes that it can, and should. But it will succeed at a price."

"Bloodshed? Men's lives?"

"That, yes. But — I was thinking of other cost. The Church."

Magda all but groaned. "Maldred has become a great churchman, of late," she complained. "Not holy, prayerful. But only in the style of it all, in rule and doctrine. He was not so before."

"When the Church, my *father's* Church, is threatened, would you have me to care nothing?"

"You see the Scottish Church as threatened by this, Maldred?"

"Can it be otherwise, Highness? Bring the great bishopric of Durham and all the Northumbrian and Cumbrian Church into Scotland, under the overlordship of English archbishops, and how shall the small Columban Church stand against them? Already you have made inroads, with your Holy Trinity here, and this of St. Andrews. Our Church is not built for fighting — save for the individual souls of men. It is a missionary Church, working from small houses, not a great united array like yours, taking commands from above, from Rome and Canterbury and the like."

"But, do you not see that your people could benefit from uniting with the rest of Christendom? Could gain greatly? You talk only of losing, Maldred. What of gaining? Is your small Church so perfect that it cannot be improved?"

He shook his head helplessly. He would never change her, convince her. And she *could* be right — although he did not think so.

They left it at that, and went to see the new church. The choir or chancel, to the east, was finished now, or sufficiently so for it to be used for services; and very fine it looked — although disproportionate in its dimensions as yet, too high for its length. But that would be altered once the huge, pillared nave was finished — which would take years yet, apparently. Even meantime, however, it was such a place as Scotland had never seen, splendid, dignified, rich, even awe-inspiring, the candle-light and soft radiance from the stained-glass windows gleaming on gold and jewelled magnificence everywhere.

"How say you to this, Maldred friend?" the Queen asked.

"It is a noble pile," he admitted.

"But . . . ?"

"But the poor will not worship here any more fervently, I think, than at the humblest Columban shrine."

"Yet the faithful poor come here by the hundred, from near and far, to see it. Pilgrims. Hence my ferries."

That silenced him. She took his arm as though in consolation.

Next day, Malcolm gave Maldred his answer to take back to Monk Wearmouth. If Cospatrick sent him word and proof that he could raise a Cumbrian army to take part in the enterprise, and that the Welsh would join in in strength, then he would agree to lead a large Scots force down into Northumbria. In the early autumn, once the harvest was in. As to the Church, that was clerics' business, not his. Fothad and Dunchad and Melmore could see to it. Maldred to return and report. That was all . . .

20

THE SCOTS MARCHED southwards in fine fettle — as well they might. For too long, thanks to Norman William, they had been denied this sort of activity, armed venturing, the spice of life. The expedition to the North to counter Malsnechtan — now turned monk in Deer Abbey, it was said — scarcely counted, for it had been very brief, against their own countrymen, with little scope for individual initiative and self-help. For seven years William's truce, if that it could be called, had held, and life had been better for such as churchmen and womenfolk than for men with real blood in their veins. During all that time the King had been irascible, at odds with all, like many of his lords, or else mooning lovesick over his holy Saxon woman — no state for any King of Scots. Now Malcolm was in his element again, doing what he most enjoyed, cheerful, even amiable in his surly fashion.

It was a great host, eight thousand strong, in the nature of things more of a demonstration in strength, a showing of the silver-boar flag, than an actual invasion force. Admittedly this might not augur too well in the important matter of spoil and pillage — but that remained to be seen.

Maldred had joined the array at the Tweed crossing, with seven hundred men of Lothian, the Merse and the Borders; so that, with the four hundred Athollmen who then put themselves under his command, he was in a position to control fully an eighth of the army — more than any other single leader, even Dufagan MacDuff — a strange situation for that young man. Madach was to come over with a force from Caer-luel by North Tyne, Rede, Coquet and Aln, to meet the host at Alnwick.

They went slowly, for most were not horsed, and fifteen or sixteen miles a day was good marching for an army thousands strong. Which gave those who were mounted a lot of time on their hands. And idle hands, especially in former enemy territory, are easily tempted, so that maintaining discipline was a constant preoccupation of the leadership. Despite the King's strict commands that, on this occasion, pillage and rape were forbidden, in the interests of local goodwill, not a few Northumbrians suffered — after all, this had been normal procedure for generations. Malcolm had to hang above a score of the independently-minded — including a group of Maldred's Borderers who looked on such activities as practically their livelihood — before he won approximate acceptance of this unnatural policy. It was all the harder for the monarch to impose, in that he himself was amongst the most tempted of all.

Well before they reached Alnwick, the second day after fording Tweed, a party of riders came fast to meet them, in the Dunstanburgh area. It proved to be Madach mac Melmore himself, with escort, in some agitation.

"Ill news, Highness," he called out, even before he drew rein. "Ligulf Thane is dead. And his Northumbrian host in disarray."

"Fiends of Hell!" Malcolm burst out. "What is this, man? Dead? Ligulf? What a God's Name are you saying? Has there been battle? Already?"

"No, sir — no. It was murder. Poisoned. Gilbert the Sheriff did it. At Gateshead. Where the Northumbrian army awaited you . . ."

"Save us — poison! What fool's tale is this?"

"No tale, cousin — truth. The Sheriff of Northumbria, this Gilbert, is kin to Bishop Walchere. Who appointed him. He was at odds with Ligulf. Jealous of his influence with the Bishop, they say. Influence which should have been his, the Sheriff's. He was against this Scottish project also, it is said. So, while they waited for you, sir, he had Ligulf poisoned. He is dead himself now. For the Northumbrians, who much loved Ligulf, went crazed with anger. They took the Sheriff and hacked him in pieces. And now all is uproar at Gateshead. They are blaming the Bishop, and others round him. Because Gilbert was his kin. Saying that they are betrayed by foreigners and Flemings . . ."

"Damnation — Ligulf dead! This changes all. He was the one I trusted. Without him . . . !" The King beat his clenched fist on his saddle-bow. "I mislike the stink of this! If such can go on in this accursed Bishop's camp. What now?"

"The Prior Aldwin of Wearmouth has gone to Durham to fetch the Bishop, Highness. To calm and reassure the army. The Benedictine Turgot he sent to Alnwick, to inform you. He was weary with travel, so I came myself . . ."

"Monks! Clerks!" Malcolm exploded. "God forgive me for being fool enough ever to enter into dealings with such cattle! And Cospatrick — what says that fox to this?"

"Cospatrick is down on the Welsh marches, Highness. With a force from South Cumbria. Linking up with the Welsh under Griffith ap Cynan. He knows naught of this."

"He should have told me, warned me, of this snake Gilbert's opposition."

They marched on for the Aln, the leaders at least in a highly doubtful frame of mind.

Turgot, waiting at Alnwick with the Caer-luel force, could tell them little more. Only that he suspected that the real mind behind this sorry business had been one Leobwin, who was the Bishop's domestic chaplain, and very close to him. His was an evil influence, Turgot admitted; and although a Saxon, some said a bastard brother of the late Earl Waldeve, he was known to be against the Scottish move, much against . . .

The monk got no further than that. Malcolm, his heavy features thunderous, dismissed him from his presence, fist raised.

So they moved on southwards, towards Tyne.

They never reached Gateshead — where apparently Ligulf had assembled his army, so as to intimidate without actually attacking the Normans building the great new castle at Monkchester across the river, with their quite small resident protective garrison. Prior Aldwin himself reached the Scots at Morpeth the next day, still a day's march from the Tyne, in dire distress. Indeed, he could scarcely gulp out his tidings, in sorrow and alarm. Brought to the King, he actually wept.

"It is all over!" he exclaimed. "All is lost. The good Walchere . . . is dead. Burned. Burned to death. God rest his soul. A blessed martyr, no less! God rest his soul. Dead. And all come to naught . . ."

"Christ God!" Appalled, Malcolm stared at him. "Another of them! Have you all run mad, man?"

"It is true, all true, Sire — the sorrow of it. The men were crazed, crazed. Ligulf's men. I went to Durham and brought the Bishop and his company. To speak and reason with them. I, I do greatly blame myself, now, God knows.

They would not heed him. Only shouted against him, that he had slain Ligulf. That he and that Leobwin, the chaplain, had betrayed them all. That they were foreigners and betrayers. They clamoured against them, threatening. I left them then. To try to get help from some of the thanes, Ligulf's friends. But, but . . . I was too late . . ." The man's voice broke.

"They slew him then? The Bishop?"

"Oh, the sin of it! Yes, slew him. They were threatening his life. He and his company from Durham, about five-score, with Leobwin, fighting off the angry soldiery, took refuge in the sanctuary of St. Mary's Church, at Gateshead. There the soldiers barricaded them in. Piled brushwood all around and set fire to it. All was ablaze when I got back with the lords. Walchere, and all within, were dead, burned. Not one escaped . . ."

"Saints a mercy! So — all comes to naught!"

All around the King stared at each other as the significance of all this sank in.

"This Northumbrian army?" MacDuff broke in. "What of it now? Who commands, clerk?"

"None seems to command, sir," Aldwin wailed. "All is confusion. With Ligulf and Walchere both dead, none knows what to do. All authority is gone. The army is dispersing, men going to their homes. All is chaos . . ."

"Then the sooner that we also go home, the better, I say!" Dufagan declared. And there were cries of agreement around him.

"But — all is not lost yet," Madach protested. "*We* are here in strength. The Northumbrians only need to be rallied — a strong hand. The South Cumbrians and the Welsh are mustered. All Cospatrick's work . . ."

"A plague on Cospatrick's work!" the King exclaimed. "But . . . this must be considered. I shall hold a council. At once. That church we passed — Morpeth. Back to it. Have the host to camp meantime in this common land. We must consider . . ."

So a council-of-war was instituted in the modest church of the Blessed Virgin at Morpeth, amongst the Scots leaders. There was much divergence of view. Most probably agreed with MacDuff, advocating an immediate return to Scotland — with, happily, no further need to restrain themselves from spoil and pillage. Some supported Madach that the project should go on, arguing that

Cospatrick's grand scheme, so painstakingly built up, so wide in its ramifications, should not be abandoned because of the death of two men, and Englishmen at that. Others again proposed a waiting policy meantime — since there was no immediate threat to the Scots army. They had come so far, and were in major strength, let them therefore wait awhile and see how matters fell out. Maldred, for his part, kept silence. He did not, in fact, know what to think. He had never favoured the venture, and so, in one way, would weep no tears over its abandonment. On the other hand, it did seem a great anti-climax, and a swift return premature. Also, of course, it left Cospatrick with the Welsh and the Cumbrians, as it were high and dry. And the Welsh had been let down more than sufficiently in the past.

Malcolm listened to the discussion dark-browed, chin out-thrust, all amiability vanished. Fairly soon he had had enough. Suddenly he slammed palm on the faldstool at which he sat, and the Earl of Angus, speaking, stopped on the word.

"I despair of your wits, all of you," he jerked. "Am I ever to be surrounded by dolts? Can none see beyond their noses? See that all is utterly changed? Ligulf dead was sufficiently bad. But this Walchere's death means that all is of no avail. He was both bishop and lord here. Now there is neither, in Northumbria. No authority. I am here at his invitation — or was. That is so no longer. We are but invaders again. Not that I care for that. But it changes all. Walchere can no longer turn over Church and earldom to Scotland. Nor is any other in a position to do so. William and his precious brother Odo will chuckle over this day's work. It will mean a new Bishop of Durham and a new lord of Northumbria, a new earl perhaps. Who will they appoint? Not any man who will bring Northumbria to Scotland — that I swear! So, that dream is over — finished."

There was a heavy pause.

"But, my lord King, you can still *take* Northumbria!" Madach said. "You are here, unopposed. None, no new bishop or earl, will be in a position to oppose you, for long, for many months, I would say."

"I cannot take the Church, the bishopric, man. And without that, and no one to command the Northumbrians to support me, I could not *hold* Northumbria. Save perhaps by constant war. No — we have lost all authority here. Save that of the sword. It is not enough. Tomorrow we turn back."

"Good!" Dufagan MacDuff exclaimed. "And must we continue to love and cherish these wretched Northumbrians, Highness? In this new situation?"

"No," the King said simply, and rose, the council over.

So, next day, without any further dealings with the people they had come to embrace, not even a royal farewell accorded to Aldwin and Turgot, the retiral commenced — as did Northumbria's ordeal. For now there was no attempt to restrain or discipline the army, and the expedition became just one more traditional harrying and spoiling rampage, this time of an utterly defenceless land. Far and wide the Scots ranged and ravaged, secure in the knowledge that there was no force, local or national, to check or punish them. They left a vast trail of fire and blood, pain and sorrow and ruin behind them. From an army, the host became no more than a mighty collection of looters and cattle-drovers, and progress homewards sank to a mere four or five miles a day.

Maldred, Madach and some others protested to the King, but with scant success. He told them that if they were so nice they could order their own contingents to cease from all spoliation and ride doucely home like monks — and see how popular that made them. For himself, he held that having been brought all this way for nothing, the men deserved some little recreation and profit where they could find it. Maintaining an army, otherwise unpaid and beholden to different lords, was not a task for the lily-livered and the chicken-hearted.

The Scots' wooing of Northumbria was over before it really started, and Cospatrick's great conception gone for nothing.

21

IT WAS THE following spring, 1080, before Maldred saw his cousin Cospatrick again. The Earl's mother-less family at Ersildoune all were now growing into their teens, and presumably their father did not judge it necessary to see so much of them; indeed "Uncle Maldred" now probably meant more to the four of them than did their erratic sire. He, Cospatrick, had spent the winter in South Cumbria and Wales, where he appeared to have made new friends — no doubt sickened meantime with the Northumbrian situation and his Scottish connections. Nevertheless, when he eventually arrived one windy April evening at Dunbar, still in his guise of wandering friar, he appeared to be his normal, cynically cheerful self. Maldred had anticipated a bitter tirade against the King and most others, but nothing of the sort eventuated. He said, in fact, that Malcolm had probably made the sensible decision, in the circumstances, however uncomfortable it had proved for himself.

"Did not the Welsh turn on you, when they heard? After their trouble in mustering and arming?"

"The Welsh are well used to such treatment. They raided over into the Marcher earls' domains of Montgomery and Powisland and Flint, for a week or two, and then went home. I had more difficulty with the Cumbrians — although some were thankful enough, I think, that they did not have to fight. They have been peaceable for too long for their good! I had promised them much Norman wealth!"

"So what did you do?"

"I led them raiding also — what else? The Church Militant! Chester and Northwich will not soon forget us! I much increased my popularity with the Cumbrians, in the end."

"So — all your fine schemes and great travels came to nothing more than the old and usual cross-border reivings? Rapine and murder."

"You could say that — thanks to the folly of others. But you would weep no tears for that, Maldred, I think? You were scarcely in favour of it all, anyway."

"I was, and am, well enough content with our border at the Tweed. But . . . do you grieve for Walchere?"

"I grieve for Ligulf. Walchere was foolish, weak, in the end. He allowed himself to be surrounded and led by worthless men. That monk Leobwin, Gilbert the Sheriff and others. Acting the earl is not for churchmen — if *I* should say so, an earl who acts the churchman!"

"Not for churchmen — save Odo!"

"Ah, yes — Odo. There is a fowl of a different feather! Northumbria will not forget *him*. For generations."

"He was worse than Malcolm?"

"As compared with Odo and his Normans, Malcolm and the Scots are but as playful lambs! You must have heard what he did to Northumbria?"

"I heard that he had come north a month past. And harassed the land. As punishment for thinking to rise against the Normans . . ."

"Harassed, you say! He *crucified* Northumbria — *my* earldom! Such savagery as no-one has ever before seen. Always the Normans have been harsh, cruel. But this was beyond all. He set Deira and South Northumberland ablaze from Tees to Tyne — aye, and used the people's blood to quench the flames! Untold thousands died. The land is left a smoking ruin."

"I had not heard. He did not come north of Tyne. So . . ."

"No. He had to turn back. When news of Gerberoi reached him. Esteeming it to be much worse."

"Gerberoi . . . ?"

"Lord — you have not heard of this, either? There was a battle, a siege, at Gerberoi, in East Normandy. William was wounded — and by his own son, the Duke Robert. William was besieging Robert in the fortress of Gerberoi. Philip of France came to Robert's aid. There was a great battle. Robert sallied out, and struck down his father. A month ago, and more."

"And William? Is he sore hurt?"

"Unfortunately, no! Less so than at first thought. He lost much blood. Men thought that he might die. So Odo hurried south from Tyne, sparing North Northumberland, his ill work only half-done. But — he may come back. That man thirsts for blood! And this is he who would be Pope!"

"Pope? Odo . . . !"

"No less. That is his aim. He makes no secret of it. Which is partly why he and Lanfranc are such foes. Lanfranc has said that he would rather die than see Odo on the papal throne."

"Save us — but even Rome would not see that fiend head of its Church?"

"Be not so sure, cousin. There have been popes almost as bad. But — he may not win it. For it is said that William

311

himself is against it. Does not relish having to kiss his half-brother's toe! William may stop it."

"William — he is still in France?"

"Yes. Nursed, will you believe it, by his son Robert! In an access of remorse, for striking down his own sire. A strange way to bring these two together again."

Digesting all this, Maldred shook his head. "At the least, it should prevent William from moving against Malcolm meantime — for having broke his oath of allegiance and invaded Northumbria."

"Perhaps. But if I was Malcolm mac Duncan I would not rely on it. William never forgets. Does Malcolm keep his armies mustered?"

"In part. Each earl and thane and lord is to be ready to have half his full strength ready to march in three days, the rest in a week. I have *your* men so ordered here and at Ersildoune."

"Aye. And I see that you keep up the watch on the Tweed crossings. Which is wise."

"That is, in part, why I am here, is it not? Although I should not foresee any attack from Northumbria in this situation, should I?"

"I think not. These new men, appointed by Odo, are not yet sure of themselves. You know of them?"

"I know that there is a new earl and a new bishop. Both Normans . . ."

"Not a new earl. Sir Aubrey de Coucy is only governor of Northumbria — and misliking the task, I hear. Only William can make a new earl, and he has other things to think on, in Normandy. This de Coucy is Odo's man. The new bishop, William de St. Calais, is likewise one of Odo's friends — but he is appointed by Thomas, Archbishop of York. So I suppose that he is truly Bishop of Durham. In time, no doubt, these two will turn their faces against Scotland. But meantime they have sufficient on their hands. I would say that, what with this and that, we might look for one year of peace on the Border. No more."

"And for that we are to be thankful?"

"Most certainly. It is more than we can usually say. And we must make good use of it. For one thing, it is a good opportunity to work young Dolfin into some responsibility in his earldom. He is fifteen years now, and should be old enough to begin to act the Earl of Cumbria. Still under Madach's guidance, to be sure. I am going to take him over to Caer-luel and let him meet and know some of my new Cumbrian friends . . ."

"I had hoped, cousin, that with this hope of peace for a while, you yourself would resume your earldoms. And so allow me to return to my own place in Atholl."

"No, no, lad — not yet. So long as William lives, Cospatrick mac Maldred must remain safely dead, I fear! I had hoped that this wound might have been the end of William — when I could have resurrected myself. He hates me does the Bastard of Normandy — I have crossed him too often. If he heard that I was alive indeed, his outlaw still, he would arise from any sick-bed and come for me! Malcolm would not weaken his position by offering me protection — that is sure. So I would be a hunted fugitive again. And if caught, either decapitated like Waldeve, or immured in perpetual imprisonment like Morkar, Siward Biorn, Roger of Hereford and Hereward of Bourne. No, I am better as I am meantime. And you serve me as deputy very well. You are comfortable enough here, are you not? Stewarding two earldoms. It is not many young men who have so much of power, not born to it. You would be none so well employed, in Atholl."

"My father is old-getting, less than strong. He has little interest in his earldom. And with Kerald dead, Madach governing Cumbria, and myself here, all is not well with Atholl."

"In a year or two Madach will be able to go back there. As Dolfin takes more into his own hands. Madach is your father's heir, not you. So it is his affair, is it not? And, talking of heirs — you now have a son, I hear?"

"Where did you learn that, on your travels? But, yes — young Melmore, a fine strong bairn. Magda took him and his sister to Bothargask a week past. I follow shortly. We have to spend *some* time in our own place . . ."

"To be sure. None say otherwise. And all is well at Ersildoune? I go there tomorrow."

"Yes. The young folk do very well. I like them greatly. But — they need their father. In especial, the lass Ethelreda. With no mother . . ."

"Would you have me bring her a new mother to Ersildoune? Friar Eadwulf!" Cospatrick grinned. "I thought of sending her to Court. To be one of the Queen's ladies. Margaret would mother her, I vow. They owe me something, there. And Ethelreda is kin to Malcolm."

"That might be best. She is turning into a young woman . . ."

"Speak to Margaret on this. On your way north to Bothargask. How is she, that sainted Queen of ours?"

"Well. Busy. Most full of good works. You have heard of her ferries? Now she has built hospices also, on both sides of Forth. Where pilgrims and passengers may wait, feed, sleep, if the weather halts the scows or if they arrive after dark. All free, at her own charges."

"A remarkable woman. Mark you, I do not think that I would wish to be wed to her, beauteous as she is! Though, to be sure, *you* feel differently, I jalouse? You always had a fancy for her, did you not?"

"Not so. Nothing of the sort . . ."

"Just so! Myself, I prefer less holy women. Yet Malcolm, whom I would have thought might feel the same, does not seem to be . . . incommoded! They have still another brat, I hear."

"Yes — they have had a fifth son — although the Queen much wanted a daughter. Prayed for one. This one she has named Alexander. Five boys . . ."

"Aye, the Scots throne is well supported with sons. But *Saxon* sons! I wonder if they ever recollect that Malcolm has two older sons — and one still a hostage for his good behaviour, in England?"

"*You* should have recollected that, when you urged the King to march into Northumbria!"

"I did, Maldred — I did. But I hear that young Cousin Duncan is well content. He is a great favourite of William's queen, Matilda of Flanders. William leaves her alone in England in all his warring in France. Her own sons grown and fled the nest, she consoles herself with Duncan, it seems. He will be seventeen years now, will he not? A useful squire for a lonely woman of middle years! He is safe there. Better off, I say, at Winchester than he would be in Scotland, unwanted. Like his brother Donald."

"Perhaps. His father never speaks of him. But Margaret does. I think that she has him on her conscience. Although it is not her fault . . ."

"Fault? Perhaps not. But she has some responsibility, does she not?"

"They are the King's sons. His business . . ."

"And she can twist the King round her two fingers! As all the world knows. Has she had Malcolm bring young Donald back from his exile in the wild Highlands, with his uncle Donald Ban?"

"No. But . . ."

"No. She would have *her* sons to dispossess Ingebiorg's sons — that is certain-sure. So do not prate to me, cousin, of our sainted Queen's conscience!"

Maldred looked unhappy. They left it there.

"Now — give me some account of your stewardship here. Start with the Dunbar earldom . . ."

*   *   *

For once, the well-informed and astute Cospatrick was wrong, and neither the Borderland nor Scotland itself was granted a year's peace. The Conqueror made a swift recovery — or perhaps it was merely that his conquering spirit was by no means wounded and drove him, unmindful of his body's weakness. At any rate, he insisted on being conveyed back to England in the late spring, and brought the touchingly reconciled Duke Robert with him. And there, swiftly taking the reins of government out of Odo's hands into his own, couch-borne as he might be, he made it clear that England had her king back. Amongst other things he created Aubrey de Coucy Earl of Northumbria, and ordered him immediately to muster all available arms. And he put his son Robert, willingly or otherwise, at the head of a large force and sent him north to teach Malcolm of Scots a lesson in allegiance.

The news came, as usual, from Cospatrick. But not in person, this time. Patie's Dod arrived at Dunbar from somewhere on the Northumbrian-Cumbrian border, weary with long riding. The Earl had sent him to say that the Duke Robert of Normandy was marching northwards and had already reached York, with an army of ten thousand. De Coucy was to reinforce him. They were coming to Scotland. The Lord Maldred must warn King Malcolm at once. So far as the Earl knew, there was no sea-borne force in support — but this was not certain. He himself was going to see to the raising of a force in Cumbria, to come to the aid of the Scots; but this would take a little time, and the Normans would have crossed the Border well before he could march. He had not thought that William could act so swiftly. But at the least, this Robert was not made of the same stuff as his father, apparently.

Maldred acted with his own celerity. He put into immediate effect the mobilisation plans for the two earldoms. He had Magda and the children pack up for a prompt retiral northwards for Bothargask — for Dunbar was of course apt to be directly in the path of any invasion from England, hence its strategic importance. He himself, however, did not wait for his family, in this instance, but set off for Dunfermline without delay.

He was again glad of the new ferries over Forth. Unfortunately, Malcolm and the royal family were not at present at Dunfermline but up at the hunting-palace of the Ward of the Stormounth, so that further journeying and delay ensued.

Maldred was very weary when at length he reached the Ward, after riding nearly ninety miles in thirty hours, with only snatches of sleep. The King was preparing to go hunting in the Forest of Clunie, with the nine-year-old Prince Edward impatient to accompany him, when the traveller arrived. Margaret, with the younger sons, cried out with pleasure at sight of him, then her voice changed to concern as she perceived his state of reeling fatigue when he stiffly dismounted.

"Maldred, my dear — you are tired, faint!" she cried. "You, you are not ill . . . ?"

"It is the tidings he brings that are ill, I wager!" Malcolm declared. "I know that look."

"Aye, my lord King — none so good." Maldred turned to the Queen. "I am well enough, Highness — only weary. I have killed three horses getting here from Dunbar."

"Then come, sir, refresh yourself. Food, wine, Maldred . . ."

"Tush, woman — the news first! Since he has come all this way with it. What is it, man?"

"The Duke Robert of Normandy is marching north against you, sir. With ten thousand men. Sent by King William. He had reached York when Cospatrick sent these tidings. From Cumbria."

"Robert? That weather-cock! In England?"

"William is back, and brought him with him. Now sends him against you. In strength. De Coucy, now made

Earl of Northumbria, is to aid him with more men. This — for your wasting of Northumbria a year ago!"

"Curse you . . . !" Malcolm began, and glanced at his wife. "Watch your tongue, cousin! So — this Robert is at York?"

"*Was*, four or five days ago. Now will be a deal nearer."

"Oh, the foolishness of it! More of war and suffering!" Margaret exclaimed. "Will men never learn better ways to settle their disputes?"

Neither of them attempted to answer that.

"Ten thousand, you say? And the Northumbrians in addition. Four days north of York. We cannot hold them at the Border, then. I cannot muster sufficient men, in time. It will take me five days, or six, to put half that in the field."

"Cospatrick, Highness, said that he would raise a force in Cumbria. And bring them to your aid. With Madach, no doubt. But it would take some time."

"Aye — all takes time. Time which we do not have!" Malcolm glared around at them all, wife, cousin, children. "God's curse on all Normans!"

"God's mercy, rather, on us sinners, husband!" Margaret said. "We break His laws and then curse when He punishes."

"Aye, no doubt. Pray you for mercy then, lass — I have more to do!" The King raised his great voice, to shout for lords, stewards, grooms.

"Come, Maldred — come within," the Queen urged. "You must have rest and refreshment. Your part is done . . ."

Malcolm heard that. "By God, it is not!" he jerked. "I have work for you. But go, eat meantime . . ."

They went indoors while Malcolm erupted orders and young Edward protested vigorously about his lost hunting-trip.

Margaret attended to Maldred's needs with her own hands. She asked as to Magda's situation — and rejoiced at least to hear that she and the children were on their way to Bothargask — which was only a few miles west of the Ward. She wondered if Maldred thought that this time it must come to actual battle? Could that not be avoided, as before? At Abernethy. By using their wits?

"William accepted an oath of allegiance — once!" he said. "Will he do so a second time? After it was broken."

"Malcolm kept his oath for seven years. Only broke it when the Northumbrians themselves besought him to come, to take them into his realm. He will not find occasion to do that again."

"Will that appease William?"

"Perhaps not. But this son Robert is less strong a man. It seems that he is easily swayed. Might we not sway him? If he was told that the Northumbrian venture had been done in the best interests of all? That his father had never really ruled Northumbria. That this way would have aided both kingdoms, removed a source of ill-will between them. And that Holy Church would have gained. The good Archbishop Lanfranc was in favour of it. Or, of Bishop Walchere's plan. I could tell him so — this Duke Robert. Commend him to Lanfranc — who is his father's friend."

Maldred was too tired for agile thinking. "I do not know. I do not know this Robert. It might help. But was not Lanfranc's concern more with countering Odo of Bayeux?"

"That evil man! Yes, Lanfranc seeks ever to undo the ill he does. But he also saw good in that the Northumbrian Church should move into Scotland."

Maldred was in no state to restart that battle-of-words about the take-over of the Scottish Church by the Romish one; but one aspect of the subject did come to his mind, as perhaps relevant, especially to Lanfranc. "Odo," he said. "Did you know that Bishop Odo seeks to be Pope of Rome?"

"Odo? Oh, no — no! Surely not that? By all that is holy — never that!"

"Cospatrick says that it is so — and he is seldom wrong in his information. The Archbishop Thomas of York is aiding him — Odo. He has been gathering in the riches of the Church and the realm, in England, for long, it seems. To bribe the Cardinals who elect the Pope . . ."

"Maldred — it cannot be true! That would be beyond all evil. A disgrace to all Christendom."

"I do not know. But Cospatrick says that William would much mislike this. If he knew. That he would not have his half-brother raised to such heights and have to bow before him. Nor would Lanfranc, I swear! Is there not here something you might use . . . ?"

"You mean . . . ? Yes — oh, yes, Maldred, I see it. Tell

Duke Robert this. Say that we . . . that King Malcolm is concerned to halt this wickedness. That Odo must be stopped. That the Northumbrian venture was part of this, not really an invasion. But a supporting of Bishop Walchere and Archbishop Lanfranc in their countering of Odo's schemes . . ."

"And is that truth?"

Margaret paused, blinked and actually flushed. She shook her fair head. "No, Maldred — no," she admitted, low-voiced now. "No — God Almighty forgive me! I, I was carried away. I thank you, thank you for rebuking me. I am a great sinner, Maldred."

Embarrassed, he touched her hand. "*I* am sorry. I did not mean . . . I was not accusing. Only pointing the weakness . . ."

"Yes, weakness. But it was sin, nevertheless. Untruth. We shall never do good by evil means — as well as imperilling our souls. No. Yet — there is something here that we could use, is there not? Lawfully, honestly . . ."

Malcolm stamped in. "You, Maldred mac Melmore," he cried. "If you have now eaten sufficiently, get you down to sleep. Instead of huddling close to my wife! I will give you four hours, no more. Then you must be on your way south again. There is over-much to do, for sleeping — or exchanging confidences!"

"We were planning a stratagem, Malcolm — to your advantage," the Queen told him, patiently. "You are much beholden to Maldred, I say."

"Leave you strategy to me, my dear." The King pointed a stubby finger at Maldred. "Go you back to the Merse at best speed. Leave parties of your Borderers at every Tweed crossing, to delay Robert's advance so long as is possible. Then, with the rest of your men, move back through Lothian. Destroying it. You understand? I want Lothian burned in the Normans' faces . . ."

"Oh, no!" Margaret cried.

"Quiet, woman! This is man's business. Robert will have marched for hundreds of miles. His men and beasts will be weary and hungry. Especially those great horses on which the Normans so rely. What they call their heavy chivalry. Any food and fodder they may have carried with them will long be finished. So I want all hay and grain burned before them, all cattle and sheep driven off into the hills. All food destroyed. You understand? Ten thousand men and thousands of horses need a deal of feeding. They are not to find any in my territories. This is *your* task. And you will not weaken in it — I know your softnesses! The realm requires it. This will give me time to gather my strength — and bring Robert to me weakened, famished!"

"It is cruel, cruel!" the Queen protested. "And not necessary. We have been discussing how to treat with this Robert, not fight him. There is much that we can put forward. That will give him pause . . ."

"Then he can pause where we can hold him — and talk if so minded. Either at the Forth, at Stirling. Or at the Carron, at Ecclesbreac. In Calatria, where Lothian ends. I shall be waiting for him there — you hear, Maldred? Hold him up for five days — I must have five days. Now — go sleep you, if you must. Then ride . . ."

*   *   *

So Maldred presently resumed his travelling, with a fresh horse but a heavy heart, the thought of the grim duty ahead leaden within him. All the way back through fertile Lothian he rode haunted by the thought of what he must bring to this fair and lovely land, amongst the most rich in all Scotland — a land of which he himself was, temporarily, lord and protector. Yet he knew that, so far as strategy went, the King was right. It was undoubtedly the most effective way of slowing down and weakening the invaders. He supposed that always the few must suffer for the many. But it went sorely against the grain. Would Cospatrick himself have done it, whose land it was? He almost certainly would indeed, being the man he was.

Maldred had one lift of the spirit on his journey, when he encountered Magda and the children, with their escort, on the way north. The parting again was the sorer trial.

At Dunbar, where the manpower of the Lothian earldom was now largely assembled, he lingered only long enough for an hour or two of sleep and a setting of affairs in order, before moving on southwards again at the head of this force of some seven hundred mounted men. Down by the Pease passes and over into the Eye valley they went, to cross the wide green Merse, making for Tweed. He argued that these men should guard the Tweed fords, under local guidance, rather than the Mersemen and Borderers themselves — on the recognition that the latter would be much more likely to burn Lothian thoroughly and effectively than would Lothian men, unkind thought as this was.

At Tweedside his own guards had sent out their spies into the Northumbrian lands across the river, and were able to inform Maldred that the van of the English host was now none so far away, having crossed Aln, and was making for the upper Till valley; but it was much strung out for almost a score of miles, and not covering many miles each day. Most of it, after all, had come nearly four hundred miles, from Winchester.

He placed the Lothian men at all the possible Tweed fords — some six of them over a twenty-five mile stretch of the great river — instructing them that their task was to hold up the enemy for as long as they could but not to throw their lives away in any last-ditch struggle. They were then to retire northwards, by Lauderdale and the hills, to make their own way through the west of Lothian to Calatria, the area between the Rivers Avon and Carron. The King would be waiting at the far side of Carron.

Then he sent word for the March earldom muster at Ersildoune to leave there and march eastwards by the southern skirts of Lammermuir, to join him at Dunbar. He allowed himself a few hours' rest, then led the Mersemen northwards.

At Dunbar again, that night, he slept in his own bed for eight hours, and required every minute of them.

Next day by mid-forenoon the Ersildoune contingent of about five hundred arrived. Maldred gave his joint force, of almost one thousand, their grievous orders. It was mid-June. All growing corn was to be trampled flat; all hay already cut and stacked, burned; all threshed grain likewise. To whomsoever it belonged and whatever pleas to spare it. All food which could not be carried away, to be destroyed. The people were to be kindly used, but firmly forced to leave their homes, and helped drive their flocks and herds and poultry up into the fastnesses of Lammermuir. Nothing was to be left to feed or solace the invader. They need not burn houses and farmeries — only what was eatable for man and beast. This was war, and they must steel their minds to it. There were to be no exceptions.

So the dire process commenced, there at Dunbar itself, Maldred, torch in hand, setting alight to the castle granaries and commanding his people to ride back and forth over the rigs of green standing oats to trample them flat, shutting his ears to the cries of the husbandmen, the millers, the women and children. The light wind off the sea blew growing clouds of smoke ahead of them as they slowly progressed westwards, so that they performed their grim work in its choking pall. Before them went fast-moving groups, to warn the folk and get them out of their homes, by force if necessary. And everywhere the sad processions of the dispossessed streamed away southwards for the secret Lammermuir valleys, with their food and most precious gear, driving their livestock, carrying their aged and infirm and infants, calling down the curses of God and all His saints on the men who ordained this wickedness.

It was as slow a proceeding as it was soul-destroying, for all had to be done on a very wide front, to be effective, stretching from the foothills to the coast; and even one thousand incendiaries and tramplers could not cover an eight-to-ten miles wide belt with any speed. Progress, if so it could be called, was very uneven too, for of course the terrain varied greatly. It was not all cultivated rigs and infields, strips and pasture and meadow, fertile as the plain was. There was much of undrained marshland, especially in the vales of Tyne and Peffer, scrub forest, whin-clad slopes and moorland and outcropping low isolated hills and ridges. By nightfall, blackened, red-eyed, sore-throated and unhappy, they had not progressed more than five miles westwards from Dunbar.

The night behind them blazed smoking, murky red.

The next miserable day they advanced for an average of eight miles, and included in that the abbey-town of Haddington, the largest in this part of Lothian, in the centre of the valley of Tyne, the abbot and monks there yielding up their food and fodder and stock but refusing to leave the monastic precincts, claiming God's own authority. The Primate's son bowed to that authority.

He had given his monarch four days.

The following red and reeking dawn was Sunday, St. Fillan's Eve, making the task seem all the more obscene. In the afternoon they were joined by the Lothian men from Tweedside, who had come up Lauderdale and over the Soltra pass — and who were notably tight-lipped about what they could see of their native province under its shroud of smoke, which now rose as a vast sun-denying brown canopy hundreds of feet into the air. They informed that they had held up the Norman advance parties at most of the fords satisfactorily, for a full day. Indeed they might still be holding them, had not one of the crossings groups failed to stand, for some reason; when the enemy had got across there in sufficient numbers to threaten the rear of all. So they had had to retire. The English van, by now, well mounted, would be half-way across the Merse.

At least Maldred now had more men for the work. He was gaining manpower all the way, to be sure. The Dunbar earldom comprised only the eastern half of Lothian, almost to Edinburgh, the western half being under a variety of independent lords and thanes. These the King had sent orders direct, and most had already departed northwards with their fighting-men. But some, more dilatory or delayed, now joined Maldred. There was no enthusiasm for the programme of destruction, but these also had had the royal command, and had to co-operate.

Nevertheless, from then onwards, the burning and trampling was less thoroughly carried out. Admittedly this part of Lothian was less fertile than the east, with more of hill and moor and forest. The town of Edinburgh, nestling beneath the great Pictish fortress-crowned rock of Dunedin, so like that of Stirling, made a troublesome place to clear, with its warrens of cot-houses and hovels — in fact took most of that day. Although there were hills in plenty round about to offer refuge, most of the folk merely fled up to the fortress itself, which was extensive enough to hide thousands behind its tall ramparts. Maldred's people left them there.

He had, of course, left a small rearguard behind to keep watch on the enemy advance; and reports now revealed that the invaders had reached the devastated area. Whether this would slow them or hasten their oncoming remained to be seen.

On the sixth day after leaving the Ward, hoarse, smoke-blackened, fatigued and depressed to his very bones, Maldred crossed Avon into Calatria, near Linlithgow. Only eight miles ahead, across extensive swampy tidal flats, was the mouth of the Carron. Behind him, flame-tinged smoke rose like an enormous towering wall. He had done his duty — to his earthly master, at least.

He found the King at Ecclesbreac, capital place of Calatria, where there was a small monastery and township near the thane's hall-house. It was no major centre, but with its own importance, situated to command the first crossing of Carron which, because of the low-lying, marshy plain of the Forth here, was wide and muddy, splitting into many channels and constituting a formidable barrier. Also it was where Lothian ended and the Lennox, the extreme southern province of Alba, the ancient Scotland, began. Here had been a Roman port — indeed this place marked the extreme northern limit of actual Roman settlement. This frontier character was how the vicinity had got its name — or names, for it was probably unique in bearing three of them, all meaning the same. Here, in the eighth century, an Anglian missionary, St. Ronan, had established a church which, being Roman-educated, he named Varia Capella, the church of the mixed or varied people. In due course, the Saxon-Danish imposition on the Picts of Lothian changed that to the Faw or Falkirk. Later the Celtic Church took over, and used the Gaelic for the same thing, Eaglais Bhreac, or Ecclesbreac, the variegated or speckled church. But the importance of the spot lay not in its name or even church, but in the strategic significance of its position, the first strong line of defence after Tweed and before the Forth was bridged at Stirling.

Maldred was not surprised to find the Queen at Ecclesbreac with her husband and the army — knowing her hopes for a negotiated settlement. She, at least, sympathised with his state of body and mind, which was more than Malcolm felt called upon to express. The King did, however, acknowledge that his cousin had given him an extra day beyond that stipulated, for his mustering and dispositions; and he appeared to accept that curtain of smoke behind the newcomers as adequate proof that they had turned Lothian into the required desert.

Maldred, to be sure, sought neither sympathy nor acclaim but only a couch in the monastery and blessed sleep.

When he was aroused, it was to be informed that the Normans were only a few miles off, and coming on fast — at least their van. He was to report to the King, at once.

He found the Scots array drawn up along the muddy

north bank of the Carron, in a line well over a mile in length. Although totalling only about six thousand men, as yet, it would make an impressive-looking phalanx from the far side. Malcolm, Margaret and the senior leadership, stood under the great boar-flag of Scotland, near the monastery, at the northern end of the stake-marked ford.

"Ah, here is my cousin Maldred, a most notable sleeper!" the King announced, as he came up. "I hope that you are sufficiently rested? I have given your command to Lachlan of Buchan — rather than disturb you, man! And the Athollmen are well enough under the Thane of Struan. Yonder is the enemy van. Do you wish to await them here, with me? Or would you prefer to return to your couch?"

There was suitable laughter at that.

Maldred gazed heavily ahead of him. "I think — not the van," he said. "More like to be Duke Robert himself and his leaders. All those banners . . ."

"So you are sufficiently awake to perceive that, are you! Yes, I judge this is Robert Bastardson himself, and his chiefest men, come to prospect the field and our strength. Think you he will find our Carron mud to his taste?"

The Queen came to Maldred's side. "Do not heed him," she murmured. "He pretends to be confident, but is not. His throne hangs in the balance, here."

Maldred nodded. "I know my cousin," he said.

They watched the enemy forward force advance, a gallant sight, all glittering steel and chain-mail, colourful heraldic surcoats and banners, on heavy war-horses, perhaps one thousand strong. Behind, a mile or so back, could be seen a much larger host advancing. The Carron here was fully three hundred yards across, just out of effective bowshot; but there was a muddy islet in mid-stream.

The Normans reined up on the south bank, a group of notables under the great standard of England directly opposite the boar-banner of Scotland. For minutes the two sides eyed each other across the water. It was too far for shouting.

"They look fine enough — but they will have empty bellies!" the King said. "Go you, Gillibride."

The Earl of Angus, chosen as spokesman, and his banner-bearer, mounted and rode forward alone into the muddy waters of the ford. There was a causeway of stones beneath the silt here, otherwise there would have been no crossing, save by boat. As it was, the Earl's horses were up to their bellies. The two men rode out as far as the tidal mud-bank, on to which the horses mounted in a slippery slaister.

"I am Gillibride, Earl of Angus," that man shouted. "I speak for the most puissant prince, Malcolm mac Duncan, High King of Scots. He demands to know who you are who come in this martial array upon the soil of his Scotland, without his leave? And your business — which had better be honest!"

From the north bank they could not hear the answer. But presently the Earl came splashing back.

"The Duke Robert, my lord King — he who wears the whitened mail — says that he summons you in the name of the King of England, Lord Paramount, to lay down your arms and come to yield up your kingdom to him. He says that you have broken your royal oath of allegiance. That you are, in consequence, no longer King of Scots. That King William has deposed you. And that your son Duncan, in his care, will now rule Scotland under him, in your stead."

"Ha — he crows so loud, does he — this tanner's grandson! Go you back, Gillibride, and tell him . . . No, wait. We shall give him his answer otherwise. Horns, my friends — all horns to sound. Loud and long. Blow, I tell you — blow!"

At first only those around the King, but soon all along the Scots line the curling bulls' horns were lifted to lips, and the wailing, hooting cacophony rose and continued, a sufficiently derisive bellowing to make the Scots attitude entirely clear.

Before it had finished, a splendid horseman and his bannerman detached themselves from the Norman central group and rode in turn into the ford and out to the islet.

"I am William de Warrenne, Earl of Surrey," this individual shouted, when the hooting had died away. "The Duke Robert requires immediate obedience to his commands. Or he will come for you, my lord Malcolm, in person. And be not gentle when he reaches you! He has eighteen thousand men to enforce his will."

The King answered that himself. "I, Malcolm, urge him to come, Norman!" he called. "I am ready for him. The only way that he will get across this river is over a bridge of his own slain! We shall see whether eighteen thousand bodies are sufficient for that — for there is a notable depth of mud! And we shall be waiting for such as remain."

Surrey turned and relayed that to the other side.

After an interval of mixed shoutings, he faced the Scots again. "My lord Duke reminds you, sir, that this river is none so long. A few miles up and he can cross it with ease. And once across, he will see that you pay for every minute that you have delayed him. Wiser to yield now — while you still have your eyes, at least!" Gouging out his victims' eyes was one of the Conqueror's methods of showing his displeasure with persons whom it was politic not actually to slay.

"Tell your duke that *his* eyes must be failing him if he has reached as far north as this and cannot see that he will get no further. And that his journey south again will be less comfortable — for such as may live to essay it! Remember that. And remember that none such will eat until they are over Tweed! As for this Carron river, I have other forces further up. Think you *this* is all the manpower of Scotland?"

While Surrey conveyed all that to his friends, the Queen spoke, strongly. "Malcolm — this is folly! Children's folly! Like bairns at play! Can grown men not do better than this? Shouting insults! Let us go speak to him, face to face. With some dignity. There is much to put to this Robert . . ."

"This one requires humbling before he will talk."

"And is this humbling him? Seeing who may shout the loudest threats? Our young sons could do better! Let us go out to that mud-bank, Malcolm. Ourselves. Call on the Duke to do likewise. And speak. If you went, he would come, I think."

"To what purpose? When he has three times our numbers."

"He may not have three times our wits, husband."

The King shrugged. "Very well. Even if we gain nothing, it can do little harm." He signed for the horses of his immediate group. Margaret insisted on accompanying them.

As about a dozen of them rode forward into the water, the Earl of Surrey and his banner-bearer decided to rejoin his colleagues.

Out on the islet, unlovely stance as it was for so illustrious a company, Malcolm, still under his royal standard, raised his voice.

"Robert of Normandy — if you have anything to say to me more cogent than these idle threats and insolences, come and say it here. I do not conduct my affairs by unseemly shouting. You will be quite safe — you have my royal word."

There was a distinct interval on the other bank, with heads together. Then a party of approximately the same numbers as their own reined forward under the English standard.

As the newcomers splashed across, they became less splendid than it had seemed at longer range. Their faces looked tired, strained and grey, actually ingrained with soot — the more easily discerned in that they were all clean-shaven and short of hair. Their fine linen surcoats, too, over the rather rusty chain-mail, were streaked with black and the char-holes left by burning embers. That last fifty miles through Lothian had left its mark. When they clambered up on to the islet, however, they did have one advantage over the fresher Scots — they sat much higher on taller, finer horses than the sturdy but squat garrons.

The man in the white-painted mail, on a magnificent black charger, was slightly-built and in his early thirties, bullet-headed and round of features. There was a distinct likeness to his father, but the strength of character was not there, even though he was scowling fiercely. Clearly he was surprised, and a little put out, to find a woman present. He jerked a mere nod.

"Lady!" he said briefly, then turned. "*You* are Malcolm . . . ?"

"I am. In granting you this audience, Duke Robert, let it be understood that I make notable concession. For your royal father's sake — whom I hear is confined to his sick-bed by grievous wounds. I should not otherwise have granted audience to an armed invader of my realm, I promise you!"

"You, sir, are no longer in a position to grant or to withhold audience — since you no longer are King!" the other gave back. "Did you not hear? My royal father has deposed you."

"Then his wounds, sirrah, must have affected his wits! Where did you strike him? On the head?"

The Duke glared. "Mind how you speak, sir — for your words will fail to be paid for! And sweetly."

"On *my* soul, man, I speak as I will. If you have aught to say to me, other than vain incivilities, then say it — and begone."

"Very well. Hear this. You, Malcolm, swore an oath of allegiance to my father. Before due witnesses — some of whom are here present. You took him to be your Lord Paramount, your kingdom a fief of his. You swore that his enemies should be your enemies. And that you would no more invade his territories. You broke that solemn oath. You invaded Northumbria, with fire and slaughter. You aided my father's rebels there. None of which you can deny . . ."

"I do so deny — all of it. I swore fealty only for my own lands in England. As must any man. I did not invade Northumbria — I went there at the express invitation of the duly appointed and lawful lord and governor there the Bishop Walchere of Durham. As to fire and slaughter, I made only some due punishment for the grievous murder of the Bishop and governor, by his rebellious levies. Then returned home."

"You burned half the North, sir! Hexham town, and others. Due punishment, you name it . . . ?"

"I but made a gesture, as was proper. As your sire's friend. Did not your uncle, the Bishop Odo, come north thereafter and do the same? Only in more notable fashion!"

Robert coughed. He and his Uncle Odo did not agree. "It was invasion, however you name it. You came to pillage and steal. We know your intent — to try to take Northumbria for Scotland. An act of war, in clearest violation of your oath . . ."

"I have stated my intent. Do you, sir, know it better than I? I came to assist Walchere the governor, who had rebellion on his hands. And died of it."

"So you say now. But I am not come to trade tales with you, sir. I am here to convey to you, and to execute, my father's royal will and commands. To pronounce your deposition . . ."

"May I speak, my lords?" Margaret put in, clear-voiced. "Of your charity, hear me. Lest there is further misunderstanding. My father-in-God, the good Archbishop Lanfranc, spoke with you, my lord Duke, before you came north?"

Warily, at mention of Lanfranc's name, the Norman eyed her. "No, lady. I did not see him. I take my orders from the King, not the Archbishop of Canterbury."

"To be sure. But he is your father's good friend, as he is mine. He was of necessity concerned to deal with much, in England, whilst you and your royal sire were away on foreign wars. Much that you do not understand, it seems."

"I understand invasion and war, lady. And my father's commands."

"Archbishop Lanfranc is not concerned with invasion and wars, my lord. Nor am I. Nor, in this present instance, was my lord the King, here. It was Holy Church we sought to serve."

Robert frowned. "I cannot see how Holy Church is concerned."

"But it is, it is. In two respects." The Queen's glance flickered momentarily towards Maldred. "Bishop Walchere's plan was for the coming together of the Northumbrian and Scottish Churches. The other, is this of the Papacy."

"Papacy . . . ?" Bewildered, the other stared from her to Malcolm, and back.

"Do you not know, my lord? What is afoot? Worse, does your *father* not know? That his brother is secretly negotiating to become Pope?"

"God's Blood — Pope! Odo? No — I'll not believe it! He is . . . this is . . . what canard is this?"

"We have it on excellent authority. That Bishop Odo has been working to this end for long. Whilst he has been governing England in King William's absence. But — your royal father *must* know of this? For we have heard that he is much against the notion. Archbishop Lanfranc would surely have told him. The Archbishop has said that he would sooner die than see Bishop Odo as Pontiff."

"If my father knows, he has said naught of it to me," Robert declared. But he looked uneasy, uncertain. "It concerns my mission nothing."

"It may be that your father does not know *all*." That was Malcolm taking up the argument. "To be sure he has been out of England for years, and is not long back. And he came back sick, wounded. With much to see to, no doubt. He may well not know all. That Odo has been milking the Treasury and the taxation for long, in order to pay his supporters in Rome — the cardinals and bishops, for the

330

election. Has been using the fines he imposed as Chief Justice of England. Has been buying many lords and their men, for his cause, with the aid of his friend William fitz Osbern. And gaining his own creatures and chaplains bishoprics in England, helped by his other friend, Thomas, Archbishop of York. Forming a party . . ."

The stir amongst the group of nobles behind the Duke had become very noticeable, particularly at the mention of these names, as jealousies and rivalries amongst the Normans rose to the surface. These men were, in the main, those who had been away in France fighting William's battles for him, and were more than ready to believe that those who had stayed behind in England had been stealing a march on them, gaining whilst they were absent. That wily veteran, William fitz Osbern, was particularly unpopular — he was father of Ralph, the Earl of Hereford who had led the late rising and was now in a Normandy prison. And Archbishop Thomas was as suspect, always Odo's man and enemy of Lanfranc.

Robert turned to consult those closest at his back, in especial one grizzled warrior, only the cross and mitre described on his surcoat indicating that he was a prelate, Bishop Geoffrey de Coutances. That old comrade-in-arms of the Conqueror shrugged and shook his grey, cropped head, tonsure just visible, clearly unable to inform.

De Warrenne, Earl of Surrey, spoke — he was Robert's brother-in-law, being married to Gunhild, William's youngest daughter. "If this is so, it will demand betterment. We shall discover, and act. But — it does not concern our business here, my lord Duke."

"No. So say I . . ."

"Does it not?" Malcolm shrugged. "That is for your decision, to be sure. But — if you fight me here, there will be the fewer of you to fight Odo later! And I promise you, I will fight! I am strongly placed — and have other forces to throw in. And you have a long road to go home to Winchester! Is it no concern of yours, to play into Odo's hands, by throwing away much of King William's army?"

Although there were growls, that obviously made some impact.

"My lord Duke — why consider fighting and slaughter when reason and exchange and wise commerce are to the best advantage of all?" Margaret was concentrating on

Robert Courthose. "When you can gain your interest by negotiation, why shed blood? You, husband, also?"

"What do you mean?" the Duke demanded.

"What is your concern here? Your principal concern — why you have come all this long road. To fight? Or to restore your father's best relationship with Scotland? If this, then surely it can be done by using the wits God gave us rather than by taking lives He gave us? You know now that the Scots expedition to Northumbria was not invasion, as seen by us. But in answer to Bishop Walchere's invitation; who, with Lanfranc was no doubt concerned with Odo's growing ambitions and power, in your father's absence. King Malcolm has declared that he had no intention of invading England. That he went as King William's friend. That he has not broken his oath. No doubt, if you question that, he will swear it again — the oath which he kept well for seven years. All should be as it was. Is that not good sense? The best for all?"

There was silence there on the mud-bank, save for the champing of horses' bits, as men eyed each other. Even Malcolm looked at a loss, uncertain.

"You would swear it again? As before?" Margaret went on, urgently, turning to him. "Would you not, my lord King? Put all back as it was, at Abernethy. None so ill? It suited King William then — it should suit him now. And this great English host can then return to him — and be to his hand for dealing with Bishop Odo."

For long moments Malcolm did not answer her, his heavy features working. Then he nodded. "Yes," he said briefly. "The same. As Abernethy."

The Duke looked at them doubtfully, suspiciously. Then, chewing his lip, he turned in his saddle to mutter to his advisers. He turned back.

"We shall consider this," he said. "We shall inform you. Presently."

"Do that," the King jerked. "Although — we would do better to fight it out here and now, I think!" And he reined round his garron and plunged back through the press of his supporters without another word to any, and into the river. In some confusion, some waiting for the Queen, the Scots followed.

Back on the north bank, Malcolm rode directly on to the monastery. Margaret lingered however, looking back.

"How think you, Maldred?" she asked. "Will they do it?

I did what I could. I . . . I did not lie. You heard — I said no lie?"

He nodded. "You did well, very well. Whether they will heed, who can tell? You have sown doubts in their minds. But Malcolm — would he take the oath again?"

"What has he to lose? He would make it with the same reservations as before . . ."

The situation across the river caught their attention. The great mass of the enemy force was now coming up, spreading widely across the levels, a daunting prospect. Duke Robert and his group were over on the south side again — but it was not at their great oncoming host that they were looking, but to the south-west, where, at a tangent, two horsemen were making for them at a gallop, lashing their mounts. Even at a distance their urgency was very evident.

"News," Maldred said. "I wonder . . . ?"

The Norman leaders waited for the two riders. After they came up there was much gesticulation, looking and pointing south-westwards.

"They are disturbed," the Queen said.

"It could be Madach, from that airt. Come from Caer-luel. Even it might be Cospatrick himself, and a Cumbrian host. If so, he has moved fast . . ."

"I shall go tell Malcolm. And try keep him to taking the oath again."

Presently the Earl of Surrey came splashing out to the islet again. "The Duke Robert of Normandy has considered your plea," he shouted. "Tell your prince that he will accept his renewed oath of allegiance. With solemn vow of friendship and support hereafter. In King William's name."

They went and told Malcolm in the monastery.

The King revealed no elation, nor even relief — although the Queen did. No haste, either, to proceed.

"If it is indeed a Cumbrian host coming up on their flank," he said, "let them sweat. It will make them the more eager, now that they have decided not to fight, to be done with it, and gone."

They waited, Margaret agitated. Then a small group of riders arrived at the monastery from westwards, and their leader was ushered into the King's presence. It was none other than the fifteen-year-old Dolfin, Earl of Cumbria, to announce breathlessly that the Lord Madach had sent him.

He had reached Camelon, about two miles off, with two thousand men, and now awaited the King's instructions.

"Only two thousand! Madach, is it? And what of your father, boy? What of Cospatrick?"

"He raises more men in Cumbria, Highness. He will bring them on."

"So — he is still in Cumbria. And but two thousand with Madach. Then go back to him, boy, and tell him to bide where he is, meantime. But to send many riders back and forth, to and fro, and to me here. That the Normans may believe his to be a much larger host, thinking to attack them. Off with you . . ."

Angus was sent back to the islet, to announce that King Malcolm was coming and that Duke Robert should join him there. Their business should not take very long. The Earl came back to say that the Duke objected to a mud-bank as being a suitable place for such an important proceeding, and desired the King to come across to the south side of the river. He was sent back again to declare that the mud island would do very well, for it was more unsuitable that either of the principals should have to put himself into the power of the other, on the far side of the river from his own host. It was the islet or nothing.

So presently both leadership groups rode out to the lowly mud-flat once more. It was no place for any ceremony — and it is safe to say that none there now desired anything of the sort. There were no gospel scrolls or similar holy objects for Malcolm to place his hand upon; also none of the Duke's people had any fluency or experience in wording royal oaths of allegiance. So, after a little awkward discussion, with everyone distinctly embarrassed and desiring all to be done with as quickly as possible, it was agreed that Malcolm should merely raise his hand, while still sitting his horse, and repeat, before all, roughly the same words as he had spoken at Abernethy — which suited the King very well.

Accordingly, with a notably disdainful expression, much less sign of deference than previously, Malcolm mac Duncan jerked off a very abbreviated version of the former affirmation, to the effect that he, High King of Scots, took William, King of England, styled Lord Paramount, to be lord of life and limb for lands held; and to uphold and support the said William, and to adjudge all his enemies as his own — so help him God.

This over — although at first the Normans seemed to expect something more — there followed sighs of relief all round. Nobody knew quite what to do next. Malcolm was most clearly of the opinion that there was no need for any further association between the two sides, even though the invaders muttered amongst themselves anent inadequacy. The King terminated these few moments of indecision by nodding curtly to Duke Robert, glowering heavily at the other Normans, and then turning his garron's head towards the northern bank.

"Sir! My lord Malcolm!" the unhappy Robert called, when he realised that this appeared to be the parting of the ways, the end of the proceedings. "What now? How shall we do? We require much. Food. Fodder . . ."

Blankly the monarch turned to look back at him. "So? Do you not provide your array with a commissariat, my lord?"

"We do, yes. But it has been a long march."

"No doubt. Too long. You could have saved yourself the pains of it! I have insufficient here to feed my own hosts. And the thousands of Cumbria yonder, also come to join me. More still to come. They will be as hungry as you, my lord Duke, I swear!"

Robert had to muster his pride. "Very well, sir. I think this goes but ill with your oath of fealty and support!"

"That was for my lands in England, man. And you are far from England here, are you not? I advise that you go there, at the soonest! Your bishop here will pray to God to provide, no doubt? I bid you God-speed, my lord."

He spurred his mount on, into the water.

When Margaret could catch up with her husband, she reproached him. "That was unkindly done, Malcolm."

"Did *they* come in kindness? You may feed your enemies, lass — I do not!"

"They have all burned Lothian to cross before they can reach land that can feed them."

"Then let them eat some of their fine horses! They should make fair enough meat, I swear!"

Back at the monastery, Malcolm relented, but only to the extent of sending over a couple of barrels of the Abbot's ale and a side of beef — more of an insult than a kindness.

As they sat down to their own repast in the eating-hall, word was brought to the King that the English army had commenced its retiral already.

"As well they might," Malcolm commented. He raised his beaker. "Drink up, my friends. It seems that the day is ours."

"Thanks to the Queen's Highness," Maldred put in tersely.

His cousin looked over at him levelly. "That, yes. And to eighteen thousand empty bellies. And six thousand full ones manning this muddy ditch!"

"Thanks, rather, to Almighty God who has this day spared the lives of many men," Margaret amended. She touched her husband's arm. "In token of our gratitude for which, my lord, I humbly suggest that we, here at Ecclesbreac, erect a new stone church to His glory, and in remembrance of our delivery, this day."

The monarch gave something between a snort and a laugh. "There is ever a price to pay, by God!" he exclaimed. "But — so be it."

Maldred rubbed his chin, as ruefully as his liege-lord. Margaret always seemed to win. A new church — a new *Romish* church. So that was to be the seal set on all his efforts and all Lothian's agony.

Kindly, warmly, the Queen smiled on him.

*　　*　　*

It was some months before accounts began to percolate through to Scotland as to the consequences of Duke Robert's abortive expedition. The principal result, it transpired, was anger, wrath, fury — on William's part. At all concerned, but chiefly at his son. Indeed, so hot was the Conqueror's choler that the pleasing reconciliation between father and son was quite shattered; and Robert departed again forthwith for Normandy, in high dudgeon. Bishop Geoffrey de Coutances, who it seemed had been sent north as adviser to the Duke, was also in disgrace, old comrade-in-arms of William's as he was. No doubt Malcolm mac Duncan himself came in for a large share of the wrath — but he was beyond its practical effects, meantime at least. However, a fourth party did feel the weight of it, in no uncertain fashion. The Bishop Odo of Bayeux was arrested, clapped in prison, his earldom of Essex forfeited, like his chief-justiceship, and even execution talked of. So much for pretensions to the Papacy and dis-appropriation of Treasury funds.

Even Cospatrick considered that the burning of his Lothian had been well worth while, whatever Maldred said.

Part Three

22

TWO SUMMONSES REACHED Dunbar Castle on the same day of June, 1085, for Maldred mac Melmore. One from the King, requiring his presence at Dunfermline, to take part in some sort of royal progress through the realm, or at least the central parts of it, to celebrate apparently fifteen years of wedded felicity; and also the completion of the main part of the great new church of the Holy Trinity at Dunfermline. Clearly, although the summons might be from Malcolm, the moving spirit behind all was Margaret, since her husband was not the man to think of celebrating either event, and certainly not by perambulating his kingdom for common folk to stare at. The second messenger arrived only an hour or two later, from Maldred's mother, the Countess of Atholl. The Earl was grievously ill, probably dying. Maldred should come at once.

He had never been really close to his father, who had always been a reserved man, detached, not good at showing affection. But he had loved him, after a fashion, and admired his quiet integrity and his scholarship. Saddened, he made hurried arrangements to leave almost immediately. Fortunately no serious problems loomed meantime, in the two Border earldoms, to complicate his speedy departure. The last four years had been comparatively uneventful ones, both on the national and the local levels, with King William never fully recovered from his wound and not the man he had been — although his rages were reported to be more terrible than ever. Only one warlike campaign he had initiated in the interim, against the unfortunate Welsh, when, despite the fact that he had been borne in a horse-litter most of the time, he had supervised retribution of an unparalleled ferocity. But he had not ventured north of Wessex, and the Scots had been left to their own devices — these by no means always peaceable admittedly; but Maldred had been well able to cope with his share of the burden of rule, mainly in keeping within bounds the normal Border raiding, reiving and feuding, and dealing out the punishment thereof. He now had a new title, of English style, bestowed on him by Cospatrick, that of Sheriff of the Merse, Tweeddale and Teviotdale — although he preferred to use the old Celtic term of Judex. Cospatrick himself spent most of the time when he was not restlessly ranging the land, at Caer-luel, nowadays, with his eldest son Dolfin, Earl of Cumbria who, at eighteen, had taken over from Madach there.

So, leaving Magda to make a less hurried departure, who was also called, as extra lady-in-waiting to the Queen, Maldred bade fond farewell to the children — they now had a third child, a son named Crinan — and set off on the long road to Atholl at maximum speed.

Even so, when he arrived at Dunkeld two days later, it was too late. His father had died the day before. His mother was prostrate, a woman who had lived almost wholly for her husband and was now all but lost. Fortunately Madach was at home and had all in hand, a practical if limited man. He was now Earl or Mormaor of Atholl, subject to the King's approval and confirmation, one of the *righ* or lesser kings of Scotland; almost certainly he would make a better one than had his unworldly sire.

They buried Melmore mac Crinan quietly next day in the graveyard of the Abbey under the soaring fort-crowned crag, beside two of his favourite hounds — for the Celtic Church allowed Christian burial for animals that had been the especial friends of men. Maldred waited on one more day, to take part, the leading part, in the ceremony in which all the thanes and chieftains of Atholl came to accept and pay allegiance to their new mormaor, if so they elected. In this case there was no dispute, and it only remained for Malcolm to add his royal agreement.

Thereafter Maldred rode south again, feeling that another chapter in his life was ended.

Again he came late, at least for the celebrations in the large cathedral-like church. These had taken place the day previously. Magda was able to give him a glowing account. He was interested to hear that the monk Turgot had been brought up from Wearmouth to conduct the service — since it had to be in the Romish rite, of course, although Bishop Fothad and some of the abbots and other Keledei had attended and even taken minor part. Malcolm had presumably swallowed his dislike of the Englishman. Incorporated in the seemingly splendid proceedings in the church had been the dedication of a vast treasure in gold and silver vessels, chalices, pattens and crucifixes, holy books and missals lovingly encased in jewelled boards, and a large number of the most gorgeous vestments, chasubles, copes, stoles and the like — all of the Queen's giving, allegedly out of the profits of her many trading ventures to foreign parts. Turgot himself was still collecting such costly things for her, as opportunity offered. According to him, via Magda, there was not a church or minster north of York itself so richly endowed as was now this Holy Trinity.

When Maldred presented himself before the royal couple that night, at the feasting in the crowded hall of the palace, it was to a more gracious reception than sometimes, evidently on account of his father's death, Malcolm actually pushing aside his old crony Angus on the royal bench to make room for Maldred at his left side, Margaret on the right giving him her hand to kiss and then holding his own tightly for a moment. Magda went to sit beyond the Queen. Even so the monarch's greetings and condolences were less than effusive.

"So you have it by with, cousin," he said. "The old man buried? He went quickly at the end, I heard."

"Yes. I did not see him alive."

"I am sorry, Maldred — sorry," Margaret said. "You will be sore-hearted."

"I doubt it!" Malcolm jerked. "Why should he be? My uncle was an old done man, who had made little of his life these many years — if ever he did! Maldred saw but little of him, mind."

"He was his father, Malcolm. One day our sons will mourn *you*. And me. Pray God, kindly!"

The King grunted, and turned back to Maldred. "You were in time for the burial? Yesterday?"

"The day before."

"Then you took your time in coming on here, man?"

"There was more to do at Dunkeld, Highness."

"I think that he delayed so as not to have to attend at our thanksgiving in Holy Trinity!" the Queen said, half-playfully. "Maldred does not altogether approve of our efforts at fuller worship."

"M'mm." Malcolm looked a little doubtful at that. "All men are not churchmen, lass. Even Primates' sons. Like Madach, his brother, to be sure."

Wondering what that might mean, Maldred shook his

head. "I had to stay another day. All the chiefs came to accept Madach as mormaor. I had to be there. He now seeks your royal confirmation, as earl."

"Aye. No doubt. That, the accepting as mormaor — that was all?"

"All? It was sufficiently important, was it not?"

"Yes, yes. I meant that there was no other talk of appointing? In your father's room. The churchmen . . . ?"

"You mean the primacy? No. That is no concern of the thanes and chiefs. It is for the abbots and the Keledei to confirm."

Malcolm cleared his throat. "Confirm, perhaps. But not appoint." He paused. "I have decided to appoint my son Ethelred, Primate in your father's room."

Maldred all but choked on his rib of venison. "You . . . ? Ethelred? The child? Primate of the Church!"

"Ethelred, yes. He is now eleven years. A lad of bookish ways. He will grow into it very well."

"But . . . but . . . ? What of Madach? The primacy is hereditary in the house of Atholl . . ."

"Am *I* not of the house of Atholl, man? Son of Duncan, Crinan's eldest son. Forby, Madach has nothing of the priest in him, a soldier not an abbot. With young Kerald it might have been different."

"But it is his *right*. At least to make the choice . . ."

"The choice is mine, as head of the house, as well as of the kingdom. Just as it is mine to decide whether Madach shall be Earl of Atholl, or no!"

Into the pause which followed that evident threat, Margaret spoke. "We should seek Madach's agreement, to be sure, Maldred. He would not wish to withhold it, I think. He shows no interest in Church matters. So long as it remains . . . in the family."

"But — a child! Eleven years. Primate of the Columban Church! You, *you* of all people, support this?"

For once Margaret Atheling, on a matter of religion, looked less than sure of herself. "He is a godly child — much more so than any of his brothers. Old for his years. Born to serve God, we do believe. In only a few years he will be a man — a fine and upright, godly Primate. Much better, more suitable, surely, than a man like Madach, with no concern for matters of religion? The Primate is appointed for life. So it could be many, many years before there is another. Important years . . ."

"Important, yes — for your efforts to turn Scotland to Rome! With the Primate in the palm of your hand!"

Margaret bit her lip.

"Watch your tongue!" Malcolm growled. "Ethelred will do very well. Some suitable appointment is necessary for him, our third son. It will enhance the primacy. And Madach will see very well what is advisable and where his best interest lies — even if you do not!"

"You will not confirm his earldom if he does not agree?"

"Have I said that, cousin? It will have to be considered — like all earldoms."

"And . . . if Madach agrees? What of the Church? Will the churchmen agree? The abbots and bishops and Keledei? To have an eleven-year-old boy thrust upon them as Primate?"

"Leave the churchmen to me. The primacy revenues are quite large. Until Ethelred comes of full age, the distribution of them will be in *my* hands. Leave the abbots and bishops to me, I say!"

"It is for the best, Maldred," the Queen said.

He did not answer further, and at the royal bench at least the meal went on in silence. Presently Margaret rose, to proceed out to the courtyard where the usual hundreds of the poor were being catered for and entertained. Malcolm, this time, elected to go with her, adopting his long-suffering expression. Maldred did not, even though Magda urged him to, as she hurried after the Queen.

The next day, St. Columba's Eve, the royal progress commenced, with the King and Queen leading a great cavalcade of nobles and chiefs and officers of state, with their ladies. The idea, Margaret's idea, was to visit as many towns, villages and communities as possible, to demonstrate the Crown's abiding interest in the people, to attract the affection and support of the masses, to show the royal children to the folk, to inspect the state of the realm and to bestow largesse. Maldred suspected also that another objective was to survey where the Roman Church influence might be established further. And Magda, privily, informed that the Queen was concerned to improve the King's reputation as father. Donald Beg, his second son by Ingebiorg, had recently been done to death in an unsavoury affair in the remote Highlands, where he had been running wild, aged twenty-two but leaving sundry bastards. And, of course, Duncan, the eldest son, was still an unredeemed hostage in England. The people, and many of their betters, were unhappy about the way these princes had been treated. Hence the taking along of all the royal children on this progress, even the latest addition, the year-old Mary. Margaret had had one more son, David, making six in all, and another daughter, Matilda. She was now in her fortieth year and presumably her child-bearing was nearly over; but she had kept her figure and remained a remarkably attractive woman. Clearly her demanding husband still found her so.

The procession, all mounted, with colourful trappings and banners, clad in the most splendid of clothing and preceded by musicians and choirs of singers, first headed eastwards through Fothrif into Fife. Margaret was particularly anxious to visit the new merchanting ports, formerly mere fishing-havens, which were developing along the north shore of the Scottish Sea as a result of her constant efforts to promote trade, crafts, manufactures and the like, source of so much new wealth to the land — and to the Crown — places such as Pettycur, Kingoren, Kirkaladin, Dysart, Wemyss and Leven. Messengers had been sent round to inform the people of the royal intention, so that there should be no lack of due attention in each place.

At first, the tour looked like being a success, the weather kind, welcoming crowds everywhere. Garrons laden with sacks of coin and grain and meats for distribution helped to ensure a suitable reception; but there was no doubt as to the Queen's popularity, at least. Throughout, she was greeted with warmth, affection, almost love, her husband neither seeking nor receiving such reaction. The children proved a major attraction, and behaved well, at least most of the time — and were left in no doubt of maternal disapproval when they did not.

It was Malcolm who grew tired of it all first, needless to say. He showed some interest in the ship and boat-building yards which were springing up along the Fife coastline, to cater for the much increased foreign trade and the fisheries for the new overseas markets — salted herring in especial. He shrewdly assessed townships and thanedoms, for the numbers of men they might produce in arms, for any emergency. He was quick to point out bad husbandry and neglected properties. But being pleasant to his subjects, concerning himself with their troubles and complaints, was not for him. Before that first day was out, he was riding ahead with some of his lords, making for MacDuff's rath at Kennoway where they were to pass the night. Maldred remained behind with the Queen's company, which scamped nothing.

Maldred had not been at Kennoway for years, making a point of avoiding Dufagan MacDuff's company. But now Dufagan was dead, killed in a drunken brawl, leaving a child Constantine as heir to the old Earl, now mountainously gross and all but senile. The daughters of the house remained unwed and soured. The boy Constantine seemed bright enough, but it was scarcely a happy household. The royal party made its own cheer, however, and there was no lack of provender. Malcolm got drunk, as compensation for a long and boring day.

The feasting finished, and the King sprawled forward over the table asleep, with Margaret and her ladies retired to a lesser chamber, the MacDuff steward came hurrying into the main hall, now in something of a riot, drink-taken young lords in noisy horseplay with the serving-wenches whilst their elders snored and musicians, not very enthusiastically, sought to provide background entertainment. Eyeing this scene assessingly, the steward seemed to decide that Maldred of Atholl looked the least inebriated of those near to the monarch, and hesitating to disturb the slumbering King, came to him.

"My lord," he said. "There is a man outby, seeking the King's Highness. A priest, a wandering friar — but with a haughty mien. He says that it is important."

"And does this friar have a twist to one shoulder, lean to one side?"

"You know him, then . . . ?"

Maldred found Cospatrick eating cheerfully enough in the kitchen premises amongst the servants, and received a sketchy benediction along with a warning glance. He was duly careful.

"You wish to speak with the King's Highness, Sir Friar?" he greeted, almost sternly. "Then, come."

When they were alone, out in the courtyard, the Earl clapped his shoulder. "God be praised *you* are here, at least, Maldred!" he exclaimed. "They say that all are drunk in the hall. And the noise is like the courts of hell, to be sure! I despaired of getting near Malcolm."

"Malcolm is scarcely sober either. But — what do you

here, in Fife? I have not known you to venture north of Lothian these many years."

"I came because it was important. And you were not at Dunbar. I am sorry about your father, lad. There was none I could send here, who could be sure of reaching the King's ear. But, sakes — I never thought that I would enter this house of MacDuff's! Whom I love as well as any viper! It must not be known who I am, Maldred."

"Is that still so important? After these years?"

"While William lives, it is."

"William is a sick man. He does not march at the head of armies, any more."

"Do not be too sure. And have you not heard how he deals with those whom he does not love, or fears? Still? He sends out assassins, secretly. Usually as *I* am, in guise of monks. To quietly poison or stab or strangle. The Conqueror is no more gentle than ever he was. If he learned that I am still alive, had duped him these years, he would have his minions after me, nothing more sure. So I wait — and live!"

"And the news that brought you here?"

"War, man — war. Fetch Malcolm, and you will hear it. But only Malcolm, mind you."

"I tell you, he is in a drunken sleep. At table . . ."

"Then wake him. I have not followed him half across Scotland to wait while he snores! And he is never witless with drink — you know that. Fetch him, cousin."

So Maldred went back to the hall. In fact, the King was not difficult to rouse, only vicious towards the rouser. He snarled his resentment.

"It is Cospatrick, Highness," Maldred whispered. "With news. Most secret."

"Eh? Cospatrick? That snake! Here? What does he want? Never trust that man." Thickly he spoke, glaring.

"News, sir. Of war, he said. He has risked much, to come thus far. To tell you."

"Not for love of me — damn him! Bring him, then." The monarch stared heavily round at the hall's noisy confusion.

"He says no, sir. He would be seen and known. He must remain secret. He asks that you come."

Grumbling, Malcolm rose unsteadily and lurched after Maldred. Few there were in a state to notice his departure.

In the yard outside the three cousins eyed each other in

the warm evening light of June. Malcolm and Cospatrick had not set eyes on each other for years.

"Save us — is this how you look, these days!" the King greeted, his speech a little slurred but his glance keen enough. "An old man, getting!"

"I could say the same, Malcolm! Since I am the younger by eighteen years, am I not? I make you sixty-four."

"Well, man — well? You have not come here to tell me my age?"

"Nor, it seems, to receive warm greeting! After all these years."

"Why should you expect that? You were never my friend, only my uncle's son."

"Yet I have served you well, Malcolm. Better than many close to you."

"For your own purposes. As no doubt tonight. What is it? What is your news this time?"

"Sufficient. The days of peace are over — such as they have been. England prepares for war, major war. This may be our opportunity."

"*Our* opportunity? Whose? Mine — or yours?"

"Both, I hope. I still seek to win back Northumbria. And you, to put Scotland's border at the Tees, do you not?"

"That tale again! A dream, man. I would have thought that *you* would have wits enough to perceive it, by now. I do not trust you, Cospatrick — but I have never doubted your wits!"

"I am overwhelmed, sir! As to dreaming, hear this. William is preparing for the greatest threat to his England since he conquered it nineteen years ago. King Knud Svenson of Denmark is claiming the English throne, as great-nephew of Canute. He has assembled a great fleet. Olaf the Farmer of Norway is to join him. Count Robert of Flanders also, whose sister is Knud's queen. And with him Duke Robert of Normandy, still smarting from his father's ire. And, to be sure, Philip of France who is always at war with William. Others, it may be — but these I name are sure. A great assault, on four fronts at least."

Even Malcolm was impressed. He tugged at his forked beard. "When?"

"This summer."

"By the Fiend — why have I not heard of this? Before now? Why have these others not approached *me*? To join in . . ."

"Perhaps because they esteem your oath of allegiance to William more highly than you do! His enemies being your enemies?" Cospatrick held up his hand as the King's features contorted with quick rage. "No, no — I but jest, cousin. I have heard that the true reason is otherwise. That Olaf of Norway's terms for joining Knud are that afterwards he has a free hand to move his army and ships against your Hebrides. He wants them as part of his realm. The Orcades also. He esteems the Orkney earls as weak — as they are — and covets their territories, with their Norse folk. So *you* are not to be approached."

"How a God's Name did you learn this, man? If it is truth."

"I have my sources, cousin — as you should know. But mainly I have friends in the earldom of Northumbria still. And in the bishopric of Durham. You know that there is another new earl? De Coucy lost William's confidence after the Walchere business, and resigned. Robert de Moubray, the new man, is bold enough, but indiscreet in his cups. He talks much. I have friends in his household. Likewise the new bishop, William de St. Calais, more soldier than priest, talks likewise. They are cronies, these two. Our friend Aldwin is now Prior of Durham — and loves the Normans no more than he did."

"You accept all this talk as truth?"

"I do. It is confirmed from other sources. Moreover, William's own actions sufficiently support it all. For England is thrown into turmoil. It is scarcely believable. William has ordered the complete emptying of the coast lands of England facing Denmark and Norway, for twenty miles inland. All to be laid waste, towns and villages and farmsteads flattened, to give no sustenance to invaders, hundreds of miles of ruin — worse, far worse, than anything he has ordained before. Most of the remaining Saxon lords are imprisoned. And he is bringing great armies of mercenaries over from Brittany and Poitou, fetching back hosts from Ireland . . ."

"Curse him — he does not sound like a man on his sick-bed!"

"Not he. Have you not heard? Before all this of invasion, he was laying waste and emptying a hundred square miles of Hampshire, on his own doorstep at Winchester, to make a new hunting forest! Every house levelled, every man, woman and child driven out — even the monasteries. Does that sound like a bed-ridden cripple?"

"It sounds like the Devil Incarnate!" Maldred said.

"It sounds like William the Bastard!" Malcolm amended grimly. "So — what now? If William makes his preparations, so must I."

"I believed that you would so wish, cousin — and so came. Time may be short."

"If I muster my armies. Ready to march south across Tweed, for Tyne and Tees. Whenever we hear word of the Danes and Norsemen landing — what of this Moubray?"

"Moubray will be mustered and waiting, undoubtedly. But waiting for the Norsemen, not for you! Facing the sea, not looking behind him. If you marched inland, down Rede and Wansbeck and Coquet, you would take him in the rear. And I, and Dolfin, would bring our Cumbrians. Once at the Tees, I say, whoever was winning, Knud or William, would be glad to treat with us, to have us on *their* side. Or not against them. We could demand our own terms."

"Aye. It could be, it could be so. How say you, Maldred?"

The younger man pursed his lips. "It smacks of a jackal's game. But . . . dealing with the Norman wolves, even jackals may justify themselves!"

"That is as high praise as we will gain from Maldred mac Melmore!" Cospatrick said. "My price is Northumbria and Cumbria both, my lord King!"

Malcolm eyed them both consideringly. "I am blessed with kindly kin!" he observed bleakly.

"You could have worse, cousin. You will muster, then?"

"Aye. Tomorrow I shall begin. Turn back from this folly. It will be better work than this of Margaret's, all but kissing the arses of my subjects! And you, man — what of you?"

"I shall be on my humble way by sun-up. I think that you, Maldred, should return to Dunbar tomorrow, likewise. To make plans, with me, for raising Lothian and the Borderland. But only plans meantime — only a few to know. Or the word of it will get cross to Northumbria, and Moubray may be warned."

In the morning, when the King and most of his nobles turned back for Dunfermline, there was no sign of the wandering friar. Margaret elected to carry on with part at least of her progress, possibly even slightly relieved at her husband's absence, intent especially on visiting St. Andrews and forwarding her missionary efforts there. Magda remained with her, Maldred accompanying them as far as the East Neuk of Fife, where, under Kincraig Point, was the little port which was the base of the Earl of Fife's ferry across the Scots Sea to his lands in Lothian. With the King's authority, Maldred got the skipper to make a special journey, and so saved most of three days' riding.

23

THE SUMMER PASSED in a strange admixture of impatience and thankfulness, for most people in Scotland at least — impatience at nothing happening when all was prepared for momentous doings; and thankfulness that the hay harvest was in, then the oats harvest, then that the reeds could be cut for thatching and the peats dug for drying for winter's fires. The mustered armies kept releasing men to go home for short periods for these activities, but to be ready for instant recall. But those who remained assembled grew bored and out-of-hand, their leaders resentful. By late August morale was at a low ebb everywhere — and nowhere more so than in the Borderland, where armed raiding was endemic, all were geared for it, and yet these months it was strictly prohibited. Maldred was hard put to it to maintain the Dunbar and March force in any sort of fighting trim.

Cospatrick had an army of Cumbrians waiting at Caer-luel, under his son Dolfin, presumably equally unruly. This was facing *northwards*, towards Galloway, so that news of it should not alarm the present Earl of Northumbria, himself mustered at points in a very long line between Tees and Aln, facing the Norse Sea.

Decision, when it did come, was totally unexpected. It was that William the Norman's luck held. Knud of

Denmark, prime instigator of the entire campaign, with his claim to be Canute's lawful successor on the English throne, was dead, murdered by his own people. Unseasonable storms had delayed him, week after week. Then there had been mutinies amongst his assembled armies and fleets. These he had put down savagely, whereupon revolt erupted amongst the Danish population, hitherto unheard-of. Knud had been overwhelmed and slain. The whole invasion project collapsed, lacking his drive, and with Olaf of Norway's interest really confined to the Hebrides and Orkney. So England remained unassailed — save by William's own terrible defensive measures.

Malcolm's disgust had to be seen to be believed. But his wife at least was thankful and joyful.

But the Queen's gratitude at the unexpected ebbing of the tide of war was all too soon replaced by general apprehension, in Scotland, as to what William would do now. He had a huge army gathered and waiting, and no invasion to face. He was not the man to overlook what had been threatened, to sit back grateful that nothing had come of it. His health was reported to be improved — although he was said to have grown very fat with the prolonged physical inactivity. He was unlikely to seek to punish the Danes and Norwegians by counter-invasion — he had not the sea-going fleets necessary. Which left the Low Countries, France and Scotland as targets for his ire and vengeance. He would know perfectly well that Malcolm had been waiting, mustered, for months, for the invasion to start; and though there was no proof that the Scots had intended to stab at him in his extremity — it might have been conceivable that Malcolm was ready rather to come to the Norman's aid, under the terms of his allegiance — William was scarcely so foolish as to believe that.

A punitive expedition, therefore, might well appeal to William at this juncture. So the Scots experienced another spell of waiting, anxiously.

The fact that the winter of 1085-86 passed without hostilities did not disperse the apprehensions of the fearful, for William might be awaiting the spring campaigning season and better conditions. Malcolm had all his earls and thanes readied once again for swift muster.

And then, at last, there was hard news. As usual, it was Cospatrick who was first with the information, received through his listening-post at Durham. William had reverted to his oldest and most deep enmity, his life-long quarrel with Philip of France, and had in fact sailed with his armies for Normandy. Before departing he had set his house in order, appointing strong men in all key positions, indeed deposing the Bishops of London, Norfolk and Chester and replacing them by three of his own warlike personal chaplains — and taking Odo and William Rufus with him across the Channel, his brother for transfer to a Normandy prison, his second son because he preferred to keep him under his own eye. Presumably he trusted his youngest son, Henry Beauclerc, for he left him in nominal charge in England.

So the Scots could breathe freely again. As well as this welcome news for the King, Maldred had tidings for the Queen also. The Prior Aldwin had died and her friend Turgot was now promoted Prior of Durham in his place.

At Dunfermline Maldred was surprised to find young Prince Edmund, the second son, mastering the palace. It seemed that the King was at Dunsinane — which was still the military centre of the kingdom — on some matter connected with his armed forces, which remained his prime interest in life; and his favourite son Edward was with him. Margaret was at the Ward of the Stormounth, comparatively nearby, with her younger children. Maldred was still more surprised at the scene he was ushered into, on arrival, by the palace chamberlain, that May evening. Edmund, now aged fourteen, was seated, or sprawled, in the King's chair at the high table in the great hall, drunk most evidently, with two serving wenches actually sitting on either side of him, both half-undressed, one indeed naked to the waist, giggling and skirling, whilst the prince fondled her prominent breasts. Such few young courtiers as were present were either asleep or similarly employed. Maldred retired, without announcing himself, to eat in the kitchen. What Margaret would have thought of this, if she had known, could be left to the imagination.

There was no sign of the prince when Maldred left in the morning for Dunsinane.

Malcolm, practising cavalry tactics in the Norman style with some of his commanders on the grassy plateau of St. Martins, was well pleased with Maldred's news, needless to say. But he was not the man to display any relief. His reaction was not that peace might now be expected to subsist for some time but rather that he was free to indulge in other warfare of his own choosing.

Maldred forbore to mention young Edmund's behaviour at Dunfermline.

It was only about ten miles to the Ward from Dunsinane, northwards, and Maldred rode on thither after only a brief halt, finding nothing urgently to detain him, certainly no pressing suggestion from his royal cousin that he should stay. Prince Edward, however, with whom a quiet but genuine mutual appreciation and friendliness had grown up, chose to accompany him.

They reached the Ward in the evening, only to find the Queen absent, and the five youngest children, the girls Matilda and Mary and the boys Edgar, Alexander and David, left in the care of the chamberlain and ladies. It seemed that, with Ethelred — whom she had collected from his favourite haunt on the monastic island of Loch Leven — Margaret had gone on some sort of jaunt round the refuges and retreats of sundry anchorites and religious hermits. Just why was not clear, but Edward declared that it sounded like Ethelred's instigation, for he seemed to think highly of such odd folk — in fact had been heard to announce that he would have liked to be one such himself. The hoots of laughter from his young brothers at this assertion made it evident that the family, at this stage, thought Ethelred very much of a curiosity.

Maldred, with memories of the hermit Keledei of St. Ethernan's Well in the Braes of Lornty, not far away, wondered at it all, but agreed that they should go to try to find the Queen, in the morning.

It was not difficult to trace Margaret's progress. She had headed eastwards, for Blair-in-Gowrie and thence down into central Strathmore, to make her first call at the cell of an anchorite who kept St. Cumin's Well deep in a woodland glade in the Bendochy area where the Rivers Isla and Ericht joined. Most of these solitaries established themselves as the custodians of springs and wells, usually linked with the name of some early saint or missionary, the alleged healing qualities of which brought sufferers and pilgrims, whose votive offerings supported the simple needs of the hermit. The fact that these were almost always sited in remote and awkward places ensured that the keeper's solitude was not inundated with floods of visitors and his chosen ascetic living-style nullified by overmuch in the way of contributions. The individual at Bendochy, extraordinarily young-looking for such a vocation and more cheerful than might have been expected, told them that the Queen had indeed been there, bless her, the previous day, with the young Primate, and had been going on, he understood, to visit Abbot Colban who occupied an islet in Forfar Loch.

So they proceeded down Strathmore a further ten or so miles, to that quite large sheet of water, not far from one of Malcolm's castles and the township which clustered round it. But if this anchorite had chosen a fairly populous area for his retreat, he made up for it by electing to occupy a tiny crannog, or artificial islet, at the west end of the loch, constructed of stones, timber and sods, with a turf hut to shelter both himself and his goat, for milk, his only companion. A bronze bell hanging on a tripod at the loch-shore was the means by which he could be summoned — and summoned he had to be, since he could be reached only by the coracle which he kept out at his raft-like island. He was noted for as often as not refusing to come for visitors. Needless to say there was no well at this artificial structure, and such suppliants as sought to approach him did so only for his blessing — which, however, was considered to be particularly efficacious, for Colban was an exceedingly holy veteran, having previously been Abbot of the important Abbey of St. Peter at Restenneth, on the other side of Forfar, and had retired here to end his days thus. How he lived on this raft, surviving on goat's milk and the large pike for which the loch was famed and which were alleged to jump out of the water for his sustenance — only faith could tell.

On this occasion the callers had to ring the bell several times before there was any reaction; and they would not have troubled to wait — for most obviously the Queen was not here — had it not been that Colban might be able to tell them where she had intended to head next. Eventually the old man emerged from his rickety hovel, bent and tottering, all straggling white hair and beard, to paddle his frail craft across to them in zigzag, splashy style. In no welcoming mood he told them to be about their business, as he did not feel like interceding for anyone that day. But he was brought to admit that the Englishwoman had been out there to see him the previous afternoon, and indeed stayed some time with him in dis-

cussion, which although perhaps verging on the imperti-
nent was also remarkable in a woman — although full of
heretical notions, to be sure, presumably Romish. To continue her education he had directed her onwards to a
fellow loch-dweller, also from Restenneth, one Gillemor,
an expert on the doctrine of the Holy Trinity, who dwelt on
a sedge-island in Rescobie Loch, a mile or two beyond the
Abbey of Restenneth, further east. The holy man, having
thus delivered himself, glared round them, flicked a finger
at them — clearly not a benediction but a command to be
off — and staggered back to his coracle, to push off, his
stick-like arms seeming incapable of propelling even such
a cockle-shell. That the Queen had apparently trusted herself to his doubtful navigation and been transported out to
the crannog and goat in his floating basket, spoke worlds
for her courage and determination.

They expected that Margaret would have spent the night
at the royal castle of Forfar, however crude a place; but
found that she had passed there and on to Restenneth
Abbey itself — where certainly she would have been more
comfortable, although that was unlikely to have been her
reason. They learned there that the monks had had an
edifying evening with her, and were much impressed with
her knowledge and authority, like no woman they had
ever known. But more to the point, they were told that
after calling at Rescobie Loch, she had intended to
proceed on to Aberlemno, to the north some miles where,
in a cave on the escarpment of Finavon Hill, beneath the
ancient Pictish fort there, a renowned seer roosted, famed
for his second-sight and prophecies. It was a difficult place
of access however, involving a steep climb, and the
Queen, on seeing it, might decide to pass it by. Maldred
privately considered that this was improbable.

In the circumstances the travellers felt that they could
omit visiting the authority on the Holy Trinity since, as
they passed Rescobie Loch they could see that no company
was present, either on the shore or on any of the many
islets of tall sedge-grass — one of which presumably hid
the Keledei Gillemor, of whom there was no sign. They
pressed on, turning northwards now into the rougher
rising ground of an isolated hilly area rising like a
leviathan out of the green centre of Strathmore.

They discovered, as they picked their way, that this
Aberlemno vicinity was indeed awkward to reach, a quite

high hanging valley between two parallel rocky ridges, modest by comparison with the mighty Highland mountains which flanked the strath on the north side, but craggy and sufficiently difficult country, with much fallen stone to negotiate. Towards the east end of this secluded valley, a particularly steep and frowning escarpment arose on the north side, crowned by the broken, grass-grown ramparts of a large fort. And at the foot of this, at the track-side, were congregated a group of men, two women and about a dozen horses. They had run their quarry to earth, it seemed — although earth was perhaps scarcely applicable here, with all eyes trained upwards.

The party at the foot of the hill informed the newcomers that the Queen had climbed the slope to interview another of these peculiar hermits, in a cave up there, and had been gone for some time. They did not comment on what they thought of such behaviour, perhaps in view of Prince Edward's presence, but their attitude was fairly evident nevertheless. Maldred and the prince dismounted and started to climb the rocky, scree-lined hillside.

A stiff clamber of about two hundred and fifty feet brought them, panting, to where a single guard stood beside a thrusting buttress of rock just below the crest of the escarpment. Saluting the prince, he pointed to a mere slit in the rock-face, tucked in at the far side of the buttress, by no means obvious as a cave-entrance. But once through this narrow aperture, quite a cavern opened out — how large it was impossible to assess in the prevailing gloom. Not much light filtered in from the aperture, and this was only modestly reinforced by a single guttering lamp set on a shelf of rock. There was a strong smell of unwashed humanity.

They heard Margaret greeting them in pleased surprise before they actually saw her, the Queen's vision having become accustomed to the gloom within whilst theirs had not. She came to kiss them both, murmuring welcome. Then, putting her finger to her lips, she took each by an arm and steered them back whence they had come, into the sunlight, blinking in its brightness. Behind her came young Ethelred, complaining in a penetrating whisper that this might spoil all.

After a brief questioning as to how the newcomers came to be there, the Queen explained the position at the cave. The Keledei Drostan here, was a noted prophet, soothsayer and godly thinker. Many had advised her to seek his advice on certain matters. But it seemed that he could not prophesy or declaim as it were to order — as was understandable — and for the moment he was awaiting inspiration of the Holy Spirit, in private prayer, deeper within his cave. How long he would be, and whether utterance would be vouchsafed, remained to be seen. They must patiently await God's decision and will.

Maldred stared. "But, Highness — why this? You, who are ever so assured? In matters of religion. So critical of our Columban Church. Seeking the words and guidance of this man! I would have thought that you would consider him heretic and necromancer, if not worse!"

"He is a most saintly man of God, my lord Maldred," the boy Ethelred asserted earnestly. "You must not call him necromancer or the like. It is God the Holy Ghost who speaks from his lips. Everyone knows that."

"If he claims to speak in the name of Christ Jesus, then surely we must believe him honest, at least — or would not God strike him down for his wicked temerity?" Margaret asked. "We must be humble, heed God's word from every source — or at least listen and seek to test it, in patient duty. And I am none so assured as you think, Maldred, God knows. I have so much to learn, so much to be forgiven . . ."

"Mother! None in this world has less to be forgiven than you, I swear!" Edward put in, stoutly. "Do not speak so."

"You do not know, son — you do not know. I have much on my conscience. Many questions in my own sinful mind which I require to have resolved if I am to have peace. Who knows, this Drostan may be used to guide me."

"He will, he will," Ethelred declared. "Abbot Ronan at Loch Leven says that he is a saint, nearer to Heaven than any in the land. I tell you . . ."

He paused, as movement behind them turned their attention. There, in the crevice that was the cave's entrance, stood the hermit. If the Abbot Colban, of Forfar Loch, had been an unchancy sight, this man was more so. Very tall but stooping, emaciated, his was the wreck of a once powerful frame, strong features now cadaverous, hair and beard tangled, eyes strangely blank in the sunlight, opaque, almost as though blind, person clad in a filthy, ragged habit which had once been monastic, tied round his middle with a rope. Nevertheless there was something undeniably authoritative and commanding about this scarecrow.

The Queen spontaneously extended her hand. "Ah, my friend — do you seek us? To have us come within, again?"

The anchorite did not seem to hear her, gazing past her, past them all. The sunlight did not appear to affect those strange eyes. Silent, he stood for long moments. Then his lips began to move, to work — but no sound came at first. Until abruptly he raised a hand high, finger pointing skywards, and words commenced, single, halting words at first, which gradually ran together and became a stream, a powerful tide of sound. But words such as Maldred for one had never heard before, sonorous, fluent now, almost musical. Margaret and the boys, assuming it to be some form of the Gaelic, glanced at Maldred — but it had no least resemblance to Gaelic. On and on this unintelligible but weirdly moving declamation went; and once started, however odd the tongue, Drostan was never at a loss for word or sequence. Whatever language he spoke, he at least sounded as familiar in it as in his own. His hearers stood as though transfixed, wondering.

For how long this continued before they became aware of a change, they could not have declared, so preoccupied were they all. But presently they began to realise that there were occasional words coming into it that they recognised and understood, incorporated in the rest, not interrupting the flow. Steadily the proportion of these increased, so that gradually the monologue grew more and more intelligible. But if this was less bewildering for the listeners, it was no more comforting. For it was a denunciation that they were hearing, a powerful indictment, with the word woe reiterated — woe to this blood-guilty generation, woe unto the faithless and the heedless, woe to the perverters of God's holy word, woe upon woe.

The strength and stern anger of this frail old man's delivery were almost as extraordinary and unnerving as what he said.

There was a pause. None presumed to speak, not even the Queen. For the hermit's hand was still upraised commandingly, weary as that old arm must have been. Then the arm came down some way, for the finger to point directly at Margaret. And the speaking resumed. But now it was different in tenor, specific not general, and addressed personally to, or at, the Queen.

"Woman," Drostan said, "beware! Beware, I say. You have been given much, permitted much, forgiven much. From you much is required. If you prove a stone for stumbling in the path of God's people, great will be the price you will pay. Grieve not the Holy Spirit, as you have done, in stiff-necked pride. Humble you! The heart is warm, yes — but the mind is cold. Let that proud mind rule and you perish. And those you love perish with you. Before you! You have it in you to do great good. But also great hurt. You worship much and often. See to it that it is Almighty God whom you worship and not yourself and the idols set up by your proud mind. Beware, I say. God can use you in His purpose, mightily. But you have it in you to hinder that purpose. Already you have caused others to falter and stumble, in your prideful haste. You have aided more, yes, and God is merciful. Be *you* merciful, woman — or you shall weep over the price others will pay for your lack."

There was a silence, broken only by the sob in Margaret's throat.

"Heed these words that I speak," the man went on, his eyes seeming to look through her, "and generations unborn shall bless you. Spurn them, and blessing shall turn to cursing. Already some price falls to be paid. It shall be paid by those near and dear to you. God is not mocked. But He is gracious and full of compassion. Repent you and cast off your pride of mind and spirit and the Almighty will be with you always, on your right hand and on your left. Be the handmaid of the Lord, that He may bless you in all that you do. As I, now, in His name bless you."

The raised hand sketched the Sign of the Cross, and he pronounced the Benediction. "Go in peace," he ended, and turning, re-entered his cave without another word.

For a while they all stood there silent, appalled, Maldred shaking his head helplessly, the boys gazing at their mother, the guard scratching his head in embarrassment, Margaret herself, head down, shaken with a great shuddering, tears running down her lovely cheeks.

Edward of Strathclyde found his voice first. "The man is evil!" he cried. "Evil — possessed of the Devil! My father will have his tongue out for that! How dared he! How dared he!"

Ethelred said nothing.

Maldred cleared his throat. "Margaret — Highness — do not grieve so sorely. Do not take it so hard. Such people are . . . strange. Wild in their talk, as in their visage. Scarcely of this world. He but berates you for your usage of his Church, the Columban Church. Heed that, yes — but do not take the rest so sore."

She shook her head, wordless.

"He ended by blessing you, Mother," Ethelred reminded. "He did say to go in peace."

"Peace . . . !" In an agonised cry that word burst from the Queen's lips. Turning from them, she started off, stumbling down the steep hillside.

They hurried after, Maldred taking her arm — and undoubtedly she would have fallen otherwise. She answered no words to their efforts at comfort. But by the time they reached the foot, she had mastered herself sufficiently not to appear broken before the waiting courtiers — although they eyed her curiously, at her set-faced, curt command to turn and head back for the Ward of the Stormounth forthwith.

By mutual if unspoken consent her sons and Maldred allowed the Queen to ride ahead of all, for some time. Eventually, after a mile or two, the boys did move up, to flank her; and presently Maldred reined nearer also. After what she had listened to, it might well seem irrelevant to speak of the lifting of the threat of war and of Turgot's promotion at Durham, but it might help to lift her mind from contemplation of Drostan's words.

She listened to him, gazing directly ahead of her, and when he had finished said evenly that it was good, satisfactory. That was all.

Unhappily, he rode on. At length he said, "Margaret — hear me, I ask you. This is less ill than you deem it. You must look at it clearly. The man may be crazed, bereft, or even an imposter. I do not know. But even if he is not, he need not be speaking God's words. Who is he to speak you so, when none of his betters, Dunchad, Fothad, abbots and bishops, have elected to do so . . . ?"

But it was of no use. The Queen merely shook her head and answered his representations with monosyllables, if at all. Margaret Atheling, for once, appeared to have had her strength, assurance and convictions shattered. Whether it was the denunciation of her spiritual pride, an awareness

362

of which had always been with her, or the speaking in tongues which had penetrated her armour; or whether some inner doubts and sense of guilt had been building up, growing, and these were now reinforced, the woman was as one stricken.

When Maldred took his departure next day, to return to Dunbar, he left her little the more happy.

24

SCOTLAND, LIKE ALL of Christendom, rang and reverberated with the tidings, the flood of news and reports, assumptions and conjectures. It did not require Cospatrick to come as special informant, for every churchman, traveller, packman and wandering minstrel was full of it all. William the Conqueror was dead and nothing would ever be the same again.

For thirty years the Bastard of Normandy had been like some monstrous shadow over Northern Europe, his military effectiveness so terrible, his harshness and savageries so vast in scale, his ambitions so boundless, that men could scarcely realise that the shadow could be lifted. His death was difficult enough to accept, the manner of it almost inconceivable and the consequences complex and bewildering. How much of it all was to be believed was a matter for individual judgement; but certainly the main and apparently undisputed facts were sufficiently extraordinary.

Pieced together, and discarding the wilder stories, Maldred was inclined to accept the following sequence. In the spring of 1087, the year after his return to France, William had got so far in his campaign against Philip that he was besieging Mantes, only thirty-five miles north-west of Paris. There, having taken the city, he was entering the burning town, when his horse reared on treading on a burning ember, and threw the King. So fat and heavy had he become, these last years, that his fall was tremendous and internal bleeding resulted. He was unconscious for some time, and on recovering his wits, was in great pain. The pommel of his saddle, on falling, had dug into his loins. He decided that he was dying. He ordered that he be carried to his own city of Rouen, in Normandy, to the monastery of St. Gervais. Convinced that he had not long, like many another before him, he found need to consider his past and provide for the future. He decided, belatedly, to forgive all his enemies, and gave orders for all whom he had imprisoned and who had not already died in durance, to be released — and that meant thousands, in cells and castles all over his territories, including his brother Odo, sundry Saxon earls, bishops and lords and innumerable French, Norman and Flemish victims. Political hostages were likewise to be freed, including Prince Duncan of Scotland. All this ordered, he had appeared to await his end more content with his chances.

However, others were less evidently content to await the end in pious hope, with an empire to be disposed of, especially his sons, as time went on. William Rufus had been kept with him throughout the campaign. Henry came over from England. Robert, still estranged, was not sent for, to Flanders. Other kin and great lords flocked to Rouen. There was a great manoeuvring for position and importuning the too-slowly-departing Conqueror, who lingered for six weeks. At first William was in no hurry to divide up the spoils of his career; but pressed continually to do so, and in much pain, as he began to sink, he eventually acceded. Forgiveness did not go quite so far as to overlook his firstborn's frequent hostility. Duke of Normandy he had made him, and Duke of Normandy he should remain. William Rufus was to get the English throne. Henry, surprisingly, got no title or rule, but five thousand pounds weight of silver and the advice to be patient — presumably referring to his brother Rufus's unwed state. Other and lesser provisions were made, some to awkward kin who had been in prison for as much as twenty years.

And then came the scarcely believable. Having heard the testamentary arrangements, made in bedside council, everyone of any prominence and importance promptly hurried off, leaving the stricken monarch to his own dying, William Rufus leading the way in a dash for England and his crown before Odo or Robert or even Henry might grab it first. Henry was not far behind, and

bishops, earls and lords raced to establish themselves
wherever their best advantage was deemed to lie, in such
fluid situation. No one of any authority and standing
remained with the helpless William; and perceiving the
way things went, the lesser men and officers, even the
house-servants, engaged in a free-for-all to grab whatever
they could of the royal possessions which were to hand,
stripping all. When at length the Scourge of Christendom
breathed his last, on the fifth day before the Ides of
September, his naked body was promptly tossed to the
floor so that the silken and furred bedclothes could be
filched, and would have lain there quarrelled over only by
the dogs had not a poor but loyal knight taken upon
himself the duty and cost of a funeral. William fitz Robert
fitz Richard fitz Richard fitz William fitz Rolf the Ganger,
Viking, aged sixty-one, was trundled eighty miles in a
farm-cart to Caen, to be interred in the knight's family
burial-ground. Even there protest was made, a local
Norman baron claiming the body as his, until certain
debts were repaid.

If all this was not sufficient, consequences in the
English South were vehement if predictable, once the
strong hand of the Conqueror was removed. The freed
Odo managed to get there first, and with the aid of the likewise freed Earl Morkar of Mercia and the Earl Roger of
Hereford, immediately raised a scratch army to grasp the
throne, allegedly for his ill-used nephew Robert; although
most believed for himself. So Rufus was faced with
rebellion from the first, and the result was still very much
undecided. Civil war raged in the South. The position was
futher complicated by one of Rufus's first acts, which was
to lay violent hands on the Lord High Treasurer and his
keys, and to confiscate and remove from Winchester the
entire English royal treasure in gold, silver and jewels —
the silver alone said to amount to over sixty thousand
pounds in weight. This, naturally, much offended his
brother Henry, whose testatory five thousand pounds was
not paid, and who now seemed as though he might throw
in his lot with Robert and Odo.

Thus and thus, and much more, the talk went.

In Scotland, Malcolm waited, on the alert. The news
which reached Dunbar from the north was that the
mustering plans were all in force again, war-training
intensified, and the King ready to pounce for Tyne and

Tees whenever the situation was sufficiently clarified to reveal his best chances. Incidentally also the word was brought that something of a rift had occurred between Malcolm and his wife. The Queen, it seemed, had become almost a changed woman, her enthusiasms gone, save for prolonged fastings and penances. No longer did she tour the country bestowing largesse and feeding the poor. Now she was reported to spend much of her time on her knees, shut up, alone. And not even usually in Malcolm's own houses, at Dunfermline, the Ward or elsewhere; for, of all things, she had elected to take over for herself a tiny islet in Forfar Loch at the other end from Abbot Colban's crannog, where, in harsh conditions and austerity, she played the prayerful anchorite herself. Why she so chose, none knew. Admittedly the distinctly gaunt royal castle of Forfar was close by, where some of her ladies were forced to roost, since she would have none on her island. Maldred, for one, saw it all as a direct consequence of that grim visit to the hermit Drostan's cave on Finavon Hill. She was still accepting the man's words as God's, stricken with some sort of guilt and foreboding. She could not share the cave with this flagellant, but Forfar Loch was in the vicinity, close enough to visit, perhaps to learn of remission. It was said that she often consulted the authoritative Colban.

Maldred and Magda were much distressed, but could think of nothing that they might usefully do. Magda pointed out that Margaret, long ago, had declared that she would have liked to live the life of a religious — as indeed her sister Christina was now reported to do, as an abbess, in England. Perhaps, belatedly, the Queen was moving towards such fulfilment.

In the autumn of that eventful year, at Dunbar, there were very different developments to preoccupy Maldred's attention. One golden late-October afternoon he was informed that a fine and gallant company, all banners and colour, was approaching from the south-west, clearly someone important. When he and Magda repaired to the gatehouse-tower to prospect, a large cavalcade was seen to be only a short distance off, gay and impressive as intimated, with even a band of mounted musicians to play them on their way, with trumpets, flutes and drums. There were, as related, many banners — but the greatest, and foremost, were to be distinguished as those of the

Celtic royal house of Scotland, the silver boar on blue, and the red rampant lion on gold of the earldom of Dunbar and March. Intrigued, wondering, Maldred hurried down to receive whoever these were. It could hardly be the young Earl Cospatrick, for he had seen him only two days before at Ersildoune and there was nothing out-of-the-ordinary occurring then.

Standing on the lowered drawbridge, as castellan, to welcome the newcomers, he saw that young Cospatrick was indeed there, near the front of the party, with his brothers Dolfin, Earl of Cumbria and Waldeve, Lord of Allerdale, and their sister Ethelreda. But these did not ride directly beneath the great banner of Dunbar — their father did that, no longer dressed in the habit of a wandering friar but splendid in a velvet cloak over chain-mail, and wearing a plumed helmet. And at his side, under the boar flag, was a richly-dressed young man whose heavy features were vaguely familiar. Then, astonished, Maldred recognised another of his second-cousins, the Prince Duncan, eldest son of the King.

With a final flourish the musicians finished. Cospatrick, reining up, raised both hand and voice.

"Ha — Maldred! Greetings! Smile, man — do not look so glum, so solemn. See whom we have here — Duncan mac Malcolm, rightful Prince of Strathclyde."

That introduction, with its implications of trouble, certainly did not bring any smile to Maldred's face. He moistened his lips.

"Welcome, cousins," he said, and could think of nothing more to add.

"Come, Maldred — is that the best you can do?" Cospatrick exclaimed, getting down with a little difficulty from his magnificent stallion — for he was permanently twisted from that long-ago wound, and the horse was a deal taller than the humble nags he had chosen to ride for years — but spurning assistance nevertheless. "How is that to greet the true heir to the throne? And my own poor self, new returned from the dead! Earl of Dunbar and March once again, monkish habit burned. Does not all this call for some rejoicing?"

Maldred inclined his head. "I rejoice, my lord — if you do. And I welcome Duncan mac Malcolm back to his own land, and freedom at last." That was the best he could achieve.

There followed a great to-do of dismounting and settling in, of hurried arrangements for feeding and quartering so large an influx. It was some time before, over the repast which Magda managed to scrape together, they heard the full story — and something of Cospatrick's intentions. Duncan proved to be a quiet and rather stolid young man, but with an obstinate chin. He left the talking to his hosts.

Cospatrick was in high spirits. With William's death he saw all threat to his life and wellbeing lifted, so that he could now resume his rightful status. This Rufus, he declared, was a very different man from his father. Not, he suggested, wholly to be trusted — this with a glance at Duncan — but with different and less menacing ideas and preoccupations. He was avaricious, more interested in wealth and fine-living and ease, than in dominating power, the reverse of a womaniser, concerned with display, entertainment, hunting and the like. And of less than good health. Moreover he had a difficult situation to face in England, and would have for some time. A weakling, compared with the Conqueror, he was unlikely to seek to pursue his sire's feud with the resurrected enemy in the North — especially with the link to be forged with the excellent Prince Duncan here, of whom Rufus was known to approve. Indeed, he had actually knighted him as one of his first acts as King on returning to England, before despatching him northwards.

"*Despatching* him northwards?" Maldred repeated. "Do you mean by that, my lord, that the prince was *sent* back to Scotland by the new English King — rather than electing to come home, himself?"

Cospatrick looked at Duncan.

That man nodded. "I was very well at Winchester," he said shortly. "I have no assurance that my father, who I think hates me, will welcome me back to his realm."

None commented on that fairly obvious assumption.

"Rufus, I think, sees our young cousin's situation in a different light," Cospatrick observed. "He conceives him as becoming something of a check and hindrance on Malcolm's hostile activities and ambitions. He, not the fair Margaret's son Edward, is the true heir. All Scotland knows that — and many might be prepared to support his claims. The old Celtic polity would prefer him, do you not think, to the younger, half-Saxon and Romish Edward?"

Maldred stroked his chin. "Perhaps. And you?"

The other shrugged. "We shall see."

"If you are right, Duncan mac Malcolm's situation in Scotland, meantime, could be an uncomfortable one."

The prince looked as though he agreed with that assessment.

"Ah, but that would depend on circumstances, Maldred. The circumstance, for instance, of *where* in Scotland he dwelt. Here, in my Borderland, see you, he would be apt to come to no hurt."

"So-o-o! You would do that? Whose side are you on now, then, my lord? King Malcolm's or King William Rufus's?"

"Say that I have Scotland's best interests much at heart!" the Earl answered easily, grinning. "And also, to be sure, those of my future good-son!"

"What! Good-son . . . ?" Maldred stared. "You mean . . . ?"

"Indeed yes. Duncan will wed my daughter Ethelreda here. A most felicitous match, do you not think?"

Maldred glanced down the table at the girl, who kept her head down. He was silent as what this meant sank in. He had always wondered whether, at the back of it all, Cospatrick had designs on the Scots throne for himself. He aimed to rule Cumbria, Northumbria, the Borders and Lothian. Would it be so unlikely a step to envisage, to aim for the rest? Malcolm was now sixty-five, himself only forty-seven. By wedding his daughter to Duncan, she could be the future Queen; or he could use the excuse of support for his son-in-law to improve his own chances of taking over the throne in due course. But — inevitably, it would mean hostility, almost undeclared war, between himself and Malcolm. The King had never trusted the one-time side-changer. This would pose the most transparent threat.

"And the King?" Maldred said, at length. "How think you he will see this?"

"Malcolm has shown no interest in his eldest son for a dozen years and more. Should he do so now?" Cospatrick shrugged. "I have served him passing well over these years. And he has never so much as said a word of thanks. Perhaps we may change that. And Duncan's prospects."

Maldred held his peace, but thought his own thoughts. Presently he changed the subject somewhat.

"If you, my lord, are now Earl of Dunbar and March again, and openly resident here, you will not require my services as deputy. I should be glad to return to my own place of Bothargask, in Atholl. Much neglected!"

"Not so, Maldred — not so. I have need for you here, still, your position unchanged. I shall make my home at Ersildoune, with my family. You will continue to manage all my lands from here. I shall take the manpower of my earldoms out of your hands — but you have besought me to do this often. I shall be much away, in Northumbria and Cumbria still, if openly now. You will do better here, man, than roosting in a small corner of your brother's lands."

They left it at that, meantime.

So, a few weeks later, at the now revived and quite flourishing monastery of Melross, Prince Duncan, aged twenty-seven and the Lady Ethelreda, ten years younger, were wed. Turgot, Prior of Durham and now much Cospatrick's colleague, was fetched north to perform the ceremony — in the Roman rite, despite Duncan's alleged requirement of Celtic support. None of the bridegroom's family were present, or invited.

Afterwards, Turgot and Maldred had a long conversation about the Queen. The Prior had heard stories about her present strange state of mind. She had ceased to write him letters. The last consignments of holy books and church ornaments he had collected for her had remained unacknowledged. He asked whether Maldred, whom he knew to be her friend, could somehow arrange an audience for him, secretly if need be.

Maldred was not hopeful. The King would be unlikely to allow it. And it would be almost impossible, even if desirable, to smuggle the monk into Scotland first and then into the Queen's presence, without authority — especially under present conditions. But he would tell her, next time he saw her, of Turgot's strong desire to visit her. That was all that he might do. He did not add that it was only for Margaret's sake and not for the Prior's, or for that of the Romish faith, that he promised as much.

25

ONE ADVANTAGE, AT least, accrued from the Duncan marriage, for Maldred — he found that Malcolm did not expect him to lead a Lothian and Border host on the next invasion of Northumbria, or even to take part himself. Clearly he was now considered to be hopelessly in the Cospatrick camp, and not to be trusted. The following summer, the unfortunate Edgar Atheling arrived back in Scotland, having been dispossessed of his countship of Montreuil-sur-Mer, given by King Philip and later over-run, but confirmed by the Conqueror to him in return for Edgar's resigning of any rights to the English throne. Rufus had now turned him out, to hand over the property and rights to his brother Robert of Normandy, in an effort to detach him from Odo's insurrection. Malcolm, despite his scorn and impatience with his brother-in-law, saw this to be as good an excuse as any to make his latest bid for Tyne and Tees; and calling on all good Saxons to rise against the Normans, marched southwards with a large army. He took the inland route by Soltra and Lauderdale to the Tweed crossings, thus avoiding coastal Dunbar but of necessity passing close to Ersildoune. However, Cospatrick could be discreet when the occasion warranted, and having no desire for a confrontation with his monarch at the head of a major host, found it convenient to betake himself, his family and new son-in-law, off on a visit to Dolfin's earldom, at Caer-luel — with a couple of days to spare.

So the Scots went harrying and burning down into Northumbria just like old times — but minus Maldred and his contingent.

The situation in England was still unsettled. Rufus had most of the South under control of a sort, but Odo was still in revolt in his earldom of Kent, even though Robert apparently was no longer his ally and excuse. Morkar had been captured and put back in a cell, but Hereford was still at large on the Welsh Marches, and much of Mercia and the Midlands not accepting the new King. Rufus had so far not ventured as far north as York; so Malcolm reckoned that his chances were good, with only Moubray, the present Earl of Northumbria and his local forces, to oppose him. He did not trouble to take Edgar Atheling with him, his part being merely to furnish an excuse for the move and to call on the dissident Saxons not to aid Moubray.

The news that filtered back to Dunbar and Caer-luel, those weeks of high summer, was of a most successful and enjoyable venture, from Malcolm's point of view, with Moubray consistently falling back without major battle and the Scots spreading satisfactory destruction far and wide, more or less unimpeded. In due course they reached the Tyne, where they found the great new castle completed, and too tough a nut to crack without a prolonged siege. So by-passing this they moved on towards the Tees in an almost leisurely fashion, making a diversion to take a swipe at Durham in the by-going, more as a gesture of warning to Cospatrick than anything else — although the ecclesiastical pickings were considerable — Bishop de St. Calais and Prior Turgot prudently absenting themselves.

Long pack-trains of booty and captives, and huge herds of cattle, kept coming back across Tweed and up through Lothian, to witness to the fair accuracy of these reports.

So passed the summer, with Maldred thankfully not involved in anything more violent than the hay and corn harvest, and Cospatrick biding his time.

It was the latter, with his excellent lines of communication, who first learned of impending change, towards the end of August. Rufus, it was said was assembling troops, further troops, in large numbers. But then he was always having to do this, and these might well be aimed against Odo or Hereford, Rufus having no lack of enemies. But when the word began to come in of a great fleet being assembled in the East Anglian ports, it seemed unlikely that this could be directed against anyone but Malcolm. When information confirmed that the objective was indeed said to be Scotland, or at least the North, and that Duke Robert was in command of the naval force, Rufus himself leading the new army, Cospatrick decided that it was time to act. It was no part of his designs to see Malcolm suffer major defeat in England, and to have the English entering Scotland as victors. Accordingly he sent messengers to warn the King, on Teesside, of the approaching menace, ordered Maldred to muster the Lothian and Border host once more, and himself collected a Cumbrian force, to march eastwards.

It looked as though Maldred was not to escape hostilities, after all.

Cospatrick and Dolfin arrived at Dunbar in foul weather of unseasonable easterly gales on the Eve of the Translation of St. Cuthbert. Maldred had assumed that the combined force would move down through the Merse to the Tweed, to guard the fords there — since, if Malcolm indeed was retiring and pursued, that is surely where he would turn and make a stand. But Cospatrick said no. They would wait here, at the beginning of the wide Lothian plain, and just beyond the Lammermuir passes of Peasedean and Bilsdean. His objective was to rescue Malcolm, and be seen to do so, not to try to defeat Rufus. The Tweed fords might have been suitable enough for a battle-ground. But they had to think of the seaborne force under Robert. That would not be affected by inland battles along the Tweed. Making for the Scottish Sea and the Forth, as it would be likely to do, it must pass close to Dunbar here. A large force seen waiting here, ready, would be apt to give Robert pause, if he arrived first. And if Rufus preceded him and was held up here, Robert would see it and presumably adjust his tactics. It was much better, too, that in any confrontation with Rufus, and possible negotiation, he should have had to fight his way over Tweed and then through these dangerous Lammermuir passes first, so that he had these hazards behind him to menace his retiral should he suffer any reverse — always an important consideration for any commander.

So they waited. But meantime Cospatrick despatched a courier over the Earl of Fife's ferry at North Berwick to bring Edgar Atheling back from Dunfermline — if he would come. He was the ostensible excuse for Malcolm's invasion, and might make a useful bargaining-counter if negotiations could be developed.

Soon messages began to come from their people along the Tweed that the main mass of the Scots army was on its way home through North Northumbria, but much slowed by immense booty. Of the English forces there was no word.

Strangely, their first real news of the southern situation came from the north. A vessel put into Dunbar harbour two days later, bringing not only Edgar Atheling but his royal sister. They brought the tidings that, as they were about to leave from Inverkeithing haven, a storm-tossed Low Countries ship had come in, whose skipper announced that he had had to shelter in the mouth of the Humber and whilst there a great invasion fleet under Duke Robert of Normandy had been driven ashore on that coast, by the fierce storm, and utterly wrecked. Margaret observed, although much less confidently than formerly she would have done, that it was, surely, an answer to prayer?

Maldred and Magda were shocked by the appearance of the Queen. Drawn, thin and pale, she seemed to have aged almost unbelievably. She was still beautiful but no longer lovely in the warm and comely way which had been so attractive. Now she was sad, reserved, without sparkle, almost ill. Magda thought that her time-of-life might have something to do with it — she was now forty-three — but more than this must be responsible. If it was the result of her penances and fastings, then she was punishing herself terribly for some reason.

They made a less than cheerful company as they waited in Dunbar Castle. All were anxious over the developing situation, Edgar particularly so, an agitated man who wished that he was not there, wished, he declared, that he had never been born. Apparently he had come in answer to Cospatrick's summons only because Margaret had insisted on it — and had come herself to ensure compliance. So she could still be strong-willed, at least. Edgar and Cospatrick, of course, cordially disliked each other, and he was by no means fond of Maldred either.

That first evening, with the Athelings declaring that they were weary and retiring early to their rooms, Magda told Maldred that she was going up to Margaret's chamber to talk to the Queen, alone, goodnights said or no. They were, after all, old friends as well as mistress and attendant. Surely she would abandon her grievous reserve and speak freely to her?

Some considerable time later, with his wife not returned, Maldred decided to go up himself. Was he not also Margaret's friend, however much they might disagree at times? He knocked at her door. Magda came and, making a helpless gesture, beckoned him within.

"Here is Maldred, Highness," she said. "May he come in?"

The Queen was standing near the window, staring out northwards across the sunset-stained sea. She held a crucifix in her hands. She answered neither yea nor nay.

Taking silence for assent, he moved in.

"Her Highness is sore at heart," Magda went on, tensely. "She blames herself. Against all reason. She conceives God to be punishing her. And so punishes herself the more cruelly."

"But . . . but, back there, did she not say that this wrecking of the Duke Robert's fleet was God's answer to her prayers? How then . . . ?"

"That was presumptuous in me," Margaret said, without turning. "Others more worthy would be praying, in this pass. To be heard before me."

"Highness — is this . . . are you still concerned over the condemnations of that crazed man in the cave? The Keledei Drostan?" Maldred demanded. "Surely that is folly? A man beside himself . . ."

"Folly? Should I condemn as folly the condemnations, when what he prophesied is fulfilled?"

"Fulfilled . . . ?"

"Fulfilled, yes." Margaret turned, to face them. "*You* heard his prophecies, Maldred. All that he said then is coming to pass. And others, as he warned, are paying the price of *my* sins. And you say not to concern myself."

"But . . . but . . ."

"My sons, my own sons. *They* are paying the price. He said that those I loved would suffer. Edmund is lost to me, lost. Given over to wicked ways, although so young. Always he was headstrong, but now he sins openly, before all, shaming me. Wine and women, lies and savageries, despising all God's commandments . . ."

"Margaret — I say that you cannot blame yourself for that!" Magda exclaimed. "You reared and cherished him to love and fear God. No children could have been better raised. And God would never cause Edmund to sin against Himself, just to punish *you*."

"God allows it. So mine must be the fault. And it is not only Edmund. Even Ethelred, my own beloved Ethelred who seeks after God, who was to be wed to Holy Church, as I should have been — even he is lost to faith and truth and all decency . . ."

"That I do not believe!" Maldred cried. "Not Ethelred. As good as a monk."

"Ethelred, yes. He is, he is . . . married! Sixteen years, and wed! Secretly wed."

Astonished, speechless, they gazed at her.

"He is wed to a young woman two years older than himself. Daughter to Malsnechtan of Moray, Lulach's son. She, she is to have a child. Ethelred, whom I taught and loved and trusted. Lost . . ."

"Not lost — never lost, Margaret!" Maldred asserted. "A young hawk, testing his wings, that is all. And honest enough to marry, not to abandon, as do most . . ."

"But he was to be a priest! A man of God. To do so much, so much before him. As Primate of the Scots Church. All thrown away, all lost . . ."

"My father, Highness, was Primate of the Church. And wed my mother, with the approval of all."

"That was different. He was not of the true . . . of the Roman Church. He was not a true priest, in orders."

"He was Abbot of Dunkeld, as is Ethelred." Maldred produced a mirthless smile. "You and Malcolm made him that, made the lad head of the Celtic Church. Can you blame him if he accepts some of the doctrines of that Church — in which priests may wed? Blame him, if he finds its customs more to his taste than some of those of Rome?"

"I do not blame him — I blame myself!" the Queen said, broken-voiced. "I am accursed, accursed, for my sins."

"Sins, Margaret, my dear — who are you to weep for sins?" Magda put in. "If you, the most sainted woman in this land, bewail your sins, what of the rest of us? Who have real sins to live down."

"You do not know what you say, Magda. My sins are as scarlet, I tell you. I have been living a lie almost from the day I reached this land. I had promised myself to take the veil. As Christina has done. I should never have agreed to wed Malcolm. He had a wife, a queen. How she died I know not — but I should not have wed Malcolm when I did. It has been on my conscience ever since. I thought, I thought to do so much, in my arrogance, for his realm, this Scotland . . ."

"And you have done much, worked wonders, no less . . ."

She ignored that. "Malcolm already had two sons. But I allowed him to put them aside, wickedly, in favour of my own. Now I, and they, are punished."

"They were *Malcolm's* sons," Maldred pointed out.

"I was made one with Malcolm, before God. His sins are mine, are they not? I let him send Duncan away, hostage. Thankful that it was not any of mine! And not only in this. I have not restrained Malcolm as I ought. His warrings and invasions and cruelties. I have not held him back from these — although God knows I have tried!"

"God knows, yes — leave it to God and His mercy, Highness. Malcolm is a hard and harsh man. No woman could ever soften him wholly. You have done great things with him and through him, for his realm. You have made his people love you — as none love *him*. You are beloved as no queen ever was. The poor all but worship you. Do not scorn the love of thousands . . ."

"Oh, I do not, I do not, Maldred. Unworthy as I am . . ."

"I think that you do. Or you would not condemn yourself so."

"It is true, Margaret — true," Magda said urgently. "God has blessed you with the love of so many. He cannot condemn you, as you think. Love is the touchstone, is it not? If you are greatly loved, you cannot be far from God."

"You think so, Magda — oh, you think so?" At last there was a flicker of hope in that unhappy voice.

"I do not think so, I *know* so, my dear. Ask yourself, is it not the simple truth?"

Abruptly the Queen threw down the crucifix on the bed and ran forward to hurl herself into Magda's arms and burst into a flood of tears. There, rocked like a child by the other woman, she sobbed her heart out.

Maldred tip-toed to the door, and out.

*　　*　　*

The next afternoon the first companies of the Scots army began to appear out of the Lammermuir passes, laden down with loot, driving herds of cattle. The King, these said, was holding the Tweed fords — for how long God alone knew, for the English were close behind and in vast strength. Cospatrick sent couriers to suggest to Malcolm that he left off that difficult confrontation and came north to Dunbar where, he asserted, a more profitable and effective stand might be made and where his own force was waiting., Whether the King would heed him was another matter.

But the following forenoon it was evident that Malcolm was coming, as more and more parties arrived, separate and strung-out after threading the hills and passes between Lothian and the Merse. Almost certainly the word that a fresh Lothian and Border host was awaiting him there had had its effect, however much he might distrust Cospatrick.

All day the Scots were coming in, burdened by the fruits of their campaigning. But no sign of Malcolm before nightfall. It was, to be sure, some thirty-five miles from Coldstream and the other Tweed crossings, and he was presumably fighting a rearguard action all the way.

The King arrived, with Prince Edward and his embattled rear, just before noon next day, weary, grim, declaring that William Rufus was out of the passes now, only five miles behind. He did not appear to be rejoiced to see his wife and certainly not Edgar Atheling, nor for that matter Cospatrick or any of them, save to find some satisfaction in the fresh force of about two thousand men waiting here, beside the previously-arrived units of his own army which Cospatrick had gathered up and prevented from retiring further.

The cousins had not seen each other for long, and did not attempt to hide their lack of affection.

"Why did you wait here?" Malcolm demanded. "If you had brought these men, these subjects of mine, to me earlier, at Coldstream, Lennel and Birgham, the English would still be behind Tweed."

"Perhaps. But not for long. If they are in the strength all tell me, twenty thousand men, then it was only a question of time. How many have you now? Eight thousand? With mine, ten thousand. Even if you had held the fords, some English would have marched westwards up-Tweed and crossed higher, at Kelso or Roxburgh. You could not have stopped them. Then you would have been out-flanked, finished, with nothing left but flight all the way through Lothian. And had to come to terms with Rufus in the end, weak, broken and in the heart of your kingdom."

"And this way, man? Here?"

"Here, I think, you may come to terms better. While you are still strong — or appear to be strong. Better terms. Rufus will think twice of giving full battle here at Dunbar, with those passes and the Tweed behind him. I have sent a small force under Dolfin to harass his rear. In hostile country, *my* country, he will be uneasy, more disposed to talk — now that he has lost his brother's fleet."

"Yes, husband — you must talk, not fight," Margaret put in, with some strength in her voice again. She looked wan and frail, but with more of spirit than when she had arrived. "Talking is a deal cheaper than battling — as we have proved in the past."

"What have we to talk about, woman? Rufus has been on my heels since the Tees. Why stop to talk now?"

"Because the further he marches from his own place — and that is the English South — the more unsure of his rear he must become," Cospatrick insisted. "He is now in Scotland, where he has never been. He is no great warrior like his father — and he leaves Odo and revolt behind him."

"And we have something to bargain with," Margaret added. "Edgar, here. Edgar has signed a paper declaring that he will yield up all his claims to the throne of England, for himself and for all time. It is a hopeless cause, to be sure — but this new William should be relieved to have it written and pledged."

"There is another reason, cousin," Cospatrick went on. "Another negotiator, of whom Rufus is known to think well. My good-son — whom you may remember!" He raised his voice. "Duncan — come you."

Out from the throng of nobles behind, the prince pushed his way. Father and eldest son faced each other for the first time in a dozen years.

Malcolm stared, speechless. Duncan had been a mere boy when last he had seen him. This was a man, a hostile, stubborn-looking, stern man with much of his sire's build and cast of feature. They had not a word to say to each other.

The Queen it was who broke the silence. "Duncan has been much misused. We owe him a great debt, my lord King. The greater if he can carry weight with this King William, his friend, to leave our land without battle."

Malcolm turned away, frowning darkly. "Here is no

time for this idle talking," he grated. "Rufus is only a few miles off. His front riders will be upon us at any moment. Whether we fight or treat, we must be doing, not tattling like old wives!"

"Agreed, cousin," Cospatrick nodded. "Let us to business now, that we may talk from seeming strength later . . ."

They positioned their forces according to Cospatrick's plan, Malcolm acceding that it was well thought-out and best in the circumstances. They withdrew the main army almost a mile to the westwards, behind the quite large Beil Water, with the marshland of its estuary into Belhaven Bay guarding their left flank, to form a solid barrier which would be difficult to dislodge. Cospatrick's own array, however, was sent to form up on higher ground in the Belton area almost a mile away but entirely visible, prominent indeed, gallant with many flags and banners, some in fact borrowed from the King's own commanders to make a better show. Because of the lie of the land it was impossible to tell how many men were marshalled there, with the ranks disappearing over the slope of a low ridge — but the impression certainly was of a large, fresh and eager host menacing the southern flank.

Long before they were finished this marshalling, the enemy van was in sight, numbers growing all the time until the entire narrow coastal plain was a mass of men and horses and the gleam of steel, a sufficiently alarming sight. Past the line of Dunbar township and about half-a-mile from the Scots front, the English leadership drew up, clearly to assess the situation, no doubt very much aware of that so far uncommitted host up on their left.

At this stage it was Cospatrick, not the King, who sent forward Maldred, Prince Duncan and an escort, under a flag-of-truce.

Halfway between the two lines, they halted and sat their horses. And presently a similar group came riding out from the bannered centre of the English front.

As they waited, Maldred pointed. "Is not that the banner of Normandy flying beside the royal standard of England?" he said. "That must mean that Duke Robert is there. Has rejoined his brother."

Duncan shrugged. "Did you wish him drowned? But . . . see who comes here. It is Moubray of Northumbria."

As the English party drew near, Maldred called out. "We come from the High King of Scots. Here is his son, the Prince Duncan. King Malcolm demands speech with whoever leads this array which has invaded his realm."

"He will get more than speech!" a haughty voice gave back. "The most puissant King William of England, Lord Paramount of Scotland, commands his immediate presence, surrender and obeisance."

"That is bairns' talk!" Maldred returned. "There is no Lord Paramount of Scotland save its High King. If your King William is there and desires speech with my liege-lord, let him come forward and King Malcolm will assure him of safe-conduct."

"Insolent! The King will not demean himself to speak with a rebel-in-arms."

"Then he must needs *fight* the said arms! You may tell him so."

The prince raised his voice. "My lord of Northumbria, I Duncan, speak. If my friend King William will not come, let him send others who may talk in his cause. We have here the Prince Edgar the Atheling, who has an offer to make. Also my goodsire the Earl Cospatrick."

Moubray shrugged, and rode back. The Scots waited.

After a little delay a simple knight spurred out to them. He announced that the King's Grace could by no means hold speech with rebels but that he would permit his brother, the lord Duke Robert of Normandy, to listen to their pleas and representations — for the Prince Duncan's sake.

With that they had to be content.

Back at Malcolm's stance, the King declared that he had expected no better, that he washed his hands of the entire business. He would challenge Rufus to battle. But Cospatrick claimed that the English reaction was good enough and that they could talk as well with Robert as with his brother, better perhaps. So long as their terms reached William it mattered not who carried them. Margaret agreed, and when her husband told her that nothing would make him speak with any of them, she said that *she* would go with her brother and Cospatrick. They had talked with Robert before and found him able to see reason, had they not?

The King acceded, shrugging, but asserted that they

would waste their breath; but to tell the Normans that *he* preferred fighting to talking.

So Maldred rode back with the reconstituted truce-party consisting of the Queen, Cospatrick, Edgar, Duncan and himself. Out to meet them came Moubray again, with Robert Courthose, looking older and distinctly dissipated, with some others. The Duke at least seemed somewhat put out at seeing Margaret.

Cospatrick took charge, from the start. "Greetings, my lord Duke," he called. "I rejoice to see you well and survived the perils of sea and storm! And through you we salute your brother, King William."

Robert nodded. "Yes. I thank you. And greet the Queen's Highness. But — I do not see King Malcolm."

"He will join us if King William does. But he would have us to declare to you that he would himself prefer to resolve our differences with the sword rather than in talk."

"So why are you here, my lord?"

"Because *I* prefer speech to bloodshed!" the Queen said strongly. "As, I think do you, my lord Duke?"

"Perhaps, lady. But . . . the speech has to be to some effect."

"Certainly."

"We bring proposals of sufficient effect," Cospatrick went on. "Prince Edgar of England, here, offers much. My liege-lord Malcolm is prepared to make suitable terms with yours. And even I, in my humble state, can make my contribution. If you can do likewise."

"We — or my brother's Highness — need to make no concessions, my lord," Robert returned. "We hold all in our hands."

"Do you, sir — do you? I suggest that you look behind you! You are a long way from home. I have a fresh army here. But think you that is all I have? All Tweeddale and Teviotdale and the Forest, all Liddesdale and Eskdale and the March, is mine, not only this Lothian. Many men, many mounted mossmen, to assail your flank on your homeward march. If I give the word. Then Cumbria — my son Dolfin, yonder, is Earl of Cumbria. I see that you have Sir Robert de Moubray there, who sits in my earldom of Northumbria. Ask him what the Cumbrians can do. If we do not talk here, like reasonable men, thus we fight. And whether you flee home thereafter, defeated, or march home victorious, you have that to face. Myself, I would not relish it."

Robert Courthose did not answer that. He turned in his saddle, to confer low-voiced with Moubray.

Margaret spoke again. "My lords, need we talk such foolishness? When all may better be settled amicably. My royal husband is prepared to make the same terms as to fealties with King William as he did with your royal sire. Is that not sufficient? And he will no longer seek to support the claims of my dear brother here to the English throne — since the Prince Edgar himself is prepared to resign all such." And she turned to her brother.

The reluctant Atheling managed both to shrug and nod at the same time. "I have here a paper," he said flatly. "In it, I make resignation, for myself and my heirs, for all time, of my lawful rights to the throne of my ancestors. It is William's, if so be he returns now whence he has come, without bloodshed. And restores to me my properties in Normandy. I can do no more."

Again silence.

Duncan spoke up. "My lord Duke, your royal brother has in the past honoured me with his friendship, released me from hostageship, even created me knight. In this coil I remain his true friend. I urge that he does not draw sword now. And I promise that what endeavour I may make, now and hereafter, will not falter in his favour and honest interest."

"Well spoken!" his father-in-law cried cheerfully. "So say I. On my soul, I would even agree to swear fealty to William for my earldom of Northumbria again!" And he grinned wolfishly at Moubray. "Go tell your brother so."

Robert looked from one to the other assessingly, and when Moubray began to speak angrily, cut him short with a chop of his hand.

"Wait," he said to his party, and reining round, spurred his mount back to the main array.

The two truce groups sat facing each other three or four yards apart, in mutual disesteem, only Cospatrick apparently at ease, Margaret relapsed into withdrawn silence.

They had to wait quite some time before the Duke came riding back. He spoke even before he had halted his horse, almost relievedly.

"The King's Grace is prepared to consider the pleas you put forward. He will see the King Malcolm."

"Good," Cospatrick answered. "Only — we make no pleas. We treat."

"Call it what you will, man. Fetch Malcolm."

"We do not fetch the High King of Scots, sir . . ." Cospatrick began, when Margaret intervened.

"I shall go bring him," she said quietly.

Maldred went with her.

They found the King less than grateful, almost truculent. "I bowed no knee to the Bastard of Normandy," he declared. "I will not do so for this puppy of a son!"

"Do no more than for his father, Malcolm," the Queen said. "It will not hurt you to do as much. That is all that is required. Now that William has conceded thus far."

"I will offer fealty only for my lands in England."

"Do that, then. Pray God it will suffice . . ."

So they rode forward again. But when Malcolm saw no sign of Rufus coming out from his host to meet him, he reined up and would go no further. So they waited, half-way out to the others. Then, after a few moments, a group moved out from the English front, under the royal standard. These came half-way to their own truce-party and there halted. Snorting, Malcolm rode a hundred yards or so further. Rufus did the same. Neither was going to be seen waiting for the other.

At length they were able to make their arrivals exactly at the same time.

William Rufus was a red fox of a man, narrow-featured, lean, suspicious-looking, bearing little resemblance either to his father or his brother. He wore magnificent armour of gold-plates, and a gilt helmet surrounded by the jewelled fraises, or strawberry-leaves, of a crown. Facing him, Malcolm Canmore seemed to resemble the hulking boar held above him as standard, grizzled head bare. They weighed each other up warily.

"You invaded my realm," Rufus jerked, at length.

"You invade mine, with less cause," Malcolm gave back. "For the earldom of Northumbria, which I entered, belongs by right of birth to my cousin here, Cospatrick."

"That I deny. And I cannot *invade* a realm of which I am overlord."

"If you are overlord here, prove it!"

"I came to do so. Then my brother told me that you would speak, make representations, renew your broken allegiance." William had difficulty with his spirited horse, which sidled continually.

Margaret spoke "I greet you, King William. It is good and suitable that you and my royal husband should speak together not as enemies but as Christian neighbours. How is my good friend, the Archbishop Lanfranc, whom I heard was ill?"

"Poorly, lady — but poorly. But I have not come here to discuss the health of clerks!"

Margaret swallowed this snub, with only an inclination of the head. "I am sorry to hear of the noble Archbishop's sickness. I pray for him — as no doubt do you, my lord King. He was a tower of strength to your father's throne."

"No doubt. Now to business."

"As you will. King Malcolm owns twelve vills of land in your English shire of Huntingdon. Of these he has for some time been denied the revenues. He desires that these be fully restored to him. Before proceeding further. He may not beseech them at your hand, lord King — so I do so, that all may be eased."

Rufus looked from one to the other, seeking to fathom this peculiar situation. "Yes, yes," he acceded. "The lands and revenues shall be restored."

"I thank you. You have my brother, the Prince Edgar's offer of resignation of his claims? And his request for the return of his Normandy lands?"

"Yes. This also I accede."

"That is well." She looked at Edgar, who edged his horse forward and held out his paper to Rufus without a word.

Equally wordless that man took it, and without glancing at the writing, handed it to one of his attendants for scrutiny.

Prince Duncan raised his voice. "I greet you well, my lord King."

"Ah, yes — and I you." The first hint of cordiality sounded in William's voice. Unmarried, he was believed to favour the company of young men to that of women.

Cospatrick spoke. "What of Northumbria, my lord King?"

"Nothing!" Rufus snapped. He turned to Malcolm. "Well?"

His fellow-monarch shrugged. "I make the same oath which I gave to your father — none other. I make fealty for my lands, held of you." He raised his hand. "This I swear."

The other blinked. "And . . . and . . . ?"

"If you would have it, your enemies are my enemies. That was it. That is all." And without another word or any valedictory salutation, he tugged his garron's head round and rode off alone. Taken by surprise, his standard-bearer hurried after him.

The rest of them eyed each other, and William, who chewed at his thin moustache. There was a pregnant silence, broken presently by Cospatrick.

"My castle of Dunbar stands yonder, Highness," he said. "You are welcome to my poor hospitality. And we could, perhaps, discuss Northumbria in comfort."

"I thank you — no!" Rufus answered, scowling. And he too rode back whence he had come, his people turning to follow, tongues busy.

Margaret looked unhappy. "Will it suffice?" she asked of Maldred, low-voiced. "I did the best that I could, over the English lands. Malcolm gives not one inch, placates nothing. Will this William accept what he said?"

"His father did, at Abernethy. And his brother did, at Ecclesbreac," Maldred mentioned.

"He will," Cospatrick asserted. "Short of battle, he can do nothing else — and he will not fight now, I think, having got thus far. He knows this is a bad place for battle. He will turn back. With ill grace — but he will go."

Duncan said, "Shall I go speak with him? Assure him that he has made none so ill a bargain? One day, it may be *me* he has to bargain with!"

The Queen looked at him thoughtfully.

"Do that, lad," the Earl said. "And remind him that so long as Northumbria remains a contention between us, he will sleep less peaceably than he might!"

From his expression as he rode off, the younger man would not convey that message.

He did not return to the Scots camp until late that evening, distinctly drink-taken. But he declared that King William would march south in the morning.

Malcolm neither thanked his firstborn nor showed relief.

26

IF SCOTLAND HAD a major escape in 1091, she was less
fortunate in the year following. Magnus of Norway,
smarting from his previous repulse, made a renewed and
large-scale assault on the Hebrides at mid-summer, this
time first having come to an arrangement with the Orkney
brothers whereby their domains were left in peace and in
return they did not oppose him or involve themselves. As
a result Malcolm was grievously handicapped, for he had
never possessed a real battle-fleet and in any war at sea he
required allies with many ships. His nominal representative in the Western Isles was the Earl Somerled mac
Gillaciaran of Colonsay; but unfortunately he was a
kinsman of the Orkney earls and made only a token
resistance to the Norse invaders. Malcolm was largely
dependent on the birlinns and longships of the west coast
Highland chiefs to transport and back up his forces, and
found them inadequate. One by one Magnus took over
the islands, great and small, without major battle, Iona
itself being one of the first to fall, the monks fleeing to the
mainland. As this process continued, the mainland chiefs
grew ever less inclined to provide men and ships for their
Lowland and south-country monarch, who normally never
looked in their direction.

Maldred was only indirectly involved in this protracted
campaign, for the King ordered Cospatrick and his forces
to occupy Galloway, to ensure that the manpower, and
especially the fleet, of that province was not used against
him by the Earl Erland, the governor; and also to threaten
Man, where Godfrey Crovan had died and his son Laoman
was now king and might think to join Magnus. It was a
very large area to cover, from the Solway up as far as Ayr,
and cut up by arms of the sea. Maldred was given the
northern section to watch.

It was in August that, judiciously and no doubt
well-informedly, William Rufus struck. For once, Cospatrick had no warning, deep in Galloway. The English
poured into Cumbria in overwhelming strength from

three different points, carrying all before them. The first Cospatrick knew of it was when his son Dolfin arrived at Kirk Cuthbert's Town in haste and alarm, seeking his father, to declare that William himself was approaching Caer-luel with a huge army.

Cospatrick wasted no time upbraiding his son for leaving his post, but sent for Maldred and every man he could bring, gathered his forces from all over Galloway, and marched south.

But it was of no avail. William had taken Caer-luel and was holding its fortified position in major strength. Cospatrick, never foolhardy, halting at the Esk, recognised that he could not retake the place, plus the general hopelessness of the present situation. He had lost Cumbria meantime, as Malcolm was in process of losing the Hebrides. Presumably William had decided that his claims to Northumbria should thus be countered.

Heedfully he withdrew his forces, to establish a defendable line in Liddesdale and over the Cheviot passes into Teviotdale and Tweeddale, in case William had further ambitions. It was a long line to hold, and taxed his manpower to the utmost.

The news, when it reached Malcolm in Argyll, confirmed in that man the grim recognition that the fates, for the meantime, were against him. The Hebrides were only of nominal and prestige value to him; and it looked as though his whole kingdom might be endangered. He should be elsewhere. He sent messengers to Magnus Barefoot on Islay, seeking peace terms — and was informed by that monarch that nothing would more gladden his heart. All that was required was a cession of the Hebrides to Norway outright. That acceded and their long-standing friendship would be unconfined.

Cursing, Malcolm signed away his Western Isles — and that, in effect, meant also his north-western mainland seaboard, for it was dominated from the sea and cut off from elsewhere by endless mountains. Then, with the autumn colours beginning to stain the Highlands with their annual miracle, he hurried his army back to Fortrenn.

William Rufus did not attack further that year. Indeed he departed for the south before very long, amidst rumours that he was ill — he had never been a man of robust health. But he left behind a large garrison at

Caer-luel, and many artisans building a mighty Norman fortress-castle, of the kind his father had erected on the Tyne, as indication that he was there to stay. Also major occupation forces at strategic points all over Cumbria.

In one disastrous season, Scotland had lost thousands of square miles of national territory, however tenuously held, to north and south.

*　　*　　*

In consequence, with the country in a state of serious unrest, Malcolm did something he seldom troubled with — he held a council-of-the-realm. And, to the surprise of all, he held it at a venue never formerly used for the like, the ancient Pictish fort of Dunedin, skied on top of its soaring rock above the small town of Edinburgh in the centre of Lothian. It was a most odd place for such a gathering, in almost every way, windy and bleak in the late October weather, with only tentage as used for campaigning, as shelter, to cover the attending nobles and churchmen amidst the crumbling ramparts. Admittedly they were to be quartered and fed down in the cashel or monastery of St. Ninian, at the foot of the narrow, mile-long spine of hillside which led from the lofty summit, on the east, to the base of Arthur's Chair. But it was an inconvenient location for the great majority of those present — who of course came from across the Forth and the Scottish Sea, and looked upon Lothian as barely in Scotland anyway, handy as it was for Cospatrick and his people. Actually, that man was grimly amused by the King's choice of Edinburgh for the occasion, asserting to Maldred that it was in the nature of a warning and gesture at himself, indicating that he should watch his step and not think that he was master of all south of Forth.

Almost one hundred attended the council, few in very cheerful or uncritical frame of mind. Scotland's fortunes were at their lowest ebb for years and scapegoats might well be looked for. Prince Duncan was not invited, but came with Cospatrick's Lothian and Borders group nevertheless. Maldred had not expected to see the Queen there, for she had been unwell — indeed while he had been away in Galloway, Magda had been at Dunfermline aiding in nursing Margaret, her verdict being that the Queen was suffering from nothing more nor less than sheer exhaustion and lack of strength, through malnutrition arising from her everlasting fasting, penances and night-long prayings. At this council she had to be helped to her chair beside that of the King by her sons Edward and Ethelred, looking heartbreakingly fragile and wasted.

Malcolm strode in, late, to a flourish of trumpets, but otherwise opened the proceedings at once and without ceremony. He called on Bishop Fothad of St. Andrews, the Chancellor.

That amiable old man uttered a brief prayer for God's blessings on their deliberations, then declared that this high council was called to consider the present unfortunate state of the realm, in respect of the aggressions of the Kings of England and Norway; and to advise the King's Highness as to how best these wrongs could be righted and redressed. Also what steps were necessary to prevent further incursions against them. But before the discussion, there was a matter of procedure. As all present knew, the Earl of Fife was premier earl and mormaor of Scotland, and entitled to lead in debate and make the first vote in council. Duncan MacDuff had died, full of years; but unfortunately he had been predeceased by his only son Dufagan (the drunken brawl in which the latter died did not merit mention). Next in line was Dufagan's infant son Constantine. But it was inconvenient and unsuitable that the realm's chief earldom, and support of the crown, should be in the hands of a helpless child. The King's Highness therefore deemed it right and proper to appoint as Earl of Fife, until the child Constantine mac Dufagan came of full age, his own well-beloved and esteemed son, the Prince Ethelred, Abbot of Dunkeld and Primate. This for the information of the council here present.

Eyebrows were raised at this announcement, but none were competent to question the decision of the *Ard Righ* on the matter save one of the other *righ* or mormaors, and these all held their peace. Cospatrick, who might have commented, was not one of the *righ*, his earldoms of Dunbar and March not being mortuaths but minted specially for him, south of Forth. But one voice was upraised, nevertheless, and few there would have asserted that its owner had no interest or right to speak.

"I make protest," Duncan mac Malcolm declared strongly. "As eldest son of the King, I should have all along been Prince of Strathclyde. That has been denied me for no good reason, and given to one of my later half-brothers, Edward. Now another, more junior still, who has already been given Dunkeld and the primacy, receives Fife. If it is to go to any of the King's kin, I say that it should go to me."

There was a murmur of agreement from many, led by the speaker's father-in-law.

"The matter is not for discussion," Malcolm grated. "Proceed to the business of this council, my lord Bishop."

Margaret hung her head, hands clutching each other.

"Yes, Highness," Fothad said hurriedly. "This of the realm. The loss by invasion of Cumbria and the Hebrides. A grievous matter calling for urgent redress. What is to be done, my lords?"

A medley of voices were raised at that general query.

Malcolm smashed a fist on the arm of his chair. "Quiet! This is a council not a cattle-fair! Speak in due order, earls first."

Since Ethelred, now of Fife, was scarcely competent to advise on national security, Angus, the oldest mormaor present, spoke up.

"What is there to do but muster again and march?" he demanded. "Firstly into Northumbria and Cumbria. We can do no other. The greatest army we have ever fielded. And whilst we are at this, be building ships. To win back the Hebrides. We should have done this long since — built a great fleet."

There was some acclaim for this straightforward if simplistic proposal, but there was dissent also. Martacus, Mormaor of Mar — he still refused the title of Earl — voiced it.

"Ships take a long time to build. And require trained masters and crews, especially ships-of-war. It would be years before we could seek to retake the Hebrides. And why should one more invasion of England prove successful? Your Highness has invaded times without number and achieved nothing."

"Save booty and plunder!" Maldred put in — and gained the first laughter of the day, although he had not meant it humorously.

Cospatrick took that up. "The Lord Maldred is right. If there is to be invasion again, then it must be better led and controlled," he asserted. "Always this of burning and raping and looting is the prime concern, not conquest of territory or lasting advantage. I say that we must have better leadership."

There was tense silence at this pronouncement, for all knew that it was the monarch himself who most favoured the looting and rapine.

Maldred, with little to lose in the matter, backed that. "Always our forces, after the first days across Tweed, are more concerned with driving back cattle, captives and gear, than in fighting the enemy. Any new invasion would require to be led otherwise, to achieve any success."

"Hark at my heroic warrior cousins!" the King exclaimed. "The Earl Cospatrick, you will all recollect, has scarcely been prominent in the lead of our arms, these past years! Or ever. Perhaps he will lead the next expedition, Maldred of Atholl aiding him? And see how they fare!"

"I could conceive worse arrangements, with Cumbria to win back."

"Ah, yes — you are touched on the raw wound now, cousin. You would not fight before. But, Cumbria — you would draw the sword for Cumbria!"

There was some exclamation and comment at that, cut into by an upraised voice from the improvised dais — the Queen's voice; and it was surprisingly strong and clear despite her frail appearance.

"My lords — already you talk of war and the sword! Surely we have learned that little advantage lies that way, only bloodshed, death, loss — and Norman success at the end. So it has been each time. In arms and numbers they are stronger than we are — it is as simple as that. Surely the time has come to attempt other persuasion than the sword?"

"In the end it is the sword which decides," her husband said flatly.

She laid a hand on his arm. "In the end it is *God* who decides," she amended. "Let us seek His aid sooner rather than later."

"*You* do that," Malcolm told her, grimly. "You are good at praying, lass. We shall say Amen — but call also upon stout hearts, strong arms and cold steel!"

"But not wits?" she asked. "God gave us wits to use, did He not?"

"What mean you?"

"My lords, I am only a weak woman — but it seems to

me that this King William can be dealt with better than by using arms weaker than his own. He is not the strong man his father was. He has two brothers, one older than he, who resent his power. He has lost his wisest adviser — my good friend the Archbishop Lanfranc, who has gone to God. And he, William, we hear to be ill . . ."

"All of which says that now is the time to strike!" Malcolm interrupted.

Patiently she shook her head. "Rather that it is the time to use our wits. By his armed attack and occupation of Cumbria, which was never English territory, William has put himself grievously in the wrong. In the sight of all men. Use that, I say. He calls himself Lord Paramount of Scotland. He is not that, all here know — but use it against him. Write to him. Declare that *he* has broken faith. Declare that fealty is a two-edged sword. Your oath of fealty to him requires that he, in turn, supports you, does it not? Does not steal from you, as he has done. Demand redress — or your oath is nullified. And, at the same time, write to the Pope . . ."

"The Pope of Rome! A God's Name — why that?"

"Because the Pope presides over the only court in Christendom superior to William's. Even the Conqueror heeded the Pontiff. Moreover, this Rufus needs the Pope's goodwill. A new Archbishop of Canterbury falls to be appointed. Rufus wishes to have the Norman, Bishop Anselm of Bec, appointed. But we know that Bishop Odo, now in France, seeks the Pope's preferment, supported by the King of France. Probably also by Robert of Normandy. His uncle is the last man William would wish to be Archbishop. So he will not desire to offend the Pope."

"But — why should the Pope heed *me*? He owes me nothing."

"You have done much for Holy Church, my lord King. More than Rufus has ever done. Have you not built the great new minster at Dunfermline? Made grants to St. Andrews? Encouraged and succoured pilgrims? Lanfranc will have kept His Holiness informed of all these . . ."

"*Your* work, Margaret — not mine."

"*Ours*, my lord. Now is the time to remind Rome." Her voice had weakened with this long speech, and having to raise it to carry against the flapping of the tentage in the breeze of that lofty place. But she summoned a new surge of urgency. "Moreover, you have something to offer. In the very area you make protest over — Strathclyde. The distant and decayed see of Whithorn, which King MacBeth held was Columban and the archdiocese of York claimed belonged to Durham, and therefore Rome. Offer that back. It is not important to you, little to pay in return for Cumbria."

There was a hush as men considered that, its ingenuity, its subtle persuasion, its likely effectiveness. Some, like Maldred, saw it all as one more weakening of the Celtic Church, one more betrayal. Especially, for the King of Scots actually to appeal to Rome. But most, undoubtedly, only saw it as a most telling weapon to be used against William Rufus, and cared little or nothing for the merely spiritual allegiance of a small and remote area of Galloway already under the temporal sway of the Orkney earls.

Cospatrick was the first to speak. "Excellent!" he cried. "Most excellent! The Queen's Highness has the wits of us all! This could trouble Rufus more than any armed invasion. It would, likewise, bring in the Archbishop Thomas of York, and the Bishop of Durham, on the side of reconciliation. And so affect Northumbria also. I say that Her Highness is right. Send the two letters, my lord King. Forthwith. And ensure that each learns what is in the other!"

There were cries of support. Margaret had at least succeeded in driving a wedge between Maldred and Cospatrick.

"It would give us time," Malcolm conceded. "Time for greater, stronger muster."

Another voice was raised, new to most there. The Mormaor Colin of the Mearns was dead and his son Malpender reigned in his stead.

"My lord King, there is more to give you pause, I think, in this of invasion, than merely Rufus of England. My mortuath abuts the Mounth. There is strong word coming from beyond the Mounth, from Druim-Alban, that revolt is seething there. That, after the failure of the Hebridean campaign, many chiefs and lords of the Highland West are murmuring against Your Highness. They say that you deserted them, left them to face Magnus of Norway unsupported, that you are a Lowland king with no concern for the Highlands. They threaten to rise against you . . ."

"Fools!" Malcolm cried. "Ingrates! They did little enough to aid against Magnus. They talk, that is all, these

Highlandmen. They cannot hurt me. Mere idle threats."

"Perhaps, Highness. But the word says more than talk. Your own royal brother is concerned — the Prince Donald. The word is that *he* will head the disaffected chiefs in your overthrow. Either of the Highland parts or of all your kingdom. He has always claimed that he should have had the crown, being, being . . ." He left the word "legitimate" to be inserted by his hearers. "If you were to march into England, Highness," Malpender ended, "there could be war at home. Donald Ban might steal your throne."

There was uproar in the council. The King had to beat his chair for quiet.

"Donald is a weakling and no fighter," he declared. "I am in no danger from him."

"Nevertheless, Highness, I would take due heed of this," the Earl Madach of Atholl put in. "I have heard the same word. There is much unrest in the West. Atholl marches with Mamlorn, where Donald Ban lives. There is much coming and going, I hear. And not only from the West but from Moray. Where MacBeth's kin still rule."

Silence followed that. Madach was a solid man and no scaremonger. And any mention of the great northern mortuaths of Moray and Ross, remote but unswervingly hostile to the present regime, was apt to cause something of a blight.

Maldred looked over at Duncan, who had for years been brought up by Donald Ban, and wondered.

"We shall watch my brother Donald, then, as well as the Highland chiefs, never fear," Malcolm assured. "Likewise Moray. But these are as nothing to the English. Bishop Fothad — you will word these letters to be sent, for my signature and seal — no doubt the Queen aiding you. Meanwhile, we shall muster, partial muster. Not at Dunsinane, but here in Lothian. That the news of it reaches William Rufus the more surely. Leaves him in no doubt that we are ready to march — if he fails to respond in fair fashion to my letter. March south, not north against rebels. Aye — and something else for his spies to report. Donald's also, perhaps. I intend to build a mighty fortress here. On this rock of Dunedin. That is in part why I hold this council here. The Normans build great castles on the Tyne and at Caer-luel, to threaten us, to command the routes into Northumbria and Cumbria. I shall do the same, only a deal better. On this rock shall rise a fortress which will make the Normans' castles seem like bairns' houses! And another on the rock of Stirling. But this one first. Never again shall the English march up through Lothian unthreatened. Forby, others shall take heed also." The King did not actually look at Cospatrick, but few doubted his meaning.

There was a buzz of reaction and conjecture.

Malcolm rose. "This council is ended," he said. "There is food and drink for all down at the cashel. Where my wife intends that a new abbey shall arise." He grimaced. "We shall tell the Pope that also!" He turned and strode out, as unceremoniously as he had entered.

"How say you to that?" Cospatrick asked Maldred. "I wondered why Malcolm chose Edinburgh for this council — which was no council! It is to be a fist shaken in *my* face, I think. As much against me as against the Normans."

"Or against your good-son, Duncan? Or both of you!"

Cospatrick grinned mirthlessly. "We shall see," he said.

27

IT WAS A strange experience to be riding down through Northumbria and the English North neither burning nor slaying nor yet opposed, indeed almost in holiday mood — although in Malcolm Canmore's company such an atmosphere was difficult to sustain. Nevertheless it was a resounding and practically unique occasion, apt for some sort of celebration. Never in living memory, or well beyond that, had a Scottish monarch progressed in style and fair company peaceably through the English countryside, all clad in their finest, banners flying but not a gleam of naked steel in sight.

William Rufus had indeed made a fair response to Malcolm's letter and the carefully leaked details of that sent to the Pope — although he had taken his time about it. But there was reason for that. All England knew, and by now most of Scotland too, that King William believed that he was dying. He had taken to his bed at Gloucester, and was in the process of putting his earthly realm in order so that he might be better received at his entry into the heavenly one — as his father, and so many another, had done before him. Just what his ailment might be remained unspecified; but it was sufficient for him to require the most influential of prayers — including the Pope's, naturally — and to send a safe-conduct to Scotland with the request that Malcolm should come in person, with his grievances, to a dying man's bedside, so that all their differences might be settled in holy amity and goodwill. Also, he suggested, that the saintly Queen Margaret should likewise pray for him. Nothing was actually said in the letter to Malcolm about the return of Cumbria, but since that was the main issue between them, surely it could be taken that a settlement was envisaged.

So the colourful and mainly cheerful throng rode southwards through the early August richness, with the English scene looking at its verdant and bountiful fairest — where it was not still a charred desert from the Conqueror's politic devastations, that is. The safe-conduct had stipulated the exact route to be taken, which first was on the east side, through Northumbria, not west through Cumbria as would have been shorter and more appropriate. Robert de Moubray, Earl of Northumbria, had met them at the Aln, with a large company, apparently to act as escort, without contributing notably to the gaiety. The two parties kept fairly carefully apart throughout.

For that matter, the Scots themselves were apt to ride in separate groups — Malcolm's own, Cospatrick's, and a gay and noisy younger company, consisting of three of the princes, Edward, Edgar and Ethelred, and the younger of the mormaors and thanes. Edmund, the black sheep, was none knew where. The Queen was not present, having been with difficulty brought to Edinburgh from her summer-time hermitage in Forfar Loch, in no state of health for lengthy travel. She would superintend the building work on the rock of Dunedin, no doubt more interested in the small personal oratory or chapel she was erecting there than in the fortifications. Duncan was travelling with them, but very noticeably avoiding his father and half-brothers and riding with Cospatrick. Maldred was in some measure able to bridge the gaps between the parties, through his friendship with Prince Edward and his link with Madach in the King's group.

Cospatrick frequently proved to be a better guide than did his enemy Moubray, his years of roaming England as a wandering friar giving him the advantage. He was also instrumental in causing the cavalcade to call in at Durham, where he carefully maintained relations with Bishop William and Prior Turgot — and where, on the 11th of August, he actually persuaded Malcolm to assist in laying the foundations-stones of part of the new cathedral to be erected there.

Turning south-westwards at York, they threaded the dales and climbed over the great moors into Mercia, and so down through the Peak country, to the valleys of the Dove and the Tame and the Avon, and finally through the pleasant Malvern Hills. It made a long journey, but there was no especial hurry and it made a welcome change for most of the travellers.

But any pleasure there was in it stopped at Gloucester. The place was an armed camp and not a friendly one. Indeed the Scots were halted peremptorily, well back from the city with its great Benedictine abbey, wherein William was lodging and where a new minster was being built. In no respectful fashion they were instructed to camp and wait; and when Malcolm demanded to be taken into the presence of King William, at once, he was informed that the King's Grace was not available, was in fact away hunting in the Forest of Dean. When they expressed astonishment at this activity on the part of a man so gravely ill, they were assured that the monarch no longer felt himself to be dying, or in any danger, God and His saints having suddenly effected an all but miraculous cure.

Moubray rode on to investigate, but the Scots had no option but to wait as instructed.

They waited, in fact, to some tune, no word reaching them before night-fall, no indication that their presence was acknowledged or even known. Next morning it was the same. By mid-day, Malcolm's offence and resentment knew no bounds. He ordered all his party to mount, brushing aside the protests of the screen of guards they had acquired, to ride into the city.

But long before they reached the stretch of Roman wall which marked Gloucester's central area, a sufficiently large and determined company of armed men came to halt them, curtly ordering them back whence they had come. With Malcolm's fury exploding in awesome fashion,

Moubray of Northumbria materialised from the midst, in most evident discomfort. After some throat-clearing, he announced that he was commanded by the renowned William, by God's grace King of the English, to declare that he, the King, did not afford audience upon demand to any, especially to rebels and faith-breakers. If there was any issue which Malcolm of Scotland wished for decision, it could be placed before the suitable English court for judgement. Meantime, the Scots would return to their camp and await instructions.

Maldred, in all the years that he had known his cousin, had never seen him in such raging anger; indeed he feared that Malcolm was going to take some sort of fit or seizure. Thickly, incoherently, he cursed and swore, all but rigid with inexpressible choler and indignation. When even choking words failed him. Cospatrick it was who reached over, first to grip the royal arm, then, when there was no reaction, to take the bridle of the King's horse and to turn the beast about and lead it back whence they had come, the monarch seeming almost dazed in the saddle. Without a word spoken, the entire Scots party reined round and followed.

For an hour or so Malcolm shut himself up alone in his campaigning tent and not even Cospatrick nor any of his sons dared to disturb him. Oddly, it was the Prince Duncan, who had little cause to love his father, who proposed to do something positive about the situation. He would go back himself, he said, alone, and see King William. They had been friends. Try to resolve this folly and indignity. William might listen to him. He would try to make him perceive that this course would serve no good to any, that only hatred and evil could come of it and both kingdoms suffer.

Cospatrick, who now had taken charge, did not see his son-in-law as likely to be successful, but he did not seek to hold him back.

At length Malcolm emerged from his tent, set-faced but calm. He gave brief orders for camp to be struck immediately. They would march for Scotland forthwith.

None sought to argue, although doubts were expressed as to whether the English would allow this. Malcolm heeded none; nor would he wait for his eldest son's return.

They rode within the hour. The guards did not appear to

399

know what to do; but they did not seek to restrain them.

For long the King, riding alone and silent, did not look back; but others did. There was no sign of pursuit, so sign even of Duncan following. They were well into the night-shrouded Malvern foothills before they camped. Malcolm remained unapproachable.

That was a strange, tense, journey home, so very different from their outwards travel, with a brooding aura of wrath and humiliation hanging over all and vengeance the word most often to be heard. Not from the King; indeed few words of any sort did he utter in those long days of hard riding — for he led them northwards at a fierce pace, telling on man and beast. They followed the same route as they had come — and as William's safe-conduct had stipulated — and never once were they held up or interfered with. Nor did the missing Duncan put in an appearance — nor his father ask after him. They had taken ten days to reach Gloucester from Tweed, but they returned in six, some of the most joyless and dreary days in Maldred's experience. Even Cospatrick was subdued, preoccupied.

Malcolm broke his grim silence only at Dunbar, but briefly, refusing to consider halting there for the night.

"Muster your every last man, cousin," he said harshly. "In all Lothian and the March, in the dales and the Forest. Wait for me here."

Cospatrick, indeed all, had anticipated this. "When?" he asked, simply.

"Soon. So soon as I can gather the greatest host ever to leave Scotland!"

Without a word of farewell, the King rode on for Edinburgh.

*　　*　　*

It was late October before Malcolm had sufficiently great an army assembled to satisfy his hatred, and marched southwards again. Certainly it was a mighty host which crossed Tweed fords, and took hours to do so, with Cospatrick's contingent of about four thousand, amounting in all to almost twenty-five thousand men. For this was to be no raid, but war, no mere attempt to extend Scotland's boundaries to the Tyne or the Tees even, nor yet to win back Cumbria; but a determined invasion of

England, to seek battle and settle accounts with William Rufus. They would march as far as they had to, to achieve that end.

From the first, then, a very different atmosphere prevailed in all ranks, with little of the carefree high spirits and cheerful anticipation of sport and loot and profit which normally characterised these expeditions. The King was at his grimmest, so that even his sons Edward and Edgar tended to avoid his company — Ethelred was left behind on this occasion, it being no work for the priestly. There was to be no looting and burning, no spreading devastation over the English countryside, no relaxation of a stern discipline and fairly rigid formation — any infringement of which was to be punished by hanging. When, a short distance into Northumbria, some of Cospatrick's Teviotdale mosstroopers were rash enough to allow their Border instincts and accustomed habits to prevail, in the sacking and rape of a small hamlet in the Till valley, a score of them were promptly strung-up on the nearest convenient trees, as indication of the royal mood and authority. There were no further breaches of discipline meantime.

Strangely, they met with no opposition. No doubt, with the Scots muster so predictable and having taken almost two months, the English would have received ample warning; so it could be taken that Rufus was not taken by surprise. He would be choosing his own time and battle-ground, presumably.

Cospatrick, from the start, sought to establish himself not only as second-in-command but as chief military adviser to the King, making no secret of the fact that he saw his veteran monarch rather as a captain of reiving bands than as an experienced general of armies. Needless to say, Malcolm saw it all differently. Moreover, the senior mormaors tended to resent Cospatrick's assumptions and influence. So there were divided counsels in the high command. Not that Malcolm appeared to care. He was a man alone, preoccupied with vengeance, ignoring his lieutenants and sons most of the time. One of his sons, the eldest, he did not ignore — for Duncan had never returned from Gloucester to Scotland and his wife. Whether this was from choice or he was again being held as a hostage, none knew.

By-passing the great castle of Bamburgh, Cospatrick's

old home, and where Malcolm had passed much of his boyhood, held against them now and impregnable, the army reached the Aln before the first reactions of the enemy became evident. Near Alnwick town, four miles inland from the mouth, where the river became bridgeable, the Scots scouts sent back the report that the bridge was held against them, but that a party waited on the far side under a white flag, and were asking for the King of Scots.

Malcolm and his leadership-group rode forward.

A company of armoured knights sat their horses at the far bridge-end. As well as the flag-of-truce they bore other banners, the largest of which, as Cospatrick pointed out, was his own rightful emblem of Northumbria. But they did not recognise Sir Robert de Moubray there. Drawing rein at their own bridge-end, a Scots spokesman shouted to ask who was there and what they might want with the High King of Scots?

Two men rode some way nearer. One called back. "I am Morel, nephew and steward to Robert, Earl of Northumbria. And this is Sir Geoffrey en Gulevant, Lieutenant Governor. My lord Earl requests audience of Your Highness."

"To what purpose?" Malcolm himself asked curtly.

"He desires to know your intentions, Sire, on behalf of King William, and submit proposals."

"I will put my proposals to King William myself — with my sword in my hand!" Malcolm gave back. "If he will present himself. Where is he?"

"The King's Grace has been marching north through Cleveland, Highness. He is now at Durham, moving on to Tyne. He has sent requesting my lord Earl to discover your reasons for bringing so great an armed host into his realm."

"If he needs others to ask such a question, then he is a fool as well as an insolent!" the King said. "He will discover from myself, in due course."

"No doubt, Sire. But he, King William, has authorised my uncle to discuss terms with you, whereby you may meet together and any differences be resolved without bloodshed. He has certain offers to make."

"Does he offer open apology, before all men, for the insults he laid upon me at Gloucester?"

"I know not, Sire. My lord Earl has not revealed to me

the terms of King William's message. Save that it concerns Northumbria and Cumbria."

"Why has your precious uncle not himself come to ask this, man? Instead of sending a steward to bespeak me!"

"He is at Alnmouth, my lord King. He is meantime stricken with a sickness. He believed that Your Grace would wish to hear King William's proposals from *his* lips rather than my humble ones."

"So he would have me, the King, ride to him at this Alnmouth? As insolent as his master!"

"Not so, Highness. But since he cannot ride to you . . . And it is not far to Alnmouth — but four miles. He offers you fullest hospitality."

Frowning, Malcolm looked at his lieutenants.

"No harm in going," Cospatrick said. "If we hear what Rufus is offering we may better gauge his intentions."

"It may be but a trick. To delay us," Angus objected. "To allow William to win closer. To gain a better field to fight on. Have Moubray fetched in a litter, if what he has to say is so important."

"Quicker to go to him, Father," Prince Edward put in.

"Yes, is it more comfortable to your royal dignity to sit here waiting for him, than to go there . . . ?" Cospatrick was asking, when they were interrupted. A thane from the rear pushed his way through the leaders' party, with a weary-looking, travel-worn courier in tow.

"A message from the Queen, Highness," he cried. "Ill tidings . . ."

The man blurted it out. The disaffected Highland chiefs had risen, on hearing that the King and his army had left Scotland, and they had been joined in revolt by the men of Moray and Ross and others hostile to the regime. They had taken Scone and Dunsinane and Stirling and were marching on Edinburgh. Donald Ban was at their head, supported by none other than the young Prince Edmund. The Queen had moved from the monastery of St. Ninian at Edinburgh up into the fortress of Dunedin. She urged the King's return to Scotland.

Much shaken by this news, Malcolm and those around him were momentarily at a loss. The King swore loud and long. His sons called for an immediate retiral; their mother might be in danger. Cospatrick declared that such would be folly at this stage, when they had Rufus prepared to talk terms. Settle with him first, gain back Cumbria and perhaps even Northumbria, then return and deal with the rebels. Donald Ban was no fighter anyway. It was unlikely that the revolt would come to anything, for these High-landers and Moraymen would soon be at each others' throats. Madach demurred. Many would support Donald Ban, considering that he should have been king. The Moraymen had remained on good terms with the Orkney earls, MacBeth's kinsmen. If *they* were to sail to their aid, possibly throw Galloway in against the King, this army might never win back to Scotland if it delayed now.

During this hurried debate the Englishmen waited at the other end of the bridge.

Malcolm made up his mind. They would go see Moubray and discover Rufus's proposals. Depending on what these were, he would decide whether to continue onwards, turn back for Scotland, or send only part of his force back.

When it was shouted to the waiting knights that the King of Scots would ride to Alnmouth, Morel called back that he was gratified. He advised, however, that they used the north bank of the river, not his side. It would cut off a series of bends and save time. They could ford the Aln back to the south side easily enough near the mouth. Malcolm agreed to this. But Madach, suspicious of trickery, suggested that they ought to move perhaps half of the army across this bridge meantime, in case it was all a delaying tactic, and whilst the King was away at Alnmouth the main English force might move up and seek to hold this river-line against them.

This was considered to be good sense, and as soon as the English party came trotting across the bridge, the Scots started moving in the opposite direction.

Most of the leadership group accompanied the King and their guides eastwards, plus a suitable escort of about seventy men. Madach was left in charge at the bridge, but Maldred went along with Cospatrick and the young princes, with the King.

At first the knight Morel sought to talk volubly with Malcolm; but getting little encouragement from that morose monarch, he presently gave up the attempt and rode on in silence. His colleague, Sir Geoffrey en Gulevant, had not opened his mouth throughout.

They cut inland from the river, through wet meadow-land mixed with scrub woodland, occasionally having to detour real marsh and fen. If this side was easier and quicker going, Maldred reckoned that the other must be bad indeed — although it did not look it from any distance. Presently, with the river swinging away to the north, from a slight eminence they could see the country opening before them to a wide and almost landlocked bay, into which, after a major meander, the Aln obviously emptied itself. The sea lay beyond. There was considerable denser woodland to cross before that bay was reached, however.

It was when they entered these woods, which appeared to flank both sides of the Aln, that Morel said they must turn down to the ford, to save following all the river's wide bend. It shallowed here, he assured. He explained that although the township of Alnmouth was on this north side of the estuary, his uncle was installed in the monastery on the south side, so they must cross.

Through the close woodland they rode down to the river. The ford proved to be not so very shallow, the water up to the horses' bellies; and wide too, fully eighty yards across. But Morel led the way in confidently enough, declaring that the monks used it constantly.

Maldred and Cospatrick, just behind the King and his two sons, were two-thirds of the way over when pandemonium erupted. Without warning a shower of arrows winged down upon the splashing Scots from both sides of the river and as horses reared and toppled, kicking and screaming, armed men by the hundred burst out of the cover of bushes and trees, swords, spears and axes in hand. Front and rear they hurled themselves into the water against the floundering company. Behind them mounted knights and men-at-arms appeared everywhere in the woodland.

Malcolm's horse was one of the first to fall, pierced by no fewer than five arrows, obviously the principal target. As the King was pitched head-long into the water, crowned helmet flying, the man Morel swiftly drew sword and slashed downwards, twice, thrice. A great gash opened on the victim's grizzled head and he sank below the surface, blood staining the current to join that of his mount.

Cospatrick was down too, an arrow through his throat, horse thrashing beside him. Reeling, staggering on the slippery pebbles of the bed, seeking to tug out the shaft, he gazed up at Maldred desperately. He tried to speak, could not, and pointed urgently instead, not at the King, nor where the King had been, nor at their betrayers, but at the two young princes, shocked, bewildered and trying to control their plunging, lashing mounts.

Maldred himself was unhurt, his horse likewise, having been part-hidden behind the others. His first impulse was to leap down to Cospatrick's aid, but the sheer command and authority in the dying man's eyes constrained him. Again the Earl stabbed a finger at the princes — his last act on this mortal scene, as his knees gave way and he collapsed into the swirling river.

Maldred sought to pull himself together. He found that he had drawn his sword. The King's body was drifting away slowly in the current, weighed down by its gold scale-armour. Clearly Malcolm was dead. Everywhere around was savage, hopeless fighting, Morel and Gulevant now turned and leading the attack from this south bank.

Dragging his terrified horse round, he raised his sword and made a furious slash at Gulevant — and had the satisfaction of seeing that knight's shoulder droop within his armour and his sword fall splashing from nerveless fingers. But with the men who swarmed out at them from this south bank almost reaching the princes, he recognised his duty, and Cospatrick's last command. Kicking his mount cruelly, he reined over to where Edward and Edgar were gazing about them helplessly.

"Come!" he shouted. "Nothing to be done here. Quickly. Back. We will . . . avenge them . . . later!"

Edward reacted, pulling his mount round. But Edgar merely stared, appalled.

Reaching out Maldred grabbed the young man's reins and jerked his beast to face the north bank. Across the river, and on that bank also, furious fighting was in progress, the remainder of the Scots party battling valiantly but hopelessly against overwhelming odds. Many had already fallen; the stony bed of a swiftly-running river could hardly have been worsened as a defensive stance — and the sloping river-bank little better. The Earl Dolfin of Cumbria and the Mormaor Malpender of the Mearns were seeking to rally the survivors into some sort of coherence, the former hampered by his brother, the young Cospatrick whom he had hoisted before him on his horse, clearly wounded sorely.

Maldred, splashing up, yelled for them all who could to close in behind him into some sort of formation, the nearest to a wedge that was possible in the circumstances. To cut their way back and out. Nothing more was possible here — although this surely was self-evident. He was the most experienced soldier there and automatically took charge. Malpender reined his mount over to Maldred's side, slashing down two men who sought to stop him. The two princes and Dolfin managed to pull in behind the older men, and those of the escort who could, ploughed their awkward way over, to fall in as tightly as possible at their backs, to create something like an arrowhead, for mutual defence, support and impetus.

Maldred did not wait for any late-comers or consolidation. Swinging his sword in figure-of-eight before him, he turned his beast's head half-left, upstream, spurring hard. This ran them into deeper water, leaving the ford's shallows; but at least it had the effect of shaking off their attackers on foot, who were soon out-of-their-depth. When the water became so deep that the horses were all but swimming, they were forced to turn in to the north bank, about one hundred yards up from the ford.

Clambering out on to dry land was a desperate business. The bank was steep and littered with debris and fallen trees; and of course many of the enemy had hurried along to intercept. The wedge formation inevitably got badly broken up, and there were more casualties. But their assailants tended to fight shy of the determined leadership. Maldred, Malpender and Gillibride of Angus who had now joined them, slightly wounded, were veteran sworders, riding close, one-and-two, formidable indeed as they breasted the steep slope, streaming water. Moreover the treacherous ambush had achieved its purpose, with the death of the King and Cospatrick; and men do not usually seek to die for a won cause. So the pressure slackened before the resolute onslaught. But just as a break-through was being achieved, an English footman, before bolting out of the way of the oncoming horsemen, hurled his spear like a javelin. It took Edward, Prince of Strathclyde, full in the chest and, coming from beneath, the point was able to penetrate under the scales of his armoured jerkin and pierced his rib-cage. With a bubbling yell he pitched to the ground.

At the dire sound Maldred wheeled about. Flinging

himself down he gathered up the choking heir to the throne in his arms, and with the aid of Malpender, somehow got him hoisted up to hang over the saddle-bow of Maldred's horse, whilst the rest of the Scots formed a milling circle round them. Mounting again behind, and with difficulty holding the twisting, jerking prince in position, he lashed his mount onwards once more.

They were pursued, but not so closely as to involve further fighting, on the three-mile dash back to Alnwick's bridge. Well before they got there however, they recognised that danger was ahead as well as behind, the clash of battle sounding. Madach had been right. The English army, or some part of it, had been watching, to come up and attack whilst the Scots awaited the outcome of their monarch's negotiations.

As they drew nearer they could see that, as might be expected, the major battle was engaged beyond the bridge, on the south side. Some fighting was going on on this side also, indeed scattered over a wide area. It was impossible to gauge how went the fortunes of war in that chaotic scene.

What to do? To plunge into the fight, with the King missing and treachery evident might be a recipe for disaster. There were not enough returned from Alnmouth — no more than thirty — to make any real difference to the outcome, although some were leaders. Edward was direly wounded, coughing blood, others also seriously injured including young Cospatrick. In this situation there were conflicting opinions, and little time for resolving them. Angus and Malpender, with contingents of their own mortuaths involved, felt bound to plunge into the battle and put themselves at the head of their men. Maldred's concern was for Edward and Cospatrick the younger, saving what could be rescued from this debacle. Edgar, now representing the royal house, was urgent that they first get his brother to some place where his wound could be tended, then home with him at the soonest. Dolfin felt the same about his brother.

So it was accepted. Malpender and Angus, with some of the men, would join the fighting, keeping secret meantime that the King was dead; thereafter they would advise retiral on Scotland, even if victorious — for there would be little point in continuing with this expedition now, and the Donald Ban situation had to be faced. Maldred and his second-cousins would hasten back to the hospice and monastery at Wooler, near the Till, where they had passed the previous night and where the monks would succour the wounded. Then make for Scotland with whatever speed was possible.

The party split up. With the unconscious, grievously-snoring prince held in his arms, Maldred led his sad little group northwards.

28

TWO GRIM DAYS later, on Scottish soil but far from home, the young man whom Malcolm Canmore had arranged to succeed him, breathed his difficult last in the bloody haemorrhage from his punctured lung. The Benedictines at Wooler had done what they could for him, but had not been hopeful — and at heart the others knew that he was dying. Bearing him in a horse-litter they had pressed on through the Cheviots, seeking at least to get him home to his mother alive, by the shortest route to Edinburgh — which, from Wooler was by the Glen Water and down to Tweed at Kelso and following up the great river to Lauderdale, where Dolfin and young Cospatrick could be dropped at Ersildoune. But in an aisle of Jedworth Forest near Makerstoun, amongst the fading brackens of a dripping November day, the Prince of Strathclyde succumbed, in his brother's arms.

Edgar, aged eighteen, was desolate. He had always been close to Edward. Now he had to go and tell his beloved mother that both her husband and her eldest son were dead.

It was a sorry homecoming for Cospatrick's sons also. The Earl had brought up his children, motherless, from an early age, and always had been popular with them however much he had left them to roam afar. And for so assured, and colourful a personality to have died so wretchedly and profitlessly, was added pain. Maldred himself realised that he would miss his dramatic and always lively cousin more than he could say.

They had not been able to travel at their fastest with the wounded, and before they reached the Leader and Ersildoune the local contingent from the Scots army had caught up with them. Their news was as good as could be looked for in the circumstances. The battle at Alnwick's bridge had been won — or at least the English had retired eventually with heavy losses leaving the Scots in control of the field, but themselves with almost three thousand casualties, for it had been a bitter fight. Apparently it had been only an advance section of the full English array, for Rufus was still said to be at the Tyne with the remainder. After the battle, the Scots had gone searching for the bodies of the King and Cospatrick; but local people at Alnmouth declared that the Earl of Northumbria's men had collected them and conveyed them to King William. The remaining Scots leaders had had little difficulty in deciding that there was no point in any further extension of this disastrous venture, especially in view of the uprising at home, and had ordered an immediate retiral to Scotland by the Coldstream fords and the Merse, where these Lauderdale men had left them.

Maldred saw Dolfin and his brother — whose shoulder-wound was painful but not dangerous — safely to Ersildoune Castle. But he did not linger there — nor indeed head eastwards across Lammermuir for Dunbar. Edgar was insistent that he accompany him to Edinburgh to help him break the grim news to the Queen, Maldred indeed feeling this to be his duty. So he sent a messenger to Magda assuring her that he was safe and well, and continued northwards up Lauderdale with the prince, travelling fast now.

Over Soltra Edge they dropped down into the central Lothian plain, with the crouching-lion outline of Arthur's Chair to beckon them on to Edinburgh and its rock of Dunedin. As they neared the town it was to perceive that they were going to have other problems to add to that of telling the Queen the evil tidings. A large army appeared to be occupying the area and surrounding the fortress on its rock. And quickly it became clear that it was a Highland army.

Anxiously they made enquiries at the herds' houses on

410

the town common muir to the south. They were told that the Prince Donald's Highlandmen had been there for five days, terrorising the neighbourhood. Nothing was safe from their depredations, women especially. Donald Ban was occupying St. Ninian's monastery below Arthur's Chair and besieging the fortress. Yes, the Queen was still in Dunedin, with her children, but said to be grievously ill. Where was King Malcolm? Why was the King not here, instead of stravaiging about in England . . . ?

Concerned, perplexed, the new arrivals were at a loss, distressed at the situation, anxious about the Queen's state and not knowing how they were to reach her in the beleaguered Dunedin. Discarding their rich armour and wrapping themselves in old borrowed cloaks which would draw no attention, Maldred and Edgar left their little party, with the body of Edward, and moved forward on foot to investigate.

They discovered that it was scarcely a close siege of the fortress, hardly a siege at all, only a containing. Donald Ban's forces were not really endeavouring to capture the all-but-impregnable stronghold, merely shutting up the Queen and her family within. No actual fighting was taking place; and Donald had even sent gifts of fresh meat and fish and fuel to the royal family, declaring that he did not make war on women and children. Townsfolk below the rock, in the warrens of huddled cot-houses, said that if the enquirers were to present themselves up at the gatehouse bearing some sort of gifts, they probably would be allowed through the rebel lines.

So, in the thin rain of the November dusk the pair of them, carrying poultry and ale which they had purchased from the market-place, climbed the steep approach, amongst Highlanders who thronged everywhere. They met with no opposition, only raillery and military wit from the pickets who guarded the spine of ridge which was the only access to the place, their only anxiety lest they had their provender stolen. But they met with more difficulty when they arrived before the massive gates beyond the wide ditch and first line of ramparts. Here the fortress defenders were unbelieving of such ordinary and uninspiring figures being the sort to bring gifts to the Queen. They were told to be off and scornfully hooted at when the pair declared themselves to be the Prince Edgar and the Lord Maldred of Atholl. Edgar indignantly shouted back that did they not have his brothers Alexander and David and his sisters Matilda and Mary there in the fort? Bring one of them, and have an end to this nonsense.

Eventually, not one of the royal children but none other than Magda herself, appeared on the gatehouse tower, to exclaim thankfully at the sight of her husband. The gates were opened promptly thereafter and a gangway run out to enable them to cross the water-filled ditch.

Magda flung herself into Maldred's arms, all but sobbing with relief and emotion. It was some little time before either of them was able to explain their situation coherently, as they climbed up to the higher inner levels of the fort.

The Queen was desperately ill, she told them. She had been frail enough before, God knew, scarcely able to walk, and had had to be carried up here from St. Ninians in a litter; but now, of all things, she had commenced a forty-days' fast prior to Christmas, similar to that she always imposed on herself in Lent. Apparently she had done this the previous year and it had even then taken great toll of her flagging strength. This time it looked like killing her. It was a sort of madness. She was blaming herself for all the ills that had befallen her family and Scotland. It seemed almost as though she wanted to die. It was the Princess Matilda who had sent for her, Magda, thinking that she might have some influence with her mother, as an old friend and close companion. She had got here from Dunbar only the day before the rebel army arrived and cooped them up in this eyrie. Did they know that the Prince Edmund was with Donald Ban? Turned renegade — a further dire blow to his mother.

Maldred glanced at Edgar, biting his lip. It was difficult enough, in these circumstances, to tell even his wife their news.

"My father . . . !" the prince blurted out, and stopped.

"Yes, the King?" Magda said. "The King — is he . . . well? For the Queen believes . . . she says . . . she deems him dead!"

Edgar drew a gulping breath.

Maldred's voice was a little unsteady likewise. "She thinks this? Really believes him so? It is not mere fears . . . ?"

"No. Four days back, when I came to her in the morning, she told me that this would be Malcolm's last

412

day on earth! She, she has been praying for the repose of his soul ever since. Is he . . . ?"

Thickly he answered her. "He was slain, that day. By treachery. Four days ago."

She swallowed. "Dear God!"

Since Edgar appeared to be unable to speak, Maldred, after a moment, went on.

"Did she say . . . more? Foretell other evil? Worse, perhaps?"

"Worse . . . ?"

"Aye, worse. For Edward is dead also. Her son Edward."

"Merciful Mary Mother of Christ — Edward!" Magda stopped, to stare. "Oh, Maldred — no! Not Edward? The sin of it, the hurt of it. This . . . this will kill her, most certainly."

"She had no premonition of *this*, then? With the other?"

"I do not know. But, if she had, she did not voice it. She has been full of sorrow and self-condemnation and punishment since ever I came. But she has not spoken of Edward's death."

Edgar sought to speak, but still could not. He was a sensitive young man.

Magda took his arm. "Oh, I am sorry, my dear — sorry! Your brother. And your father. And, and now this . . ."

"We are accursed," he got out, wildly. "Rejected of God! Our family . . . is . . . damned!"

They shook their heads, but found no answer to that.

Here they had reached the topmost levels of the great rock where the royal quarters were being erected, these not any sort of palace. Some part was sufficiently near completion to be occupied. Nearby was a tiny, absolutely plain gabled building, little more than a stone cell, featureless save for some small windows and a door.

"The Queen's new private chapel," Magda explained. "To house the Black Rood. She says that Dunfermline no longer requires it. But that this chapel requires no better ornament than her piece of Christ's True Cross. She, who has built the great Holy Trinity, the minster at St. Andrews and restored Iona — this is what she erects for herself — a hermit's cell!"

They entered the royal house, a bare place also, where they found the four youngest of the children, Alexander, David and the girls Matilda and Mary, all looking pale and strained. These ran to embrace their brother. The youngest of all, the nine-year-old David, slight, great-eyed and fine-featured, asked for Edward, obviously favourite. None spoke of their father. Edgar forbore, meantime, to inform the others of their double loss. Magda, with manifest reluctance, said that she would go in to prepare the Queen. The two travellers gulped down proffered beakers of ale, to sustain them for what lay ahead.

Presently Magda emerged from the royal bedchamber, tears welling in her eyes. She gestured within, but shook her head.

"She will see you. She knows that you bring ill tidings — knows it, of herself. But . . . I have not told her."

Maldred hung back, to allow the prince to meet his mother alone. But Edgar grasped his arm. Together they moved in to the ordeal they had been dreading for days.

Strangely, the atmosphere was superficially cheerful in that room. A bright wood fire crackled on the wide hearth, candles illuminated the rich and colourful wall-hangings and evergreen branches, even some roses decorated the chamber. And on the great bed Margaret smiled, actually smiled at them, the first smile they had seen for long. She was desperately thin, her face like alabaster, her eyes huge and dark-circled. But she managed to smile, and raised a quivering hand.

"Edgar! And . . . Maldred!" she whispered.

The younger man ran forward, choking, to lean over the bed. He would have embraced her, but her obvious weakness and brittleness restrained him and he threw himself down beside her instead, head on her pillow, to kiss her hair, her cheek. He did not speak.

"Edgar, dear Edgar," she murmured. Over his head her great eyes sought Maldred's and held them. And they were fearful no longer, nor agonised, but calm, deeply assured, as they had used to be — accepting.

He wagged his head, also wordless.

Her lips moved but he could hear nothing. He moved closer.

She tried again. "You both . . . have come far . . . with a sore burden . . . to carry. I grieve . . . for you."

Like a weight lifted, Maldred recognised that they need not have feared, that their ordeal was not to be so unbearable, their burden so heavy — for Margaret herself was going to carry most of it. She was, indeed, in command, not they, weak as she was in body.

"Margaret!" he exclaimed, thickly. And again. "Margaret!"

"Tell me," she ordered. "How . . . it was."

Edgar raised himself. He glanced over at Maldred. "It was, it was . . ." He weakened. "It was none so ill," he finished lamely.

Maldred shook his head. That would not serve. The prince, seeing how shockingly fragile was his mother's state, thought to spare her, thought no doubt that the truth would kill her. But she knew, she *knew*. And however frail her person, her spirit was strong, stronger than either of theirs.

The Queen's hand reached to touch her son's arm. "The truth," she murmured. But it was a command.

"They are gone, Highness," Maldred said. "Both. Both gone."

She closed her eyes, and slowly nodded her head. "Yes," she said.

Edgar glared at Maldred, clenching his fists. "It was treachery," he exclaimed. "Foul Norman treachery. They came to us, under the white flag. Led us to speak with Moubray. To hear Rufus's proposals. Then turned on us, when crossing a river. In great numbers. Arrows, spears, swords. Father was slain at once. Edward . . . Edward was wounded. He, he died later. We were bringing him home . . ." His voice trailed away.

There was silence for a little, save for the crackle and hiss of the log-fire. Margaret's eyes were still closed, and two great tears welled out to run down her wasted cheeks. Her lips moved, but she was speaking to herself, or more probably to her Maker.

Strangely, when she did find words to utter aloud, and opened her eyes, her voice seemed to have gained an unexpected accession of strength.

"Edward," she said. "Edward." A pause. Then, "I praise . . . Almighty God. Now . . . at the end. That Thou hast willed it . . . that my soul should be cleansed by . . . this anguish. That Thou hast given me time . . . time to endure it. And so, I pray . . . wash away some of the stain . . . of my sins!"

Exhausted by this effort, she seemed to sink away. Maldred thought that her breathing had stopped, and took an involuntary step forward to the bedside. Edgar sank on his knees.

But then the large eyes opened again. "I come," she said, with distinct authority. "It is finished. Fetch me . . . the Holy Rood. Quickly!" That last was urgent.

Maldred saw the Queen's eyes turned towards a corner of the bedchamber. Expecting to see the famous relic there, he was surprised to perceive a man kneeling there in the shadows, the Cluniac friar Thurstan, the current confessor found for the Queen by Turgot. Silently this priest rose, bowed and hurried from the room.

"Quickly!" Margaret sped him.

"Mother . . ." Edgar began, but stopped when he saw that the Queen's lips were working again. He leaned close, to listen. "I cannot hear what she says," he exclaimed, in agitation.

Maldred bent, ear down. "It is the psalm," he said softly. ". . . from the rising of the sun unto the going down thereof . . ."

As though it was desperately important that they did not miss a single word, they listened to those painfully-panted well-known phrases of the Fiftieth Psalm.

"Out of Sion hath God appeared: in perfect beauty . . ."

It took them a little while to recognise that seeming mistakes and stumblings in the faint recital were in fact the Queen inserting the word 'quickly, quickly' here and there, with a sort of feverish impatience. Her hearers looked at each other helplessly.

The murmuring had all but died away when the priest came hastening back from the Queen's chapel outside, with the Black Rood in its silver casket, the same relic which Maldred had first seen in that dark ship's cabin at Wearmouth, twenty-four years before. Thurstan brought it and laid it on the bed.

Thankfully Margaret reached her trembling hand to it, fumbling for the lid's catch. Unable to raise her head and see the thing, she groaned, fretting. "Merciful Lord — quickly!" she gasped. There was even a touch of temper there.

Edgar leaned over and released the reluctant clasp, to open the lid and lift out the fragment of dark wood studded with the diamonds, two fragments, bound together to form a cross, to put into her hands.

She clutched the wood to her breast, panting shallowly.

"Thank God!" she breathed. "Thank God!" She looked up, then, at her son and her friend, and the tortured, desperate look had quite gone from her eyes. The old assurance and serenity were back, leavened with love, affection, understanding, even the hint of a smile. She raised the cross. "It is good," she whispered. "All . . . is well. At last!" She sought to make the sign of the cross with the relic towards each of them, but could not keep her arm up. "Bless," she got out. "Bless."

They waited, hardly daring to breathe. There was nothing that they, or any, could do. Besides, the Queen was still very much in command in that chamber.

Then, seeking again to sign with the cross, but over herself this time, and in a slow but quite confident and quite curiously different voice, she began to repeat the prayer after communion received, in the Roman office. "Lord Jesu Christ who by the Father's will . . . hast given the world life . . . through Thy death . . . deliver me . . ."

The whispering stopped. Again they waited, willing her strength. The Rood drooped.

It was the priest's voice which next spoke, presently, however. "God in His infinite mercy has received her soul," he declared simply. "*Requiescat in pace!*"

The other two stared, at Thurstan, at each other, and then back at Margaret Atheling. She seemed no different from moments ago, just gathering her strength again, the light not faded from her lovely eyes. But when they leaned close they perceived that she no longer breathed.

Strong again, she was on her way.

Later, when Edgar could speak coherently, he picked up the cross from his mother's breast.

"This was her guide and strength and solace always," he said. "One day, when I am King — and it may be that I am King now — I shall build a great abbey here, in her memory. To contain this her Holy Rood. God aiding me."

Maldred shrugged. "Perhaps. But her memory will require no stone-and-mortar monument. I think, so long as there are Scots, they will remember her. They may not all bless her, always — but they will never forget Margaret the Queen . . ."

HISTORICAL NOTE

THE QUEEN'S BODY was taken from Edinburgh to be buried in Holy Trinity, now Dunfermline Abbey, along with Edward's. Discounting alleged miracles *en route*, we can take it that Donald Ban allowed passage. Malcolm's body was buried by the English at Tynemouth, but in time was disinterred and brought to lie beside Margaret at Dunfermline, the first King of Scots not to have been interred at Iona. William Rufus, although almost certainly implicated in Malcolm's death, made a show of anger over such an end for a royal personage, and confined Moubray, Earl of Northumbria, to perpetual imprisonment. Cospatrick, for some reason, possibly on the urging of Prior Turgot, was taken to the new cathedral of Durham and buried there.

Edgar did not become King of Scots for over four years. The mormaors, under the Celtic law of tanistry, accepted Donald Ban as rightful monarch. But he only reigned for six months, when his nephew Duncan marched north at the head of a large English army, having sworn fealty to William Rufus for Scotland — an action which was to give rise to much trouble for centuries thereafter — and unseated him. But Duncan reigned for only six more months, when he was slain at Mondynes by Malpender, Mormaor of the Mearns, who supported Donald. Donald then resumed the crown for three years, and seems to have reigned well; when Edgar at last, also with English aid — for the Margaretsons were in exile in England — overthrew his uncle, and ascended the throne; and the long regimes of the Margaretsons commenced. It is to be feared however that his mother would not have approved of Edgar's revenge, indeed his general behaviour. He had Donald Ban's eyes put out and sent him to be a scullion in the royal kitchens. When Donald died he was the last Scots king to be buried on Iona.

Edgar died unmarried in 1107 and was succeeded by his

next brother, Alexander the First. He seems to have made a better monarch, and continued his mother's work of Romanising the Columban Church. One of his first acts was to have Prior Turgot installed as Romish Bishop of St. Andrews and Primate, thus ending the hereditary primacy of the Dunkeld line. He reigned for fourteen years, during which his sister Matilda married Henry Beauclerc; who when Rufus died in 1100, became Henry the First of England. Alexander produced no heir, and was succeeded by David the youngest of the Margaretsons — they were never referred to as the Malcolmsons — who occupied the throne for no less than twenty-nine years, a great king by most standards, of whom his mother would have approved. He completed the Romanising of the Scottish Church and added his own Normanising policy in the state. By the end of his reign both the Celtic Church and the Celtic polity were largely a thing of the past, and Scotland had moved from the patriarchal and tribal into the feudal age, with Papacy triumphant. So Margaret won her battle in the end. She was officially canonised in 1250. Bishop Turgot wrote her biography, the earliest such production in Scotland, although it is to a large extent hagiography.

Edmund the black sheep, on Donald Ban's downfall, found it wise to reform, and entered Holy Church. Ethelred in due course had to give up the earldom of Fife to its true heir; and lost his primacy to Turgot. Oddly he seems to have been more or less converted to the Columban faith, and as his brothers turned towards the Normans, he turned to the Gaels, indeed Gaelicised his name to Eth, or Hugh, and lived in the Highlands, producing a son MacEth who in due course became Earl of Moray and whom some claim as the founder of Clan Mackay.

St. Margaret's influence on Scotland has been enormous, much greater than that of any other woman, and few men have had as much. Whether the pulling down of the Columban Church was a good thing or a bad, is still a matter for debate. Certainly the non-hierarchal, independent and more homely faith seems more in keeping with the Scots character; also more akin to the Church which arose out of the Reformation and is now the Church of Scotland. But the change-over might well have been inevitable, in the Middle Ages.

It is perhaps of interest that, while a descendant of Malcolm and Margaret still sits on the throne of the United Kingdom, in 1963 a direct descendant of Cospatrick, Alec Cospatrick Douglas-Home, 14th Earl of Home, became Prime Minister thereof. He still lives in the Merse.

NIGEL TRANTER

THE YOUNG MONTROSE

James Graham – the brilliant young Marquis of Montrose.

One man alone could not change the course of history.
But James Graham was determined to try. A gallant soldier, talented leader and compelling personality, his
fame has echoed down the centuries. For the young
Marquis of Montrose was to give his utmost in the
service of his beloved monarch.

The first of two magnificent novels about THE MAR-
QUIS OF MONTROSE.

CORONET BOOKS

NIGEL TRANTER

DAVID THE PRINCE

Set in the twelfth century, the incredible story of one of
Scotland's greatest kings. Half-Celt and half-Saxon, determined King David who took hold of his backward,
patriarchal, strife-ridden country and – against all the
odds – pushed and dragged it into the forefront of
Christendom's advancing nations. A story of indepen-
dence, singlemindedness and hard-headed leadership.
But also, through the turbulent years of his reign, a story
of devotion – to the woman he admired and loved,
Queen Matilda.

CORONET BOOKS

NIGEL TRANTER

LORDS OF MISRULE

In turbulent 14th century Scotland, the ruling House of Stewart was a house divided, beset by hatred and jealousy. Descendants of the Bruce's daughter, they only kept the throne by an astonishing genius for survival – and, many said, the luck of the Devil himself. Their rivals were the Douglases; and when the second Earl was slain in battle, the Stewarts were suspected of foul play.

Young Jamie Stewart vowed to avenge his master; but he had only his wits, courage and integrity with which to challenge the most eminent and unscrupulous men in the kingdom. And while vengeance still burned in his heart, he could not prevent his fatal attraction for the beautiful and spirited Stewart women – and one in particular.

CORONET BOOKS

NIGEL TRANTER

MACBETH THE KING

Across a huge and colourful canvas, ranging from the wilds of Scotland to Norway, Denmark and Rome, here is the story of the real MacBeth. Set aside Shakespeare's portrait of a savage, murderous, ambitious King. Read instead of his struggle to make and save a united Scotland. Of his devotion to his great love, the young Queen Gruoch. Of the humane laws they fought for, the great battle they were forced to fight. And the price they paid.

CORONET BOOKS

ANYA SETON

GREEN DARKNESS

Perhaps the greatest gifts Anya Seton brings to her historical novels are the zest of her narrative, the life she breathes into the most insignificant characters, and the atmosphere of the era she evokes around them'
Books and Bookmen

The young Celia de Bohun has fallen helplessly in love with Stephen, the resident priest in the Catholic household of Sir Anthony Browne. Against his will, Stephen returns her love. Gripped by the sweetness of their forbidden passion, the young lovers become the victims of their savage times.

Centuries later their tragedy threatens the life and happiness of another Celia. She can only be saved by piercing the green darkness of the past and revealing its mysterious truth.

CORONET BOOKS

HISTORICAL NOVELS FROM CORONET

All these books are available at your local bookshop or newsagent, or can be ordered direct from the publisher. Just tick the titles you want and fill in the form below.

Prices and availability subject to change without notice.

CORONET BOOKS, P.O. Box 11, Falmouth, Cornwall.

Please send cheque or postal order, and allow the following for postage and packing:

U.K.—50p for one book, plus 20p for the second book, and 14p for each additional book ordered up to a £1.63 maximum.

B.F.P.O. and EIRE—50p for the first book, plus 20p for the second book, and 14p per copy for the next 7 books, 8p per book thereafter.

OTHER OVERSEAS CUSTOMERS—75p for the first book, plus 21p per copy for each additional book.

Name ....

Address...

....